In sixth century Constantinople—the New Rome—how does the daughter of a bearkeeper, one who fashions her life as an actress and prostitute, rise to become the Empress of the Byzantine Empire? How does a poor Syrian boy, who is violently forced to become a eunuch, rise to an esteemed position in the Palace of Justinian I? How do the two meet and become such allies that one day Theodora asks Stephen to write her biography?

"James Conroyd Martin not only unfurls the vast canvas of history, but he paints the deeply personal side of the men and women who lived it. His settings and characters come to life in meticulously researched detail. I felt like I was there."

—Lisa Wingate,
New York Times bestselling author of *Before We Were Yours*

D1569292

"*Fortune's Child* is a treasure for historical fiction fans—richly detailed, immersive, and heart-pounding. Martin paints a vivid and satisfying portrait of one of history's most remarkable women."

—Olivia Hawker,
bestselling author of *The Ragged Edge of Night*

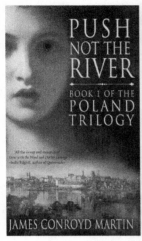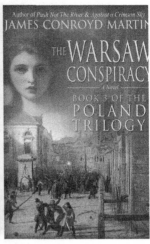

Check out The Poland Trilogy: https://goo.gl/93rzag

Based on the diary of a Polish countess who lived through the rise and fall of the Third of May Constitution years, 1791-94, **Push Not the River** paints a vivid picture of a tumultuous and unforgettable metamorphosis of a nation—and of Anna, a proud and resilient woman. **Against a Crimson Sky** continues Anna's saga as Napoléon comes calling, implying independence would follow if only Polish lancers would accompany him on his fateful 1812 march into Russia. Anna's family fights valiantly to hold on-to a tenuous happiness, their country, and their very lives. Set against the November Rising (1830-31), **The Warsaw Conspiracy** depicts partitioned Poland's daring challenge to the Russian Empire. Brilliantly illustrating the psyche of a people determined to reclaim independence in the face of monumental odds, the story features Anna's sons and their fates in love and war.

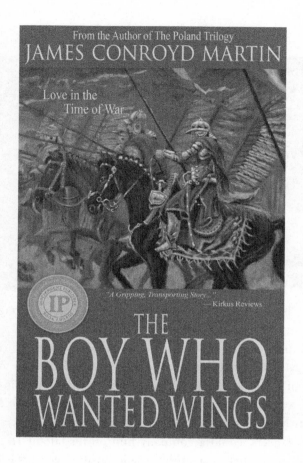

From the Author of The Poland Trilogy

JAMES CONROYD MARTIN

Love in the
Time of War

"A Gripping, Transporting Story..."
— Kirkus Reviews

THE
BOY WHO
WANTED WINGS

Aleksy, a Tatar raised by a Polish peasant family, wishes to become a Polish winged hussar, a Christian lancer who carries into battle a device attached to his back that holds dozens of eagle feathers. As a Tatar and as a peasant, this is an unlikely quest. When he meets Krystyna, the daughter of the noble who owns the land that his parents work, he falls hopelessly in love. But even though she returns his love, race and class differences make this quest as impossible as that of becoming a hussar. Under the most harrowing and unlikely circumstances, one day Aleksy must choose between his dreams.

FORTUNE'S CHILD

A NOVEL OF EMPRESS THEODORA

JAMES CONROYD MARTIN

HUSSAR
QUILL PRESS

CHICAGO

Fortune's Child: A Novel of Empress Theodora
Copyright 2019 by James Conroyd Martin Trust All rights reserved
First Print edition: November 2019
http://www.JamesCMartin.com

Edited by Mary Rita Perkins Mitchell
Cover and Formatting: Streetlight Graphics
www.steetlightgraphics.com

Hardcover ISBN: 978-1-7340043-0-4
Paperback ISBN: 978-0-9978945-9-2

Art:
Front cover: *La Emperatriz Theodora*, 1887
By Jean-Joseph Benjamin-Constant
Museo Nacional de Bellas Artes, Buenos Aires
Public domain

Back cover: *Empress Theodora and Her Attendants*
Mosaic, Basilica di San Vitale, Ravenna, Italy, Public domain

ALSO BY JAMES CONROYD MARTIN

The Poland Trilogy:

Push Not the River
Against a Crimson Sky
The Warsaw Conspiracy
and
The Boy Who Wanted Wings
Hologram: A Haunting

ACKNOWLEDGMENTS

Many sincere thanks go out to those who have travelled with Theodora and me along this journey: Scott Hagensee, Mary Rita Perkins Mitchell, John Rdzak, Kathryn Killackey Mitchell, Pam Sourelis, Elizabyth Harrington, and members of Portland's 9-Bridges Downtown Saturday Meetups.

For Kathryn Killackey Mitchell
and John Rdzak

Thank you for reading **Fortune's Child**! I think you will enjoy it, and I'm hoping you'll reward me with a brief review afterward on Amazon, B&N, Goodreads, KOBO, Smashwords, or i-books. Thanking you in advance!

PLEASE subscribe to my **Newsletter** for rather infrequent announcements about freebies, bonuses, booksignings, contests, news, and recommendations: **http://jamescmartin.com/announcements/**

LIKE me on **Facebook**: https://www.facebook.com/AuthorMan/

Follow me on **Twitter** @JConMartin

Follow/add me on **Goodreads**:
https://www.goodreads.com/author/show/92822.James_Conroyd_Martin

JConMartin on **Instagram**

AUTHOR'S NOTE

Long ago and far away in Los Angeles, I took an adult Art Appreciation course. When we studied the Byzantine mosaics located in Ravenna, Italy, the professor pointed to the figure of Theodora and said, "I'm not a writer, but if I were, that is the woman I would be writing about."

Click!

I immediately went to the Hollywood Library and took out a dozen books on the period and the empress. I had already started my first novel, *Push Not the River*, so I planned for Theodora's story to be my second. As the first novel was going to press, I started work on Theodora. Ah, but St. Martin's Press had a different idea: they wanted a sequel to *Push Not the River*, so that led to other books and the passage of years. Like the woman herself, the story is resilient and now ready for the light of day.

That teacher was so right! Theodora is absolutely fascinating.

Enjoy …

Ravenna

Rome

Carthage

W E

S

The Byzantine Empire
550 AD

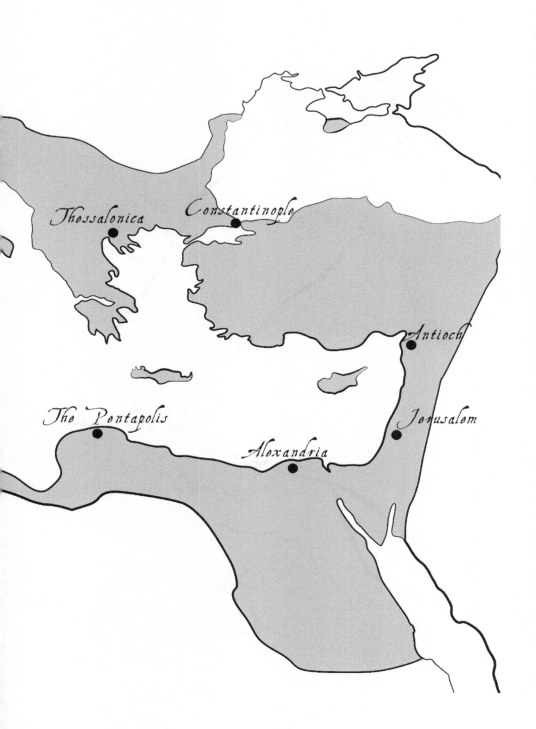

Thessalonica

Constantinople

Antioch

The Pentapolis

Jerusalem

Alexandria

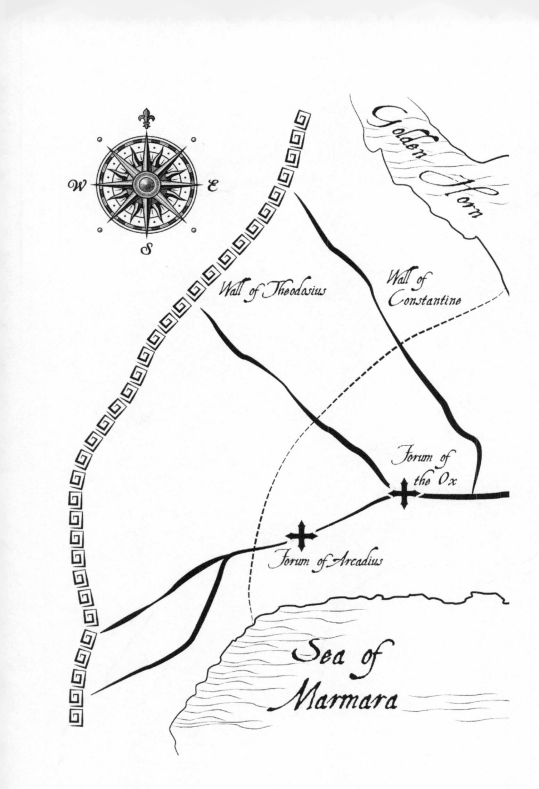

W E

S

Golden Horn

Wall of Theodosius

Wall of
Constantine

Forum of
the Ox

Forum of Arcadius

Sea of
Marmara

Bosporos

1. Hippodrome
2. Palace of Hormisdus
3. Milion
4. Church of Holy Wisdom
5. Augustaion
6. Baths of Zeuxippos
7. Chalke
8. Kathisma
9. Prosphorion Harbor

Forum of Theodosius

Forum of Constantine

Great Palace

Constantinople

For amazing pictorial reconstructions of Constantinople,
visit the website of French artist Antoine Helbert.
http://www.antoine-helbert.com/fr/portfolio/
annexe-work/byzance-architecture.html

GLOSSARY

ANASTASIUS (Emperor 491-518): Was a Monophysite, placing him in conflict with the Orthodox Church.

ATRIUM: center of a Roman house, the open roof sheds light on the rooms nearby; contains an impluvium, or pool, directly under the opening to catch rain water for use within the house.

AUGUSTAION: The public square at the east end of the Mese, south of the Church of the Holy Wisdom, and north of the Great Palace.

BATHS OF ZEUXIPPOS: Luxurious public baths named after a Thracian deity and located on the northeast side of the HIPPODROME.

BLUES: Supporters of the charioteers of the Blue faction.

CHALKÉ: "The Bronze Gate" serving as the ceremonial entrance or vestibule to the Great Palace.

CHURCH OF THE HOLY WISDOM: (also called the Hagia Sophia) Significant edifice on the Augustaion. The first burned down in 404, the second during Justinian's reign in 532. The third was built by order of Justinian and it still stands.

CISTERNS: An ingenious system of aqueducts and cisterns, open, covered, or underground was built to effectively supply fresh water to the city population, even in times of siege.

CODEX (Plural, CODICES): A book constructed of pages made of papyrus or the more durable parchment and enclosed with hard covers.

CURSE TABLETS: Scrolls of thin lead engraved with curses thought to be harmful to those cited in them.

DALMATIC(A): A wide-sleeved and heavier garment worn over the lighter tunic by both sexes, but mostly by men. A robe.

DAPHNE PALACE: Complex of buildings on the western side of the Great Palace that houses the Imperial Apartments.

DIOPHYSITE: One who believed that two natures existed in the person of Jesus Christ, the divine and human, adhering to the view of the Orthodox Church.

EUNUCHS: Men who have been castrated and who often performed important parts in the church, army, and civil or palace administrations.

EUPHEMIA: Empress and wife of Justin I; desired that the diadem be passed to Justinian, but much opposed to his marriage to Theodora.

EXCUBITORS: The Imperial Guard.

FACTIONS: Supporters of the BLUES and GREENS, chariot teams named for their colors. The REDS and WHITES had fallen out of favor and been assimilated into the other factions.

FOLLIS (Plural, FOLLES): Largest of the copper coins, it was valued at 40 NUMMI or 1/288 of a NOMISMA.

GREAT PALACE: A complex of many imperial buildings created at the southeastern end of Constantinople amidst pavilions and gardens at the edge of the Sea of Marmara.

GREENS: Supporters of the charioteers of the Green faction.

HALL OF THE NINETEEN COUCHES: One of the Great Palace buildings used for imperial ceremonies and banquets.

HECATE: Greek Goddess of magic, witchcraft, the moon, and ghosts.

HESPERIDES: Nymphs of the sunset in Greek Mythology, usually depicted as three in number and as caretakers of Goddess Hera's garden near the Atlas Mountains in Africa. In the Garden of the Hesperides there grew a grove of apple trees that bore golden apples capable of dispensing immortality when eaten.

HIPPODROME: Capable of accommodating 50,000 to 60,000 citizens, the U-shaped race track next to the Great Palace was used for chariot racing, public entertainment, imperial ceremonies, as well as military and political demonstrations.

JUSTIN I (450-527; reign 518-527): Sought his fortune as an excubitor in the reign of ANASTASIUS I, became commander and then emperor upon Anastasius' death; adopted his nephew Justinian, who was named co-emperor with him, and who became emperor in his own right four months after Anastasius' death.

JUSTINIAN I (483-565; reign 527-565): Succeeded his uncle, Justin I, as emperor; ordered the codification of Roman law and sought to regain parts of the empire lost to barbarians, including Rome, North Africa, and Spain. Went against most of society by marrying actress Theodora.

KATHISMA: The imperial loge at the Hippodrome attached to and accessed from the Great Palace.

KNUCKLEBONES: An ancient gambling game like dice adopted by Romans and Greeks and utilizing the bones from the ankles of sheep.

LEVANT: An approximate geographical term referring to the eastern Mediterranean; a broad definition roughly refers to the territory from Greece to Egypt.

LORD (or GRAND) CHAMBERLAIN: Highest ranking attendant (usually a eunuch) to the Byzantine emperor, with whom he held great sway.

MAGUS: A member of a priestly caste of ancient Persia; a sorcerer; wizard; conjurer; charlatan; trickster.

MESE: Main thoroughfare traversing Constantinople from the MILION west to the outer city walls.

MILION: Marble arch near the Church of the Holy Wisdom and just outside the AUGUSTAION, it served as the point from which distances in the empire were measured.

MITHRA: Pagan Sun god. Also known as MITHRAS.

MONOPHYSITE One who believed that Christ had a single divine nature, whereas the Orthodox Church held that Christ had both a divine and human nature and considered Monophysites heretics.

NARSES: A eunuch serving Justinian as a steward, Commander of the Imperial Guard, Grand Chamberlain, and finally, as a general and commander of the forces that reconquered Italy.

NOMISMA (Plural, NOMISMATA): Gold coin.

NUMMI (Plural, NUMMUS): Smallest copper coin.

PALACE OF HORMISDAS: A palace within the Great Palace complex located at the water's edge of the Sea of Marmara and used by Justinian before coming to power.

PATRIARCH: Head or bishop of a diocese. The five dioceses in Theodora's time were Rome, Constantinople, Alexandria, Antioch and Jerusalem.

PROCOPIUS: A contemporary of Theodora and Justinian, he was a lawyer and the chief palace historian, one known for his biased accounts of the royal couple and their reign. His especially damning and vitriolic work, *Secret History* surfaced many years after the deaths of the principals described.

QUADRIGA: A chariot drawn by four horses harnessed abreast.

SHADE: the spirit of a dead person.

SHATRANJ: Indian board game and forerunner of chess.

SILENTIARY: An official of the court acting much like an usher, staying silent while standing guard over imperial personages.

STOLA: A long, pleated dress for women worn over the tunic, usually woolen or linen, but sometimes silk for the rich citizens. Often worn with a belt placed just below the bustline.

STYLITES: Holy men or "pillar saints" who lived atop tall columns.

TARTARUS: In Greek Mythology, the abyss used as a dungeon for the wicked.

TESSERA (Plural: TESSERAE): Small pieces of stone or glass used in the creation of mosaics.

THREE FATES, The: In Greek Mythology, the three goddesses who determined a person's fate. They were Clotho the Spinner, who spun the thread of life; Lachesis the allotter, who determined the length of life; and Atropos the inflexible, who cut the thread of life, ending it.

THUCYDIDES: (460-400 BC) A well-respected Greek historian.

TUNIC(A): Replaced the toga, over which upper class males often wore a DALMATIC and females wore other garments, like the STOLA or a mantle. *Tunica intima*: A woman's under tunic.

TYCHE: Greek Goddess of Fortune, Fate, or Chance; as the daughter of Aphrodite and Zeus (or Hermes), she was thought to direct the destiny of a city and to be responsible for unexpected turns in people's lives, both good and bad.

PART ONE

PART ONE

1

Constantinople 547

I AM DREAMING ABOUT HER YET again. Theodora: Goddess. Theodora: Nemesis. The woman I once adored.

I suddenly come awake in a cold sweat, eyelids flying back. Is it the dream that awoke me? I think not. Memory holds to some vague noise. All is quiet now, a thin silence stabbing me with dread.

I listen. In a dungeon any sound other than a rodent's skittering on stone bodes ill. A minute passes. A long minute before I recognize the metallic clicking of a key in the lock. I draw in breath and hold it, listening. The recalcitrant gears do not give. Wrong door? Wrong key? My heartbeats triple. I pull myself up on my filthy pallet, back pinned against the craggy stone wall.

One expects no changes in routine here. No benign changes, I mean to say. Panic courses through me like a fever. I had already been given my second and last meager meal of the day, a kind of lentil mush. Any unusual occurrence in routine after that—a footfall or rattle of keys at an odd hour—is enough to raise the hackles of the most hardened criminal in the underground maze. I feel the blood draining from my face, a clenching at my middle. The lazy workings of the lock should not turn again until morning—but they are being tested. And yet, even as I mindlessly make the sign against an evil eye cast from afar, the gears are giving way.

The rust-pocked iron door bursts inward, spilling torchlight from the hall. Two prison guards in short woolen tunics advance and pull me to my feet. The single chair and the scrolls and codices on my small table are sent flying. "What is it?" I dare to ask. One guard answers with a grunt. Their faces are no more than outlines in the dark.

Giving me no time to find my ragged sandals, the guards strong-arm me out into the hall and prod me toward the stairs. I make no further attempt to question them. The day I feared has come. In my time here, I have heard others dragged off, begging for mercy. Some were returned mute and broken; most did not return. Some begged as they were hauled away. I will not beg. My fear is hardening into a sense of grim fatalism.

At intervals, low-burning torches light the passage. As we move up the narrow, stone staircase, I hug the rough and weeping wall, struggling to keep my feet from slipping on the damp, uneven steps. The absence of railings sparks the old vertigo I have not felt for years. Oddly, the sensation of dizziness is like an old friend returning after an extended absence. We continue up, higher, higher, one guard in front, one behind. The air grows less corrupt, less damp. Still higher.

I become light-headed. My enfeebled legs, so unused to exercise, quiver and threaten collapse, but the alien fresh air piques all of my senses, and from somewhere nearby the sharp scent of myrrh evokes my first visit to the great Church of the Holy Wisdom, after Justinian had it built anew. The balm affords me the needed reserve to take the steps, one upon the next.

Then come the ground floor and a flank of windows. Sunlight. Day is moving into dusk now, but sunlight nonetheless. Strange, I had thought it the middle of the night. Below it is always night. My eyes blink at the sight, so suddenly do my lenses have to adjust. My heart beats fast. If my crude record keeping is accurate, I have not seen the sun in five years, have not felt it on my skin. Blurry bursts of colors fly at me, a prism of reds, blues, yellows that at first offend and then feed my emaciated sense of sight.

The joy I feel at the awakening of my senses is stunted by terror. What has caused my release? The Syrian blood now coursing through my veins at an accelerated rate is said to carry the seeing skills. But it takes no clairvoyance to know where I am being led—and who has sent for me. I tremble to think of it.

We pass through marble hallways, familiar hallways. My movements stiffen as if ice is enveloping me, hardening me. A cold sweat breaks out on my forehead.

Supper is in preparation. The aroma of herb chicken in orange sauce comes wafting up from the palace kitchens. It had been a favorite of mine. Ahead, servants in long gray dalmatics are lighting the sconces for the fall of night. They are trained not to take notice of anything, but I can intuit their curiosity as I pass, for they recognize me, as I do them. One old man, a lamplighter with whom I often jested, approaches, his eyes growing round as thimbles. He looks as if he is about to speak, but when his gaze sweeps over me as we pass, he is struck silent.

Fear comes in a second rush, intensified by the certain knowledge of whom I am about to face. Something in my chest tightens and my gait slows, but the strong arms of the guards pull me along. Then come the final stretch of columns and a marble floor that shines like black ice. The huge bronze double doors loom ahead, seeming now to recede as I walk toward them. My heart pounds. This is a dream, I tell myself. Before I get to those doors, I will awake to my tiny cell. The details are vivid, I assure myself, much like they are in a dream. I look down. I can see the hem of my dirty and tattered tunic moving with the motion of my legs, bare feet slapping the cool floor.

Suddenly we are at the doors of her private reception chamber. Silentiaries stand on either side. I glance up. Purple brocade drapes the doorway. A new addition. How she loves the purple.

I long to be back in my cell. My world is secure there. It took months to adjust to the cold and cramped cubicle. I fell into raving fits in the first weeks, the guards told me later. After the surprise arrival of candles and my manuscripts, life became less miserable. I knew that they had come from her, and I accepted them with a grateful bitterness. I dared not ask for writing instruments.

The doors are open now. I did not see them opening, distracted as I am. Dreams operate that way, too, I know, propelling one from scene to scene with no transitions.

But this is no dream, much as I wish it were.

I see her now. At the far end of the vaulted room, in a high-backed, cushioned throne of ebony, she sits. A pair of exquisitely carved leopards comprises the arms and front supports of the chair, the blue gemstones in their eyes glinting at me. No hint remains of the baseborn actress she had been, only the empress she has become. She wears a mantle of purple silk, open enough to reveal a collar of pearl ropes draping from her shoulders to her breastbone. Instead of her diadem, a black veil covers her upswept coiffure and falls to cover her face. *Strange.* I have no memory of her veiling her face within the palace.

She motions the guards and silentiaries away. They hesitate. A second flick of the royal wrist and they dare not disobey.

The doors close. She and I are alone.

The last time I had seen her—so very long ago—we played a board game and I had no hint of what lay in store for me. Two days later, her secret police knocked at my door, polite as you please. What am I to expect now?

Her hand draws me forward. Clairvoyance aside, basic espial skills elude me. There is something different about Theodora, I realize, something enervating in her move that gives me pause. But the thought is fleeting. For one just released from Tartarus, I am too saturated with sensations, with emotions.

I draw close to her, feeling her eyes upon me from behind the veil.

I stop and prostrate myself in the fashion she had brought back from the past—to the loathing of senators and nobles. Face down, arms outstretched. Some things one does not forget.

"Rise, Stephen," she says. It is the Greek name that a long-ago magus assigned me, my boy's name of Sufian all but forgotten. "I've never required that of you." Her voice is snappish, yet soft as air.

I rise. My body is unsteady and stiff as a plank of wood.

"It has been a long time, Stephen."

"Yes. Five years, Mistress," I say, employing the epithet demanded of the Justinian and Theodora regime.

"So—you've kept a calendar?"

I did manage that. The omission of even a basic reed pen was intended, I knew from the first. What was she afraid I would write? "Yes," I say, "I make scratches on the wall. One scratch for every two meals. That makes for one day, Mistress." I resist saying something about the quality of the food.

A silent nod.

"But your codices—you were given your codices?"

I nod. "And tapers. It was very gracious of you." Best to keep my answers short, I think. Best not to reveal too much.

In gesture, her hidden right hand disturbs the mantle that envelopes her. "Dispense with the formalities, will you? You and I knew each other well once upon a time."

"We did, Mistress—once upon a time."

"Ah, the old irony is in your voice. I like that."

"I practice on my fellow tenants so as not to fall out of habit. I don't think the rats always understand my humor. Or perhaps I have less of it. They are more concerned with having a share of my morning stale bread." I immediately regret my answer. I know where such words could lead me.

"Bitterness, too." Her shallow intake of air is audible. "Ah, who can blame you?"

After a few moments, she says, "You have not lost your looks, either, Stephen. That Syrian handsomeness. A bit dirty and malnourished perhaps, although you were always slender, unlike most of the palace eunuchs."

I shift from one foot to the other, aware of the stink of my tunic. This invitation to intimacy unnerves me. Though her comment about my appearance touches on a pride long thought dead, a flame of anger ignites at my center.

"We came through some times, did we not?" Theodora asks. "Some times."

Her voice is still sultry, but I cannot tell whether her wistfulness is real or a guise. She is good at donning masks, always had been. I do not answer and an awkward silence ensues.

"You hate me, Stephen," she says, employing one of her theatrical sighs, causing her veil to shiver. "Of course, you must."

"No," I say. The answer is impulsive. I give my reply no thought, no thought to the hours and days and years spent cursing her in the labyrinthine stone complex beneath the Great Palace.

"I wonder," she says. "I wonder."

"It's just that—" Tears of fire suddenly ignite in my eyes.

"Yes, Stephen?" She tilts her head slightly, addressing me as if I am a child. "What?"

"It's just that I had no hint of what my sin was." My words, my tears, are childish. I feel small and despise her for it. I feel something else, too, an emotion long since thought dead, and I hate myself for that. Could some shred of my long-ago love still endure?

"Ah, but you were close at hand. Too close." Her voice hints at a thin smile behind the veil.

Too close? Her meaning escapes me.

"Fate betrayed you. Oh, it is hard for any woman to admit her wrongs, Stephen, much less an empress."

My head spins. Is this an admission of wrongdoing on her part? Why? Or is it possible she is toying with me as prologue to the sentence held in abeyance for so long? Has my execution been ordered?

"Stephen, you are wondering why I have sent for you."

I attempt to smother a laugh. "It must be your mother's Syrian blood that tells you so."

She laughs, too, from behind the veil. "I never had the gift. You know that."

When our light laughter—mine more forced than hers—fades, I lift my gaze to the veil and the occasional glint of eyes that it hides, eyes like black, depthless pools that had entranced a prince and won an empire. I straighten and push fear from my voice. "What do you want with me?"

"Ah, to the point, yes?" Now comes the intake of air behind the veil again, this time sharper. "Stephen, I need your skills."

"What skills?"

"Your memory. Your fairness. Your education—and your eloquence with the pen."

"But I've been denied kalamos, as well as parchment."

"Your pens will be given to you.—Stephen, I want you to remember the years of our friendship, as well as the stories I have told you."

"What shall I write?" I ask. "The story of your life?"

Long moments ensue before she releases the answer in a sad hiss: "Yes."

I meant the question as a joke. Now I stand speechless, numb, feet locked to the floor. Maybe I have the gift, after all.

"You know how I came to be here, my friend. How I came to wear the purple. My God, you helped me! A bit unwittingly at first, but for you, I might not be here."

I swallow hard. Astonishment washes over me like water over stone, so cold it stings. *My friend?* Are the past five years to be expunged as if of no significance? I am trying to fashion something to say even as she is removing her veil. At the sight, any choleric words that I might venture fall away.

This is not Theodora. Not the Theodora I once knew. Not that her beauty is gone or the change dramatic. The heart-shaped face is still magnificent, the brows still richly dark and thinly penciled so that they meet, but her visage is gaunt—not overtly, just enough for me to notice. The skin, of Greek and Syrian extraction, is just a bit more pale than I recall. As she removes the veil, the purple mantle falls away from her hands and arms, and I notice that they are veined and thin. Theodora had never looked her age, had always held a decade at bay, but now her forty-seven years are in evidence.

My eyes meet hers, and my heart catches. She is studying my reaction. My effort to mask surprise comes too late.

She sits straight and stiff. Her right hand goes to the dimpled area at the base of her neck, her first two fingers gently massaging. It's a gesture I've witnessed her make in moments of uncertainty, whether at a board game or at someone's death. "Remember how others were amazed at how much alike we looked? Is the likeness less?—It is, your expression tells me so. Oh, don't pity me, Stephen. I will not have it!"

"The physicians, have they—"

"I knew you would see it, Stephen." Her hand falls into her lap. "No one else has, not even Justinian. It's a cancer, the physician says. Oh, he claims I have years—but who knows?"

I feel light-headed. This is all too grotesque. An hour before, I had been in my cell, and it was a day like any in the nearly two thousand that had preceded it. And now I am in the empress's reception room, my mind unable to adapt as quickly to her presence as had my eyes to natural light and color.

"Will you tell my story, Stephen?"

"Why me, Mistress?"

"Because others will tell it slant. I trust you to tell the truth. And you have been with me from the day I met Justinian. Who better? And as for the years before, I think I have told you many of the particulars, but I shall refresh your memory."

"I remember all of your stories, Mistress." I stifle my rage. What had I to do in recent years—other than rely on my memory to keep myself sane?

Theodora takes on that snappish tone again. "In private, as we are now, you are to address me as you once did." She pauses, drawing herself up, her fragile frame leaning slightly forward. "The stories I told you comprise my journey, my life.—And I will not have them vilified by Procopius!"

"Procopius?"

"Yes, Procopius, Stephen."

"But he records the empire history, does he not? Or has Justinian dismissed him?"

"Oh, he still has his place. Some even call him an *eminent* court historian." She manages a laugh, a bitter laugh that evolves into a painful coughing. Many seconds elapse before she recovers enough to continue: "Others may think him eminent, my husband among them, but he is a snake in the royal household. You can be certain he writes works that flatter the empire and flatter Justinian and flatter me, but I have it from house spies that he is at work on a secret manuscript in which I play a leading role. It is a web of lies he will bring forth after I'm gone, you can be sure. So—I must leave behind my own record.... Will you write it, Stephen?"

Theodora does not ask me to forgive her. I try to understand this woman whose word had plunged me into darkness. Now a word and a whim have brought me into the light. She no doubt thinks my bitterness can be transformed into gratefulness. *If she gives it any real consideration at all.*

My own thoughts seize on my five years out of favor, five years' imprisonment—unjust imprisonment. An impulse possesses me now to feel for my belt and dagger. I do not follow through on it, of course, for I have neither. I want to fly at Theodora, nonetheless, fly at her and strangle her fine, snowy neck, denying her the months or years she has left.

Instead, my eyes settle onto that exquisite visage, those dark, proud eyes, and I hear myself answer like any bootlicker to the throne: "Yes, Mistress."

Is it by design or by chance that a poor boy is taken from a failing farm in the hills of Syria, schooled in languages, made to meander the great cities of the East, coming at last to the greatest, whereupon he becomes friend— and enemy—to the Empress of the New Roman Empire? Whether my life has been guided by direction of a god or fate—or merely chance—I, myself, am choosing this turn in the road.

And so begins my unexpected career as a biographer.

I do not return to my subterranean hell. I am given a room that could compare to one that Christians would call an upper chamber in Heaven. Oh, it is not the suite of prior years, but I don't care, for the room has a niche that will serve as an office, windows, and a terrace. I will see the rising and setting of the sun, the waxing and waning of the moon, and—if my luck holds—the cycle of the seasons.

This first night, I leave my bath to find that the attendant has left. I immediately go to the door, draw in breath, and grip the handle. The door opens and I sigh in disbelief that it does.

A fine tunic, dalmatic, and sandals have been laid out for me. In fact, the wardrobe, empty when I entered the bath, has been well stocked. The white linen dalmatic slides on as if made of silk. The long, voluminous sleeves, neck, and hem are trimmed in gold. I reach up to the shoulder and touch the purple-threaded badge in the shape of a kalamos, a reed pen. My fingers glide over it. My status as a royal scribe and Secretary to the Empress has been returned to me.

I walk barefoot out onto the terrace. Here is my adopted and beloved Constantinople, wonderfully cacophonous with the cries of peddlers and children, its skyline burned red with the sunset. I think my heart will burst. I cry now, releasing long-held tears and shaking like an old woman, for all the sunsets that have come and gone without me. And for this one that embraces me like a lover.

Something claims my attention, something I swear not to take for granted again. I marvel at the mere movement of air upon my skin. A spring breeze sweeps up from the Sea of Marmara, bringing with it the sweet, heady fragrance of the jasmine vines down near the water.

My God, I am alive again!

I look out to the waters that undulate gently, their sparkle pinkened by the dying sun. My eyes take in the shores of Constantinople, surrounded on three sides by bodies of water. The lapping ripples of the Golden Horn, the Bosporus, and the Sea of Marmara bedeck The City like a coruscating necklace of diamonds that leads the eye to the seven hills, as to the contours of a beautiful woman. I look out, luxuriate, and remember.

More than thirty years before, I had entered The City—as many call it—by ship through the Sea of Marmara. My coming had not been by choice, of course, but nevertheless the sight of this twelve-century-old maritime colony had been that of a siren to a wandering sailor. My eyes widened at the sight of the acropolis—so mysterious and majestic to me then—where it rose on a triangular bit of land that jutted out toward the sea. The ship sailed along the eastern shore, one marked by a long sea wall that was interrupted by two small harbors. Above the wall rose the buildings of The City: grand and small, rich and poor, public and private. We sailed north toward the famous harbor of the Golden Horn, passing as we went the Church of the Holy Wisdom, the Senate House, the Hippodrome, and the complex of the Great Palace. How could I have guessed that in short order the palace would be my home?

The sun is fully set now, and my thoughts come back to Theodora. *Yes*, I had told her. I would write her story. Why had I agreed? I owe her nothing, nothing but what repayment I might give for five years sealed in a tomb. Oh, for the moment I had been moved by her illness and pity and maybe even the old love. Our bond had been too close for me not to feel something. Was that why I had said yes?

Perhaps.

The word had fallen out of my mouth without thought. Had I immediately assumed that agreement meant release? Certainly, that was a possibility. Scruples can be elusive when freedom is the prize. In any case, the hatred and thirst for revenge bred by countless hours in that cell were not to be dispelled so easily, like my childhood nightmares had been quelled by my mother's soft voice and soothing hand to the forehead.

No, it is only now, after agreeing to tell her story in manuscript that I come to realize my prayers have been answered. I will have my day. I will be redressed. And as the moon emerges above me, my heart sings as if I am fifteen and in love.

But to take revenge on a dying woman—an empress forged in steel, nonetheless—would demand cold determination and a cunning mind. I vow to meet the challenge. Why, to think I could have strangled her right there in her bedchamber, so imperiously certain was she of herself and my unflinching fidelity that she had dismissed her guards. Has the sickness entered her brain? Does she truly think I could forget so quickly? Does she think me such a spineless sycophant?

Only one of the two chairs in my new quarters is cushioned and lends any comfort. The desk, so highly polished I need no mirror to see my thin face, is laden with manuscripts, paper, pens, and ink. My fingers tremble to once again hold a writing instrument. The sleeping couch is wide and so soft I cannot sleep that first night.

Two days later, my task begins.

It is late at night when a soft knock, almost imperceptible, comes at the door. I open it to find Theodora standing there, a finger to her lips. She is dressed in a purple bedchamber robe. She wears no veil or headdress. Her hair falls about her face like an ebony frame about the portrait of a ghost. I stand aside and she enters, gliding like some visitant saint into a monk's cell.

But she is no saint. And since I am no monk, I take the comfortable chair.

"You know the circumstances of my birth, Stephen, how my mother kept me from being ... abandoned—exposed to the elements."

I nod, taking up a kalamos.

"The story is legend by now. Of course, it may be quite accurate, but my mother would relate it as a way of upbraiding a thoughtless and unappreciative daughter who would drolly mimic the ways of the adults around her, as well as the pretentious airs of an older sister. I was two when the mid-wife was called again and Mother gave birth to a third child—alas, another girl." She pauses, appraising me, her biographer. "Take what I tell you, Stephen, and bring my life to parchment. Breathe life into my past." The empress grimaces as she settles in without complaint against the hard back of the chair, bringing her hands together in her lap, the interlocking fingers pale as moonbeams against the purple of her robe. "I shall begin, Stephen, where my memory begins."

For my pettiness in my choice of chair, I feel a tinge of guilt, but I dust it away and begin taking the notes that will become her biography.

2

Constantinople

THOUGH THEODORA WAS PALE AND thin at birth, she was not a sickly child, and as time went on, she thrived. The midwife who had suggested she be exposed would have wondered at the outcome. She was long since dead.

Theodora was five years old when her Greek father died in 505. He had been a longtime circus worker for the Greens, one of the two main competing factions—scarcely more than gangs—whose influence dominated the games and chariot races in the massive amphitheater, the Hippodrome. He took great pride in his training of bears, and his skills were remarkable enough for him to be promoted to Master of the Bears. But with his disappointment upon the birth of the third girl, Anastasia, he indulged in drink, an avocation especially to be avoided by a bearkeeper. He escaped injury for a few short years, but one day he drank himself into a stupor and was fatally mauled by one of his dancing bears. Death often has a more profound effect on the young than on the seasoned, and so it was that the loss of her father bitterly stung Theodora. She had been his favorite.

Her Syrian mother, Asima, a dancer and actress past her professional prime but still darkly attractive in her early thirties, was not long without a man in attendance. The suitor, Militiades, had experience in bearkeeping in Cyprus but currently had no means to support a future wife with three young girls. Asima proved ever-resourceful, and soon after their marriage contrived a scheme that was to involve Theodora and her sisters.

She bartered well with one of The City's best seamstresses, sacrificing the furnishings of her little home so that lovely white mantles of muslin with borders of brocaded gold could be made to dress her daughters. White and red flowers were fashioned into bracelets and into crowns for their dark tresses. The three exchanged silent, questioning looks as their mother fussed, behaving like some stranger, preoccupied and nervously tense. At three, Anastasia was too young to understand, but Comito and Theodora, at seven and five respectively, knew that they were being groomed for something very special.

Their mother coached them in a simple dance and on the appointed day, they were ushered into the immense Hippodrome, a place open to all on ceremony and parade days but restricted to men on game days such as this. As they passed near to the side occupied by the Green Party, Theodora saw someone waving and calling to her from the lowest bench. She recognized her dearest friend Antonina, whose father was a charioteer favored by the Greens and who no doubt had used his status to allow his daughter to attend. Theodora waved back and drew herself up. "Proud as a peacock" her mother had told them. "Walk as proud as a peacock."

It was the first time the three girls had been inside, and as they were led out into the hollow of the U-shaped structure and onto the hard dirt concourse, Comito began to cry. "It's all right, Comissa," Theodora said, employing her older sister's diminutive, "Just remember the steps Mother told us. And hold your head high." Still, she had her own fears to face down. *Why are we here?*

The kathisma, the imperial box, stood empty but the stadium was nevertheless filled near to its capacity of sixty thousand. The crowded stands resembled an enormous canvas of color set in motion. The noisy audience, completely masculine as a matter of course, was here to view and wager on the races. Theodora had never seen so many people.

They stood, three delicate and trembling figures, thrust before the mob of thousands in the stands. The dirt raceway on which they were placed would soon be clouded with dust and vibrating to the wheels of chariots and hooves of madly-driven horses. The Blues' faction was favored by the emperor so that they gathered in the tiers nearest the kathisma on the shady eastern side, while the Greens, inveterate enemies of the Blues, assembled on the western tiers. Asima positioned her three girls on the concourse closest to the Greens. At a word from her, they began the little dance they had practiced for a week. Joining hands, they moved in a circle for three slowly-paced revolutions. Their hands dropped to their sides then, and they bowed to one another. Their right arms reached up into the air, and clasping hold of one another's hands, they moved in the opposite direction for another three revolutions. Several variations followed before they stopped, dropped their heads in obsequiousness, and came to stand directly before the Greens, the faction that had employed their natural father. The man that her mother had pointed out as the leader of the Greens—the demarch, she called him, stood stone-faced.

"Smile," their mother called from the side, mimicking the expression.

Her sisters may have needed the prompting, but Theodora did not. From the start, she found that she was enjoying herself. Theodora peered up into the masses and felt a prickling upon her skin.

The audience, packed together on the benches of wood planking and brick supports like a roosting murder of crows, row mounted upon row—seemingly to the sky—remained unaware of their presence. The men continued with their clamorous conversations in anticipation of the day's races. To those more concerned with wagers, drivers, and horses, the girls were but three tiny insects on the vast concourse.

At a signal from their mother, they knelt.

The herald's deep voice cut through the din as he presented himself to the Greens. "These children," he proclaimed, "kneel as suppliants to the Green faction! The oldest is Comito, then Theodora, and the littlest is Anastasia, whom they call Tasia."

The girls rose, in turn, and curtsied as they had been coached.

The herald fought to hold the attention of a crowd interested mainly in the impending races. "I ask you to listen and hear their plea!" he shouted. "Their father, Master of the Bears, Acacius by name, has died in the line of duty! Their mother—see her there—implores the Green faction to give the post Master of the Bears to her new husband so that he can support her offspring!"

The children knelt again. Theodora's heart beat fast. The initial thrill she had felt dissipated with the realization that few seemed to be interested in them. Her little body tensed. Even at her tender age, Theodora sensed that this was the moment for which her mother had planned. This was her moment of truth.

No signal, no call, came from the Green benches. The demarch looked away. Those who might have listened remained unmoved. Shouts went up. "What is this delay? Away with those girls! Let the races begin!"

"The father of these girls must have a position!" The announcer was becoming hoarse and red in the face. "He comes from Crete with much experience with dancing bears. Hear me! These girls beg you to make Militiades Master of the Bears!" He pointed to the father.

Theodora's stepfather took a step forward from his place at the side of his wife, his plain face impassive. It was his only part in the little drama.

The herald's further attempts were shouted down with chants of "Take them off! Take them off! Take them off!" Years later, Theodora would learn that to launch her scheme, her mother had bribed the amphitheater's herald, as well as others deemed necessary, with what little she had in the world, her favors.

Theodora's heart caught when she saw her mother's face whitened with shame and streaming tears. Her scheme was slipping toward ruin. This woman whose name meant "protector" and to whom she looked for strength was suddenly so vulnerable and shaken. Theodora had not fully understood the events of the afternoon, but her mother's hurt was not lost on her. Oh, how her heart ached for her. What had her mother done to deserve the taunts of so many?

The three sisters had been tutored only to this point, so they had no idea what they were to do now. Their dance had ended in ignominious defeat. They knelt, helpless and frightened by the deafening impatience of the mob. Theodora looked to her mother, who had been transformed into a weeping Madonna. The concourse was stony and unforgiving to the tender knees of the three. Little Anastasia began to cry.

Theodora prayed that her mother would regain her senses and take them away. On impulse, she stood and ran to her mother, burying her face in her mantle and begging her not to cry. Then she began to tug on her mother's arm and plead to be taken home. Her mother pulled back, resisting and imploring Theodora to return to her sisters. "You must dance again."

Theodora did not know that across the stadium her actions must have provided an entertaining dumb show that was quickly gaining the attention—and sympathy—of the Blues. To them, out of earshot, this pathetic pantomime of a mother and her daughters was entertaining.

Suddenly, she and her mother became aware of a competing commotion that rose, like a tidal wave, distant at first, then taking on power until it drowned out the jeering of the Greens. She turned and looked across the stadium. Men were standing on their benches waving them over. "Come here, girls," they were calling. "Come!"

Theodora's mother immediately sprang to life, and even while swiping at her tears, she shooed her three around the spina—the low wall with obelisks and sculptures that divided the racecourse into two lanes—and toward the benches of the Blue faction, like a hen chasing her chicks. Militiades followed.

They stood before the cheering Blues, ever-antagonistic foes of the Greens. "So," the demarch of the Blues bellowed, stepping out onto the raceway as if onto a stage, "Demarch Asterios and his Greens have no heart? They would turn you out into the streets?" he asked, making wide gestures. "Well, we will not! As fortune would have it, our bearkeeper has recently died, so your new father may take his place."

Tears started flowing once again down her mother's cheeks, this time from surprise and relief and joy. Theodora was happy, too, because her mother was happy. Later, they would learn that Asterios had accepted a bribe to give the post to another.

"Now, come sit with us, girls," the Blue demarch said, "the jugglers and acrobats are about to begin."

There, on the side of the Blue faction—the shady east side—they watched in awe as a splendid display of entertainment usually denied to children—and to women—unfolded before them. In time, after the acrobats, jugglers, mimes, and animal acts, a herald announced the names of the drivers, after which the blast of a trumpet pierced the air, signaling the first of twenty-five races. Theodora looked in awe and pointed to the starting gates where, on a roof high above the gates stood a life-size gilded sculpture of a quadriga, a chariot drawn by four horses galloping abreast. "They look so real," her mother said, "except that they are made of gold."

"Not gold," her stepfather responded, "copper, through and through."

Theodora gave little thought to the difference between gold and copper, for in moments real quadrigas—two driven by Blues, two by Greens—came thundering out of their stalls, each attempting to hug the low wall down the center as they flew down the length of the track. Each team of horses moved at breakneck speed. At the far end of the concourse, workers removed from the spina the first of seven metal cast sculptures of dolphins, indicating that the chariots would have to pass by six more times, and as they returned to the starting turn, the first of seven metal ostrich eggs was removed, signifying to the audience the completion of a full circuit. Gold emblems, silver helmets, and purses of gold coins imprinted with the emperor's image were presented to the winners. At intervals between races, the sand covering the hard dirt concourse was raked as musicians, singers, and mimes performed. It was indeed a charmed afternoon.

The low wall of the spina supported an array of sculptures, statues and obelisks, and Theodora found herself mesmerized by a particular bronze column of three serpents interweaved when she noticed that across the track Antonina was waving again. She returned the gesture.

"Who is that you're waving to?" her mother asked.

"That's Antonina, Mother—my friend. Her hair is golden!"

"Indeed? I see that. But her father is a charioteer for the Greens. Her grandfather had been one, as well. From now on, Thea, you are not to play with her, do you hear? We are beholden to the Blues now."

Her mother's order hardly seemed fair and while she sank back a little on the bench and gave no response, she knew even then that she would not obey it. Antonina's connection to the Greens was not one she had chosen.

The Blues may have been merely trying to humiliate the Greens, without any real regard for the plight of Theodora's family, but she was somehow changed by the event. She would never forget their act of kindness, nor would she forget the black-hearted reaction of the Greens. She was changed in a more important way, too. From the moment they were placed—like actors on a stage—before the swarming audience, as frighteningly awesome as it was, a certain foreign excitement pumped into her heart, coursing through her like liquor, an exhilaration that was to become for her, in the years to come, as necessary as life itself.

But the three girls were to learn early in life that Tyche, Goddess of Fortune, could be capricious. Militiades owned sandals that shifted with the sands, and within a year, he deserted the family. A series of men, each of whom their mother insisted they address as "uncle," paraded through their lives, staying only for brief periods.

Acting as speaker for her sisters, Theodora once pointed out to her mother that they didn't care for a particular uncle. Her mother slapped her hard across the mouth and sternly scolded the three, saying that were it not for their uncles, they would not have their little house on a rise just above the city of Constantinople but would be quartered in the squalid tenements below. Theodora learned the value of silence.

In the next few years, her mother's darkly radiant beauty faded at a rate that outdistanced her years. As Asima continued to worry about the support of her family, her once buoyant disposition became increasingly morose. Visits from "uncles" became more sporadic, lessened in tranquility, shortened in duration.

Theodora was put to work at the age of ten. Her mother had been an actress and so had the necessary connections in theater. At twelve, Comito—darkly beautiful and more than a head taller than Theodora—was already a rather successful comedic actress at the Old Royal Palace so that her younger sister's initiation to life on the boards was a logical one. Theodora studied Comito's performances with the absorption of an understudy. "I want to be as beautiful as you," she would say. "I want to be tall, too!" Theodora played small, non-speaking parts. Until one day.

It was one of Comito's typical one-act comedies. Theodora was playing a servant girl, as usual, with no lines or interesting stage business. She resented the fact that she was but a tiny cog in the workings of the play. On this particular night, Comito was reclining languidly on a chaise while spouting funny lines to several other key players. Often, the humor escaped Theodora, but the tittering of the audience indicated that her lines held some secret meaning. Only later would she learn that the lines were double entendres, often lewd.

"Girl!" Comito called. "Hurry with my supper. Even idols must eat."

Dressed in an undyed tunic of the lower classes, Theodora entered from the right, balancing a heavily laden tray. She started moving to upper center stage, toward Comito. A stool that was out of place stood in her path, but with the tray she failed to notice it. She fell headlong over it, sending tray, dishes, and silver clattering and crashing to the floor.

The audience gasped and snickered, but Theodora took little notice. For the moment a childish anger rose up from within, causing her to forget that she was onstage. She pulled herself to her feet and put her hands on her hips in much the same way her mother did in moments of chastising her three daughters. "What idiot left that stool there?" she demanded.

Beyond the footlights an eerie silence descended, silence that did not last long before the audience erupted in laughter, sustained laughter.

Suddenly, Theodora remembered where she was and that she had no lines. Hot blood rushed to her head. Her sister's face registered dumb surprise and the jaws of the other players went slack, too. A deadly lull fell now upon the play. Everyone, players and audience alike, was at a loss for how to react. She felt every eye in the theater on her. A heat came into her face. Her immediate impulse was to run. She was scanning the stage for the most direct egress when she spied Ivan—the theater owner and director—across the way in the wing, his face beset with panic.

Instead of running, she drew herself up, deciding now to play the scene she had started—she had been too long without lines. Besides, Ivan—who had treated her with nothing but disdain—was now wildly gesticulating for her to leave the stage, his face flaring red with anger. He had given the boot to players for lesser infractions, so she concluded that her stage career had met with a sudden end. She ignored a flutter in her chest, drew in breath, puffed out her cheeks and grimaced in mock pain. "Who put that stool there?" she raged, her voice escalating unnaturally. "I could've been killed!"

The crowd roared. But Comito rose and started downstage toward her sister. It was not laughter gleaming in her black eyes. It was murder. "How do you dare?" she spat. She raised her hand to Theodora, who turned her head with the movement of her sister's hand so that while contact produced a sudden sting, the brunt of the slap escaped her. The audience fell into hysterics. Comito's reaction, like Theodora's, had been unconscious and real. Now, the realization that they were spontaneously creating comedy flashed across her face, a realization Theodora had already taken in. The sisters' eyes met in a moment of conspiracy. "Take that!" Comito cried, her hand coming down on Theodora's cheek in a mock slap. And again Theodora turned her face with the blow, this time allowing only a whisper of wind to come near. She stamped the floorboards with a pummeling motion of her legs and feet. "I won't have it," she screamed. Her nostrils flared, and she screwed up her face as if to punctuate her little mutiny.

The playgoers responded uproariously—Comito's plays had never been received so warmly.

And so, for two years, Theodora became her sister's apprentice in comedy. As she found herself closer to center stage, a fascinating and potent power enveloped her. A power she would not willingly relinquish.

3

"WHAT ARE THESE ENTERTAINMENTS?" THEODORA would ask fourteen-year-old Comito. She was twelve now, a curious child maturing into a curious adult. Her eyes were always moving, ears always pricked.

"Be still, Theodora."

"But perhaps I can be of help. You know I am good in the comedies."

"Yes, Theodora, you are very good. Sometimes you show up your older sister. And your body is developing—you are becoming very pretty."

"Well, then?"

"It's just that … well, you have yet to fully blossom. You are still very young, but the day will come. All too soon you will know the ways of The City."

Carrying her three-legged stool on her head, she would follow Comito through the tangled, narrow streets of Constantinople, stopping for indeterminate durations at private residences where her sister would be admitted, leaving Theodora at the stoop to set up her stool and amuse herself. The houses of the wealthy had largely blank walls facing the street, so that when their doors closed on her, she felt both excluded and inquisitive.

There on her stool, Theodora would keep her mind occupied—for a time—by the variety of people and the bustling activity, for these great villas often rose up side by side with the more modest wooden houses of the middle class and even the ramshackle hovels of the poor. Sometimes her younger sister, Anastasia, accompanied her, providing a diversion. Usually, though, boredom set in and she would retreat into her own inner world of thoughts and dreams.

Theodora could not wait to grow up. She was certain that she would become a great lady of The City, that everyone would know Theodora. She longed to dress in luxurious silks and brocades, to buy jewelry and perfume at the finest shops along the Mese, the main thoroughfare, to have a respected and handsome husband, and to be admired for her charm, beauty, and wit.

These were the imaginings of an innocent girl, imaginings that came long before the understanding that one's status could be limited by one's class, bloodline, and sex.

She was one of three daughters in a community where sons were most prized. The little family was of the lower class, but they had their freedom. And Theodora had her dreams, wild and absurdly naïve, but without them the course of her life and history would have been very different.

Any naiveté associated with childhood was wrenched from Theodora without warning in that twelfth year, on a day like many others preceding it. She sat alone on her stool outside a patrician home, brooding over her continued exclusion. She noticed one of the house servants, a large woman burdened with two baskets of fish, fruits, and vegetables, struggling up the incline toward the villa. A white snood did not serve to hide hair that had not fully grayed, but to someone as young as Theodora, the woman seemed ancient.

Theodora jumped up. "May I be of some help?"

"Ah, thank you, child!" the woman said, wheezing. "You are a gift from God."

Theodora took one of the baskets. "That is my name."

"What, child?"

"Theodora. I am Theodora. Gift from God."

The woman laughed. "Most appropriate!"

They made their way to the side entrance. "I am too old to go to market," the woman said between labored breaths. "And my legs are weak nowadays. But if I send the younger one, she brings home produce that never ripens or is on the verge of rotting. What can I do?"

A male house servant came to the door, admitted the woman, and took the basket from Theodora. The two disappeared into the house. Hands full, the servant had kicked the door behind him, but the lock did not engage, so the door remained slightly ajar.

Heart thumping, Theodora stared at it only momentarily before slipping into the villa. She paused to listen. The sounds of the servants came from the left, to the rear of the house. Quickly removing her sandals, she ventured forward into the first room on her right. The mirror-like black marble floor was cool on her feet as she moved through a wide, colonnaded reception room. Breathlessly, she stole from column to column, pressing close to them for concealment while gaping at the gilded ceilings and rich furnishings. The rooms of the Roman villa were grouped so as to open out onto a beautifully landscaped courtyard, the centerpiece of which was a fountain with quick flowing waters that gurgled and flashed in the sun. Exotic birds of brilliant hues were cloistered in bamboo cages. Astonished, Theodora stared for what seemed a long time. She recognized nightingales, starlings, and two parrots.

Other than the warbling of the starlings and intermittent squawking of the parrots, the house was strangely silent. She wondered where Comito could be; she could hear none of the usual sounds of entertainment. Might she have left by another door, forgetting her little sister?

A noise.

Theodora went rigid with fear. Her eyes darted about, but she could not detect the source of the noise because the highly vaulted chamber allowed for deceivingly placed echoes. It had sounded like the catching of a door latch, but she could not be certain. She felt unsafe and thought it best to retrace her path and reclaim her stool outside.

Theodora had taken only a few steps toward her point of entry when a powerful hand gripped her shoulder, a man's blunted fingernails cutting into her skin.

"Ah, what have we here?" a deep voice demanded. He roughly turned Theodora to face him. His dark olive face loomed large over her. His brown dalmatic had wine and food stains.

Her heart pounded heavily and she felt a pressure at her temples. Words would not come.

"A thief, so it seems. Is that it?"

"I am not a thief!" Theodora blurted.

"So there is a tongue in that pretty head. You are trespassing, are you not?" His breath reeked of garlic.

She bowed her head. "Yes, sir, but I am not a thief."

"What is your name?"

"Theodora."

"And if not for thievery, why do you trespass?"

"I was waiting for my sister at the entrance … the door was left open … I came in."

"Curiosity, eh?"

"Mama says I would have died at birth if I hadn't been so curious about what I would miss."

Disarmed, the man laughed heartily and released his hold. "Tell me, Theodora, who is your sister?"

His shift in mood prompted Theodora to relax. "Comito."

"Comito—ah, yes, Comito."

"Do you know my sister?"

"Oh, yes—yes, I do." He paused now and lifted Theodora's chin so as to study her face.

His touch sent a chill through her. She was immediately on guard again. The thick-set man's face was bearded, his features blunt. It was the piercing eyes, however, brown and flecked with red, that made her wish she were still on her stool outside.

"The resemblance is clear," he was saying. "The same creamy coloring, black eyes under heavy brows. Your father, the bearkeeper, was Greek, and your mother Syrian, yes?"

Theodora nodded. Her heart beat fast.

"A fine pairing, to be sure. Ah, but your features are even finer than Comito's. Your face is more oval. You will be a magnificent woman, Theodora." His finger moved caressingly under her chin.

Theodora drew back.

"Why is it that you must wait outside?"

"I am not allowed to attend the entertainments."

"But you would like to?"

"Oh, yes, but—"

"Come, then."

"But Comito—"

"Never mind. Put your sandals on and come along."

Theodora felt compelled to obey. Regret would come later. The man led her to a stairway. She was frightened—of the eerie silence, of what her sister's reaction to her audacity would be, of the stranger who held her by the arm.

"I had better wait outside," Theodora said, stopping halfway up the stairs.

"You wanted to see your sister, did you not? And the entertainments?"

"Yes." The word was scarcely a breath.

"Well, come along, then." His hold on her tightened.

She swallowed hard, caught like one of the birds in the courtyard.

They ascended the stairs and proceeded along the balcony that fronted the second-story rooms. A pungent scent of incense hung in the air. She could hear voices now—low, muffled whisperings and what could only be moans.

They came upon the last room at the far end of the balcony. The double doors were but half closed. Leaning down, the man fastened his hands on her shoulders so as to position her and whispered, "Comito is there."

Theodora peered in. The shades blocked the windows so that the chamber was dark as Hades' lair. Somewhere in the room wind chimes tinkled. Here, at the source of the incense, the air was thick, the scent sickeningly sweet. Beneath it, she detected a musky whiff that somehow reminded her of her mother's sleeping area.

As her eyes became accustomed to the dark, she could ascertain vague shapes in the interior of the large room. On the matted floor, intertwined torsos writhed as naked limbs lifted, swayed, caressed. Unable to determine how many men and women were engaged in this activity, Theodora listened as the sighs and moans of the many rose and fell and rose again in a collective force of what she realized was pleasure-taking.

The scene was foreign to her—and terrifying. Yet she could not look away.

The man bent forward. "Comito is there," he said, his foul breath hot upon her ear.

Theodora turned and glared up at him, her eyes challenging him.

The man's thick lips curved upward in a smirk.

Theodora pulled free and ran. Her agility was slowed by the slippery marble. There was no time to remove her sandals, for she could hear his steps behind her.

She was nearly at the stairhead when his one hand closed on her shoulder like an animal's claw, and the other covered her mouth.

Her balance gave way now as he dragged her into a nearby room, and the door closed behind them with a thud.

4

SOME MIGHT THINK THAT THE years that passed since Theodora's rape would have ameliorated the humiliation and pain of a twelve-year-old. Such is not the case with the empress. As I listen, the tears wash down her face as though she is experiencing the terrible event anew, bringing an end to our first session and I am left to wonder whether there would be another. Had the retelling brought out from hidden places so much distress that the dying woman would forego the venture? Does she have the desire to continue? The strength? And if she does not? Where would that leave me? I would no longer have a purpose and a use that afford me the new luxury of breathing fresh air. I brood over that uncertainty—and more.

I, too, live with a painful past. There are eunuchs who are admired and envied, ecclesiastical singers whose crystalline voices echo in the cathedrals or palace ministers who have the emperor's ear and who aid in overseeing the empire in significant posts. And there are those who chose the life, I had learned. But I am not one of them.

The choice had been made for me. And in spite of it, I ascended like a royal eagle within the hierarchy of the Great Palace. At the time of my imprisonment I had few friends but no enemies that I knew of. Well, maybe one, the very man Theodora has placed at the top of her enemies list: lawyer and court historian Procopius, who also climbed high in the palace ranks. He is a bearded one, that is to say, he is not a eunuch. I believe he disliked me because he had seen me rise from nothing to become the closest confidante of another outsider, one who rose from the streets to the highest throne: the empress. I'm certain he thought that in my relationship with the empress I had already risen too far above the station of most eunuchs. It was true, I know. I smile at the thought, painfully honest with myself now—the years in a damp and cramped cell made me so. Oh, I do admit to possessing hubris in those heady times.

But I stroll the halls lightly these days, wearing a mask of humility foreign to me in the old days—and acutely conscious of those around me.

I become uneasy when two days pass without word from Theodora. Has she changed her mind about the task she has given me? My anxiety is tempered by the deliciously rich meals delivered at appropriate times and the royal tailor who arrives to take measurements for my wardrobe.

On the afternoon of the second day, I happen to pass Procopius in the hallway near the Royal Library and Scriptorium where I once worked. I expect no warm greeting. When he sees and recognizes me, his facial expression shifts quickly from surprise to displeasure to bewilderment. He averts his eyes, no doubt at a loss as to what my release means. I wonder if he knows that the empress is aware of his plans for a secret codex about her.

It comes as a surprise to me that I am free to come and go within the palace and without. On the third day, I venture out into the serpentine streets of The City. It is a hot and dry August day. The noise of a city of 750,000 at midday—a varied cacophony of children's cries, peddlers' pleas, donkeys' braying, and dogs' barking—comes as a happy assault on the ears of one who had been buried alive in a soundless chamber. I hear the usual mix of foreign tongues, my native Syriac among them, but for the most part people speak Greek, the language I had learned well enough, along with Latin, even before my initiation to the palace.

Little seems to have changed since my imprisonment. The streets, teeming with people, are as varied and colorful and vibrant as ever. The odor of bodies too long unbathed and the smell of fresh dung deposited by donkeys trafficking rotund officials and rich patricians in carriages coalesce with the sharp cinnamon and clove scents of the spice quarter and the tantalizing balm and bouquet of the perfume shops, and to me it is all the same and all beautiful. It is life. The spice and perfume shops, I might add, are located closest to the complex of the Great Palace so as to keep at a distance the malodorous elements of the city.

Once in a while, I cast a backward glance, expecting to catch sight of a palace guard—an excubitor—shadowing me. In time, I realize I am indeed untethered. Free. Why, I could go … where? It dawns upon me now: I have nowhere to go. Nowhere at all. The palace is my home. The strongest chains are invisible ones. Theodora, shrewd as ever, knows as much, too.

In returning to the palace, I find myself walking along the colonnade of the Augustaion, the public square where city founder Constantine had set up a great statue of his mother. Children are running around the base of the sculpture, gleefully frightening and setting to flight the flocks of pigeons that have long made the square their home. I look up at the regal Augusta Helena. What might she have thought of the Augusta Theodora, I wonder, this low-born woman raised so high?

With its paved slabs of dark marble, the square is enclosed on three sides by the great edifices that are the heart of The City: the Church of the Holy Wisdom that had replaced the fire-damaged—and less spectacular—church of the same name, the Great Palace buildings, and the colossal amphitheater—the Hippodrome.

Theodora's early years—the years before I met her—were spent in the shadow of the Hippodrome. It could not have been an easy existence, for it was here that the masses were encouraged to give vent to their lowest impulses. Oh, the hand-to-hand gladiatorial contests had been abolished in the fourth century, but the lust for violence was carried forward in the often-fatal chariot races, and in blood sport among animals and between animals and men. Within a Christian Constantinople, this remains a place of the old ways, a haven for the ancient fickle gods and ruthless men. Here, the die-hard, uneducated leaders of the Blue and Green factions could be most cunning and cruel at manipulating and inciting their unemployed and rebellious youths. Why is it, I question, that the young must fight and die for the grudges and greed of the old? Is it any wonder that Theodora never forgave the Greens for their treatment of her mother? Life among such types no doubt toughened her in ways I could not imagine.

My worries about the empress's absence come to nothing. I had no cause to doubt Theodora's intent in her little literary venture. If her wish for me to tell her story were a whim, it was made of iron and forged by Hephaestus himself. For my moment of misgivings, I had forgotten that it was only she who had the backbone to persuade her husband not to flee when a bloodthirsty mob threatened the throne. She is no more about to abandon the telling of her own life in order to vanquish Procopius at his own game than she had been willing then to give up the wearing of the purple.

Under cover of night, Theodora comes again to my chamber. As I stand aside to allow her entrance, I smile to myself, for lest anyone witness her visit, she herself is carrying cushions for the uncomfortable chair.

And so, my life and work fall into a pattern as steady as the seasons. At each interview I take copious notes as Theodora speaks with great emotion of her early life. I then take pains to transform her narrative into a formal history of the empress. For now, I do not tell her story slant. I dare not, for at any moment of any given day Theodora might ask to see—or hear—the progress of our work.

All the while I crave redress just as I craved untainted water in my rodent-infested cell. I decide early on the approach I will take. I recall Olin, the Keeper of the Imperial Pantry, who had been driven from his high post in disgrace. The greedy eunuch had kept two accounting codices, one that recorded all the monies spent on kitchen matters and another that nearly doubled the amount with fictitious expenditures that over the years were meant to provide a treasure-trove for his anticipated retirement. He was found out when a fellow eunuch became jealous of the hidden cache and turned informer.

Like Olin, I will keep a second manuscript, one in which I will weave and embellish the gossip and whispers that had always swirled like a tempest around Theodora. I will lie on my sleeping couch, taking great pleasure in inventing scenarios of lust, greed, and violence that had never happened. I will care nothing for truth. What had she cared for me in the five years I was in the palace dungeon, good as dead?

And so, as Theodora resumes her narrative now, regally assuming she has my confidence, my loyalty, I put a steady kalamos to parchment, my blood all the while afire with the thought of revenge.

5

"Well," Comito said, clicking her tongue, "now you know everything, Theodora. Does it satisfy you? Of course, I will go to Mikos on your behalf and demand a respectable sum. He should be made to pay for what he's done. Virgins should command a good price."

They were seated in their little sitting room. Comito was sewing a stage costume she had torn. Theodora stared at her sister through wet-stained eyes. "Oh, Theodora," Comito exhaled in staged exasperation, "you cannot mean that you did not know the specifics—about intercourse?"

"Of course, I knew. It's just that … I didn't know women were to be used in that fashion—outside of marriage."

"Well, they are. We are. It is expected." Comito looked up at Theodora, her crisp reply deepening with anger. "But what is not expected is that a man would have the nerve to take you by force. Mikos must pay, damn him! I will go to him on your behalf and demand a respectable sum."

"What if he refuses?"

"Oh, he will pay, don't worry—I know men who will make him pay." Comito's gaze moved down to her stitching, but her hands remained idle. "You know, an actress in the theater is to play the role of prostitute like any other when bargained for by a spectator. She accepts her fate. If she enjoys it, so much the better! Men will start asking for you, so you might as well become accustomed to the idea."

"I will not!"

"You will have to, Thea. Men have asked about you already. I've always put them off."

Theodora glared at her sister.

Comito compressed her lips and continued stitching. "How long do you think you can go on playing the impish clown? It was all very fine two years ago, but you are too old for such a threadbare routine now. Your antics get fewer laughs with each performance. Have you not noticed? Yet, what can you do? You have no talents."

Theodora bristled in humiliation.

"Can you sing? Dance? What is left for you? You do not show the aptitude for my kind of adult comedy."

"Nor the inclination," Theodora countered. She felt fresh tears beading in her eyes.

Comito looked up. "Oh, Thea, I know this whole episode has been a trial for you, but you must put it behind. After all, we have problems that pertain to all of us."

"What do you mean?"

"Mother and I have been finding it more and more difficult to support the family."

"I've been working, too!"

"Your nightly pay, a copper follis or two, is nothing." Comito snickered. "It takes nearly three hundred folles to make a gold nomisma. For all your prying, where are your eyes? Mother and I have been maintaining the household by entertaining men. Why do you think you have had to follow me house to house?"

Theodora could only stare dumbly.

"It is so your nosiness does not interfere with Mother's assignations. Though they are fewer these days. She is not the young and desirable woman she once was."

Comito paused, waiting for a response, but her sister had none. "Your body is maturing, Theodora," she continued. "You are still girlishly slender, but there are many men who find that attractive." An intensity came into her eyes now that held Theodora captive. "Thea, you must gradually step into Mother's place. And in a few years—Tasia must help, too."

Theodora groped for words. "I will not ... be passed from man to man like a coin. And neither will I allow such a life for Anastasia!"

Comito's gaze went back to her work. "What choice is there for us? We are three half-breed daughters born into a circus family. We have no protector. There are limits set upon us.—Ouch!" Comito cried, having pierced a finger with her needle. "Well, at the very least, perhaps you could assist Irene, and then I would not have to mend my own costumes."

In Theodora's dreams there had been no limits. She stood, turning her back to Comito, and walked to the window that looked down on the shabby tenements below. Her dreams seemed silly now, with no connection to the real world. After a time, she spoke. "Do you like it, Comito—your life?"

Comito looked up, taken by surprise. "My life—well, yes, I suppose I do."

Theodora was certain her sister had not given the question any real thought, ever. Acceptance came easily.

"It is like any other life, I imagine," Comito continued. "Some things to the good, some to the bad. We cannot do much to change them."

"But—what if we could?"

"What?" Comito scoffed. "Change things? Not very likely, little Thea."

Theodora stood staring out the window for some time, mute as a stone.

Comito continued sewing. "Come now, Thea," she implored with an amused impatience, "what is it you are thinking?"

"I am thinking about our little family of women," she said. "And I am thinking about how quickly a coin becomes tarnished and worn when it is passed from hand to hand."

Comito shrugged her shoulders and said nothing.

That night Theodora cried herself to sleep.

Theodora's attacker, Mikos, evaded paying restitution by leaving The City for a political position in Alexandria.

Theodora set about to prove wrong her sister's assertions regarding the roles of women. She wanted to affirm that her own role in life was not pre-ordained—and that she had some talent, some gift. Progress came first on the latter; by the age of seventeen, she discovered and nurtured a talent. She learned that she could remove her clothes quite adeptly. Not quite a reputable skill, she knew, but one that set her on the road to independence.

Theodora spent many tears over her lack of height; neither did she have the fleshy vitality of women from Rome and other western provinces, and yet the day came when Theodora fully blossomed, as Comito had foretold. She was put to work by Ivan, the director who had rescued her from non-speaking parts. He was also the producer of "living pictures," and it was in these that Theodora began to make a mark, creating a sensation within the theater community and within The City. In these stage presentations of various biblical and mythical scenes, Theodora appeared nude or as nearly undraped as possible. She found herself center stage, and while the audience number was but a tiny fraction of those who had watched her dance in the Hippodrome, her success was intoxicating.

Theodora felt an obligation to help support the family and did so. However, she did not have any wish to follow in her mother's and sister's footsteps, footsteps that led door to door. Only those who were prepared to pay most handsomely did she reward with her favors. With a new stream of revenue, she was able to rent a tiny house not far from the theater.

Theodora became determined that her fate and that of her mother and Comito not befall her youngest sister Anastasia. She demanded top price for her companionship, saving money, too, so that a different life would be possible for Tasia. For the time being, her dreams and expectations were not for herself, but for her young sister.

Her meeting with Hecebolus began much as others had. One evening at the theater she noticed him in one of the front rows as she took her bows. Even from her removed position on the stage, she could see that she held him bewitched. Who could have guessed where it would lead?

That evening she performed her Aphrodite triplet, one of the most popular series of living pictures—and one of her favorites. As Aphrodite, goddess of love, she appeared in the first tableau alone in a garden setting. She was attired in an ice-blue tunic made of a gossamer fabric. One hand clutched the folds of the material near to her breasts where the tunic appeared to be threatening to pull away; the other hand held an apple.

In the second picture, Theodora was joined onstage by a well-built Ares, god of war. The love-smitten deity seemed to be tugging at her, while she feigned to shrink from his advances. The interaction had caused the tunic to slip, exposing her firm, round breasts and dark nipples. As if in unnerved saintliness, her eyes were uplifted.

In the third tableau, a nude Aphrodite reclined on a bed designed to tilt forward for the benefit of the audience. Ares, stripped to the waist, sat on the edge of the bed. Both deities stared above them in numbed surprise at an elaborate net that was about to descend and entangle the illicit lovers. An ugly hulk of an actor portrayed Hephaestus, smith to the gods and husband of Aphrodite, who stood stage right, smirking at the genius of his enterprise.

The actors held these poses for several minutes each while an actor offstage presented in stentorian tones a dramatic reading of the myth.

The director came to Theodora's changing cubicle after the performance. Like the mythical god Hephaestus, Ivan was a hunchback. But his unattractive appearance did not preclude a keen eye for ferreting out unusual attractions that drew large houses—and sometimes even critical praise.

"You were wonderful tonight, Theodora! It was no surprise to me, though. You are always at your best on the boards."

"What is it that you want, Ivan?"

Abashed—or appearing so—Ivan lowered his eyes. "There is someone in the audience—a friend of mine, Theodora—who wishes to meet you."

"The one in front with the grizzled beard?"

Ivan's eyes came up, widening. "Ah, you are always ahead of me, little Thea." His look was calculating. "May I say that you will receive him?"

"Show him to the stage after the show."

"But Theodora!"

"Yes?" she asked, playing at his game. "Isn't that where we receive our well-wishers?"

"I ... have assured him of a private audience."

"You presume too much, little man."

"I know, I know. But could you not—"

"No." Theodora smiled slyly. "Give him back half of the folles you have palmed and send him to the stage with the others."

"He was very generous. What are a few coppers to you?"

She thought how every follis was important to the family. "Do as I say."

As he left, Ivan muttered an aside meant to be heard: "She is but an actress and yet she earns more than I."

"Not on the boards I don't!" Theodora called after him.

Theodora took her time in dressing. As she stepped onto the stage, she saw the bearded man helplessly caught up and grappling with the swarming flow of cohorts and admirers who moved in to congratulate the cast. Her eyes passed over him with deceptive speed. He seemed unaware that she had even noticed him, and yet she forged her own impression of him.

He was shorter than she had imagined when she had seen him from the stage. He was painfully plain. No Ares here. Yet the man interested her in some indefinable way.

Theodora chatted and laughed gaily with those surrounding her, pretending to ignore the nervously intent stranger. She knew that his eyes never left her.

Finally, when conversations began to wane and most of the people filtered from the theater to other private places of late-night amusement, the strange little man summoned his courage, squared his slightly-stooped shoulders, and approached Theodora. "I did so enjoy your performance, my lady," he said.

"Did you? I'm glad." He was dressed well and stood exactly at her height. For once, she was glad she was not as tall as Comito.

Silence. It seemed that in all the time he had studied her, he gave no thought as to where he would lead the conversation. His eyes darted about. Theodora's lips tightened, affording no assistance.

At last he ventured, "I am Hecebolus."

She suppressed a smile, nodded. "I am Theodora."

"I was ... hoping to speak to you."

"And here I am, Hecebolus."

His eyes were tiny dark windows to his ardor.

"Well?" she pressed.

"Is it possible ... that is, may I spend the evening with you?"

"An easy request. You may join us. There are three parties tonight and I intend to put in an appearance at each."

"I meant ... if it is possible ... for me to be alone with you."

"You are a quiet one, but you come to the point soon enough." Her eyes captured and held his. "So shall I. Hecebolus, do not imagine for a minute that I can make a decent living by performing here. I am forced to rely on— other means. There is not a party-giver of any worth in all of Constantinople who will not pay me quite well to brighten up a dull gathering with my wit and a certain art of mimicry I possess." The lie came easily to Theodora's lips. While her mimicry was duly appreciated, no host or hostess had ever paid her.

"You will find that I am not a parsimonious man, Theodora." Hecebolus silently removed a ring from his little finger and placed it in her hand. "I am certain," he whispered, "that a good jeweler can mold a setting more suitable for one such as you."

Theodora stared at the finely detailed talons of some bird of prey, talons that clasped a large, perfectly faceted emerald. She felt a sudden lightness in her chest. No one had ever given her such a gift. Placing the ring on the third finger of her right hand, she smiled, drew in a long breath and said, "Why, Hecebolus, I think the setting is just fine."

6

That night, Hecebolus stayed at the little house in the shadow of the Old Royal Palace and just four weeks later, after a few assignations, he pledged his undying love as they lay on the sleeping couch. Theodora lounged on her back, eyes to the ceiling. She did not return his pledge.

"Make a life with me," Hecebolus pleaded. He was lying on his side, his finger tracing a path from one of Theodora's nipples to her naval then moving up again to encircle the other nipple. "I swear you will not regret it. I would be selfish only when it comes to you. Give up this wretched existence you lead. You will have everything. You will be able to provide money for your family. You will worry about nothing. It is only a matter of time before I am given a governorship."

"A governorship?"

"Yes. It will be an important post."

"Of what province?" she asked, feigning a lack of interest.

"It has not been determined."

"I see." Theodora shifted to her side, one arm propping up her head. Her eyes fastened on his as he lay across from her. "Does this mean marriage?"

The muddy brown eyes beneath the dark brows were suddenly sad. Sheep's eyes, she thought.

"You know that is impossible for us. I am of a patrician family, forbidden by law to marry a woman of the theater."

"So that renders you safe then?" Even as Theodora spoke, she knew her snideness was misdirected. She made an effort to rise from the sleeping couch.

Hecebolus held her back. "Do not think that I would not marry you if it were possible. I would! But think, my darling, how self-defeating it would be. Why, my position would be denied. We would be ostracized."

"But it is acceptable for me to become your mistress?" She lay back in submission.

"Hypocrisy is the lifeblood of society, I admit." Hovering over her, the sheep's eyes pleaded. "What have you here? A life with me would be a better life than here—having to degrade yourself by selling your body to the highest bidder. How many years do you think that can go on?"

Theodora's blood ran hot. How she resented his audacity. More than that, she resented the truth of his words. She lay quiet for a long time.

Finally, she said, "I possess something here that you would take away."

"What is that?"

"Freedom. My comings and goings are only my concern, regulated by no one. It is one of the few things that I can point out and say, 'This is mine.' You would deny me that."

Hecebolus could offer no protest, nor fair compensation, for such a loss.

"Fine as it is, I cannot accept your offer."

The man seemed to realize that he could not counter her claim, and his face fell into folds of disappointment that seemed to add years to his real age.

"Take heart," Theodora said. "Don't look so downcast. Come to the theater Tuesday next. Tuesdays will be yours, if you wish, only yours. But make no further demands of me—and come only on that day."

He did go to see her whenever he was in The City, reluctantly keeping to Tuesdays, always tearful at their goodbyes.

Hecebolus hailed from a prominent Greek family that had resettled in Antioch, Syria's trading crossroads. Over the weeks, Theodora plied him with earnest questions about her mother's homeland and the people whose blood flowed in her veins, along with the Greek of her father's. As yet, her world did not extend beyond Constantinople, and she longed to travel, to see other peoples, other ways of life.

Hecebolus assured her that his was a noble family fallen on hard times. He had been reduced to acting in the stead of a merchant from his city while he waited upon the promises of officials in The City.

Theodora knew well enough how hollow the promises of officials could be. She had come to know a number of the city officials, some high up, and she was aware that their pledges—both political and personal—could be forestalled year after year, and that many would never come to fruition. Such was the way of matters of state.

Despite Hecebolus' country naiveté—which even a girl half his age could discern—she liked him well enough. It was this facet of the man that drew her to him. He stood out from the usual menagerie of theater characters and hangers-on. He chose not to thrust and parry in meaningless wordplay. He was direct and sincere as sunlight. His attentions to her were unfettered by the pretenses with which she had become acquainted. Another girl of seventeen might have imagined herself in love. Theodora knew that this was not so, yet sometimes she fancied it true. She longed for passion in her life. Still, she felt something for Hecebolus, and for the time being, his adoration of her came like a cool mountain spring to sooth a life parched for genuine affection.

Before meeting him, Theodora could apply no tangible meaning to love. It had merely been a shopworn word in the plays at the Old Royal Palace, nothing more. Men were not to be trusted. Even her father—in his reckless behavior that led to his death—had dashed her sense of expectation. But now, with someone in love with her, vaporous notions of love took up residence in her head.—She knew that she did not love Hecebolus, and she wondered when—or whom—she might love.

Theodora's childhood gift of mimicry grew with her. She transformed it into a mischievous, yet genuine, talent and came to take an unabashed pride in it. She thought it great fun to take on the mannerisms and foibles of those around her. At nearly every party she was asked to do a turn.

Her talent elicited unforeseen repercussions at one particularly raucous gathering. She had already executed for the theater crowd a number of her more familiar imitations: the proud patriarch of Constantinople; the glib Emperor Anastasius; and an effete jeweler of some fame. She employed no costumes, wearing only her sand-colored tunic, and mining humor from her variety of facial contortions, gestures, and off-color commentary.

"Do another!" several called from their couches. "Yes, do, Theodora!"

Theodora never played the coy actor who needed coaxing. Perhaps, too, the wine made her feel a bit devilish. She looked about for the theater director. Ivan had already left, so for the first time she performed an imitation of him. She hunched her back and dragged herself up and down the length of the room, sputtering and muttering a slurred series of complaints having to do with money and uncooperative actors. Her drunkenly receptive audience caught on immediately and cheered.

"Do Miranda," someone called.

"Yes, Miranda!" another echoed.

"Oh, do," a woman's voice intoned more sharply, "It is so seldom that she is not in the midst of things."

"But I have never done Miranda," Theodora said. And yet, her mind, already tickled by the colorful subject, had already moved on to a plan of execution.

Miranda was a mediocre actor of the troupe, effective in tragedies, for the shrillness of her cries could empty the theater, if not the Hippodrome. In other ways, too, her lack of moderation became apparent. Having developed a penchant for sweets and baked goods, Miranda had transformed her once well-endowed and well-kept figure to an overt plumpness a pound or two short of obesity. She tried to disguise the flatness of her features with heavy and colorful face paint and a monstrous mane of red, red hair, coarsened and given a will of its own by years of dyeing. Though she was on the high horizon of her thirties, she persisted in portraying twenty-year-olds on stage, as in life. And Miranda dearly loved men.

Scarcely a challenge for Theodora. Her friends assured her later that her interpretation was flawlessly funny, but her single recollection of it was at the end, with her standing, legs apart, warrior style, on a cluttered supper table, tunic hiked to her uppermost thighs, breasts thrust out in blatant seduction.

It was but a moment later—as she lifted her head from a deep bow—that she spied there in the doorway, Miranda herself.

Theodora suddenly sobered as all sound died away.

Miranda tossed her head now and swept into the room, smiling broadly and calling out greetings. She gave no evidence of having witnessed anything unusual. She must have only just arrived. Relief ran like a river through Theodora.

Later, someone whispered to her that Miranda had seen the entire scathing performance. Had the mirror image not penetrated her dye-abused scalp? Or had she chosen to ignore the incident rather than enlarge it? Theodora decided the latter the most likely case and applauded Miranda for genuine—heretofore well-hidden—acting talent.

But her laurel for Miranda proved premature.

Ivan came to her changing room the next evening as she prepared to go on. She was in a good mood. "If you have come to scold me for being late to the theater you are justified in doing so, Ivan, but just the same I will be ready in time if you don't trouble me with lectures."

"There is no need to hurry, Theodora."

His ominous tone slowed the stroke of her hairbrush and made her glance up from her makeup table. "But I'm next on."

"You will not be going on, my dear." The deeply set black eyes were in earnest.

"What?"

"I am releasing you from the troupe."

"Releasing me? But why … for what reason?" Of course, she knew the reason even before Ivan spoke.

"For your lack of discretion, shall we say?"

"The party?"

He nodded.

"But it was merely in fun!" Slapping the hairbrush on the table, she stood now.

"Such fun can exact a high price, my dear."

A part of Theodora could not believe he was serious. "Why, Ivan, this is not like you. I've seen actors mock you openly and your hide has never been thin. Believe me, there was affection in my satirizing of you." She approached and tried to embrace him, but he stiffened at her touch. "If you had seen it, Ivan, you would have led the laughter. You have always taken a joke as well as the next man."

"I still can, Theodora. A hunchback can't afford a delicate disposition. But you must realize that my authority as a director would be put in question if I allowed you to stay on. The incident is not to be overlooked. You will have to leave."

And then it came clear to her. "It's Miranda, isn't it? She's put you up to this!"

Ivan looked at the floor. "I'm afraid you won't be able to persuade Miranda that there was affection in your imitation of her."

"Perhaps not, but never has my art depicted life so accurately." It was an impulsive and cutting remark that she immediately regretted. "Oh, don't be so dour, Ivan. I will apologize to Miranda and the incident will become history. She was late to the party and I wasn't certain whether she was aware she was being mimicked."

"Oh, she didn't know at the time. Someone told her later."

"She had to be told?" Theodora snickered. "Pity—were it not for some talking viper—anyway, I shall apologize."

"I'm afraid she won't let it go at that."

"*She* won't let it go?" Theodora's amusement was giving way to rage.

"She will leave the troupe if you aren't sent packing."

"Let her! And good riddance! You'll find that the boards no longer creak under her. What is this talk? *You* are the director. Who is she but a third-rate howler? I am one of your biggest draws. They stand in line for me." She knew even as she spoke that she should stop. But she couldn't. "You would lose me to hold on to someone whose talent has the vitality of the Dead Sea and whose figure must this very moment appear to the front row patrons as a fully-measured bag of grain."

"Theodora!" The shout was wholly uncharacteristic of the director. Ivan would mutter and complain and fall into dark moods, but he never raised his voice.

"What is this?" Theodora asked, suspicion surging. "What is Miranda to you?"

Ivan's eyes swept the floor.

"Sweet Aphrodite, Ivan!" Theodora's hand went to her throat. "She's your lover!"

His face ran red. "She won't have it known about."

Theodora's rage was suddenly deflated by her utter surprise that such a secret had been kept among theater folk where the wine was watered with gossip. "And you mean to do this to me?"

"I must."

"What of me? What am I to *do*? I know nothing outside of theater work. I need the money, Ivan; my family is dependent upon me! Besides, I've only just rented a little house for myself."

"You'll land on your feet, Theodora. Don't underestimate yourself. You are not without your assets. And you can be very charming when you have a mind to be."

Theodora knew his meaning. "I have seen too many passed from hand to hand. They are the fashion of a year and then they are left to the streets. I mean to be more!"

"Perhaps we can find a spot for your little sister. I noticed her waiting for you the other day, and I can tell you she is a very pretty little thing—"

"No! Tasia will never know this kind of life. Do you hear? Not ever!"

Ivan sighed. "We are caught up in a difficult situation. Believe me, my dear, when I say that it is not only my business sense which makes me regret doing this; I have affection for you. But what can I do? Look at me, Theodora. I am gaining in years. I am ugly and misshapen. When I was an infant, my mother stole me from the stone ledge where my father had placed me to die. I was raised by a family she paid regularly until her death. Then I was on my own. I never knew her. I didn't fare badly, and in the theater world I command a certain amount of respect. But women—with women I am the object of ridicule, hate, and worst of all, pity. Oh, I know that I purchase Miranda's interest with starring but ill-suited roles. I know that she would be ashamed to reveal our relationship, and I know that she has other lovers. But if I let her go, who would there be to love me—or let me at least pretend?" He stepped closer. "Would you, Theodora?"

Involuntarily, she stepped back.

"I thought not," he said. "Please leave quickly now, child—and without commotion." He turned to go.

"Wait!" Theodora called. "There is no other troupe of any consequence in The City. I will do anything to stay on, take any position, no matter how lowly."

Ivan turned back at the doorway. "Theodora, you are a great beauty now. You could not play an extra any longer. You are meant to be featured. I would be severely berated as a director to so misuse you. And Miranda was specific— she wants you off the boards."

"I don't mean a position on the boards. I mean backstage in whatever menial job there might be. Irene the costumer needs a girl. Everyone knows she's overwhelmed. You've said so yourself."

"You know nothing about—"

"I am not slow. I will learn! Oh, Ivan please let me stay on!"

His head dipped, moving side to side with uncertainty. "Miranda will not like it."

"Why shouldn't she? She'll be glad to see me in my reduced state. It will be sweeter than one of those greasy meat pies she so treasures."

"Well, perhaps then." Ivan paused and waved a crooked forefinger. "But you will have to apologize."

"Of course."

"And you must not say a word to the others about Miranda and me."

Theodora nodded. Words failed her—for she knew that would be the hardest part of the bargain. The taste of humility was bitter, but she learned the danger of unnecessarily making enemies.

For me, an enemy had come early in life.

During the course of my initial interviews with Theodora, I begin to experience visions from my past—often fleeting—but always real, teeming with color and sound. They are memories from which I have tried to escape all of my life.

Unlike Theodora, I am fully Syrian. I come from a large family that lives on a sheep farm in the hills north of Damascus. We were very poor with many mouths to feed, but I could remember being carefree and happy. More than anything I remember my mother. Her face was not unlike those of the Madonna found here in Christian painting, sculpture, and mosaic. Oval like Theodora's, darker, and nearly as beautiful. My life forever changed when I was ten, the third of three boys; I had two sisters, one older, one an infant.

A stranger in rich, gold brocaded robes arrives at our three-room farmhouse. He is Persian and fits my romantic idea of an emperor; he isn't, of course, although my parents behave obsequiously, especially Father. My siblings and I had been washed and made to wear our good long tunics. We are called to line up before the guest, who sits at the family table, a cup of wine in hand.

Some wordless communication passes from the bearded man to my father, who immediately dismisses the two girls; Maya takes Baby Rima outside. The visitor then inspects my older brothers. Ahmed, the oldest of us, is strong but wiry and thin like a stick. Sami has more meat on his bones, but his nose had been broken by Ahmed the year before. And then the man's piercing black eyes settle on me. His oiled black hair falls to the sides of his face like curtains and his mouth curves into a smile. "Turn around, boy," he says. When I do so and then pivot back, he insists that I imitate his smile. I make the attempt. Then my brothers and I are sent outside.

After what seems a very long time, Mother comes to the door, takes the baby from Maya and motions for me to come in. The others are left outside. Moving toward the table, I see that the man is smiling again. Father's face is serious, though, and Mother's face—I will never forget—is wet with tears. She takes her seat and puts Rima to her breast. I look to her and my heart melts away. Though her life is hard, she is always full of joy, always with a smile. What happened to make her so unhappy? I feel at once protective and sad. She stares at me long moments, then looks down at Rima. Her eyelids close, flushing out tears that roll down her cheeks.

"Leave us now," Father says.

I draw myself up before realizing that he is looking at Mother.

She pauses, fear darkening the wet eyes.

"It is best." Father's tone is firm. We know that tone well.

Mother rises and—without a look to me—takes the baby into the sleeping room.

A motion from my father sends me across the room, near the wall. My father and the man sit at the table, finishing off cups of wine. Something gold glitters there. I sit alone on the dirt floor, afraid for my mother, afraid that the stranger in brocades would turn in my direction and insist that I smile.

Just before dusk and the evening meal, the Persian makes ready to leave. I stay rooted to my place. I hear my brothers laughing as they play outside and wonder how they can be so light-hearted. But I have always felt different from them.

The man turns in his chair, and his hooded eyes fall upon me. My heart races.

Father calls me over to the table. "You will be leaving with this man, Sufian." He takes hold of my upper arms, almost gently. Emotions float there in his dark eyes, emotions I could not decipher. "You're to be a good boy, do you hear?" There is no time for thought, no time for tears.

The Persian rises, upsetting his chair, and takes me by the hand. I have no opportunity to take my everyday short tunic or few childish belongings, no opportunity to say goodbye to Mother.

I had been sold.

7

As Theodora went about in her reduced capacity, she was conscious of the gloating Miranda but chose to ignore her, busying herself with her work. She knew that she could have used her knowledge of the affair with Ivan to her advantage, but she kept her tongue, knowing that Miranda would have left him. It was a difficult thing to apologize to a woman who had to be told she was being played the fool, but Theodora suffered through it. It became more difficult when Miranda refused to accept the apology. The woman did not, however, balk at Theodora's new position.

Work went well with Irene. She was a stoic to the marrow and although gray-haired with a face deeply lined, she possessed features that testified to a bygone beauty.

Irene's manner could be cold, abrupt; this Theodora put down to her calculated way of putting off actors, who could be at times—Theodora knew from experience—demanding and full of conceit. In the first weeks of Theodora's apprenticeship, Irene's patience ran thin, her attitude toward her apprentice clipped. "Stupid girl, put the needle down until you learn how to use it!" But there was something swimming in her fathomless gray eyes that belied the stony façade, giving only the very observant a glimpse of a singular soul well hidden.

One day as the two left the theater for the evening meal at their respective homes, they came upon a man posting a sign on a nearby playhouse, the Theater of Euripides. They stopped to watch.

"What do you suppose it says?" Theodora asked. "Do you think he can tell us?"

"I will tell you, Theodora," Irene said drolly. "It is an announcement for the Dion Dance Troupe, which is to arrive next June. I hear it is quite extraordinary in a very odd sort of way."

Theodora's mouth fell open. But it was not the sign's message that so caught her off guard.

"Surprised, my dear?" Irene swirled about and began moving down the Mese.

"Astounded is the word, Irene!" Theodora hurried to catch up. "Where did you learn to *read*? You have never dropped a clue."

"Oh, sweet Gemini!" Irene cried without missing a step. "My child, you must learn that to lay down all your cards is tantamount to an invitation for an enemy. In a little company like ours, especially where a woman is concerned, the ability to read is likely to breed resentment and jealousy." Theodora would come to wonder at this philosophy many times, but for now it passed over her. Irene stopped suddenly before continuing along the crowded thoroughfare and pivoted toward Theodora. "So I ask you not to put it about. Some things are best left unheralded." The corners of her mouth turned up in mischief. "Oh, I know you can keep a secret," she said, "because you've not given Ivan and Miranda away."

Now Theodora was doubly surprised by this woman and her face must have reflected her incredulity because Irene's lashes flew back and she laughed heartily. "A costumer in a theater is much like a housekeeper in a large house—she cannot help but know all."

Theodora laughed with her. Her mirth was more than the humor of the moment, for she realized that in the space of a thunderclap they had become friends.

"Come to my home, Thea, for a meal. But don't expect anything special."

Theodora accepted, thrilled for the invitation, as well as for hearing Irene call her by her diminutive for the first time.

At Theodora's prompting, Irene spoke of her history during the course of the next hour. Like Theodora's father, hers had died when she was a child. Her mother married again—to a much older man, a Roman—and it was decided that Irene would be educated to act as governess to her patrician stepfather's grandchildren.

Over a meal of olives, cheese, bread, and watered wine, old grievances played out in her carefully controlled tone and hand tremors that held her two-pronged fork. "I occupied a niche in that household no higher than that of a servant, no more revered than a pet might have been. Out of sheer rebellion, I would neglect my studies, preferring to sew and embroider. I excelled at these occupations, and they did help lessen my loneliness—as well as hide my resentment." She paused and Theodora could sense a thousand long-buried hurts struggling to surface. They ate silently for a while. "Ah, Fate! That Tyche is a crafty goddess," Irene expelled in a sigh. "When Anastasius took power, the family fell out of favor and returned to Italy. I was of age, so I elected to stay, choosing a career to my liking—and independence."

"No regrets?"

"What is there to regret? I've led my life the way I chose." Irene lifted her wine cup as a salute—and drank it off.

"I mean to do the same."

The mischievous smile again. "Drink it down—or live as you choose?"

Theodora laughed. "Both!—Tell me, do you read and write well?"

"Reasonably so. My written Latin, though, is superior to my Greek."

Theodora stared dumbly. "You know *both*?"

"Yes, now let's not tarry." Irene rose from her dining couch. "We should be getting back to work. You know that someone will split a seam or tear a sandal before going on."

Theodora joined her and they started out for the theater. Even at fifty-one, Irene stepped so sprightly that Theodora was nearly running to keep up with her in the teeming and noisy Mese. Her thoughts returned to the sign they had seen. "Why did you say," she called above the din, "the Dion troupe is so extraordinary?"

Irene stopped and turned to Theodora. "I said it was extraordinary in an odd way. Had I not only heard of it the other day from some circuit actor, I would be at a loss to tell you. Even so, I hesitate to say." She turned and picked up her step.

"What is it?" Theodora followed, repeating her plea. Then louder: "Irene! Do tell me!"

"I am certain you'll find out soon enough!" she called back.

Theodora knew Irene enjoyed keeping her in suspense. "Irene, please!"

"Ah, well," she said, stopping, turning about, and motioning her toward the shade of an arcade. "I suppose you will be impossible until I tell you. It seems, my dear, that this troupe has taken some absurd new notion of dance from the mountain villages. They call it leaping dance. Can you imagine!"

"Leaping dance! That's ridiculous."

"That is precisely what I told that grandstander of an actor. But he swore on his life that it is, indeed, true. Dion is the name of the man who took the crude country dance of the lower class and somehow made it palatable for city theaters. That I should live to witness—"

"Oh, Irene, don't you want to see such a thing? At the very least it should prove amusing. Where is your sense of adventure?"

"Left behind with my youth, I suppose. I expect the experience will find me in the end. Like death. But in the meanwhile, we will be late to the theater."

Theodora gave a light and absent laugh. Her friend's fatalism left little impression. Her own mind had reverted to an earlier path. She detained Irene as she started to move away. "Irene, will you teach me to read and write?"

A sparkle came into the woman's eyes. "You are bright, Theodora. You know that your beauty will not sustain you indefinitely. One can usually find a position if one is educated."

"Oh, I do not mean to be a governess to some city official's brats! Such was not your choosing, either."

Irene's eyebrows arched, the furrows in her forehead deepened. "Ah, you have loftier ambitions, do you, Theodora?"

Theodora's face flushed hot. "I do. I have my ambitions, as you say." She told her of the feeling, innate within her—or perhaps borne the day that she and her sisters were ushered out into the wondrous Hippodrome—that something great lay in store for her.

"The Goddess Tyche has something in store for all of us, Theodora. Your fancy is no different from those of clever young girls everywhere." Irene lifted her hand to cradle Theodora's chin in a motherly fashion. "But if you give yourself too much over to fancy, disappointment will surely club you down."

Theodora wasn't about to argue. She knew she would have sounded very conceited, and she was thankful for the warmth of Irene's touch and concern. Her mind became fixed on one thing now. "Irene, will you teach me to read and write?"

"I gave up teaching long ago."

"I want to learn."

"My work consumes all my time."

"I will come mornings or nights, whenever you wish. I will bring meals to the theater for both of us so that we may use our supper break. You make the conditions and I will agree." Theodora held her arm then. "I beg you, Irene. I must learn. I must!" She paused for a moment. "And, of course, I'll pay you with whatever I have. It may not be much—"

Irene pulled away. "Don't insult me with talk of money. I would only ask for an enthusiastic student."

"Then you *will* teach me?"

Irene pursed her mouth as though on a lemon wedge, turned and moved off in the direction of the theater, her head shaking as if in exasperation.

Theodora stood there smiling to herself at Irene's pretended pique.

Theodora continued to see men on the sly, for Ivan would not have approved of the assignations of one of his seamstresses. A fervent Hecebolus persisted in his courting, and although Theodora had grown quite fond of him, she still restricted him to Tuesdays, wishing no deeper commitment. She did not know what love was—she knew only she had not tasted it, with him or with other men who sought her company on other days of the week. She would answer his oft-voiced and impassioned pleas with an adroit avowal that only marriage would do. Of course, she knew full well that his family and ambition forbade it.

By the time June brought the dance troupe to The City and its banner was being hoisted in the square fronting the Theater of Euripides, a curious crowd gathering about it, Theodora could read it.

The Dion Dance Troupe
Presents
Myra as Psyche

Theodora and Irene watched with interest. Her mentor gave out with a sigh and said, "Dion's coming will give our troupe a little competition. I do hope Ivan will cut back on the number of our performances so that I can catch up on a dozen little projects—and you, my dear, can do some reading!"

"How can I read when the Dion Troupe is upon us?" Theodora spoke in a mocking tone. "A pretty comedy it should be."

"Theatrical nonsense, indeed!"

A tall, slim woman standing in front of them—also watching the business with the banner—turned now and looked at Theodora and Irene. She was dark, beautifully dark. Dramatic Eastern features and thinness almost startling. She stood stiff as a reed, black eyes glaring.

"Well," Irene said, "what is amiss, young woman?"

Her response was so slow Theodora thought she would speak a foreign tongue. Finally, she asked in an even tone, "Have either of you seen the troupe?" Her Greek was quite good.

They replied that they had not.

"Yet you would condemn it?"

"Not necessarily," said Irene, "we merely deride its concept—leaping dances from the mountain villages."

"That sounds like a condemnation."

Theodora looked up at the woman. "You've seen it?"

"Yes."

"And?" Irene asked.

"I can only say that I hope the good citizens of such a huge and illustrious city do not attend the Dion Troupe's performance with such preconceptions, or worse, stay away."

"Are you," Theodora asked, already certain of the answer, "a member of the troupe?"

"See there," the woman said, her thin, dark arm pointing to the banner, "I am Myra."

Her tone held no inflated pride as her two questioners might have expected, even deserved, and the embarrassment on Irene's face reflected that of Theodora's, who wished a fissure would open up in the ground and swallow them whole.

Theodora attended the dance opening with her childhood friend Antonina, with whom she had remained close. Antonina was a confidante and yet Theodora had yet to reveal to her—or to anyone—that she could read.

Theodora was not unaware of the magnitude of the gift Irene had bestowed upon her. Her teacher had done what teachers do—bring their charges into the light.

Earlier in the day, Theodora had asked Irene why the Church conducted a war against dancers and dance. "Ah, Thea," she responded, "like theater itself, dance has been in a state of flux. The Church regards those who partake in such professions to be of a low class with questionable morals." The corners of her mouth crinkled impishly upward. "And sometimes that is the case. But neither interdict nor threat of damnation has met with success, for dance remains a cherished and innate part of private and public festivals, feasts, and ceremonies. Why, it's traceable to the comedies of the master playwrights and, further back, to the threshing floor worship of Demeter, Goddess of Grain. No decree could eliminate dance from the soldiers' drill, nor from the charioteers' expression of joy upon winning their races at the Hippodrome. Dance is a part of the Greek soul."

Settling into their seats in the elaborate Theater of Euripides, Theodora hardly knew what to expect. Rumors and heated discussion had long preceded the arrival of this new dance, and the theater was filled to its capacity of several hundred. There were those who expected—perhaps hoped for—failure. But there were many present who were drawn to dance in any form.

Theodora and Antonina had only just taken their seats when the gangways were barred to any latecomers. Theodora found this precaution amazing. At any performance she had given or attended at the Old Royal Palace, the gangways were left open, allowing for not only latecomers but for patrons to move freely at any time during the performance. What kind of theater is this, she wondered, that compels the audience to stay seated in order to aid in the illusion?

The orchestra area was crammed with at least ninety players of cithara, lyre, flute, harp, drum, and cymbals. All but the stage lights along the front of the stage floor were extinguished. The crowd hushed.

"This is quite something, Theodora," Antonina said. "What was the entrance fee?"

Theodora turned to her, whispering, "A nomisma each."

"You're not serious—gold! Really?"

"Yes, now shush, Nina." She made no mention of the fact that it had taken a good bite out of her savings.

Flute and cithara were set to playing an eerily haunting passage. A sudden chill rippled through the crowd, catching everyone unaware; when one's life is in the theater, one can discern even the most subtle audience response, and Theodora now felt her arms go to goose flesh. Then the other instruments began to converge, one by one, coalescing into a strange but beautifully lush sound, its power underplayed. The corpulent conductor seemed lost in a world of his own.

Theodora looked around at the potpourri of patricians, politicians, their stiff wives or rouged mistresses, foreign businessmen and merchants, women of society and notoriety, and in the farther reaches, the motley brew of ruffians and prostitutes. Contrary to their usual deportment, no one was speaking.

No one at all! Even the Persian businessmen, who regarded the theater back benches as a fancy brothel and bartering place, were attentive.

As the overture drew to its conclusion, the sounds built into a wall of substance and height, climbing, climbing, still climbing after one thought the apex reached—then finally falling quickly with crashing cymbals into a reverberating silence and the "ahhhs" of a spellbound audience.

The faintly lighted stage stood bare but for painted flats depicting nature in spring. A lonely flute sang the first cadence. All was expectation.

Then, as the other instruments took up the theme, a sextet of intertwined maidens in short tunics, three in blue and three in yellow, floated in from the right wing and commenced a carefully orchestrated dance meant to celebrate the season of renewal. Antonina, to Theodora's right, was one of many to let out a gasp. The six visions flowed in serpentine fashion across the stage and back, falling into a circle and out again. Theodora stared in awe. She was accustomed to seeing dance troupes in soft, cloth slippers that made for a shuffling sort of motion; she saw now that these dancers wore high boots of supple leather. As the music accelerated, so too did the dancers' movements. Their hands fell free of one another's hold, each dancer becoming a separate part of a single, flawless vehicle. Their tunic sleeves were voluminous, the motion of which caught and pleased the eye. And all at once, in perfect unison, the chorines were leaping, leaping, leaping across the stage! The idea, once preposterous, conquered its doubters immediately. What a brave and wonderful new form of art, Theodora thought, watching what seemed to be deer in a symmetrical rout. It was apparent that the pliable soles of their boots afforded them a precision that slippers—and the clogs of old—could not. Their steps, whether tiny or long in stride, were quick motions of one machine, precise in its lightness, charm, and grace.

When the joy of the music and dance had played out, the six became as motionless as marble, beautiful and delicate. Almost imperceptibly, the music began to rise again—flute first, then the lyre and cithara. It was only when the harps made their timely bow with sweeping, heavenly tones that one of the six stepped out from the chorus, as Thespis—Irene had taught Theodora—had done so many years before at the dawn of theater.

It was one of the women in blue who portrayed Psyche. Theodora recognized her only now, so blurred had been her thoughts and the marvelous motions of the dance. It was Myra. Her fitted bodice displayed the modest contour of her breasts. On stage, the reed-like, almost manly, thinness did not detract. Her body itself was a lithe tool as she took the lead, waving the leader's traditional kerchief as the others followed. Myra seemed not so much to dance as to emote in a vision of expressive movement. Led by the lyre and flute, the music whipped up, faster and faster, until the leaping began again. The five chorines did not try to fully imitate the amazing leaps of Myra, and Theodora was certain their skills were not as great—they couldn't be! Myra lived the part of Psyche, the lovely maiden who fell in love with Cupid; there was no alternative to the audience but to believe it. With feline litheness, she moved with such poise and speed and fluidity in her flight that one could hardly imagine her as human. And just as the audience expected the piece to culminate in frantic chaos, the music stopped suddenly and the dancers dropped to the floor in dramatic fashion. The audience gasped in surprise and wonder.

The handsome actor portraying Cupid entered, wearing a short red tunic open at the chest, and even though he performed admirably, Theodora some-how felt jealous that he was sharing the boards with Myra. She was so very exceptional.

The work was divided into two acts. In the first, Psyche was smitten and seduced by Cupid, who visited her in the pitch of night, bidding her never to seek his identity. Myra's dancing was acting; no playwright could have written words to better convey her innocence, temptation, desire, blissful surrender, and love, all on a shadowed stage. Psyche became curious, however, and when she lighted a lamp to look at the sleeping Cupid, a drop of hot oil fell upon his shoulder. He awoke and fled. The full majestic force of the orchestra sup-ported Psyche now in a heart-rending dance of despair, rising subtly from the evocation of loneliness to a series of more complex emotions—and complex leaps—to a height of near madness—until Psyche finally fluttered to the stage floor like a wounded butterfly in a dance of death.

Act Two soared still higher, entrancing the audience. The abandoned Psyche wandered far and wide in search of her lover. When she became a slave of Venus, Cupid's mother, she was treated with extreme cruelty. Ultimately, at the stirring and bewitching climax, Psyche was united with Cupid, thus attaining immortality.

At the dance's finish, Theodora could scarcely breathe, lest she start sob-bing as so many others were doing. The effect was staggering. It seemed that everyone recognized that this was a grand moment in theater.

Antonina, now nearly a head taller than Theodora, walked her home bubbling over with enthusiasm for what they had just witnessed. Theodora's mother's interdict against Antonina and all things associated with the Green Party had not broken the friendship between the two. Following in her mother's profession, Antonina was employed at the Theater of the Three Coins as a chorus girl dancing in the orchestra pit. Even though such chorus girls were ranked well below actresses like Comito and considered little better than street harlots, Theodora remained loyal to her friend.

At home, alone, Theodora could not put the performance out of her mind. She appreciated dance, yet had not dreamt what the art could be. She inwardly burned to think of her own presentation of Psyche and vowed never again to portray that goddess in a living picture. No, she thought, this new leaping dance was a medium that would live as long as man. How she longed to meet Dion—and Myra!

8

"SO YOU WISH TO ATTEMPT the leaping dance?"

Theodora's jaw fell slack at Myra's greeting. "I do … how did you know?"

"My dear, there is always some young girl wanting to speak to me the morning after a performance in a new town. What is your name?"

"Theodora."

Theodora learned from a stagehand friend that Myra was staying at a villa of a patrician family, and she had come early so that she might speak to her alone. A servant informed her that she had not yet risen, and so she spent a fretful hour in the courtyard. When Myra did come out to greet Theodora, her appearance was startling. Her hair, drawn close to the head and knotted at the back for her performance as Psyche, had been released, allowing it to shoot out in one great tuft of wiry expression. Theodora was drawn to the deep-set ebony eyes that gazed down at her in an oddly appraising manner above a strong but imperfect nose.

"Is this not," she asked, "a change in disposition in but a few days?"

Theodora felt the heat of her blush as she recalled the derisive tone she and Irene had taken in speaking of the newly arrived troupe of leaping dancers.

"Yes, I recognize you." The timbre of Myra's voice resonated with amusement rather than accusation. She stared for a long moment. "You have a magnificent complexion, Theodora. Are you Greek?"

"Half. My mother is Syrian. Oh, do forgive me for the other day."

"The mixture was good," Myra continued in her own train of thought. "To say that I am Egyptian, I think, implies that I carry the blood of many races. My grandmother was Nubian, this I know."

"What beauty and talent you have, Myra."

"So! You have been inspired by the mountain village dance, yes? " Here again was the amusement in her voice.

"Oh, yes! I would want nothing more than to move an audience the way you did last night! I cannot—will not—settle for less."

"You are eager." Myra took Theodora's hands in hers. "It is in your eyes as well as in your words. That much is good. I eat early. It's best for a dancer. Join me now and we shall talk more. Though when you witness my dreadful diet, you may have second thoughts about this career."

The morning flew by. For all her genius and acclaim, Myra seemed to Theodora as unspoiled and genuine as a country girl. Upon parting, she promised Theodora an interview with Dion.

Two days later Myra kept her promise. They found the director in the lobby of the theater. When Myra introduced her, Dion turned to her and made an immediate judgment. "You are too old, my dear."

"What? I am but fifteen," Theodora said, subtracting two years in the blink of an eye. She had expected him to critique her lack of height—but not her age.

When Dion took a second look, Theodora prayed he would not see through her lie. "And a budding beauty," he said. "This I understand. But as far as a career in dance is concerned, you are past your prime."

Theodora stared at the man in disbelief.

"A girl," he continued, "should begin studies by eight or nine, earlier if possible."

"But I have danced." Theodora fought for composure. "I have taken classes at the Women's Gymnasium. And I've danced at the theater when a play required it."

"What sort of dancing?"

"Country and formal," she said defensively. "And I have always kept myself in condition with a daily regimen of exercise."

She knew, even before Myra warned her, that he was a strong director—no man could have achieved such phenomenal success without having set himself up as a supreme autocrat. He took stock of her now, his dark Greek eyes seeming to stare right through her. Lifting her head slightly, Theodora dared to return the look. Myra had said he was fifty. Ironically, this director of such sophisticated dance possessed a stocky frame, overly large head, bulbous nose, and receding hairline. He had come to the theater late this day, looking more tired than his years warranted. His troupe had taken Constantinople by storm, so Theodora suspected he had been making the rounds of parties the night before. She noticed the redness in his eyes now and cursed her luck, figuring the night's carousing had made him short-tempered and eager to dash a young girl's hopes.

And yet the interview continued. Theodora spoke quickly and at length in an effort to demonstrate that she had the necessary capability and determination, that she should at least be given a chance. Dion grew distracted even as Theodora regretted her aggressiveness.

Finally, Myra, who had been keeping her distance, approached. "Dion," she said, "I think Theodora should be given the chance to prove herself."

It was a bold move and Theodora's heart caught.

Dion cast a glance at his star that decried her mutiny, yet it was clear her status held no little sway. Sighing loudly, he turned back to Theodora. "I will tell you what, my dear. I have no desire to see you do a turn today. In that you may be lucky, for I doubt I would be pleased. Come to me in three months, just before the end of our run. Come with a leaping presentation—of course. We will be leaving for a tour of Smyrna, Antioch, and Alexandria. If you show promise, you may accompany us and begin what will be a vigorously difficult apprenticeship. If you do not show promise, I shall not mince words."

His stinging eyes fell on Myra. "Perhaps you can give your newest novice some pointers in your art."

Myra returned an enigmatic smile.

Theodora witnessed a current pass between Dion and Myra. It was the sort of unvoiced knowledge that was indecipherable to anyone other than the two parties. Theodora felt a slight quiver at her middle but shrugged it off.

And so Theodora resigned her position as seamstress—to Ivan's dismay. He gave no indication that she might have her job back one day, but she didn't care. She was convinced she wouldn't need it. A career in dance was in the wings.

Dion no doubt expected failure, so her fervor was doubled. She worked like a Spartan, sleeping a mere five hours a night. Only through strain and sweat, and the abstinence of pleasures that had become lifeblood to her, would she be ready in three months' time. She attended no parties, accepted no callers—not even Hecebolus. With little money to sustain herself, she nevertheless became determined to manage somehow.

For the first time in her life, Theodora had set a goal that was truly challenging. She felt as if there were certain long-secreted juices within her that had awakened and begun to flow. She vowed to herself to be up to the test.

Theodora had always thought herself to be in good condition. A sudden and grim new reality dawned. Her daily routine of stretching and walking long distances, often uphill, had been no preparation at all. Myra began to coach her, pushing her to limits—and pain—unimagined. She put Theodora on a strict diet. Like Myra, she took an early meal—no more than a slice of barley bread splashed with a bit of wine and a few figs. Pounds started to fall away, pounds Theodora previously did not think excessive. As before, she began her day at the Gymnasium, only earlier. Her walking distance trebled, her stride lengthened. She thought her tendons would tear or her lungs burst. For variety and her own sightseeing amusement, Myra would insist on climbing what seemed to Theodora the steepest of Constantinople's seven hills. Then came the morning warming sessions at the theater, a leisurely limbering process for all the other dancers, except for her; for her it was grueling. She managed to keep up for the most part, knowing there were curious and censorious eyes about and praying that her face masked her struggle. *I am an actress, after all.* When the session ended and the dancers began rehearsing for the evening's performance, Theodora rushed home to make a lunch of soup—usually lentil—accompanied with bread and olives, after which came a very short nap, and then three hours of reaching, holding, bending, holding, stretching, holding, lifting, holding. Myra would occasionally appear to oversee the afternoon's regimen. It isn't so much the action, Myra would tell her, as it is the holding that strengthens and tightens the muscles. Sometimes, to demonstrate form, her hands pressed lightly, almost caressingly, between Theodora's sweat soaked shoulder blades and at the small of her back. Theodora thought the holding would do her in and fought off the urge to curse Myra.

Theodora prepared a supper as spare as lunch, but it usually included fish, as she was clever and flirtatious in her dealings with the fishmongers along the bay's shore. Another rest then and a final hour of toning.

And with night came the supreme pleasure of her day. Taking only a fraction of the time it usually took to prepare her face and dress, Theodora hurried to the evening's performance of the troupe, her admittance secured by Myra. She had not missed a single performance, and had not once been disappointed. Invariably, by evening's end a new inspiration took root, one that would get her through the next day. She avoided friends, chatter, and invitations, slipping off, like a thief in the shadows, to her home, a basin of hot water for her feet, and bed.

One evening at the end of that first month, a knock came at the door of her tiny wooden house. Theodora limped to the door and opened it. Her mother stood on the other side of the threshold, her eyes widening as they moved over her, coming to rest on Theodora's feet. Theodora looked down at her own bare and bloodied feet and when she lifted her gaze, she saw that her mother's mouth had turned down in an old familiar expression of disapproval. "You are *bleeding*, Theodora, and you've gone bone thin."

"I'm in training, Mother, I told you."

"You are killing yourself, that's what you are doing."

Had Theodora the strength, she would have put forth an argument, but her body wanted to side with her mother.

"Do you need money?" her mother asked.

"No," Theodora said. There was truth in her answer, too, for Myra had taken to leaving Theodora sums of money. "Ah, money," she would say when Theodora attempted to refuse it, "what do I need so much for? And you need to eat and have a roof over your head, do you not? You can pay me back sometime."

Her mother's uninvited visit served to strengthen Theodora's resolve. Oh, she wanted to make her mother proud, but more than that, she wanted her to be secure in her old age—secure and happy.

Theodora's younger sister, Anastasia, was more supportive. Theodora had taken her to the Dion troupe's performance twice, and she was duly impressed. While Anastasia still lived with their mother at home, Comito, like Theodora, had taken her own place, but it was located in a seamy area down by the docks. There she worked the boards, if one could call it that, playing a grotesquely bawdy routine in a tavern. She was seen often along the Mese, one of countless harlots. Theodora and Anastasia saw less and less of her. Like the rest of The City, they came to know her by reputation. Theodora wished for some way to redeem her.

Her own feet would follow a different path. And she was determined to see to Anastasia's future, as well. Daring to assume that she would be leaving Constantinople with the troupe, Theodora contacted a local matchmaker and employed her to find a suitable husband for her sister. After all, Tasia was fifteen and blossoming nicely.

To dance the leaping dances and to do it with a degree of grace, Theodora came to realize, was more than a skill—it was an art that she was determined to possess. Myra brought her a pair of boots of the kind that the dancers wore, and by the second month, she was instructing her in the basic beginning steps and leaps. Theodora fell often at first, so awkward were her landings. She burned with embarrassment but nonetheless undertook the challenge as a mathematics student might approach a test of many problems, that is, one by one. She repeated them again and again, checking and rechecking with an analytical eye until the steps were mastered, always the same and always correct. Her body had begun to accept and respond. Her leaps became less clumsy and began to lengthen. She drove herself even harder than Myra urged.

In the third month, she chose her audition piece.

"It is," Myra said, "one of the most difficult dances you could have chosen, Theodora. Should you be so daring?"

"Exactly! Dion will be all the more impressed." Theodora had set her heart on the dance of despair which Psyche performed after Cupid fled from her. Of all the performances she had witnessed, this one had moved her most, and so she reasoned that she could put all of her soul into it.

"I can't allow it. It is not a dance for a neophyte."

"Your words and your eyes doubt me, Myra. But, wait, I will surprise you."

"You always surprise me, dearest," Myra said, pushing Theodora's dark hair back from her forehead.

That Myra's response seemed favorable conspired to make Theodora overlook the fact that the woman's tone and touch had momentarily chilled her.

The individual steps depicting Psyche's dashed love were fitted into one flowing movement, like so many bits of a mosaic into a whole design. The difficulty, Theodora found, was the great variance of pace; the movement accelerated, by subtle gradations, from the languorous to the frenzied of one gone mad. The turns and spins—so integral to the piece—needed to become more and more fluid and precise. So too did the leaps need to broaden. But Theodora believed that she could do it.

By the end of the month, she was foot worn and enervated but had made incredible strides in a very short time. She knew that she radiated confidence and well-being.

Theodora wondered whether her teacher was as confident so that when

Myra said, "We shall be ready tomorrow," Theodora's head whirled with euphoria. She had said *we*. It was an unexpected compliment that made her forget her fatigue and bask instead in thankful wonder at the devotion Myra had shown for so many weeks and months.

Theodora was about to extinguish her ceramic lamp and retire when there came a rapid knocking at her door. It was the night before the audition, and she had avoided going to the theater so that she would be well rested.

Hecebolus stood in the doorway. "May I come in?" His dogged attempt at a smile buckled all the lines of his face into an expression of despair.

Theodora attempted her own smile, one that she hoped would belie her surprise and annoyance. "Of course."

The two sat on a couch. Hecebolus' manner was oddly formal. Unlike his previous visits, he made no effort to kiss or embrace her. "You're thin as a stylite, Theodora," he said. "Have you been ill? Is that why—"

"No, of course not! I have never been in more perfect form."

Hecebolus drew in a long breath. "Then—why have you refused to see me, Theodora? When your last note came, I, well … I was beside myself."

"I wrote that it could not be helped, Hecebolus, that it had to do with something of the utmost importance to me."

"It was all very vague. You are trying to put me off."

"No, Hecebolus."

"You are. Do you lack the courage to say so? It would be an easier end than this limbo I find myself in. You know that I adore you. Is there another who has caught your interest?"

"Look about—do you see a man? Had I anticipated your reaction, I would have written more. I am so sorry, Hecebolus. My time has not been diverted by a man, but by an art." Theodora told him now of her love affair with dance and her deep desire to make a life of it.

He believed her, naturally, yet his desperation increased. "Then you mean to leave with this band of nomads and fritter your life away, trekking city to city, one dirty room to another?"

"If that is the way of life that calls me, I will gladly accept it—if I can dance as Myra dances, leap as she leaps. Oh! You must see the troupe! What has kept you from it? It is the talk of The City. When you see it, you will rejoice for me."

"You can't do this, Theodora. I could not bear to lose you. Stay here and give up this whim."

"It is not a whim. It is my chance to be … someone."

"Theodora …" Words failed him. His tongue wet his dry, tightened lips.

"Yes?" Theodora asked, her heart going out to him despite the unannounced visit.

He took her hands into his own. His palms were moist. "Thea," he said at last, employing her diminutive for the first time. "I will marry you."

Theodora felt her heart quicken. "What?"

"I will. I will not lose you. May our marriage take place as soon as you wish. Yes, let it be very soon!"

"You speak without thought, Hecebolus. You're being impulsive."

"No, I have given it much thought."

"Really? What of your family? Their reputation?"

"Hades take them! I have thought it out. You are all that matters."

"And the position you hope to gain?"

"I am tired of silken-tongued politicians. I am tired of anterooms. I am tired of waiting."

"Upon whom do you wait?"

"Senator Leontini. If he were to recommend me to Emperor Anastasius, as he had promised my father, my own qualifications would win the governorship."

Theodora's eyes must have reflected her knowledge of Marcus Leontini.

"You know him?" Hecebolus asked.

"I know of his hypocrisy." She placed her hand on his arm. "Leontini aside, there are laws. A marriage to a woman of the theater would negate any chance of your attaining the position. You must think about yourself."

"Having you would make my life full enough. We will move to a city where such things do not matter. We will get by."

Theodora braced herself to deliver the blow. She spoke slowly. "Hecebolus, *I* will not be content with getting by."

"Then … you refuse me?" He paled and his mouth fell slack. "You have always said—"

"I know what I have said. But I have no intention to marry you or anyone else. I doubt that I ever shall." Theodora went on at length, singing the praises of Myra and the new form of art, but it seemed that she could not convey to him the possibilities that dancing with Dion's troupe held for her. That she could not put this new found quest aside. That she would prevail.

Hecebolus stayed the night. Theodora could not turn him away. Their bodies lay together after lovemaking. Their minds, she knew, moved in different orbits.

Theodora refused the several nomismata he offered before he left at dawn, a silent and dispirited man. She was certain he felt as she: that their affair had run its course. Neither dared look the other in the eye.

Shaking off a vague feeling of emptiness, Theodora began to prepare for the audition.

9

ALL WAS IN READINESS AT the Theater of Euripides when Dion arrived. Theodora noted that the stage floor had been cleared, cleaned, and lightly layered with a gritty substance to prevent one's slipping. The troupe's limbering exercises had been scheduled late to accommodate the audition; still, a number of the curious were scattered about, waiting to see the testing of a neophyte. For the occasion Myra had made for Theodora a short, azure-colored tunic with a bodice perfectly fitted to her breasts, which were by now nearly fully developed. Myra advised against makeup and fashioned her pupil's long, black hair in a simple upsweep style held with pearl pins. The supple reddish boots that Theodora had broken in with hours of practice had been polished, Theodora noticed. So many thanks to be given to her mentor.

"I see you have not given it up, my sweet," Dion said. The director was smiling. "You do have spirit. Well, we shall put you to the test."

Years later, Theodora would recall his insufferable condescension, but in her youth she was unable to recognize it for what it was. She knew only that she was suddenly frightened—terrified—and surprised at her fear.

"Are we ready?" Dion asked.

At Myra's nod, Theodora drew herself up and said, "I am."

"Are the musicians here?" Dion called out.

"Musicians?" Myra's face paled.

"But, of course! What is my dance without music?"

"Dion," Myra protested, "Theodora has not yet danced to music. In but three short months, we could not have—"

"I am certain, Myra," Dion said, "that if the girl possesses creativity as well as spirit, she will adapt."

Myra stepped close to Dion, and in a stage whisper that Theodora could hear, said, "You are making it as difficult as possible for her, aren't you?"

"This way of life," Dion said, his smile evaporating and his whisper no softer, "is a difficult one, as I'm sure I don't have to remind you. A prospective member of the troupe, even a favored protégé of yours, Myra, will not be pampered. One must rise to meet expectations. I expect music. It is that simple."

Myra and Theodora watched wide-eyed as a small contingent of the orchestra assembled in the pit, some ten or twelve players in all. Dion had prearranged their appearance. Theodora wanted to say something—what, she had no idea—but her jaws had clenched involuntarily. And she sensed an almost tangible tension between Dion and Myra. Was he in love with his star? Was he jealous of the attention Myra had shown to her?

"What is your piece, my sweet?"

Theodora swallowed hard. "Psyche's dance at the end of the first act."

His eyes widened in surprise, but he chose to say nothing, pivoted, and called out the dance to the conductor.

Theodora had spoken before Myra could contest further. Although it was clear to both of them that Dion meant to humiliate and reject her, Theodora's eyes beseeched her instructor's silence now with a message that an argument could only do more harm. She would attempt to match her dance to the music.

The difference between dancing with or without music might seem a petty one, but to the dancer it is not. Theodora's movement, which had been choreographed to a mental beat, had to now coincide with a melodic flow over which she had no control. Her steps and the strains of the orchestra had to appear seamless. She knew the risks. Without benefit of rehearsal or even a single run-through, her concentration could easily be diffused and her performance scuttled.

The orchestra began. Because of its reduced size, the thin sounds it produced compounded Theodora's plight by making it difficult for her ear and mind to grasp the rhythmic phrases so that her body could respond. Today only a weak facsimile mimicked the powerful nighttime orchestra, music without magic.

Just the same, Theodora focused on her dance as she had learned it, closing off from her mind everything else.

The piece began with the dropping of oil on Apollo's chest. Theodora had no male dancer to work with and so had to react facially and bodily to an imaginary Apollo as he awoke and fled from her. This audience knew the story well enough—another factor that could work against her.

Theodora began unsteadily—and a beat late. Her first steps were awkward and rushed as she attempted to synchronize her movement to the music. This was, indeed, a very different thing for her. She prayed that the real panic she felt usurping her would be interpreted by Dion and the others as Psyche's reaction to Apollo's desertion.

But this little hope did not hold. She faltered badly, recovered, faltered again. She was failing. Concurrent with this realization, her temples began to pound, deafening her to the sound of the orchestra. She lagged farther behind, so that when the first series of leaps came they were unsteady, short, the landings clumsy. Her audition was a disaster and she thought of ending it immediately. Her face burned with humiliation. Still, her body danced on, gracelessly, impervious to thought, impervious to the music.

As Theodora advanced numbly into a series of spins and leaps across the full width of the boards, she saw not the revolving faces of the concerned, the curious, and the condescending in the wings and audience seats; her unwilling mind spun in many directions at once. Vivid images flew up at her. Later, she would recall just one image: that of her mother ignominiously weeping before the Greens. Theodora had promised herself once that she would laugh when she was hurt. She wondered if she would be able to do so at the conclusion of the audition.

She fought anew for control. She fought to put everything from her mind and to dwell only on Psyche and her lost love. Her mind seized full control of her body now and every muscle, sinew, and nerve followed suit. Her blood vibrated with the music and she fell into its flow of movement, allowing herself to be swept away, coming to live the despair that was Psyche's and to forget her own. Blocking everything else, Theodora propelled her body through the second half of her dance as if on wings of fury, leaping, leaping, leaping as if she had been born to the mountain village art form. She performed the second part of her dance better than she had thought possible. As she dropped to the floor, she became certain of it.

The generous applause fairly lifted her from her prostate position. She was fully winded and perspiring profusely. Myra was there to offer her a towel and embrace her. "Oh, Theodora, I think you've done it," she whispered in her ear.

"If it's true," Theodora said, catching her breath, "*we* have."

Dion approached. "A rather good piece, Theodora. A shaky beginning, but understandable. All in all, commendable for just three months' work."

"Thank you." She thought it prophetic that he had dropped the "my sweet" epithet for her name.

"Have you traveled much?"

"No, sir."

"Would you like to?"

"Oh, yes!"

"Good. It will not be an easy apprenticeship, you realize. It will be some time before you take your place on the boards, but if you apply yourself in this same manner, you will make a very capable chorine."

"Oh, I will! I know that I will. And *more*, you will see. Thank you, Dion." Theodora turned to embrace Myra, whispering in her ear, "And you!"

Dion coughed. "Theodora, what do you mean by *and more*?"

She turned to raise her eyes to his. "Why—that I intend to put body and soul into becoming like Myra."

"Is that what you wish?"

"Of course!"

Dion shot a nervous glance at Myra, then trained his gaze on Theodora, who detected pity in his dark eyes. "Myra," he said with deliberateness, "possesses the genius that glitters once in a generation, like the rarest of comets."

"Oh, I am aware of that," Theodora said. "I am not so bold as to think I could ever be that good." Her words seemed to assuage his uncertainty. "To dance," Theodora continued, "some of her stage roles, the less demanding ones, if you will, will be my goal. To hear and sense the approval of the audience—this will be enough."

"You have your heart set on featured roles?" The edge was in his voice again.

"Yes. Oh, I know it will take a great deal of time and work. I shall surprise you!"

"Theodora, listen to me. I came here today prepared to put you off. But you performed well. You are lithe and you have ambition. I can make a fine chorine out of you, as a sculptor might create a statue from a piece of marble. But you must believe me when I tell you that you cannot hope to play a featured role in this troupe or any other. You do not possess that large of a talent. Besides, you are not tall enough."

Theodora felt her legs quaking, her head reeling. "Something to do with the quality of the raw marble?" The words, she realized, were her own.

Dion did not reply. The pity was in his smile now, and Theodora hated him for it. "Can you be so certain?" She sensed Myra stiffen at her side.

"Yes, Theodora."

She felt a falling sensation at her middle, a trembling at her chin. Here was one man who spoke the truth.

"Being a chorine," he asked, "will that be enough?"

A long moment passed. "No," Theodora said, lifting her head and forcing her jaws to work, "it will not. I do thank you for your time and evaluation. I'm sure you're right. It was naïve of me to think—" Words failed her now. And so, she laughed. A quick look at Myra's stricken face killed the laugh, however, and she turned and made for the exit.

Myra must have stayed on to talk to Dion because Theodora had changed into her sandals, thrown a cloak over herself, and covered a street length's distance from the theater before Myra caught up to her.

"Theodora, wait!"

She turned. "Forgive me, Myra. My mind ... I didn't thank you for your help. I do thank you ... with all my heart. It was a good attempt, was it not?" She laughed. "I'm to seek my fortune elsewhere."

"What is it, Thea?"

"What is it? Did you not hear Dion?"

"He said that you would make a very able chorine."

"That was not my intention. You *know* that it was not."

"But you will be dancing. You will have your career." She took Theodora's hands into hers. "And ... you will be with me."

"It is not enough." Theodora tried to disengage herself but Myra held on.

"Perhaps Dion is wrong. He's been wrong before, I can tell you."

"Tell me, Myra, for you have seen more of my ability than he—do *you* think he's wrong?" Theodora's hard gaze dared her to be dishonest. "Do *you* think I could attain featured status? For one thing, I doubt that I will grow any taller."

Myra drew breath as if to speak but exhaled without making a sound. Her compressed lips rendered a clear answer.

"Again, I thank you," Theodora said, pulling free. One by one, she removed the pearl pins from her hair and handed them to Myra. She began to walk away, her dream of dance vanquished. She would not show her tears.

"Why must you be so proud and stubborn?" Myra asked.

Theodora could not deny those traits, and so she walked on.

"Do you," Myra called after her, "have no feeling for me? Why do you think I invested time and effort in training you?" An angry tone vibrated in her voice, one Theodora had not heard before. "Do you think me a fool to train someone good enough to replace me on the boards? No, you may not be the best, but you will *dance*!"

Theodora spun around and closed the distance between them. "Why, then, Myra?" she countered. "Why did you give so freely of your time and talents? Oh, and your money, too! *Why*? I've often wondered."

The folds of Myra's face softened, as did her voice. "For you, dearest. For love of you."

Myra's intent was suddenly defined and unmistakable.

Theodora felt the hot flush of blood rising to her face. She stared for a long minute before she could bring herself to say something. She drew in a long breath. "Then I am sorry to disappoint. Truly I am." She turned, leaving Myra standing there. She did not look back.

Theodora walked home, wondering why it was that Myra's declaration had surprised her. Oh, she was no innocent. She had known of such love and had ignored flirtatious overtures from other actresses, usually older. Why hadn't she seen beyond Myra's mask? The hints came back to her now—sometimes it had been only a word or an inflection of the voice, sometimes a touch.

The truth was, she admitted to herself as she lay in bed that night, sleepless, some part of her had known, but it was smothered by a stronger part that held the knowledge at bay so great was her desire to learn the leaping dance.

Theodora fixed her gaze at the ceiling. *Oh yes, I had planned to be as good as Myra. I had aspired to be better!*

Her disappointment, bitter and sharp, was not to be cushioned by the knowledge that, while she was young and had yet to discover love, she had already claimed the love of two people: Myra and Hecebolus.

With one, it was impossible, with the other …

Mindless to the vibrations and jolts, I sit cross-legged on the hard boards of the wagon as it trundles along. My parents have sold me, this I know. Fear looms large while sorrow and anger are merely brewing. I cannot accept as fact that I would not be going home. The thought invades my mind, and I attempt to crush it, to no avail. As the wagon moves down, out of the Syrian hills, jumping and jolting along, I hold back tears, numb and frightened for the future. The man has not bound me, but this is my prison cell, nonetheless. The vision of his smile sends a chill running through me.

A black curtain separates me from the Persian, who sits on a bench in front, directing the single horse. I attempt to gather my thoughts. Most children's imaginations would be filled with dread about what is in store for them, and so is mine, but as the wagon rattles along, fear fades a bit and I become inquisitive about its strange contents. My parents often upbraided me for my curiosity. My father would make his point by slapping me on the back of the head. Mother would shake her head and say, "You are the most meddlesome child."

A few feet from me sit two large trunks made of weathered wood and bound with iron. They fascinate me. How I long to know their contents!

After some hours, the man halts the vehicle and hauls me down so that we can piss in the nearby foliage. Oh, I consider running away. I know the wagon could not follow me into the forest interior. I ponder my opportunity. Would the Persian leave his belongings and give chase? I am certain I could outrun him. But the densely forested surroundings—and the eerie noises of birds and animals—are not of the welcoming variety. Had not my mother told me that the evil one himself abides in the forest, awaiting wayward humans? I know that I am very far from home—and what if I were to return? What greeting would my parents have for me? They had struck a bargain with the Persian, and intuition tells me that I would be given over to him again. No, I decide, I will run away—one day. But for now it is an unthinkable feat. And, truth be told, I am determined to discover the contents of those trunks.

We are scarcely back on the road half of an hour when curiosity gets the better of my sense of propriety—and safety. I know I will have a little time before the man bothers to check on me again. It takes all of my strength to lift the heavy lid of the first trunk, so very quietly. That done, I peer into it in, heartbeat accelerating.

I spy rolled papyri. Unrolling one scroll, I see writing for the first time. The figures and markings mean nothing to me, of course, but I know instinctively that they mean something to others, that they are symbols for something. Underneath them are folded thin sheets that open into a kind of tablet. I believe they are made of lead. These, too, have symbols. The markings have been made by purposeful scratching in the lead. I shiver when I notice that two of the tablets have nails piecing them, as well as drops of what looks like dried blood. I have no key within my unschooled brain to unlock the meanings behind the symbols on the papyri and tablets, so it is perhaps the mysteries they hide that reach up to me, like so many beckoning fingers. I go to close the trunk, and the heavy lid slams down with a thud. Fear runs through me like a lance. I can't move. My eyes become fixed on the front of the wagon, waiting for the Persian to throw back the curtain and pounce on me. A full minute passes. Nothing.

Two more minutes and my tenacious trait reasserts itself. The second trunk holds its own surprises—and questions. It is nearly filled with strange dolls, wax figures of men and women and children, most about as long as a man's forearm and bound with rag-like cloth. I hesitate to touch them, yet cannot resist. I pick up a pair wrapped in papyrus that is covered with markings. The scroll opens easily. The wax figures are naked and in an embrace. I hold back a gasp, feeling an odd embarrassment come over me. I wrap them up again. I look at several others, then come upon two that raise gooseflesh on my arms. One figure of a woman has had her leg removed and placed in her mouth. Six or seven needles pierce her torso. And there is a young man, naked, kneeling, his hands bound behind his back. Unlike some of the others that possess genitals, this one has none. A red dye had been smeared where his private parts should be.

As with the items in the first trunk, I sense a symbolic meaning behind the objects. But there is a difference here. My curiosity, heightened by the papyri and tablets, is snuffed out now like a candle by the grotesque wax figures. This doll, in particular, sends a cold shiver along my back. As if stung, I drop the figure and in a hasty attempt to quietly close the trunk, I somehow manage to bring the lid down on two of my fingers. The pain bursts from the source and speeds to every extremity. I draw in breath rather than cry out.

I retrieve my hand, thankful that the fingers are not crushed or broken. When the hurt eases, I attempt to come to terms with what kind of man the Persian is, what kind of man now controls my life. Mother had told me, Maya, and my brothers an abundance of tales, and so many of them had at their heart a magus.

I had been sold to a magus. I take in a mouthful of air. I am traveling with a wizard. My head reels like a wheel being spun by a cartwright, so difficult it is to comprehend the fact. I am filled to my hairline with a dichotomy of strong emotion—I am at once horrified and awestruck. *What does a wizard want with me?* I ask myself, once—and again.

I vow to run away—but my fear battles with the meddlesome prying I am prone to entertain. I want to learn more about my captor. My owner. There will be time later to consider running away, I tell myself, trusting that I will recognize the opportunity.

10

DRESSED ONLY IN HER *TUNICA intima*, Theodora went to the door as soon as she heard the knocking. It was the first time in months that she had not ignored the knocking of friends or family.

Irene stood there on the little stoop, her expression one of relief. "Well, you do live, I see. Hidden away, but alive just the same. People at the theater have doubted it or have had you sailing the Middle Sea with that fellow—what is his name?"

"Hecebolus. Come in, Irene."

Theodora led her to the little table, turned, and in good time produced an amphora of watered wine and a cup for the guest. Irene sat at once, still chatting on about business at the theater—until she noticed what even Theodora's *tunica intima* could not conceal.

"Why, Thea, you're … you're—"

"Yes, Irene, I am." Theodora sat.

"Surely you don't wish—"

"To have a child? No. Few women ever plan it, do they? Especially women in the theater, like us."

"You look far along, Thea. You've been so clever in the past. Why haven't you done something?"

Theodora offered a tight smile. "I have. I sent for you."

"But what can I do?"

"You mean to say it's too late?"

Irene nodded.

"I did try the potion once my courses stopped, but it had no effect. I've been in such a state since—I've just let time slip by." Theodora's gaze met Irene's. "Has Dion's troupe left The City?"

"They have, long ago.—The father, is it someone in their troupe?"

"No. I think I conceived the night before the audition. I was so caught up in preparation for it that I neglected to do the immediate precaution. The child is Hecebolus'. That night he offered to marry me, intending to give up his hopes for a governorship in some God-forsaken part of the world if I said *yes*."

"Well, he's still in The City. At least, he was. I saw him walking along the Mese not more than a week or two ago. If the child is his and if he's of the same mind—"

"Irene, think! He would have no hope of advancement if he were to marry me. I don't want that for him—or for me."

"Ah, I see."

"Oh, that doesn't mean I wouldn't go with him if he wins his governorship. He's not to know about—*this*, do you understand?"

"I do. You don't think he would accept the child as his?"

"If it's a boy, he might consider it."

"But not so much a girl? A sad situation, that is. And, Theodora, I'm so sorry I'm unable—"

"Oh, I knew it was too late for that, but there are two things I would like you to do for me."

"Anything, dearest."

"Find out what you can about Hecebolus' situation. If he *is* still here in The City, find out where he lives. And also find out where the home of Marcus Leontini is located."

"Leontini? The senator? What is it you are weaving?"

Theodora gave out with a genuine laugh. "I've been taught to sew by you, Irene."

Irene's hand reached across the table for Theodora's. "You can't stay here by yourself, you know, with no one here when your time comes."

"Thank you for coming, my friend. And for your concern. I have thought about that. I've written a note to my sister Comito. Would you see that it's delivered?"

On the raised bed, Theodora attempted to stir herself in the damp, chafing straw. The ordeal of birth had left her limbs heavy, her pulse weak. The enervating effects of the herbal tea she had been given during labor lingered, and she was thankful for it. She fought off a dark—but somehow welcoming—void that threatened to descend.

Someone entered the stone dwelling's single room now. Her heavy eyelids lifted. Without a word and no more than a sideways glance, the midwife's stooped husband went to the well-worn wooden birthing chair, picked it up, and made his exit. She saw that the rushes where it had been positioned were darkly stained.

It was unusually hot for May, and the thick heat of the afternoon afforded no breeze. From the other side of the window's drawn leather shade, she could hear street noises as though distilled through the fog of the rose and witch hazel brew. Then came murmuring in serious tones that put her on edge, chilling her despite the heat. Comito was conferring with the midwife. What was the woman saying, urging?

Theodora looked down at the dark little head in the crook of her arm. The baby was tiny, dark eyes wide as if in pain or fear. In labored fashion, its naked chest rose and fell, fell and rose. Theodora's slender finger worked at curling a wet wisp of the baby's hair. She would not allow herself to fall asleep. She pulled the child still closer.

Someone had placed a vase of purple spring crocuses on a table nearby, and she found their strong scent oppressive. Outside, the two disembodied voices droned on like bees corked in a bottle. How much time had passed since the birth of her child? Why had the midwife not gone home to her own family? What could they be discussing?

Theodora laid her head back and stared at the webbed cracks in the plaster ceiling. Fatigue crept in like fog off the Golden Horn, weighting her eyes until they closed.

"The child will not live."

At the sound of the words, final and terrible, Theodora's eyes fully opened.

It was the old midwife speaking, Comito peering down from behind, her pretty face creased in concern. The woman stood before Theodora, stooped, face weathered, hair grizzled and frowsy. The sparkle of her dark eyes belied her message. "It has come before its time," she said. "See how weak and frail it is. Listen to it wheeze and gasp."

Theodora had no intention of keeping the girl-child, and yet the midwife's words pierced her herb-infused thoughts and sped to the heart. Time lengthened between beats. She stared at her until her figure blurred before the tears beading in her eyes.

"It would be best," the midwife was saying, "if you allow me to take it."

The suggestion validated Theodora's terrible presentiment. The midwife and Comito had been debating whether to expose it on the stone ledge where the deformed and unwanted were given up. The practice was of the old ways and outlawed decades before, but it was nonetheless still observed on occasion. The enormity of the midwife's words unleashed a scream from her soul, but by the time it traveled up from her core to her throat and to her mouth, her voice was but a breath: "No."

"But it is hopeless—"

Theodora summoned her strength. "She gasps because she strains for life. If my child insists on living, who are we to deny her?"

"It is a girl-child," Comito whispered, stepping to the other side of the bed and taking Theodora's hand. "You told me there might be options for a boy-child, but for a girl-child ..."

So, Comito is taking the woman's side. Is she about to back out of our agreement that she see to its care? Theodora felt the child twist and squirm in her grasp. She was holding her too tightly. Some unseen strength shored her spirit now. "If my daughter's ambition is great enough, she will have her place."

Comito sighed. She took several copper coins from her purse and handed them to the midwife, who shrugged, accepted payment, and turned to leave. "What future can there be," the midwife hissed, "for a weak and sickly girl-child?" Some indecipherable look passed between her and Comito. Were they merely humoring her? Comito saw the midwife out.

Theodora lay back but could not ease the strain within her body. The voices moved beyond the house, then out of earshot. She could hear only the distant whine of a dog. Would her sister conspire with the midwife? *What if,* Theodora thought, *the woman had something to gain by taking the child? Is there a market for babies? A slave market?*

Theodora looked down at the child. Was it her imagination, or did her daughter's breathing now seem more regular, the lift of her chest less labored? Her eyes were closed, and she was sleeping.

Comito returned at last, an uncertain smile on her face. She came close to the bed, her smile deepening. Would she live up to her promise?

The moment hung suspended.

Then, at last, Comito asked, "What are we to call her?"

"Come, take her up. It will be for you to name her, Comito. You will keep to the bargain?"

Comito lifted the child from the bed and settled her into the crook of her arm. Glancing down at her younger sister now, she nodded, then looked lovingly at the child in her arms.

"I have nothing to leave her, Comissa." Theodora thought for a moment and pointed to a nearby table. "Take those earrings over there and save them for her. She'll like the little dangling pendants."

As she watched her sister obey, her hand moved up and made a quick brushing motion at her eye, as if to bat away a fly.

The villa of bleached stone stood like a forbidding fortress on a grassy bluff above Constantinople, not far from the mausoleum of Constantine. It was the home of someone who had done well for himself.

Theodora would not give her name at the door. "Most irregular," the servant muttered, squinting as if to see the face behind the veil. He showed her into a well-appointed reception room. "I will speak to the master," he said, his lips drawn thin, "but without a name, I can assure you—"

"Tell him, then, that Aphrodite has come to call."

The poor old man's eyes beneath a high forehead turned to saucers. He drew himself up and hurried away. In a short time, a servant boy brought her a cool drink. His passive face allowed only a ripple of surprise when Theodora thanked him. Clearly, the master class of which she was a pretender did not often thank a servant. She tucked away that bit of knowledge.

The old servant's message brought quick results. Senator Marcus Leontini appeared in the doorway. "Good morning, my lady," he said. His words rang with that hollow cordiality one too often finds in public men.

"Good morning, sir."

"And you are—?"

Theodora had come to his home as a lady of polite patrician society, face veiled and in a shapeless mantle of blue brocade borrowed from Irene's costume storeroom. She removed the veil now.

Leontini's jaw fell slackly into his fleshy jowls, and an audible hiss escaped through his small teeth. His facial features were unrefined, more of the baseborn than a noble Roman. His large head was shaven of what few hairs he had. He was a sturdy, brutish sort, late fifties, Theodora guessed. In earlier days, he might have possessed a gladiator's body, but she suspected that beneath his voluminous blue dalmatic his body had run to fat early on.

"You know who I am, Senator," Theodora said, allowing a smile to play at the corners of her mouth.

He squinted and in moments raised his bushy gray eyebrows. "How ... how dare you come into my home!" he ranted. "Are you insane? What do you mean by this?"

Theodora spoke evenly. "I have business to discuss."

"I maintain chambers at the Great Palace complex; anyone could tell you that. What business could you possibly have ..." His voice dropped to a whisper now. "Did anyone see you arrive?"

"As you saw, I came veiled. And in garb suitable enough for a grandmother. No one would have taken notice."

"Then I ask you to leave just as discreetly."

"I will leave when our business is concluded, Senator. And only then."

He sneered as if Theodora were one of the beggars along the Mese. "I have no business with the likes of you!"

"But I have with you." His arrogance rankled her, but she recalled Irene's advice to lay down one card at a time. She looked him in the eye. "However, I know a man of your importance must be very busy. I would not want to detain you. If I've come at a bad time—you won't mind if I leave off the veil as I depart? It is a bothersome thing for one so unused to it and it's so very warm today." She stood as if to make an exit.

"W—wait," he stammered. He moved quickly toward the exit, and with a covert side-to-side glance into the vestibule, closed the door.

He rejoined his visitor. "Very well, Theodora," he grunted, "what is this business? Be quick about it. I'm expecting visitors."

"I believe that you know a man named Hecebolus—a Syrian?"

"I do not recall every ... yes, I think that I do. A rather short man, swarthy. Altogether a nuisance with his petition!"

"He has been promised a governorship."

"Yes, yes. Too many have been promised." Leontini glanced down at his manicured nails. "That is the problem in politics."

"He is qualified?"

"It would seem so, but there are older men higher up the list. Men with more—sway."

"But you promised his father!"

"Promises are easier to make than to keep. What is your concern in this?"

"I have come to intercede for him."

"You!" His laugh was harsh and mean. "His chances grow dimmer by the minute."

Theodora waited until his humor dissipated, then said, "Do you recall your assignation with me?"

His color went the way of his humor. "I admit to nothing of the sort!"

"I see. You are forgetful. It could not have been more than a year past, Senator. You were a brash and passionate suitor, but, alas, very drunk. No doubt your forgetfulness was to blame for your failure to leave the appointed sum. I had been forewarned of your tactics, and that is why I slipped a certain ruby ring off your chubby little finger."

"You!" he boomed. "Then that is where ... where is it? Give it to me at once!" He thrust out his open hand, stupidly expectant.

"Oh, I have it. Do not fear—it is safe." She paused, baiting him. "Is Chryse well? Is she visiting her relations on Cyprus, as she did last year at this time?"

Leontini glared at her.

"When is she due to return?"

He fashioned his mouth into a half-smile half-sneer. "Ah, I see your little game."

"Good. We can come to terms quickly, then. You will recommend Hecebolus to the emperor?"

"You are demented! Get out!"

"And the ring?"

"Keep it."

"And I thought I wouldn't have to explain everything to you. You see, Senator, I have no wish to keep a ring that belongs to another. When your gracious wife returns, I shall pay her a call."

Leontini grunted. He paled slightly.

His reaction was enough to validate her theory that his wife had given him the ring, that it might even be an heirloom.

"She will be glad to have it back—along with the details of how I came to have it. I will have no need to embroider."

A twitch was working almost imperceptibly within the folds of his left cheek. He understood completely. "You are quite the accomplished criminal for your years, Theodora."

"I am merely trying to gain what has been promised. Is that so terrible?"

"I will buy the ring from you."

Theodora remained impassive.

"That is all I can do, Theodora."

"I have heard of Chryse's temperment—and pride. If she leaves you, what then? It is no secret where the wealth lies."

Leontini moved closer to Theodora, his face empurpled. "Your pretty neck," he said through clenched teeth, "could be wrung as easily as a wren's."

The danger was real. Murder flared in his eyes, and for a moment Theodora did think herself out of her depth. "Do not dare to touch me!" She was suddenly and genuinely frightened—but not without quick-wittedness. Her sedan bearers were waiting outside, but he could dismiss them with some bogus excuse. "I have left word of my destination. Even for a senator, murder is a hard thing to conceal."

He stopped, the dark, hooded eyes assessing her. He let out a great sigh and gained control of himself. "You think you are very clever, my dear, don't you?"

"Clever enough to strike a bargain with one who knows his best interests." Theodora smiled.

"A governorship for a ring. It is extortion."

"You are merely being reminded of a pledge you made."

He turned and walked across the room, his right hand at his chin. "There is one vacancy imminent, one of importance. At the Libyan Pentapolis. Do you know Africa?"

"No."

"The Pentapolis fronts the Middle Sea to the north and is sheltered from the desert by mountains to the south. It is as lush as Eden. A stellar province."

"Is it?" Theodora wondered if he was overpraising the province. Was it truly an Eden? Hecebolus would know. She was about to question him regarding the posting when he suddenly turned to face her.

"You are in love with Hecebolus?"

The question took her by surprise. She did not respond.

"You don't love him, do you?" he muttered, moving closer. "But by raising him you are raising yourself, that's it, isn't it? Do you intend to marry him?"

Theodora smiled, the tightest of smiles. "You know that I cannot. Doing so would deny or rescind the governorship."

"Well, you are not to have your way in all things, then, are you?"

She remained silent.

"Very well," he said, sighing, "I shall go see my friend Tribonian. He has the emperor's ear."

"You'll recommend him? I have your word?"

"You do."

"Just the same," Theodora said, playing her final card, "I have placed the ring and a letter detailing your assignation in the hand of a friend. In the unlikely event of something happening to me, the authorities would be contacted and the ring and letter would be sent to your wife's family."

The man's face went white as a ship's mast. Theodora doubted that he had ever deferred to any woman in private or public matters, much less one as young as she.

She took her leave. Outside, her two hired men were waiting. She had been carried to the Leontini villa to be in keeping with her pose of a patrician woman, but now she found herself quite enjoying the luxury of the cushioned sedan chair. She became lost in thought as she was borne down the narrow crushed-stone road to the stone paved Mese and into The City's true heart. She loved Constantinople, and yet she would be glad to be gone from a city that had spurned her dreams, dictating to her the role of prostitute. In the Pentapolis, she would be someone, even if it was merely the mistress of the governor.

Theodora looked down to see that when she climbed into the sedan chair an object that hung from her neck on a gold chain had been freed from the folds of her *tunica intima* where it had been hidden. She gasped and pressed it to her racing heart, thankful that she was the sole witness. Had it happened just ten minutes before, she would have lost more than the ruby ring. She had no doubt that Leontini would resort to murder rather than lose his link to his wealthy in-laws.

11

"MUST YOU LEAVE?" ANTONINA ASKED. "You are my one true friend."

"And you are mine, dearest, even though I've always been jealous of your light hair and blue eyes. For now, yes, I must. I'll come back a lady, just wait and see."

"Ha! In that case you won't have anything to do with a mere chorus girl!"

"Not so. We shall always be true friends, Nina. Always!"

It was no exaggeration. Theodora would miss Antonina terribly. But as she returned home, she did wonder whether they would meet again.

In the last few days before Theodora and Hecebolus left, The City stayed on her mind. After all, she had known no other. Her attitude toward Constantinople softened, a change ignited in part to her fear of the unknown, for as her days there dwindled, she came to see her birthplace as a friend. Just as with a friend, it had been exciting, changing, challenging—but also unsettling, abrasive, and dangerous.

Theodora said farewell to her mother and younger sister, promising them shares of her success. She had not seen Comito or the child since the day after the birthing and could not bring herself to return to her sister's home for goodbyes.

On the day before the departure, when she knew she should have been at home seeing to the details of the voyage, she found herself walking along the colonnade of the Augustaion. The public square was enclosed on three sides by the great edifices that she knew as the heart of The City. While the Great Palace belonged to the emperor and the Church of the Holy Wisdom belonged to God, the Hippodrome belonged to the people.

It was only natural that the sweet and bitter happenings at the amphitheater were the most vivid of her memories of The City. She had grown up in its shadow, relishing the excitement of the circus and theater crowds, yet awakening to the unseen chains her birth imposed.

She entered the cathedral. She had been baptized there and could remember attending Mass regularly as a child, always wide-eyed at the colorful pageantry. The sharp scent of the incense made her sneeze. But that was in the years before her father's death—when her mother's dark beauty was enough to startle people on the street. After she married again—to a pagan—they went no more to church.

The click-clack of her sandals echoed now on the glasslike gray marble in that great, cool cavern. She moved up the main aisle. Several old women prayed in lilting and lisping whispers. Theodora's eyes became transfixed by the interior, a masterpiece of stone, marble, mosaic, and light. How had she avoided this place for so long, this deeply quiet other-world? She stopped. A triangular shaft of shimmering light that emanated from a window in the main dome fell at a narrow angle onto the subject of the mosaic that dominated the sanctuary. Mary, Mother of God, illuminated that way, appeared to be lifelike, her face radiating a soft fragility and humanness so unlike other mosaics she had seen that projected brittle, artificial poses.

She prayed now—though she hardly knew the way of it. Hers was not a prayer of words. It was a great flowing out of feelings, a blind reaching for … she knew not what. The vivid memory of the black-haired child in the crook of her arm came back to her. "Let Comito do the right thing," she said aloud.

A sense of peace entered her. Theodora felt something … though she wasn't able to explain it then, or later. Was it her soul that became light … light, as if gossamer wings were bearing it up toward the painted image of Christ in the dome high overhead. Had her prayer been heard?

"Are you unwell?" someone asked her.

Theodora was startled to see the weathered face of an old priest just before her. "What? Oh … no. Thank you, Father."

She turned and hurried from the darkened church out into the blinding sunlight. She walked toward the palace.

Upon her stool, she had spent countless childhood hours observing those of nobility and influence parade along fashionable streets to the Mese, then toward the Sea of Marmara and the Augustaion. She witnessed the elite enter the Chalké, the royal vestibule with its roof and doors of gilded bronze. Of course, no one of her station in life had access to the grounds of the Great

Palace, so she contented herself with imaginings rich in color and plot as to what lay behind that brazen entrance.

She sat on a stone bench now. She had seen the emperor on several occasions, but her clearest, most vivid vision of him came by way of others.

The incident had occurred when she was twelve. Rioting had erupted in the streets. Word began to spread that The City was to have a new emperor. The people demanded it. Anastasius had made the error of mixing into the people's religion by changing certain words in the *Trisagion*, the people's paean to God. When the patriarch of the church objected, the emperor deposed him. Anastasius could not have guessed that the entire city, empathetic to the patriarch, would take up the cry, "Give The City a new Emperor!"

From all parts of Constantinople, they marched to the cathedral, singing the *Trisagion*. "Holy, Mighty, Immortal Lord!" were the defiant words. Houses were fired and deaths reported. It was later put about that much of the chaos and violence was incited by the Greens, the faction Theodora had neither forgotten nor forgiven.

At the cathedral, the emperor's guards were put down and the people claimed the church as their own. Emperor Anastasius sent out criers calling the men to assembly at the Hippodrome on the next day. Of course, women were excluded, so Theodora received her account from Dorian, a theater friend.

The stadium was filled to overflowing and all eyes were trained on the kathisma, the imperial box. Anastasius let them wait. While they did so, the leaders of the political factions, farmers, merchants, and craftsmen each, in turn, gave vent to their grievances with the emperor. The speeches were interrupted often with roars of "Give The City a new emperor!" These Theodora and the women and other children heard plainly enough in the streets.

At last, the curtains in the box parted and there stood the withered and white-haired Anastasius.

All heads turned, eyes on the emperor whose face, Dorian said, was a colorless mask of tragedy. The crammed tiers fell into a deathly silence soon broken by men gasping like startled old women.

The emperor had put off the imperial diadem, the purple robe, the scarlet sash and shoes. He stood, visibly trembling, in the undyed tunic of a common citizen! Before the crowd could recover, the imperial announcer stepped forward. "The Ever-August, the Emperor Anastasius stands before his people, innocent in his heart, yet yielding to their will who find him guilty. In all humility, Emperor Anastasius puts off the imperial diadem and resigns as emperor. He asks you now whom you will have in his stead."

A single whisper among the sixty thousand could have been heard by all. That the crowd had vented much of their hostility before the emperor appeared worked in his favor. The crowd's leaders, dissatisfied as they were with both important and petty things, knew that whomever might be installed, The City would be run much as before. The riot had gone further than they had expected, and they had to admit to themselves that they were not truly prepared to choose another emperor.

Anastasius' humility and willingness to accept the will of his people had maneuvered the enemy into a state of confused frenzy. A low discordant murmur, then a universal hue and cry ran through the crowd. The amphitheater was suddenly a bee's hive whose queen had abdicated. This chaos went on for long minutes.

Finally, a deep voice far back from where Dorian was standing bellowed above the din. "You are Emperor, Anastasius, until your last day. Take up your diadem!" Another called: "Take back the purple!" and the chant was taken up by another and another—until even the women and children in the streets were nearly deafened by it. Then they, too, took up the cry: "Take back the purple! Take back the purple!"

Anastasius humbly bowed to the will of the people.

Some said the emperor's resignation was a ruse, a clever gamble. Now, years later, Theodora supposed as much. Even so, the event robbed Theodora of her respect for Anastasius. She would long remember thinking—even at her tender age—that had she worn the royal color, she would rather have had the inciters slain in their seats, or would have gladly died herself, than put off the purple.

Theodora shook herself free of her memories. She would miss The City, but it had been unkind to her. She vowed not to give herself over to self-pity. Neither would she listen to a little voice inside her that accused her of running away. She was running toward something, something significant—and as yet unknown to her. Of this she was certain. Some greatness lay ahead for her, not theater, not dance. What? She stood and hurried home. There was much to be done.

On the next day, Hecebolus and Theodora set sail for the Libyan Pentapolis.

"You had high hopes, then?" I ask.

Theodora nods.

"What is it you wanted?"

Theodora pauses, looks away. "Well, there was love. I imagine every person longs for love, yes? Perhaps learning the leaping dance was my attempt to regain an audience's admiration—and love."

"And when that failed …"

"Yes," she says, "there was Hecebolus."

"Did you love him?"

"He loved me, I was certain. And I thought he could make a lady of me. That became my secret wish. If he could do that for me, I could not help but love him. Or, so I thought."

"You would start a new life at the Pentapolis?"

Theodora gives a tight smile. "How long could I have gone on living on the fringes of the theater circuit? From my days of sitting on my little stool in front of the houses of the wealthy, watching the great ladies arrive and leave, with their rich brocades and jewels, their heads held high, I knew what I wanted. I wanted to be a great lady."

"More than love."

"Ah, well, you see, he promised me marriage—and that one day we would return to The City, man and wife, rich and respected.—But, between you and me, I don't know that I believed in love."

"Really?"

Theodora's dark eyes narrow. "Do *you*, Stephen?"

Her question ices my heart. Does she know the object of my love? How can she not know? I draw myself up in my chair, praying my expression reflects humor. "I am writing *your* story, Theodora."

PART TWO

PART TWO

12

A T MY NEXT INTERVIEW WITH Theodora, I find myself interrupting her when she starts to relate details of the voyage to the Libyan Pentapolis. I have a question about her life on the stage, one she will not like.

"You sailed in 518, Theodora, did you not?"

"Yes, Stephen. In June, my birth month."

"You were eighteen?"

She nods. "I turned eighteen on the ship."

"Your daughter was born before you left."

"Yes."

I pause, unsure about my next question, anxious about her reaction to it.

"Come, come, Stephen—what else?"

"Well—" I'm nervous. And it takes some doing for me to become accustomed to using her name again. "Theodora, there is one theatrical piece that people talk about."

"Yes? Which?"

"*Leda and the Swan.*"

"Oh, what is it they say?" A light blush comes into her cheeks.

I wonder if she is toying with me, if she knows very well what they have said about it for years. In any case, I am not about to tell her that the legend has her posing naked in the most lascivious positions while several geese peck away at her privates which have been covered in grain that is being held in place with olive oil. Instead I say, "They say live geese appeared on stage with you."

"What nonsense! What would geese have to do with the myth? Yes, yes, I appeared naked, but it was one of my living portraits, and it was fairly well executed, I must say, but not one of my favorites. In the first tableau I appeared as Leda in my garden, scantily dressed. In the second, Zeus was present in the form of a great swan. It was a wonderful costume made of real feathers! I was a bit jealous for the attention he received, but as Leda, of course, I made the most of my ability. She had no idea it was Zeus once again transforming himself into an animal so as to stray from his vigilant wife Hera. In the next tableau, I lay naked splayed upon a sleeping couch with him atop me, his wings spread wide. It was wretchedly uncomfortable so that my pained expression came naturally. The director often held the curtain longer than usual so that every wide eye in the back row could take it in. In the final scene, Zeus had unmasked himself and I was staring in wonder.—You know, I never did know whether Leda's wonder stemmed from surprise, delight, or horror."

"Maybe it was a little of all three," I say.

"Perhaps, but you must see that the very idea of live geese in a living portrait is ludicrous. How would they ever be made to stand still for minutes at a time?"

I feign to laugh. I am not so certain this is all truth, but I know it is best to allow the matter of feathered gods and geese to come to an end. There is enough here for me to creatively twist when I find the time to write my own secret life of Theodora.

I move on to the subject of the Pentapolis.

On ship, Theodora exulted in the thought that she would celebrate her eighteenth year in the Pentapolis a woman of some consequence—if not yet a lady.

The great pagan god of old, blue-haired Poseidon, smiled on her and Hecebolus, and the first leg of the voyage progressed as though charmed. A swift and steady wind caught the bleached sails of the *Horizon,* propelling the trireme across the royal blue of the Aegean. Tranquility continued to reign on the third day out—and into the Middle Sea by now. The chanter's song, a euphonious but unintelligible jumble of some Bulgar words, and the endless thump of his drum were controlled in rhythm, dictating a moderate pace for the rowers. This song of slaves was for Theodora a song of gaiety, for the synergism of muscled arms manning the hundred seventy oaken oars on three levels were bringing her, span by span, toward what she hoped would be her kismet. The shoulders and backs of the slaves—their skins of varied hues, dark and light—glistened hotly in the sun as they leaned into their task and pulled back, leaned and pulled, their faces alike in masks of grim resignation.

On these days, the azure sky was clear but for the faintest whiffs of white, clouds like cobwebs against the brilliance of the sun. The nights were star-hung, the waxing moon's reflection shimmering on the horizonless sea in every wave and ripple. Theodora stood now at the stern, reveling in the brisk and salty wind against her face. She was sorry to see the last of the gulls that had followed the ship as far from their coastal nesting places as they dared, cawing gratefully as they fed on waste thrown into the sucking wake of the ship. Soon her attention was drawn to where a little miracle was unfolding. On either side of the ship, cresting the waves in orderly formations were glass-gray dolphins, like soldier-escorts of the sea. Theodora's heart and breath caught at the sight. For a girl whose farthest path from The City had led to a feast in a meadow during harvest-home, this was an adventure.

Theodora exulted in the knowledge that her scheme had been successful, recalling how she feigned surprise when Hecebolus came to tell her of his reversal of fortune, his face at once happy and uneasy. "Leontini sent for me. I can't understand it. I was resigned to returning home to Antioch when he sends for me and offers me the governorship of the Libyan Pentapolis. It's very strange."

"No doubt you're the best candidate, Hecebolus," Theodora said. "He's probably had his eye on you all the while. Your persistence tipped the scales."

"I don't know. Somehow the man seemed false. I sensed something hidden beneath his words, like a sand snare that can swallow a man whole."

Theodora became dizzy with fear that her scheme had been in vain. "Hecebolus, you *accepted* ... didn't you?"

He nodded. "I did ... and yet—"

"I'm sure it was *nothing*," Theodora said, kissing him on the cheek. "Your life is to change now."

"It's just that I don't wish to be played a fool. You see, friends here have cautioned me that the Libyan Pentapolis has had its measure of troubles, not the least of which is the native population. There's no telling what I'm letting myself into."

Theodora offered a smile. "But without challenges, my dearest, achievement is nothing. What sort of troubles?"

"Weather, crops, poverty, insurgent natives."

"You know I am unskilled in politics, Hecebolus, but aren't these standard obstacles in any of the outer provinces?"

"That may be, but—"

"Did Leontini himself warn you of these things?"

Hecebolus shrugged. "He did mention them in passing. He spent more time talking about the fertility of the land and its potential. Others I've talked to are not so enthusiastic."

"I'm sure Leontini is right. The others are but envious. Do you think *they* would refuse such a commission?"

"To hear them tell it—"

"Hades take the liars! Do you think Leontini would have made a second offer? Did you expect him to say 'Here, Hecebolus, here is a prosperous province without a single challenge.'? No, a settlement without problems would be a settlement without people." Theodora purposely held Hecebolus' gaze with her own. "Whatever challenges arise, we will meet them toe to toe."

"We?" His distraction dissipated immediately and his lips widened in a smile. "You mean that you will come with me?"

"Didn't you mean to ask me?"

"Of course, and beg if I had to." His dark eyes went glassy. "You will go?"

Theodora smiled.

"And your dancing?"

"I've grown tired of it."

He laughed. "I'll never understand the fickle ways of women. You won't grow tired of *me*, will you, Theodora?"

Theodora kissed him again. "I will not."

Hecebolus' face darkened. "You … know that we cannot marry here, but there—there I am the highest law. I will marry you, Thea."

"You'll need a dispensation."

"To hell with that!"

"No, Hecebolus, it must be done properly. We will want to come back to The City one day, yes? We won't want to spend all of our days there, will we?"

"Who knows? If it's with you, I could!"

Theodora smiled sweetly. "But I could not."

The moon was still waxing on the third night. Theodora awoke with a jolt to find she had been tossed like a doll from her raised pallet. Hecebolus lay beside her on the floor of the tiny compartment. "Are you all right, Thea?" The ship was rocking violently. Before she could answer, they heard shouts from above.

"Leeward! Leeward!" someone was shouting, the order faint against the elements and the din of men.

"It was a wave," the pilot told them later, "the height of eight or ten men, a marvel it was. It rose right up out of a calm sea like Poseidon's hand itself and came crashing down upon us."

Theodora and Hecebolus got to their feet. The ship veered sharply, heaving heavily as it plowed headlong into angry waters. Salty spray and rainwater splashed down into the shafts, spilling under the door into their compartment and collecting on the floor in a pool, only to wash out like a shallow tide as the ship listed to the far side. The rush of water that returned was deeper each time. Wind whiffled shrilly through the flues and any unplugged apertures. Buffeted by high waves throughout the long night, bearing up under wind and rain, the vessel pitched and groaned as a thing alive.

Hecebolus and Theodora clung to one another, saying little. Theodora thought his fear was as great as her own, and the thought made her uneasy.

The storm lessened by dawn, but by that time Hecebolus was nearly unconscious with cold, fever, and seasickness. He had vomited during the night, purging himself, yet he still convulsed, as if to spew forth his very insides.

Hecebolus looked up from his pallet at Theodora, who had been closely attending him. "The fools," he muttered, a helpless grimace tightening his face. "They claimed this was the best sailing weather."

"Don't try to speak." Kneeling, Theodora took and held his hand. "It's only a summer squall, they told me. It will pass any moment."

"Yes," he said, "taking us with it."

"The danger is past, my dear. Try to rest. You will need all your strength when we reach the Pentapolis."

"I tell you, it's a poor omen, Theodora. Who knows what might be waiting for us there?"

"Take heart, it's the sickness, Hecebolus. Like the storm, it will pass."

But he lapsed now into delirium, his mouth still rounded as if to repeat "omen."

It had taken no coaxing on Theodora's part for Irene to accompany her to the Pentapolis. Irene was eager to take up a more relaxed lifestyle, to travel, and to stand by Theodora. With Irene came a shower of blessings. Though Theodora called her a companion, she cheerfully played the roles of maid, tutor, advisor, and—most importantly—friend. Like the two newly appointed minor officials who traveled with Theodora and Hecebolus and numerous hirelings awaiting them at the Pentapolis, Irene would be paid from public funds, and Theodora saw to it that Irene's wages were generous. She had heard that loyalty overlooked was often the undoing of kings.

At mid-morning the pilot, a burly man of good humor, checked on them, assuring them that the worst had passed. Theodora was relieved to give over care of Hecebolus to Irene, who cheerfully added the role of nurse to her skills. Theodora wanted to go up on deck to look about, but the pilot would not allow it, so she went to Irene's tiny compartment to rest.

Despite her exhaustion, sleep would not give Theodora any respite. She lay sleepless, her body still as a corpse, her eyes tracing the boards above her. She worried over Hecebolus' health, of course, but she was confident he would beat back his sickness. It was a different aspect of him that frightened her to the quick. She wondered of what grain, what character, was this man who ventured into one of life's junctures, paling and trembling as though at the entrance of a dragon's den. It's only the sickness and not a flaw in character, Theodora told herself, yet she found her fingers in mid-air, making the ancient sign against the evil eye.

She had written her own part, and she knew she must play it out to the fall of the curtain. Money and pride would mark her steps and feed her lines. On her own, she was destitute. A Greek merchant's son had been found for Anastasia, so most of the savings Theodora had accumulated were left behind for her younger sister's dowry, the fall wedding, and the matchmaker. What sum was left she gave to her mother. Theodora was now fully dependent on Hecebolus and what she would be able to make of the position she had schemed to acquire for him and herself.

Theodora knew that the tides are but the playthings of the moon, and on the fourth night of the voyage, the moon led them into the seething vortex of another storm, this one no summer squall. This was a thunderous tempest beyond her imagination, and the consideration struck her for the first time that they might never see land.

Into the evening, Irene came down with the seasickness, and Theodora had two to care for. She insisted that Irene take her pallet. "I want you in here, Irene, so that my patients are in but one ward." Irene laughed. Of the two, she was the better patient. When Theodora herself felt the nausea coming over her, she repelled it, as if she could will it away. She held to her precious store of physical and mental energy.

The chopping, swirling sea whipped and tossed the ship about like a paper sailboat. Theodora could hear the great confusion overhead of orders barked, the chanter's tuneless shout and the quickened drumbeat, oars in motion, and running on the deck. And then a great thunderous crash. A mast falling, she guessed.

Rain and lightning and thunder besieged the ship while wave upon wave, each more forceful than the one before, lashed the vessel until every board and timber creaked and cried out. While Hecebolus and Irene slept fitfully, Theodora waited in horror for the moment when the ship would be torn asunder, splintering into ten thousand pieces, and dropping them, like marbles, into the deep.

The night crept on. The holds below became submerged, and the water level in the compartment continued to rise. It was all Theodora could do to rouse Hecebolus and Irene, forcing them to sit straight upon their pallets, backs against the compartment wall. Still the water rose, until the level reached her knees. In time the cold and wet broke through her patients' delirium, and they sat with sober and fearful faces. No one spoke.

By morning the sea calmed and the waters in the compartment had risen no higher. Though the ship listed, it had steadied. Theodora thought it a miracle they were still afloat.

"She's blown over!" the pilot called down. "It was a beauty, a blisterin' beauty! I'm sending some men down to help the governor and you ladies up to the bridge while we bail and see to repairs."

The ladder proved a struggle for Hecebolus and a deckhand had to assist. On the bridge, the trio joined the two government officials, who wordlessly reflected the amazement of everyone that they were still alive.

The pilot offered a litany of the losses. Everything in the lower holds—the ship's lading and the travelers' belongings—was ruined and was being unceremoniously chucked out into the sea. The second mast was lost and a number of oars damaged. Two of the pilot's mates had been washed overboard, and a number of rowers in the lower bank had been lost, drowned while still chained to their benches.

Theodora spoke for everyone when she thanked the pilot for seeing them through.

"Bad as it was, milady," he said, "I've been through worse."

Theodora did not for a minute believe the man but smiled nonetheless, for he had called her *milady*.

They lost a day and a half for repairs and bailing, another two for having been blown off course. During this time Hecebolus and Irene both recovered. Hecebolus' spirit seemed to revive, along with his health, so—together with the nightmarish memories of the storm—Theodora put from her mind the needling doubts about the man she had chosen to follow.

13

MORE THAN A WEEK AFTER their setting sail, the continent of Africa loomed ahead. Theodora stood with Hecebolus on the pilot's bridge, excitement ignited in her heart. The sea sparkled in the sunshine that rained down like gold from a blue, blue sky. Leontini had not lied. As the Libyan Pentapolis came slowly to float before their eyes, the splendor of the panorama—like Eden—beckoned them.

The pilot spoke exceedingly well of the Pentapolis. The province of the five cities lay mainly on the plateau of Barca, its threshold a one-hundred-and fifty mile stretch of coastland, its depth, at the furthermost point of a very wide arc, some two hundred miles. The position, formation, soil, and climate coalesced to make this a garden even the Hesperides would have coveted. The center of the arc was a moderately raised tableland, its coastal edge dipping down in a sequence of terraces arrayed with verdure and hill flowers. Frequent rains and cool mountain streams running through ravines kept vegetation plentiful and lush. The multiple terraces possessed a diversity of climates, each suited to nurturing particular vegetables, fruits, and flowers. Green Mountain, an especially fertile track on the north and northwest side of the tableland, could yield eight months out of the year. The five cities of the Pentapolis—Apollonia, Cyrene, Ptolemais, Arsinoe, and Berenice—were nestled snugly against their protector, a mountain mass that shielded the province from the hot winds of the Great Desert. Dozens of other settlements—tiny rustic villages—speckled the interior.

This was to be their home for three years, the length of Hecebolus' term as governor. If the province was managed adroitly, Hecebolus could look forward to advancement or, at the very least, an extension of his term.

The battered ship dropped anchor at Apollonia, the coastal port city. From the harbor, a train of horse, cart, litter, and pack mule would take the new governor and Theodora up the steep cliff side path to the Governor's House in Apollonia, the provincial capital.

People were streaming down to the docks, drawn like ants to a dropped honey cake. "Look, Hecebolus!" Theodora cried. "The city has turned out to greet you."

It was then, when she spoke of people hailing Hecebolus, that it was brought home to her what the status of mistress meant. Had she not bitten her tongue at the last, she would have said *us*. But—unless a marriage could be arranged—she and Hecebolus were to be separate in all things public, separate and unequal. No one would ever announce the Governor Hecebolus and his wife Theodora. Hecebolus would be announced with some fanfare and Theodora would be left to covert glances past righteous noses and appropriately hushed tones. "And that is his low-caste mistress," they would whisper.

So be it, she thought. She had chosen her own lot. She would endure it. And in time she would be his wife. He had promised.

"Meaning no disrespect, milady," the pilot said, "but these people have not turned out to greet the governor. The poor of the Pentapolis seem to collect in the capital and these poor devils you see here live only on what they scavenge from the sea. They will dance attendance on any ship coming from The City. Hoping for mail or money or supplies, they are. Ah, what with everything that went overboard, they will be mightily disappointed this day."

Theodora masked her own disappointment. After a time she inquired of the pilot how the people had regarded their former governor. "Governor Adrian was," he said, pausing, "removed, you might say, from the people. He had failed to win their hearts, you see, and when he died of the spring sickness … well, there was little breast-beating to be seen."

Theodora knew the pilot was measuring his words—and that more had been left unsaid. She looked to Hecebolus, who seemed not to be listening. His face darkly serious, he was squinting in the sunlight, looking past the hordes of ragged, rushing people. His eyes were directed up to the city at the edge of the plateau. He turned to the pilot. "I was under the impression that the capital was a walled city."

"Oh, it is that, my lord. On every side, except for the seaward side."

"I see," Hecebolus said with a grunt. "No need, what with the elevation. How high is the cliff?"

"I'm told about eighteen hundred feet, my lord."

Theodora and Hecebolus sat in a rocking, jerking cart as the driver negotiated the heights via a series of terraces. Irene and the two silent and bedraggled functionaries sat in one that followed.

The welcome was not quite what Theodora had expected, but as they came to the city gates, she pointed down at the harbor and put on her most optimistic face. "Look there, Hecebolus, what a wonderful view."

He looked down. "Indeed," he murmured, as if distracted.

Theodora wondered at his lack of enthusiasm. Did he share her uncertainty? For one whose only residence had been the glorious Constantinople, this seemed a wild land and she felt within an aching void.

Once inside the city gates, they traveled along a wide avenue, passing a stone basilica abutting one of the city walls. "Impressive," she said, although she knew it did not compare to a single one of Constantinople's many dozen churches. Roman baths had been built nearby and they, along with a large public square, an aqueduct system, and homes of wealthy planters and merchants, served to raise her spirits.

In size—if not grandeur—the Governor's House did not disappoint. It was an imposing structure of limestone built on a hillside overlooking the Roman baths. Dozens of palace inhabitants stood outside as Hecebolus and Theodora climbed down from the cart.

The household, they found, was run by Simon, a corpulent Greek who dressed as flamboyantly as a Persian satrap, and Pythia, whose mixture of Libyan and Asian blood accounted for a dark complexion and refined features. Not much past thirty, she was not beautiful in any conventional way, yet there was something birdlike and exotic in her visage and slender frame that caught the eye. These two hirelings, several minor officials, dozens of servants, and as many slaves turned out to meet their new master.

When Simon announced he had prepared for the new governor a proper tour of the palace complex, Hecebolus spoke up, introducing Theodora and saying that she would be coming along, as well.

After Theodora was introduced, Pythia remarked, "Forgive me, I had been told that the Governor was not married. And—well, we didn't expect—I mean to say, you may find us ill-prepared, milady. I will see that all is set to order immediately."

Cloaked by effusive courtesy and concern, the insult was nonetheless sharp. Theodora sensed eye movement all about her. Simon and the officials had not been taken by surprise—that much was clear. They had known of

Theodora's arrival and of her relationship to Hecebolus. Theodora was convinced that Pythia was aware, too, and deliberately chose to create a scene meant to embarrass her. It was the performance of an amateur. Theodora smiled now, burning inwardly at the woman's audacity. Here is someone to watch, she thought.

Erected on the southeast side of the baths, the palace was no more than twenty years old. Assuring the couple that the two-story palace boasted a hundred rooms, Simon took them through the first of two sections. "This side of the palace is devoted to the ceremonial chambers of the governor," he announced, leading them through an audience hall, guardroom, armory, chapel, and various offices used for government business. They came then to the residential side of the palace. Its many rooms were less majestic in style but still very much more luxurious than any home Theodora had experienced. The governor's second-floor bedchamber was richly furnished with imported marble and red bed hangings. Simon hurried them out to the terrace without comment on the walls that were colorfully painted with erotic frescoes. From the terrace they looked down on a Roman villa and a dozen small houses that were also part of the complex.

Throughout the tour of city and palace, Hecebolus listened carefully and observed everything but said almost nothing. Whatever misgivings he and Theodora entertained in those first days they did not disclose to each other.

The summer passed peaceably. Theodora was pleased to note that Hecebolus took to the responsibilities of his office. Of the various minor officials under him, some were frivolous, some merely stupid. Theodora could not identify a leader in the lot. Hecebolus took up his mantle and moved as a man of purpose. He investigated every graveled street, every cistern in the city; he rode to the tiniest and most distant of the villages in the green interior. At supper he would seize the conversation and run on, his declamations jumping from crops to aqueducts and sewers to buildings and this plan or that. He relished the responsibilities of his position while hardly tasting of the meal.

On one occasion, Theodora had enough. "Why," she pouted, "must there always be talk of sewage at the supper table? You haven't even noticed my new stola!"

Hecebolus smiled indulgently, apologized, paid his compliment as if it were a coin, and in short order turned the talk back to business.

In truth, Theodora could not have been more pleased with the emergence of his leadership qualities. Hecebolus wrote to the palace at Constantinople, requesting city planners, artisans, slave-laborers, materials and supplies, horses, and most especially, soldiers, for they had found the Pentapolis pitifully lacking in military protection. And there was cause for concern: in the past, the province had been preyed upon almost yearly by nomadic bands of Libyans, the warlike neighbors to the west. Only a month before the arrival of the new governor, a mere war-scare had prompted more than half of the soldiers, with neither governor nor pay, to have done with the province whereupon they departed for Alexandria or some other eastern port. Luckily, the Libyans had not struck in any great force. Theodora was certain those dullards temporarily in control would have handed the city over with honeyed phrases of politeness. It was imperative now that Hecebolus hold tight to the reins—and urge the emperor to send men for the defense of the province.

Because the province's future was no less her future, Theodora made an effort to learn of its history and geography. She listened, questioned, stored away knowledge. She kept herself acquainted with each of Hecebolus' plans and decisions. When she thought her opinion of some value, she voiced it when she was alone with Hecebolus. But as her confidence in him was shored, she began to turn her attention to setting the household in order.

One day, Theodora was being measured and fitted by a seamstress for the beginnings of a new wardrobe when Pythia came into her suite, carrying a supply of clean linen. Before leaving, she stopped to admire a bolt of sheer golden material that Theodora had selected. "Such quality," she remarked, "extravagant for the Pentapolis. It is lovely, though, so very lively and different from what so many of the women here wear. It well reflects your background in the theater."

Theodora felt a surge of blood rise into her face. Pythia's sly but sharp reproach proved gossip to be tenacious and impervious even to seawater. She took in a breath. From the first she had known that she would have to unstring Pythia's bow, and now was the time. She caught the retreating housekeeper by the arm and turned her about in an ungentle fashion. "Yes, Pythia, it's true. I have been an actress. But it is not an uncommon thing in The City to hear of one who has improved her lot. My story is short and lacking in sensation. I shall take the trouble to relay it to you one day. Let me say, however, that it takes a certain talent to conquer the stage." Theodora put the knife to her text now. "Take notice, dear Pythia, if you do not take caution and bridle your

James Conroyd Martin

tongue, you will find yourself in the street.—You must be—what? Thirty? Too old, I think, to learn the ways of the street."

Pythia's brown complexion blanched to the cast of dirty stone. The woman stared, as if she didn't know whether she stood on her head or heels. "Yes, Lady Theodora," she mumbled, collecting herself and scurrying away.

Theodora turned now to the witness of the exchange, assuring the trembling seamstress with a sudden smile that her anger was in no way directed at her. "Do continue with your measurements."

In a few moments, Irene entered. "What in the name of Hera is going on? As I was ascending the stairs, Pythia came flying down like a duck in thunder!"

Theodora laughed. "Her role here was explained to her, you might say, and it came as something of a thunderclap that she had no lines."

"You would do well to be rid of her and be done with it."

Theodora dismissed the seamstress now, requesting that she return the next morning.

Once they were alone, Theodora said, "I think we shall see a marked change in her, Irene."

"Just the same, she is dangerous."

"Oh, Irene, I think not."

"Oh, *do* you?" Irene tilted her head with the flare of an actress. "Do you know what her position was under Governor Adrian?"

"From your look I think I can guess—a position not unlike my own?"

"Exactly so—and with his wife living in the same building! These rooms you're settling into, Thea, once belonged to her."

"Oh, that hardly seems possible, Irene."

"Why, because she is no beauty? Oh, do not underestimate her, Theodora. Women to whom the mirror has been unkind learn to survive on their wits."

Theodora scoffed. "In that last part you mentioned, we are alike."

"Women like her—with their docile and wily manners have their ways to please men. In my long life I've often marveled at what men can find attractive."

"Well, she has had her comedown. I think she knows her place now."

Irene sighed. "Theodora, what king who has ever fallen and been allowed to live in his homeland has not plotted to regain his days of glory?"

Theodora's eyes widened. "Why, Irene, you don't mean to say—ah, I see that you do! By Venus! She's as ugly as a dead monkey! And more than a decade older than I. Not to mention it, but I *shall*—Hecebolus is in *love* with me."

102

"A decade older, perhaps, but not yet on the cusp of senility. True, she hardly seems a match for you, Thea, but a cunning woman is not to be discounted. She'll speak words of spun sugar to one while spitting venom at another. One thing is certain: Pythia is a woman accustomed to sailing near the wind.—How did the previous governor die?"

"The summer pestilence, I was told."

"And I wonder who might have nursed him."

"Oh, Irene, you're not serious. You don't think—Why, his death was her undoing, as you can see. You've been working in theater too long."

Theodora fully intended to speak to Hecebolus and have Pythia packed off, a little gold in her pocket. But in the days following, the woman's attitude and behavior changed abruptly, becoming as different as cheese from chalk. She became pleasant and eager to please, seeming altogether a different person. No one could argue that her performance as a housekeeper was laggard or inefficient in any way. The house hummed like a well-ordered hive. It was an easy thing to put off her dismissal.

Theodora realized, too, that without Pythia there loomed a host of mundane and distasteful domestic tasks that would require close overseeing, a duty for which no other servant was prepared—and one which little interested her. Planning the afternoon and evening meals, cooking, churning, spinning, sewing, polishing, cleaning, and a hundred other daily and torturously repetitious chores with which women busied themselves had always left Theodora bereft of patience. So Pythia continued in her position, and when Hecebolus fell ill, Theodora had no time to manage the household and was grateful for the woman's services.

It occurred in late August. Senator Leontini had not mentioned to Hecebolus the summer sickness that appeared at the Pentapolis every year, redoubtable as a tax collector. With his illness, the brief period of tranquility that he and Theodora had enjoyed came to an end.

Myron, a physician in Cyrene, took a room on the first floor of the palace and visited Hecebolus daily, treating him behind closed doors. He was no more than fifty, but strain and overwork had sculpted deep creases in his face and fully whitened his hair. Little wonder, for it was not an uncommon thing for a third of the population to come down with the sickness, as was now the case. Many of those citizens, despite clean and proper care, did not survive.

A week into his care of Hecebolus, Theodora put her usual question to Myron: "How is he, Doctor?"

Myron pursed his lips. There was, understandably, no sense of good humor about this man. "He is no better and no worse than my other patients. Boil his water well and make him drink large quantities."

Theodora nodded.

Myron's answer was always the same. He might just as well have said, "He may be on his feet tomorrow—or he may be dead."

"I'll make him drink until the bed floats."

The physician looked askance and proceeded to make his exit.

Theodora's concern over Hecebolus ran deep, her sleep short and unsound, her own health flagging. She knew she had not come to love him; indeed, she had come to doubt in the word *love*. She did feel affectionately close to him and was not unresponsive to his worship of her. And she saw their lives as permanently linked now, if not by marriage, then by a bond almost as strong. Their futures in the Libyan Pentapolis were becoming increasingly interlaced, like two young transplanted vines climbing a single post.

The fact that they weren't married, that she was not the Governor's wife, pushed itself to the fore. What if Hecebolus were to die? What then? What would become of her? Linked to that worry was the trepidation that came with the memory of the days at sea when Hecebolus seemed lacking in determination and bravery.

And yet, the enthusiasm and pluck with which he had undertaken his post as governor rebounded now, stirring hope that they would be enough to carry him through. He drew breath after the physician's visit, as on days previous, but this day he asked whether ships had arrived from The City.

"Yes," Theodora said, her tone flat. It was true. There had been ships, come with regularity to collect the fruits of the province: corn, oil, wine, figs, dates, almonds, truffles, saffron and the like. In turn, what the ships brought was a pittance.

"Men?" Hecebolus asked, trying to sit up. "Soldiers?"

"No.—Lie back, dearest."

"No horses? No money?"

Theodora shook her head, sorry for the answer but glad he was taking interest again. Later, she would tell him the disconcerting news that Emperor Anastasius had died and that his successor, Emperor Justin, was almost seventy years old.

Hecebolus fell back against his pillows, disappointment clouding his face.

Theodora mustered a smile. "I will direct that another letter be written. It can be sent with a ship that leaves tomorrow."

Hecebolus nodded. "Go ahead, but I am afraid that by the time it arrives in Constantinople, the gale season will be upon us and they will not risk another ship until spring. They have had our letters. Why haven't they responded?"

"Drink this," Theodora said, passing him a mug of warmed milk and honey and laced with the pressing of a poppy. "You need to rest."

"Ah, the cup of humiliation," Hecebolus joked. He sat up and raised the mug. "It is not for us to question, but to drink!"

"Hush, now."

Theodora turned to see Simon enter the anteroom of the Governor's suite.

"My lady, the province's officials have assembled in the council chamber. Is the Governor ready to present himself?"

"No, he is still much too ill.—How many are there?"

"At least a dozen."

"That must be the whole lot, yes?"

"I expect so.—Shall I send them on their way?"

"No, Simon. I sent for them and I shall speak to them."

Simon's small, dark eyes dilated. "You, my lady?"

Theodora turned to the mirror and adjusted a wisp of her black hair. She wore her hair swept up and plaited at the crown. For the occasion she wore a borderless brown dalmatic, one belonging to Hecebolus that she had altered. In the mirror her eyes caught Simon's reflection. His fleshy cheeks had fallen into folds of perplexity. She turned to face him. "Yes, Simon, I will be speaking to the ministers."

He nodded, whispering, "Yes, my lady."

Theodora smiled inwardly. The Governor's mistress was to step well above her station and address the city's highest officials. Simon looked as though she had just told him she would jump from the city's battlements at midnight.

14

THE SPIRITED VOICES SUBSIDED AS Simon pushed open the double doors and Theodora glided into the room. The last whisper died away at the sight of her.

The officials stood, thunderstruck.

"Good afternoon, Gentlemen!" Her voice pealed crisply. She felt the old stage tremors but—as she had done on The City's stages—channeled the energy to a show of confidence.

Their mouths fell open in murmurs of greeting.

Without missing a beat, Theodora moved to the governor's place at the head of the long and heavy table made of ebony. "We regret," she announced, "that the Governor's illness prevents him from business of state. Your patience notwithstanding, I ask that you allow me to sit in his stead." Theodora meant the question as rhetorical, and as she busied herself in sitting, she did not look up so as to give the ministers a few moments to mask their reactions.

She drew from her sleeve a parchment on which she had scratched the necessary topics and concerns. She then launched into her little oration. At some length, she addressed the most serious challenges facing the province, arriving at—in short time—the threat of an impending attack from the Libyans, a threat compounded by the Pentapolis's woeful lack of soldiers, horses, and weaponry.

Theodora called for opinions, comments, information.

A few spoke sparingly, but most remained closemouthed and the discussion quickly grew strained.

"Come, Gentlemen, this is no time to keep your tongues between your teeth. Speak up."

The hush was stifling.

Finally, a man at the far end of the table stood. His features were Latin and fair, his hair gray, thinning and tortured to the fore. "Begging no disrespect ... Lady Theodora, but I think some of us are ... reluctant to put forth our views."

Theodora focused on the man. "If anyone here has a view, I want to hear it voiced. This matter is grave."

"My lady, I think that they feel, that is, *we* feel that this business is best held over until the Governor is well."

Theodora's eyes moved about the table, making eye contact with everyone that dared look her way. "And who," she said, "in the meantime is to hold off the Libyans? The matter will *not* wait!"

The minister cleared his throat. "Then leave us, if you will, to discuss the matter, Lady Theodora. Talk of warfare and defense is not for women."

Theodora held down her anger. "I am to submit with good grace then—because you stoop even now to speak to me? Do you think life is less sacred to me, or to any woman?—*All* lives are at stake!" Her eyes moved over the other faces. "Any action that can be taken, must be taken, and without delay. The Governor is to have his representative in this concern. *I* am that person."

The minister's eyes searched the others in hope of support, but when it didn't come, he seated himself.

Still, it was impossible to make them speak; they sat like mute monks.

Theodora inquired who had charge of the military. A small, unassuming man stood.

"How many soldiers do we have in real numbers? How many are Greek, how many are mercenaries?"

He stared at her with clouded eyes. "Well, now, my lady, it would be difficult for me to hazard a guess—"

Theodora shot several more questions at him, becoming more and more alarmed at his ineptness. He knew very little. "Are you sure you are not minister of the dairies?" she asked, feeling her face flame up. Perhaps you know how many cows we have and what condition the goats are in?"

She wasn't trying to elicit the titter that her comments drew and knew that she shouldn't be so irreverent, knowing it would make her no friends. Her patience, however, had evaporated. At first, she had thought he was feigning ignorance as a way of putting off a woman who had forgotten her gender, but as she looked at the stunned and empty face, she saw that he was in earnest. She wondered how the Pentapolis had operated at all under the likes of him.

Gripping the arms of her chair and drawing her head up and back, she asked with a deliberate calm: "Who is the Captain of the Guard?"

Finding he could answer this question, the minister brightened a bit. "Ambrose, my lady."

"Thank you." Theodora stood. "Then, gentlemen, if no one else has anything further to say, shall we call this council closed?"

The officials quietly filed out, each bowing in turn while they mumbled their respects. Theodora could imagine them going home to pale, plump wives and raving on about the audacity of the governor's mistress.

No sooner had the last one bowed before her than she called out for Simon.

Simon entered. "Yes, my lady."

"Have Ambrose, Captain of the Guard, brought to me at once!"

In the council chamber Ambrose stood before Theodora, his blue uniform recently brushed. She had to look up, for he was tall, thin as a broomstick, and plain of face; his dark hair, slightly silvered and tousled, fell in longish and uneven fashion around a face that reflected curiosity. She studied him closely, recalling how her father had been a drinker and—even though she was very young when the habit led to his being mauled by one of his bears—she recognized similar traits now: a cast in the eye, a ruddy complexion, a faint sweet odor, a nervous carriage.

Theodora motioned him to sit at her immediate right at the great table. He did so, clumsily. No urbane minister this man.

"I expect you are no less surprised than anyone else that I should take interest in matters of state. I must have cooperation from you, Ambrose. It is imperative. The summer sickness has its hold on the governor, and so these things are left to me. And to you."

The man's curious look transformed into one of shock that he was sitting before the governor's mistress and answering to her.

As Theodora waded into the business at hand, his expression took on the seriousness of the issues. Theodora judged him a man who drank to excess—but one who did not take lightly his position. He was only too aware that the previous governor and the current military councilor had failed in the execution of proper defense. As their talk went on, he gave every indication that he was willing to follow whoever might lend the authority to mend the situation—even the Governor's mistress. In his words and expression she sensed qualities that in higher Pentapolis officials had gone wanting. With a unique and fresh blend of shyness and confidence, he answered all of her questions competently, sketching out a detailed analysis of what the province had in strength—and what was most needed.

In the event of attack, the Pentapolis had scarcely enough men to protect even the walls of the five cities. To think of setting up command posts or allowing even a single detail of troops out into the interior was put by the side. Assuming the defense of the cities was their first consideration, they set to work constructing plans. For the interior, a network of lookouts—spies— would ride the boundaries, most especially the western demarcation, from where the Libyans had come in the past. These lookouts would notify the cities immediately of any danger, of course, and—at Theodora's insistence—they were to alert hamlets and villages as well so that the simple folk, whose work was crucial to the well-being of the province, would be able to hasten to the safety of the city walls in time.

The Pentapolis's slave force of some four hundred were to begin repairs on the city gates and walls. Supplies and food to last a winter's siege were to be stockpiled within each city. Weapons were to be created and made ready.

When Theodora requested that she be allowed to visit each city, each arsenal, as the plan went forward, Ambrose blinked back his surprise—but agreed.

"Now," Theodora asked, "what is the situation with the men?"

Ambrose averted his eyes. "Not good, my lady," he mumbled. "Morale is low. And I must admit that I have not pushed them, but I'll see that they fall into line in short order."

"How long since they've been paid?"

"Ten months."

"I'm not surprised. Our requests to the capital have fallen on deaf ears." Theodora thought for a few moments, then drew herself up in her chair. "I will meet with our wealthy planters and merchants and shake some coins free. I'll see that as much of their back wages is paid as possible."

Ambrose's forehead wrinkled upward. "That would have its effect, my lady."

"You realize that only the Governor is to be credited in all this? It must not be put about that orders or money have come from me. No faction would deem it proper. While the Governor is ill, the Pentapolis is in our keeping— yours and mine. Do you agree?"

He nodded.

"His ministers are mere fools," Theodora added, wishing at once she had filtered her words.

Ambrose's eyes flashed surprise, and the corners of his mouth twitched, drawing upward in amused concurrence. "We will do well with it, Lady Theodora."

For once her title had been spoken with sincere respect, and Theodora's back straightened at the sound.

Theodora was certain that Ambrose needed respect, too—along with the responsibility—so as to move forward with purpose and honor, even if they came from a woman so young. She wondered whether he had been commissioned to the Pentapolis as a reprimand for his drinking bouts or the wine habit had sprung from the assignment. She suspected the latter.

Theodora dismissed Ambrose now, remembering to thank him. She sat for some time staring at the gray stone wall, working on her plot to conjure up an untold amount of gold pieces.

15

THEODORA'S SENSE THAT THERE WAS a great immediacy to the military threat was soon borne out. Preparations for defense had been underway for just ten days—with much to be done—when the alarm reached the cities. The Libyans had struck.

As expected, they came from the west, far to the southernmost Pentapolis boundaries. The governor's rear balcony allowed for a splendid panoramic view of the country's lush interior, and each day Theodora could see the encroaching smoke of the enemy descending on the cities, like vultures swooping toward the staked form of a condemned man. Whatever they could not eat, use, or cart off, they destroyed and burned so that, day by day, the brown fields ate into the green, all the while moving closer, closer.

On the fourth day of pillage, Theodora awoke in the early morning from a fitful sleep to the kind of panic and clamor that convulses a city only when it is struck by enemy or earthquake. The streets teemed with shouting men and screaming women. Had the attack come to the cities? Ambrose had assured her that the Libyans would not risk an attack on the cities, and that they would leave when their damage to the interior was done. She had not fully believed him, thinking it very likely that the Libyans had intelligence that the province was, in truth, weakly fortified, the soldiers so demoralized.

As Theodora ran room to room, her sandalless feet slapped the marble flooring, lightly resounding through the seemingly empty house. She came to the balcony where she found Irene, Simon, Pythia, a few ministers, and several servants, their duties momentarily forgotten.

"Are they at the gates?" Theodora demanded.

Many eyes turned to her. Without a word, Pythia pointed.

Theodora's eyes followed the line of her finger. She saw then what had raised the city to fever pitch. Far out into the eastern interior there billowed high into a still blue sky great clouds of dark smoke. The unmentionable had occurred. A second assault—this one by eastern Libyan tribes—was underway, and the cities were their targets. There would be thousands of them, swarming down like bloodsucking swampflies.

Many of the villagers were able to reach the safety of the cities' walls. But many did not, and grim details of atrocities came to light.

Within a few days the eastern tribes had camped against Apollonia and Cyrene, just beyond bow shot.

Even though Theodora had found funds to pay the soldiers, dividing their military strength into five parts had quite crippled what they had. Overcrowded with hungry, frenzied citizens, villagers, and slaves, the five cities boiled like cauldrons at high heat. The province's officials, as frightened as everyone, were forever underfoot at the Governor's House in the event Hecebolus' fever would relent, allowing him to deal with the crisis. The Governor lay in his bed, erotic frescoes all around him, his limbs like lead and mouth and ears resistant to sounds. It was as if he were lying in state. Indeed, Theodora began to think he would not recover.

She sent for Ambrose again. When she demanded that the Libyans be driven from the cities, he told her plainly that he had too few soldiers.

Theodora paced the council chamber. "Why have they not already stormed the walls?"

"I suspect," Ambrose said, giving a little cough, "that they are waiting for the western tribes to join them in the effort."

Theodora studied his face. "It's more than a suspicion, yes?"

Ambrose shrugged and nodded.

"They will have enough men to storm ten cities! Good God! If your dog has a few ticks, Ambrose, you don't wait for them to breed a colony before you take the pincers to them."

"I can't argue with that. But in order to act, I need orders."

"You shall have them. Orders that give you free rein to rid us of our enemy."

"Signed by Hecebolus?"

"Of course," Theodora said, without a missed beat. "Now, you can rally our men to the offensive?"

Ambrose took good time in answering, and Theodora could sense the scales tipping in his mind.

He stood now. "I think it can be done, my lady. The soldiers who have stayed constant are the best and bravest of the lot. And the money was of no little help. Now they have the added incentive of fighting for their lives."

"Let's start planning now, then, Ambrose. Time will either destroy or deliver us."

"May it be the latter, my lady."

The nighttime plan itself was principally Ambrose's. Theodora would steal none of his thunder. The daring scheme was formulated and stealthily disclosed to the five cities that very day, its execution set for some thirty-six hours afterward.

At the second bell of a clear but moonless morning, Ambrose's forces attacked. The massive gates of Apollonia and Cyrene opened and every soldier and male citizen, servant, and trustworthy slave spewed forth like silent lava until they were upon the enemy's startled sentries. The dead calm was shattered at once by trumpet blasts and ear-splitting war cries. The troops from Ptolemais, Arsinoe, and Berenice, already in hiding close by, converged now, riding and running into the scene of battle.

Theodora stood between the teeth of the city's battlements, her eyes straining into the darkness, heart hammering as if she were herself carrying sword into battle. She could see little at first. She could hear the terrible din of weapon on weapon—steel on wooden shield, steel on steel—and the war cries and wailing of dying men. Soon, though, the tents of the Libyans flared, lighting up the night like a hundred staked torches, and she could make out—she thought—the movements of sword and axe shimmering in the glow like the silver threading in an exquisite tapestry.

By full light, it was finished.

Theodora watched Ambrose return, stained in blood and the stink of death upon him, but on his face and in Theodora's heart there were only the flush and exhilaration of victory.

"Apollo be praised," he said, bowing, "they have been routed to the hills like so many rabbits."

"And our losses?"

"Surprisingly few, a hundred twenty. The enemy has left behind five hundred on the field, dead and dying. I don't think any of the tribes will take the cities now, my lady."

"Thank God, Ambrose, and you, too."

The Pentapolis had scarcely a week's respite before nature unleashed the fall gales. Torrential rain and winds lashed and pummeled from the maddened sea to the north. With the damage of the storms, however, came the near certainty that the threat from the Libyan tribes had passed.

Theodora continued to fear for Hecebolus. His complexion was white—nearly gray—and each day he seemed to wither away until his slack skin could scarcely conceal the outline of every bone. One day she spoke her fear to Irene.

The woman's lips tightened, as if to withhold comment.

"What is it?" Theodora pressed. "We are too close for you to hide your opinions from me.—You think he will die, is that it?"

"He *will* die … unless something is done."

"What?" Theodora found herself short on patience. "What can be done that is not being done?"

"The physician must be stopped."

"Myron?—Stopped?"

Irene nodded. "The bleeding."

"Myron is bleeding Hecebolus?"

Irene nodded uncertainly. "You didn't know?"

"No. He always insists on privacy with Hecebolus. How long?"

"All these weeks, from the start, I suspect."

"But doesn't he mean to purge the poisons?"

"He's purging the life out of him, that's what he's doing."

"Why have you waited to tell me? I've seen no marks. Are you certain?"

"His body servant told me only today. The blood is being drawn from his legs—that's why you haven't noticed, but the marks are there. His legs are riddled with them."

"You don't believe in the practice?"

Irene shrugged "Oh, done in moderation, bleeding might drain the poisons in some cases, but with Hecebolus, the doctor has gone to extremes. I'm certain that the bleeding itself is killing him. Quickly so."

"How am I to tell the physician his business?"

"It would be best, perhaps, if you just dismiss him."

"But what of Hecebolus' care? We're not skilled at such things. If he should die after I dismiss Myron, I would be blamed."

"Theodora, he is going to die if you do not keep Myron from him!—I've heard of a wisewoman in Berenice. With your permission, I'll go there and if I find her creditable, I'll fetch her back. Believe me, I would place a good wisewoman above most of the physicians I've encountered."

Theodora spoke to Myron herself, and he appeared oddly unruffled at the news of his dismissal and offered no argument. Theodora thought perhaps that his prognosis for Hecebolus was less than optimistic and that he was relieved to have done with the responsibility of the Governor's living or dying.

When she gave orders to Pythia and Simon that, under no circumstances, were they to admit Myron into the house, Pythia scowled and mumbled something under her breath.

Theodora chose to make nothing of it, closing the matter without discussion. It was the first time Pythia had shown even a hint of insubordination since her sly comments about Theodora's wardrobe, so she felt inclined to let it pass.

The wisewoman, Kuba, an eccentric old native Libyan, was quickly installed to care for Hecebolus. A large, unattractive woman, she moved about in a brisk manner despite her size and years. Her knowledge of herbs, potions, and country healing, Irene insisted, was formidable.

Theodora prayed that it was formidable enough to save Hecebolus.

The northern gales continued to strike with unrelenting fury, day after day, through the fall and into winter. The native citizens claimed it to be the worst season in memory, its destruction beyond that which the Libyans had dealt. The entire length of the aqueduct system, designed to carry fresh water to the cities from the hills and mountains, as well as carry off waste, became choked with mud, for the rains had washed down the topsoil of the fields that had been burned. The system was useless and no two consecutive days went by when weather permitted workers to clear it. Good water was at a premium. Pots, pitchers, leather buckets, and various containers could be seen all about the cities, laid out to catch the precious rainwater. A solution for clearing away the waste was harder to come by.

The ruin done to the harbors, though, was the most terrible. The once secure breakwaters had been battered away to nothing and the harbors filled with sand and mire, becoming unserviceable swamps. As for new breakwaters, it would be spring before weather would allow for booms to be stationed and caissons sunk.

16

D AY BY DAY HECEBOLUS SLOWLY regained his health. Kuba had managed to bring color into his cheeks and flesh to his bones. Theodora credited the reversal of fortune to the wisewoman and to Irene's wisdom.

Still, as Hecebolus' condition improved, he seemed different to her, more distant. His enthusiasm for his position and the desire to once again take up his duties came back, but his old affection—even worship—for her seemed to remain dormant. She put this down to his illness, confident that when his manly needs asserted themselves again, her spell upon him would be as potent as on their first night.

Elated with his recovery and a respite from the bad weather, Theodora planned a supper more magnificent than any staged before in the province. It would be a night of nights.

Nothing escaped her exacting preparations: not the invitations; nor the menu; nor the color of the servants' and slaves' starched attire; nor the polish of the black marble flooring throughout the house. On the evening of the event, all was in splendid readiness.

Two hundred had been invited: the Bishop of the Pentapolis, the ministers and minor officials, leading citizens, planters, wealthy merchants, and all of their wives or mistresses. Theodora hired three minstrels, insisting that all the music be light-hearted. She arranged for a troupe of comedic actors to perform at midnight, after the minstrels and wine had loosened the mirth-bones.

Despite the scarcity of food, two cows had been butchered, and for days prior, hunting parties had been returning with hare, wildfowl and the like. Neither good wine, nor butter, nor bread—despite the province's shortage of grain—would be stinted.

On the evening of the supper, wall torches and a thousand sandalwood-scented candles lighted up the great hall. Supper couches crowded the room—but for the center where the entertainers would perform—overflowing into the adjoining rooms. The sandalwood blended with the scents of incense and wine that had been spiced and warmed. Theodora was preparing herself in her rooms, drinking in the fragrances and allowing an old excitement to awaken and tingle within her. She was reminded of those nights on stage when she had premiered some new and startling portraiture. It seemed so long ago that she had trod the boards. The memory caused her to realize that she missed performing. But she smiled to herself, thinking that this night she had a performance of sorts to render. One of great importance.

No, it was not the role of a lady. She would not be billed as the Governor's wife. She remained his mistress. But one day that would change. Hecebolus had promised.

In the meantime, no one this night would doubt her stage authority.

Over a white silk tunic, Theodora wore a robin blue stola, elegant in its simplicity, its drape such that it made her seem taller than she was. Setting it off were several bracelets and a stunning choker, all worked in gold and cloisonné. Her use of face-paint was subtle, yet effective. Kuba had given her an herbal conditioner for her hair, making its jet like color gleam and glisten. Irene helped her in the hair styling, loosely curling it and drawing it up from her nape. Tortoiseshell combs held it in place.

Hecebolus, dressed in a stately blue dalmatic, came to bring her downstairs. His hand trembled slightly as he took hers, but he seemed much his old self. Theodora had kept his ministers from him for weeks, so she imagined he was a bit nervous at taking up the mantle of leadership again. He led her to the stairhead. The guests would have arrived by now.

The two descended and entered the great hall to applause.

Theodora came to stand before her place at the governor's supper couch while Hecebolus remained near the door, where a receiving line had formed. Her eyes fully drank in the sight now. It was a bitter brew. No more than fifty had deigned to attend. And how few women! A few mistresses, but not a single official's wife.

The evening proceeded at a crawl. Theodora sat, seething inwardly at the number of absent guests, while attempting affable chatter with the ancient Bishop Andrew, who sat on her right. Very few others spoke to her and when they did, icicles hung on their words. For the many, it seemed clear that they were glad Hecebolus had assumed his yoke again, but what came clearer to her was the hard fact that she was considered the Governor's low-caste mistress and that the evening was an affront to her. She longed for it to be done with.

The minstrels performed during the meal. They—and the fine supper—elicited no more than polite enthusiasm. Even before nine o'clock, many guests had begged their leave.

Theodora motioned Simon over and instructed him to dismiss the comedic troupe and to pay them extra, for she remembered well the disappointment a poorly received or cancelled appointment brings an actor.

When she felt she could manage the false face of gaiety no longer, she whispered to Hecebolus: "I am going upstairs. Will you come to my rooms when it's over?"

He looked at her questioningly, but nodded.

At the bottom of the stairs, Irene stopped her. "Theodora, do you wish company?" Her friend's expression told her that she had noted and felt Theodora's discomfiture.

"No, Irene.—Thank you." Theodora started up the stairs. "Tomorrow, perhaps."

Theodora entered her room, picked up a vase she was fond of and sent it crashing into the hearth. She collapsed onto her sleeping couch and lay there, her eyes unfixed yet staring, her mind reeling with hurt and spite.

A part of her was not surprised at all by the evening's outcome. She had overstepped herself and she had known it from the first, but she had wanted to believe that the success she had achieved would be enough to ameliorate the damaged pride of the councilors and other officials. She had badly miscalculated.

Inexplicably, two hours passed. She couldn't imagine what kept Hecebolus. Everyone had seemed ready to depart when she had come upstairs. Neither could she predict how he was to react to the evening.

At last, he came in.

Theodora bolted upright and stood. "How did they dare!" she cried, her temper blazing. It had been harnessed long enough. She would remember little of the tirade that lasted some minutes as she went on about the ignorance shown by the guests who had not come and those who had.

Suddenly she realized that Hecebolus was not sympathizing with her in the least. In fact, his sheep's eyes had been transformed into small, hardened discs. She was immediately put on guard. He had never looked at her in such a way before.

Her words—and anger—fell away as she came to realize she had more to contend with this night than social censure. "What is it?" she asked.

"I have much to say to you, Theodora." He took several steps into the room but kept his distance.

"What have they been telling you?"

"A good deal."

Theodora bit at her lower lip. "They took time enough. Will you not sit?"

"No."

He seemed so formal, so hostile. She remained standing, as well, her heart pounding like that of a novice Cretan bull dancer who chooses his ground and stance to face his opposition.

Hecebolus drew in a long breath and spoke: "In the name of Zeus, Theodora, what made you think you could play governor while I was ill?"

Theodora wet her lips. "I did not *play*. There were things that had to be tended to, important things that no one seemed prepared to face. I saw them *done*. Otherwise, the province—"

"Otherwise," he interrupted, "the province would have survived. A woman—scarcely more than a girl—has no business in the affairs of government. *Otherwise*, I would not have my ministers ready to mutiny! And they *are*, thanks to your interference."

"What have they told you?" Theodora kept her temper reined in now. "Has it really taken hours for them to spin their webs? As in everything else, they are slow spiders. Their miserable heads would be on Libyan pikes on the city walls had it not been for me."

"They are not the only ones you've offended. What made you take it into your head to pay the army its back pay?"

"If a man's wages have been stopped, so too will his pride in his work be pinched. We were losing them to desertion every day. How many of those soldiers who risked their lives while protecting the province would have done so had they not been paid? And those who died?"

"Such things are to be left to the proper authorities, not—"

"They are blithering fools! Surely, you must see that, Hecebolus." She took a step forward, but something in his eyes held her there. In truth, Theodora felt a fool for not having told him all that had transpired during his illness. The excitement and preparations for the night's celebration tempted her to put the business off. Now others had told him, embroidering their stories with their hatred of her.

"Where did the money come from?" he asked.

"I'm certain that they would have told you that, as well. Why do you need to ask, then?" It was difficult for Theodora to avoid a querulous tone. "It came from the rich Italian and Jewish merchant and planter families. Who else would have that kind of money?"

"And they are greatly put out over the matter, demanding to be reimbursed. Where am I to get such funds? Where? They say that you personally extorted the money from them!"

"I merely spoke the truth! That without it their businesses and very lives would be placed in jeopardy. They received good value for their money."

"You said it would be returned?"

Theodora nodded. "I said that they would be repaid when funds come from Constantinople."

"The City has sent us precious little thus far. How could you assume—"

"And if they never see their money—so what? They have held to their miserable carping skins. They should complain? If it were not for Ambrose and the army—"

"Ambrose!" Hecebolus bellowed. "What possessed you to fraternize with a soldier and not expect talk? And to invite him to tonight's affair, seating him at one of the front couches, no less?"

"Without him, my dear, all of the couches tonight would have been occupied by Libyans."

"You assume too much, woman!" He closed the distance between them now. "Do you think that men two and three times your age and wisdom could not run this province?"

"Into the ground!" She would not be cowed into retreat even though he stood close enough that he could strike her. "They are conjoined in a conspiracy of idiocy. Can't you see that these incompetent fools were assigned to this distant outpost by more clever ones in Constantinople only to be put out of the way?"

"Oh, is that what you think?—And perhaps you think I have been appointed governor for the same reason?"

"No! You were assigned here because I saw to it." The words were scarcely out of her mouth before Theodora regretted them, wishing she had cited only his leadership skills, wishing she could take them back. Her heart raced.

Hecebolus' jaw went slack, his expression blank.

The moment hung suspended.

"What do you mean by that?" Hecebolus asked at last.

A voice within Theodora told her to lie, and she did feel up to the task. She had done enough lying in her time. But pride swelled within her, as well as hurt that she should be so little respected for what she had done. In a steady voice she told him about her visit to Leontini, carefully avoiding mention of how she used her previous assignation with the senator to strong-arm him into granting the governorship.

Hecebolus fell silent.

Theodora watched him, fear growing. Her pride had taken precedence over his, and she wondered now if their very relationship was in the balance.

By the time he collected himself, his mood had shifted. A sort of dark resignation enveloped him—tinged with what—sadness?

"There is something else in which you've meddled," he said. "I have put it off on several recent occasions, but we will speak of it now."

Theodora's eyes questioned him. Her heart quickened. What more could be laid at her feet?

Hecebolus drew a deep breath. "Why did you dismiss Myron? What could have compelled you to make *that* decision? Was it a personal difference? My life was at stake!"

Yes, it was sadness on his face and now in his voice. And hurt. Theodora reached out to touch his bearded cheek. He pushed her hand away.

"He was killing you, Hecebolus," she said softly and more flatly than she intended. "You would have died had I allowed him to go on attending you."

Hecebolus' brown eyes assessed hers. He didn't speak.

"Sweet savior! What do you think? That I would place some personal grudge above your well-being? That I would want to hurt you?"

"I don't know—I've gone over it in my mind many times. What am I to think?"

"And what should I gain, may I ask? If you died, Hecebolus, where would I be? What would I have profited? I am but mistress to the governor."

"If only you had acted as such. I want to believe you—"

"My dear Hecebolus! Understand me. Myron's ineptness would have killed you. You began to recover only when he was released."

A strange smile lifted the corners of Hecebolus' mouth. "Theodora, he did not stop attending me. He never stopped coming."

"What?" It was her turn to be surprised.

"He came here to the house during the hours you were out, or sometimes in the middle of the night."

Theodora's voice struggled to catch up to her runaway thoughts. "But ... *how?*"

"He was let in," Hecebolus said off-handedly.

"Let in?" she said through clenched teeth. More than surprises, Theodora hated disloyalty. "He was slowly bleeding you to death!"

"Only to drain the poisons. When this was done successfully, he stopped."

"How long since he stopped?"

"Three weeks."

Theodora deduced that the bleedings had stopped when the clandestine visitations began. "And Kuba's potions?"

"Myron scoffed at them, but I continued to take them so as to humor the old native woman. She insisted on watching me drink down those bitter drafts."

"But don't you see that your health was revived by the potions—and because the bleedings were discontinued?"

"I am sure Myron is competent."

"Oh? Did you know that it was in his care that Governor Adrian died of the same pestilence? And that he was bled to the very end?"

Hecebolus seemed to think on this for a moment. "I wish I could be certain that you had my interest in mind, Theodora, in all of these unwise decisions."

"Unwise? Hecebolus, do you—"

He waved his hand dismissively and made for the door. "I am most tired. We will talk more of this in the days to come."

"You will not stay here—with me?"

He turned around. He did appear tired—but distant, too. "No, Theodora."

"It was Pythia, wasn't it? Against my orders she made the arrangements for Myron to come under the cover of night like a bat! Was it fully her idea? She must have delighted in the subterfuge. Since we arrived, she has hated me, mumbling and casting the evil eye in my direction. It is she who has whispered these doubts in your ear."

"What she did, she did from a sense of duty." He paused now, his eyes narrowing. "I can see your mind at work, Theodora. I have assured Pythia that her position here is safe. You are not to have back at her—not in words or deeds. Do you understand?"

Theodora felt her face flushing hot with anger.

"Do you?" Hecebolus' voice dropped into a low register she had never heard before, a growl that frightened her.

Theodora turned away, all but certain she had lost him. And with him—her future. "Yes, I understand," she muttered.

17

"KUBA KNOWS POISONS AS WELL as healing herbs," Irene whispered. "There are a few that can work quickly and without a trace."

On the balcony off the second floor of the house, Theodora was observing a pair of marsh wrens held in a cage. Her words failing her, she turned toward her longtime confidante who sat on a stone bench nearby.

Irene's mouth puckered with impatience. "Oh, Thea, do not look at me in that manner. Your choices have narrowed. Don't think for a moment *she* is above using poison. I won't point fingers, but whose fault is it that you are in such a quagmire?"

"Mine," Theodora admitted. "I should have put her out at the start ... but you can't be serious about this?"

"Survival comes at a price, Theodora. You see it in nature. You see it in men—and women."

Theodora lowered her head and did little more than mouth her words. "But to kill her—"

"You might have had her displaced once, but that door is closed to you now."

"And you think she means to have my place?"

Irene nodded. "Can you doubt it?"

"I don't know—I just don't think I could—do *that*."

"It's self-preservation, my dear."

"They would know. Everyone would know. For Pythia to die at thirty of no apparent cause—"

"There will be talk, of course, but if you—rising as you've done from the streets—aren't used to talk, you have need of getting used to it. Oh, Hecebolus may marry you, but that will not stop the gossip."

"But, Irene, you're talking about—"

"Oh, there are other ways, if poison is not to your taste. There is a low parapet about the balcony which fronts her room. The bluff is sheer there, and rocky. A single misstep—"

One of the birds began to sing, prompting Theodora to move closer to the cage. "Do you suppose these two mate for life?"

"Not those two," Irene said with a laugh. "They're both males."

"Really? Well, why does Pythia keep them?"

"I'm told the former governor liked to hear them sing. They're Marsh Warblers. They sing very complex songs. If I thought Pythia the sentimental type, I'd say they remind her of him."

"But she's not…. How are they to breed?"

"They won't. Oh, if they were free they would fly back to Europe in the spring and find their mates."

"It's cruel to keep them so."

"Cruelty sometimes has its place." Irene sighed. "My dear, one cannot have lived so long a life as I without learning to recognize at a glance foe from friend—and their potential. Pythia's potential is lethal."

Theodora kept her back to Irene. "Have you … have you ever killed someone?" When she didn't answer at once, Theodora turned back toward her.

Irene patted the bench beside her and Theodora accepted the invitation. "Yes," she said, nodding slowly as she called up a memory. "I've told you about the Italian family that raised me in Constantinople. Shortly after they left to resume residence in Rome, they sent for me. A big brute of Goth extraction was sent to collect me. I was of age by then and did not want to leave my city and my friends. Besides, I always felt a servant to them, rather than a daughter. A servant to their natural children. Well, he took me against my will. Along the way, I plotted ways of escaping—or even killing my captor. But I couldn't bring myself to do it. Then one night, just a day's journey from Lake Garda, where I was to live, he got roaring drunk and came after me. I put up such a struggle that it was only at knife point that he was able to have his way with me."

Irene paused for a moment, as if to hold back the pain that came with the memory. "Afterwards, I lay there a very long time, listening to his breathing become regular as he drifted into a deep stupor, still atop me. His mouth was partially open and I felt his spittle on my neck. My hand moved at my side, searching for the knife. I found it and clenched the cold, carved ivory handle in my hand. Not daring to move out from under him, I reached up and sliced a wide gash in his throat. He gave not a sound other that the sharp hiss of hot blood that shot out like a fountain, drenching the wall, drenching me." She paused, exhaling deeply. "I returned to Constantinople. I don't know what story the family may have gotten, but they did not send for me again."

Theodora sat speechless.

"Oh, don't think that I am proud of it, Theodora. But I would do it again.—Know your enemies."

Theodora was on her feet in an instant. "It is a harrowing tale you tell, Irene, but the situations are very different. I have lost neither my position nor Hecebolus. And I will not, you will see. I do not intend to resort to killing."

Irene shrugged, as a teacher might to an obstinate pupil. She rose and went to the door. Over her shoulder, she said, "Do as you must, child."

Theodora was left to marvel at the friend she thought she had known— but had not.

Do as I must, she thought. She strode to the Marsh warblers' cage and opened wide the gate that held them captive.

"I am a magus, Sufian," the Persian says as we sit on the ground that first night, eating bread and cheese under a shadowy sky. His richly embroidered robe had been shed for a brown one, considerably more plain and utilitarian and smelling of sweat. He speaks in my native Syriac.

I nod, too afraid to say I had guessed as much, afraid that my investigation of the man's trunks would be found out. I stare out into the velvet black of night. The moon is scarcely a sliver, like the cuticle of a baby's thumb.

"My name is Gaspar." The Persian drinks wine from a goatskin.

"Does it mean something?"

"It means *treasure master*.—Friends used to call me by the diminutive 'Gazsi'—years ago."

"Which shall *I* call you?"

The man snarls. "Neither! You are to call me *master*! Is that understood?"

My heart accelerates at his sudden change in tone. "Yes."

"Yes, *master*!" he bellows, bits of bread flying from his mouth.

"Yes, master."

"Good.—That is your first lesson. Do not forget your place. Do not forget that I *bought* you, my young urchin."

"Lesson?" I ask, my mind already moving on to ways in which I might escape.

"There are to be many as we travel." His voice is at once warm again.

"To your home, master—in Persia?"

"No, although the roads there are better than any other country's. No, you are to see the world with me—little hamlets, towns, and great cities." The Persian goes on to speak of exotic places, buildings, ships, monuments, people, strange tongues and all manner of marvelous entertainment.

I half-listen, my mind simmering with thoughts of the discomfort of living one's life in a wagon, eating on the ground, relieving oneself by the side of the road, and having to sleep side by side with the mysterious and mercurial Persian. It was the life of a slave, for that was what I had become. And yet, the notion of travel intrigues me, the idea of seeing the world I could merely have wondered about while tending sheep at my family home. But it is the notion of magick that makes me—for the moment—discard thoughts of escape.

"Of course, you must have lessons in Greek." The Persian finishes off the wine, red droplets spilling down his beard.

"Greek, master?"

"Yes. Knowledge of Greek is better than any currency, you can be certain. We will be traveling the coastline of the Middle Sea. Much of it is now a Greek world. The language is our bread and cheese. Oh, and wine for me. Without Greek, you would be nothing but a third-rate wanderer. With it, your value increases. You must have a Greek name—so, from today forth, you are Stephen."

"Yes, master," I mutter. We eat in silence a long while, my mind in a daze.

In time Gaspar lies back, using for a pillow the rim of a wagon wheel. His eyelids become heavy. He would soon be asleep.

I think how this opportunity might afford my escape. And yet—where am I to go? My father had sold me. My own family would not accept me back. I think of my mother, the tears in her eyes when I saw her last.

I lie back now, head on the stony earth, eyes on the twinkling constellations above. Never had I seen so many stars.

"Will you teach me magick?" I blurt impulsively. "Master?"

"Hmmm?" The Persian mumbles something. Its content escapes me, but it was not in his often sarcastic tone.

"Magick—will you teach me, master?"

"Yes, yes.—And one day you shall teach me."

"What, master?"

Another mumble.

"How shall I teach *you*, master?"

The sky, the air, the earth all hold to the same stillness for the longest minute. And then, quietly at first, but growing in volume, comes the snoring of the Persian. I am left to wonder how learning Greek would increase my value.

18

THEODORA FOUND THE WINTER INTERMINABLE. The gales persisted, and the cities teemed with sickness, hunger, and malcontent. The failure of the aqueduct system aided in the spread of the pestilence, but even a greater number of people were dying from starvation. Governor Hecebolus saw to the systematic and stingy doling out of grain, but the day came when the people plundered the granaries so that none was left. A quarter of the population did not survive the season.

Theodora learned that people, no matter the race or religion, are a superstitious lot. In desperate times, especially, a rumor begun out of idleness or spite often takes on unimagined proportions in the timespan of a wink. Theodora milked the gossip from Irene, who got about the cities much more than she did. The people were turning against her. What right had the Governor to bring his low-caste mistress here? Why should the Pentapolis be governed by a former actress, a whore? Forgetting that the plague was a regular visitor, they blamed her for it, declaiming that Hecebolus should cast her off.

Theodora knew that in the old days of the city-states, she might well have been dragged to the outskirts and stoned, the city's scapegoat offering to the gods. She knew that the weeds of treason sprang from her lover's ministers, her own house, and Pythia. But she could do little.

She waited impatiently many days for Hecebolus to come to her sleeping couch, and when he held back, she took the initiative. Her charms and considerable skills at pleasure-giving had not deserted her. Hecebolus was not immune and started coming to her rooms again.

Theodora sensed by now—through a furtive guilty look of his or a secret sneer of Pythia's—that he had bedded the housekeeper. She wondered if the affair continued. She was wise enough, however, not to press the issue or even let on that she knew. "I have enough confidence in myself," she told Irene, "that I will hold Hecebolus. I am certain that whatever unlikely allure that homely viper possesses will burn itself out, like some minor comet."

Then, with the new year of 519, life at the Pentapolis witnessed an abrupt upturn. The gales abated, then died away, and spring with its warm whiff of promise was upon the land and work was begun on the aqueducts and harbors. The people rallied with the warm, placid weather; rumors and grumblings went the way of the gales, and superstitions seemed no more than that. The land was worked and the spring planting done. A ship called, going east to Alexandria, then to Constantinople. Hecebolus sent word with it to The City of the province's urgent need for food, money, horses, city planners, soldiers and workers.

"If they ignore us now," Theodora said, "why not sell our products to other traders, other cities? Why should we send them on to The City and not be properly repaid?"

She felt buoyed that he did not dismiss this bold suggestion out of hand. He seemed to give it some thought although he didn't pursue the topic.

In the scheme of things, this little interlude lasted no longer than the life of a spring flower, for an undulant fever swept the cities. It claimed few lives but almost no one seemed immune to its persistent fever, pains in the joints, lack of appetite, and severe depression.

In the Governor's House, Pythia was the only one to escape it, and from her bed Theodora cursed the smiling woman, who attended her in the most cursory manner and addressed her with a mix of sarcasm and scarcely disguised scorn. "What would you have now, milady?" she would ask. Theodora held her tongue, thinking how easily the witch could do her in.

Only later would Irene tell her that Hecebolus had begun to castigate Theodora from his sleeping couch. And why shouldn't he? Theodora asked herself. It was she who had done dirty work to have the post offered to him— and to convince him to accept it when he had been undecided. It was she who had belittled the significance of the problems coming with it. And it was she who earned the contempt of the officials and citizens, the good she had done notwithstanding.

Would she be able to hold him? She remembered his lack of courage and resolve during the storm at sea and shivered with foreboding.

The fever lingered, like an unwelcome and implacable relation. Theodora lay on her sleeping couch for weeks, partner only to her doubts, overcome by a bottomless malaise. All of her life she had been certain that she was destined for wondrous things, that she would be a great lady one day. What had led her now to such ignominy? Had it been her scheming against Leontini? Is this his revenge? Is *this* my destiny? Her doubts haunted her and faded only with the forgetfulness of sleep.

And then—at last—one day the fever lifted, and her old hope and confidence rose with it, phoenixlike. From her balcony she saw the promise of spring in the rolling hills of the Pentapolis that were alive again with green things growing, and she steeled herself with the determination that this year their fortunes would turn.

One morning at summer's end, Theodora suddenly became aware of a bustling and rising confusion of voices and movements within the house. Barefoot and in nightdress, she moved from her bedchamber into her anteroom calling out for Hecebolus and Irene. "What is happening?" she cried.

Her questions were answered by her own echoes. The house had suddenly stilled, like a just-closed tomb.

Her curiosity was always enough to stir her steps, but it was more than that this time. She felt a tingling in her chest as she experienced a presentiment that something important and terrible had happened. *What more?* She attempted to run, her feet slapping along the marble flooring. Still very weak from the fever, she stumbled.

Then Irene was at her side, taking hold of her, concern tight upon her face.

"What is it, Irene? Another uprising? Is Hecebolus all right?"

"I don't know, Theodora. They've all gone outside. Go back to bed and I'll check and see."

"I will not! Let's go to the balcony." Theodora was already on the move. Irene followed, hurrying to lend support to Theodora as they went.

The day had dawned bright as gold, but as they stepped out onto the balcony—crowded with other curious faces—they saw that the sun had seemed to dim, like a lamp draining the last of its oil.

"Has there been foretelling of an eclipse?" Theodora asked.

"I've heard of none," her friend replied.

Facing east, the onlookers stood near the parapet, Hecebolus among them, his face—like theirs—a mask of horror. Below, in the streets, citizens were not nearly so mute.

Theodora knew it could not be an amassing of Libyans, for they had no supernatural sway over light and dark. The sun's warm glow had been choked by a great gathering of dark clouds in the far hinterland of the province. Theodora shivered, more by the chilling sight than any breeze breaking on the balcony, for there was none. The storm was moving toward them in a strange, still vacuum."

"Sweet Jesus," Irene muttered. "This is a storm of storms."

Pythia heard the comment and turned about. There is a certain breed of person, Theodora knew, who by character takes dark delight in the accounting of bad business. Pythia was of this mold, but only later would Theodora recall the subtle arrogance and glee in her voice. "That is not a storm. We are doomed," Pythia said, her face so distorted in the dimming light that she might have been one of the Gray Women looking into the future.

Baited thus, Irene questioned: "What is it, then?"

"*They*," Pythia snarled, "not *it*. They are the *desert locusts*."

The words at first held no meaning for Theodora. She peered into the darkening sky. Surely this was a storm. What was this woman talking about?

Pythia continued in a haughty tone. "If our city's managers have done their accounting correctly, the devils are early by a year. The plague always comes in the seventeenth year. The province has always made certain to have harvested the crops early."

"But the harvest has *not* been done! This must be a storm!" Theodora cried. "It *must*!"

Hecebolus turned to her now, his face angry and defeated. "No, listen, Theodora! Listen!"

She heard it then, the harrowing drone of the little devouring insects, its volume seeming to increase even as she listened.

"They come in the tens of millions, they do," Pythia said, her voice oddly flat, as if reciting something for a tutor. "They will eat every growing thing in the province until neither leaf nor stem remains."

It was true. The strange, changing formations of the hovering swarm as it moved toward the cities dictated not storm clouds but the concerted motion of millions upon millions of tiny winged creatures, darting like life-given grains of sand, their uncommon beating wings making constant cracking sounds.

Field by field, orchard by orchard, they swooped down upon the budding province like a dust storm. The speed of their destruction was astonishing.

In a field nearby, frenzied farmers ran to and fro.

Theodora looked to Hecebolus. His face was ashen with resignation, the sight of their future being spent.

"We must go in now," someone said.

Theodora's mind reeled. One disaster followed another, like the biblical plagues. She could not accept what was happening. She could not. She pulled at Pythia's sleeve. "What can be done?" she implored.

"Nothing," Pythia said, her tone sharp and one side of her mouth curled into a sneer. "Oh, they won't eat your flesh, Lady Theodora, although they'll nip at the salt on the surface. When they have eaten every other living thing, they will leave. They will die not long after their spree."

"No!" Theodora cried. "It can't be. We can't just stand by! They must be stopped!" She started pulling at Hecebolus' arm. "You must issue orders at once. They must be stopped somehow—"

"It's hopeless," Hecebolus blurted, as if he, too, was annoyed with her. He shook her free and joined the others moving toward the balcony doors.

"No! No!" Theodora screamed, but no one looked back, no one listened.

Theodora would not remember pulling free of Irene and running down the exterior balcony steps and out into the governor's garden.

"Come!" she called to a dozen farmers and slaves who were fleeing their fields for the safety of the city. "Come! We must beat them back!"

By now, the forerunners of the legion were alighting and beginning to gnaw on the nearly grown vegetable plants. They were no longer speck-like objects, but brownish-green whirring grasshoppers, one to three inches in length and as ugly as anything in creation. And yet, ironically, the sound of them amassing and eating was almost musical, as if made by an orchestra of stringed instruments.

She found a shovel left behind by some farmer. It was heavy, but she lifted it high and brought it down in a hammering motion, striking repeatedly at the voracious creatures as they landed. "Do you see?" she shouted. "They die! They are not invincible—we must kill them!"

If those fleeing the field paused at all in their flight, it must have been only to gawk momentarily at this bare-footed woman in nightdress, this shrilling madwoman.

Theodora continued to scream until she was hoarse. Again and again, she struck until the shovel, the ground, and the hem of her nightdress were wet with putrid slime. The little beasts only multiplied. No one had listened to her; they had all run for shelter like hares to their warren.

She would not cry; she would not run.

They came on thick and quickly; the sky blackened with them. Theodora could no longer scream, for she had to close her mouth against them. And their deafening drone would only drown out any sound she'd attempt.

A farmer tried to drag her from the garden, but she struck him with the shovel and he gave up the effort.

Theodora could not believe that the Goddess Tyche—or God—could be so cruel to have sent this latest test. Her strength weakened, but still she hammered the ground with the shovel.

Then it was as if night had fallen and they were everywhere. She was forced to abandon the shovel so that she could try to keep them off her person as they swarmed about her. In a frenzy she brushed them off her arms, neck, and face. They became entangled in her hair.

Her senses left her and she stood stupidly for what must have been a minute, the creatures covering her.

She turned to run, slipped in the slime, and fell.

She felt them on her, heard them about her, felt them biting. Her mind's eye recalled how as a child she had seen a fly-covered carcass of a lamb. It had horrified her and haunted her dreams.

Theodora hadn't the strength to get up. She opened her eyes, focusing on one locust gnawing on a nearby pepper plant. This is the last thing I shall ever see in this life, she thought. So be it. She prayed: *Let me die quickly.*

A human hand, then another—stronger—tugged at her now.

PART THREE

PART THREE

19

THEODORA CAME AWAKE TO STARE at a stained and patched ceiling, one unfamiliar to her.

She moved her eyes, the only parts of her that seemed willing to respond. To her clouded mind, ragged gaps in the plastered wall next to her seemed more like lines of demarcation on a map. She blinked, tried to focus. The tiny, shutterless window allowed for a slanting of sunlight to pierce the stale-smelling room and light a piece of the earthen floor not far from her narrow pallet.

Something other than the smell of must caught her attention. What was it? Salt? Yes, salt. The sea was very close by.

She was no longer in the palace. *Where am I?* She wanted to rise, to peer from that tiny window, but her limbs were leaden. She could only lie there. In time she dozed.

She awoke to Irene's gentle shaking.

The older woman brightened at finding her alert. "You are a sight, my dear."

"How long have I—"

"Two days. I've brought some warm milk and honey, along with a potion from Kuba. Are you able to sit?"

Irene helped Theodora to a position at the side of the pallet and made her drink. Every bone, every muscle, every tendon posed painful resistance. She took a sip, then looked up. "The locusts?—How did I—?"

"Kuba helped me pull you out from under them." Irene paused, as if uncertain how to continue the story. "The crops are in ruin, but that matters little to us now, Thea. What is important is that your fever broke last night, praise God. You did give me a scare, I must say."

Even while she drank the nourishment, her eyes scanned the miserable hovel from this new vantage point, coming in good time to fix questioningly on Irene.

Before Irene spoke, Theodora instinctively sensed that this was one of those rare occasions in her life when she knew beforehand every nuance of a conversation, even the tone and hesitation in Irene's answers. She wondered if she did have something of the second sight.

Hecebolus had cast her off.

She had been blamed by one and all for this latest misfortune to fall on the province, Irene told her. It came as no surprise. Dissatisfaction on the part of his ministers and superstitious citizens—as well as Pythia's influence—had coalesced into a power great enough to break Theodora's hold on Hecebolus.

Irene had hired a litter to carry Theodora down the terraced pathway to the huddle of buildings crammed near the docks, where she paid dearly for the one-room hut in which they were to await a ship for their return to Constantinople. "He," Irene said, avoiding the name of Hecebolus, "gave us little more than ship fare. But I've managed to save a bit so that we have a roof and something to eat while we wait."

Irene helped Theodora to lie back and pulled a chair to the side of the pallet. Unable to return Irene's gaze, Theodora went quiet for long minutes as she tried to grasp what had happened to her. All of her hopes for a life of meaning and significance had come to this—this degradation. She wanted to run, but run where? Into the sea? But her limbs would not obey. She should have seen it coming—the flaws in Hecebolus' character, the treachery in Pythia's. Oh, Irene had warned her about Pythia and she had not listened. The responsibility was hers.

"I'm so—so sorry, Irene," Theodora said, turning her face to the wall.

"For what, dearest?"

"For bringing you halfway across the world—to this."

"Nonsense! I would not have missed it."

Theodora's eyes moved toward her friend, hot tears coming fast. Here, at least—in this friendship—could she celebrate one little success.

Irene took Theodora's right hand in hers and lifted it, as if to kiss it. Theodora glanced up at her own hand and noticed the pale circle of skin on her ring finger. She raised her head and pulled her hand away, gasping. "My ring!" The emerald ring had been Hecebolus' first gift to her.

Irene sighed. "The governor kept all of your jewelry, Theodora."

"I see." Theodora allowed her head to fall back on a straw pillow. "What does it matter?" The reply blended bitterness with resignation.

"But he hadn't noticed your ring," Irene explained. "You were placed on the litter that brought you here and I was pulling a cover over you when *she* noticed it."

"Pythia?"

"Yes," Irene hissed. "The witch whispered something to Hecebolus, and he gave a nod. It was she who then took it off your finger in so rough a way that I wanted to strike her."

Theodora could see that Irene took these setbacks very hard and so tried to make light of them so as to assuage her friend's heartache. "Ah, well, it's all for the best. It will be good for us to return to The City again, Irene. I think we have both been learning all along that the Pentapolis is best viewed from the stern of a ship—when does the ship sail?"

"At the end of next week."

Within three days, roles were reversed. Even as Theodora regained her health, a fever took hold of Irene. Theodora hastened to Berenice to fetch Kuba.

The wisewoman provided a potion but was less than hopeful. "She is not so young anymore," Kuba whispered, "this makes for a worse time of it. She must fight if she is to rally."

Theodora knew that Kuba was right, that a wish is the father of fact, and so she urged her friend to fight for her life.

Irene drank down the brew, gave a little smile, and said, "My time is coming, Thea. I'm only sorry to be leaving you."

"Nonsense! God would not take you from me."

Irene's smile widened even as her eyes closed. She slept.

The day came when their ship docked. It would stay at port five days and then set sail for Constantinople. Irene's condition had not improved, and Theodora knew they would not accept an ailing passenger. If it had to sail without them, she would not worry. Surely there would be another before winter made voyages treacherous. Her concern of the moment was for Irene.

Theodora nursed her friend, daily emptying the chamber pot, fetching fresh water, and seeing to their meals which were meager because there was little food to be had—by poor or rich—in the cities. She performed the chores of a servant girl and did them gladly for this, her one friend on this side of the world.

Irene seemed to improve.

One morning Theodora rose to find the pallet next to her own unoccupied. She stood staring in astonishment, panic welling up. Where had she gone? How?—she had been so dreadfully weak. Had she wandered off in a delirium?

Theodora sprang to life, pulling on the only tunic Irene had been allowed to take for her, an undyed one of appropriately humbling simplicity. As she was adjusting her sandals, a terrible thought came to her: Had Irene been of a mind to kill herself?

Theodora spent the day wandering the lengths of every stink-ridden nook and back-alley of the harbor. People who recognized her sometimes stared and pointed. Undeterred, she questioned dozens of citizens, but no one had seen Irene.

Theodora spent a sleepless night sitting in a cushionless chair, head in her hands.

At dawn she heard the creak of the door and looked up. There, beneath the wooden lintel stood Irene, carrying a cloth bag and dripping perspiration. Theodora caught her as she collapsed.

"Where did you go?" Theodora asked much later, after she had put Irene to bed and given her watery goat's milk laced with juice of the poppy. "What possessed you?"

"I shall not live long, my dear. There was little time."

"You will outlive me, you crusty old fox!" Theodora realized even as she spoke this line that it rang false as any from a bad play. Irene's recovery seemed unlikely. "And where did you disappear to? Tell me. I scoured the harbor, so speak true to me."

"To the house."

"The Governor's House?" Theodora gasped. "You climbed the terraces?"

"About half way up I was able to beg a ride. Some people still hold respect for their elders." Irene managed a little laugh. "But I came down on my own two feet."

"In God's name, why did you go there?"

Irene withdrew her right arm from beneath the covers. She unclenched her fist then, revealing the magnificent emerald gleaming in its delicate setting of a bird's tiny talons.

"My ring!" Theodora was dumbfounded—and incensed. "You risked life and limb for *that*? Irene! You crept up there in the middle of the night for my ring?"

"Not only for that." A strange smile played on her cracked lips. "One must catch a weasel when it sleeps."

"Pythia?"

The white eyebrows arched in mock-innocence.

"What have you done?" Theodora asked, this too as if a line from a play.

"Did you know, Theodora, that Pythia takes an herbal potion every morning without fail? She carefully prepares it the night before." Though the woman's voice was weak and the glassiness of her eyes indicated the poppy was at work, a lilt remained in her tone. "To keep herself young. She is obsessed with the fear of growing old."

To Theodora, not long past her nineteenth birthday, Pythia—in her early thirties—was already old.

"Well," Irene continued, "that obsession will trouble her no more."

Theodora blinked, taking her meaning at once. Conflicting thoughts and emotions flew at her in a frenzy. "Irene, I—"

"You should have allowed me to do it long ago."

Theodora couldn't speak.

"Listen to me, Theodora. The ship leaves tomorrow. They won't take me, of course, but you must go."

"Hush, now get some rest."

"If an issue is made over her death, they'll come questioning."

"It was a poison?"

"Yes. It was easily done. Her room was empty and the drink was prepared and at her bedside."

"She was with Hecebolus?"

Irene's eyes evaded Theodora's. "I expect so."

"Were you seen at all?"

"Only by the slave girl that let me in. I paid her well and trust her silence. Once the death is discovered she will be too afraid to admit allowing me entrance."

"Nonetheless, I will not leave."

"You must, Thea. I insist. Make a new start. If you look in that cloth bag on the chair, you'll find several of your other jewels."

"Oh, Irene, you scoundrel!"

"And—your favorite silver strapped slippers are there, too. They are like a talisman to you."

Theodora gave out with a great laugh. "What a friend you are. Sleep now. And get well. We shall depart this hell-hole and return to The City together."

Irene tried to argue further, but the spell of the poppy was too great.

On the next morning, Theodora stood outside the ramshackle structure and watched the ship sail away, toward Constantinople.

That evening, Irene died. "Begin again," the woman had whispered. "I once scoffed at your notions, your dreams, Thea, but it was only to make you strong. To make you wish them into being."

Her heart in shreds, Theodora thought about those words as she watched Irene's body being burned. Afterward, she knelt at the pyre and cupping her hands, she scooped a quantity of the ashes into a clay vessel made for carrying water. She buried it herself, near an olive tree on a little bluff overlooking the harbor. It was a beautiful place, but she silently promised Irene that one day she would come back in order to return the ashes to Constantinople. And then—for the briefest time—she allowed herself to come apart and cry. She was alone, with only Irene's words to push her on.

Pythia's body would have been found by now, she knew. Whether or not the slave girl had talked, they would come to question her. To accuse her.

It was imperative that she leave the Pentapolis. But where was she to go? How?

Checking at the docks, she found no ship was expected for at least two weeks. She had not the luxury of time and so began to get ready. In the cloth bag that Irene had brought back from the Governor's House, she found a favorite stola, along with the silver strapped slippers. The tears came again. She realized now that something remained at the bottom of the bag. She reached down into it and withdrew the makeup case she had travelled with since her days in the theater. "Oh, Irene," she whispered. She wiped at her tears—and laughed aloud.

She learned, though, that a caravan had left for Alexandria two days before. Knowing that options were few, she hired a young Egyptian, Abasi, to catch her up to it. Even with nearly continuous riding on the best of camels, it would take three or four days.

"You are a handsome young man," the woman says. At the door to her well-maintained villa, she takes the heavy basket from me and rewards me with a smile, as well as with a coin. I thank her, finding her quite pretty even though she must be twice my age or more.

Her smile lingers. I flash my own quick smile, cast my eyes downward—and hurry away.

Her comment on my handsomeness lingers, also. By now, I know that Gaspar uses my innocence and good looks to attract potential customers when the wagon rolls into some settlement. He places me next to him on a little collapsible platform and goes on at length before the crowds about how I have been cured or made handsome by some spell of his. The story varies with the town and with the telling, but it is all fiction, of course.

I return to the wagon now, my home for three years. Memories of my family have paled just a bit, but not my desire to escape. I carefully take the copper coin I have just earned and add it to the little hoard of copper, silver, and gold coins I keep hidden beneath the false bottom of a carved box I purchased in Palestine. I have mixed sand into the compartment so as to keep the coins from tinkling. Gaspar is not to know about it. I return the box to the corner of the wagon where I place it under two extra tunics Gaspar has purchased for me. "You must look your best," he says, "when I place you before my customers. You must have handsome clothing to match your face." Sometimes—when I know Gaspar is to be away a long while, I take out the coins, dust and polish them, and hold them to the light, relishing how they might help in my escape one day. Until that day I know not to emit even a whiff of discontent.

On our many travels, invariably I am able to find some little side job to do out from under the eye of the Persian: making a delivery, sweeping a shop, carrying the bundles of a wealthy shopper. Oh, I know it is often my youthful looks and smile that coax the women into employing me. Their attraction to me is etched into their faces. I am thirteen now and growing straight and tall, like a reed in springtime.

I find myself to be singularly adept at languages. Not only do I shine at my Greek lessons, but as we follow the crooked curves of the Middle Sea, I take to Latin, Aramaic, Coptic and various dialects of the Levant. Also under the tutelage of the Persian, I learn to use a kalamos and write in both Greek and Latin.

"I am treasure master," Gaspar would say from time to time when he is in his cups, "and you Stephen, are my treasure, my pretty treasure."

The comment never fails to make me uneasy. I feel as if I myself am a coin he polishes, one gaining in value as I take direction from my Persian tutor—and owner.

However, I no longer feel that same vulnerability the man's fixated stare and smile incited in those first few months. I become convinced that I need not fear for my physical well-being. Gaspar has not touched me in that way. His possessiveness stems not from physical attraction, an attraction I do some-times encounter on the streets from men of high and low birth. No, Gaspar's interest in me is intense and emotional and mysterious. But what is at the heart of it? I am, in a way, a mystery to myself.

"You are my initiate," Gaspar announces one day, quite soberly. And in-deed I begin to learn the ways of the wizard. Our wagon bears on its side a large painting of a blue eye and black pupil—symbol of the magus—and when we trundle into a village or city, no other advertisement seems necessary. Customers—often desperate to alter something in their lives—are seldom in short supply.

The rites of exorcism that Gaspar allows me to witness concern healing. These are beneficial rites that call for health, success in business, love, and trials, legal or otherwise. Gaspar claims that his words and amulets counter the holds any demon, witch, or sorcerer might have on the worthy and cash-ready customer. The exorcisms bring the petitioner out from under the spell of an evil one and into the protection of the Divine.

As to what power the wizard actually wields, I cannot be certain, for we are always up and rolling on to the next destination before word of the customer's satisfaction—or lack of it—could be verified.

I question the character of Gaspar, and while I have serious doubts about this profession, I admit that it does support us both well enough.

As time goes on, my suspicions are validated. Gaspar allows me to witness more and more of his client sessions, and I come to realize the teacher is a Gemini of a wizard. The master possesses another side. Gaspar is prepared to meet the needs of any customer, and as often as not, this means he employs curses, dolls, and binding spells. I can read the Greek and Latin tablets in the trunk now, and their contents—spells calling down evil on someone at the whim of another—chill me.

At about this time, he teaches me about auras and how he can judge a worthwhile customer by a mysterious emanation surrounding their person. "I chose you, Stephen, for your pink aura," he tells me. "It denotes sensitivity, art, affection, and love."

This is a mystery that catches my imagination, and I become obsessive in my effort to attain the skill. I work hard at the meditation day after day—until finally I am able to read the aura of several of our customers. The power thrills me.

However, before I tell Gaspar of my triumph, I attempt to read his aura. I surprise myself with immediate success. But it is a stormy, pulsing gray that comes through—enveloping his large frame—the shade of unclear or malevolent intentions, and my eyes go to his hands and fingers that drip red—not the deep red of power but a scarlet red that denotes pain to specific parts of the body. Fear runs through me like a current and I rush away from the wagon and into a small stand of trees where my stomach empties out. After that, I make no more serious effort to read auras, and when Gaspar asks about my progress, I lie, saying I do not have the power.

After this experience, my obsession turns to earning every coin possible. I will escape this man one day. *I will.*

20

THE CARAVAN MASTER LOOKED WITH no little surprise at Theodora and his fellow Egyptian Abasi as he learned the reason for their sudden appearance well into the caravan's trek to Alexandria. His name was Haji. He was a husky fellow with owl-like eyes as black as his full beard. The caravan had been stopped mid-afternoon at a watering hole when they caught up to it. Haji listened to Abasi, casting unwelcome and unfriendly glances at a dark-robed, dusty, and tired Theodora, whose face remained veiled to the elements. She felt blood rising into her face. It irked her that she had not been introduced and, worse, that they quibbled over her as if she were merely baggage. Abasi spoke in a pleading tone to his elder while Haji spoke quickly and with certainty.

Theodora listened to their confusing Coptic, failing to catch even a word or phrase, but Haji's strident tone rang clear. He was unwilling to take her.

Although it occurred to her that his hesitancy might be a ruse to double or triple her fee, she could not stand by in silence. She removed her veil. "Tell him, Abasi, I will pay him well, just as I have paid you. It will be worth his while."

Abasi obeyed. Haji listened, his eyes narrowing, then shifting to her face and widening again. He spoke to Abasi now, saying something in a more restrained tone.

"Haji says he wants to see the jewels first," Abasi announced.

Lucky for her, Theodora had thought to remove two of the large rubies from their hiding place in the hem of her austere brown robe. She had given two of the smaller rubies to Abasi. She held the stones out now, one in each palm, where in the rippling heat waves they glittered a liquid red, as if she had the stigmata.

Haji took a pace forward and Theodora's hands closed. She had been too trusting at the Pentapolis. From this point on she would be cautious.

When Haji kept his distance, she opened one hand again and motioned him forward. One by one, he held them up to the blistering sun. He studied each stone for a full minute as if through a jeweler's glass. He returned them now, his hooded eyes moving up to her face, still assessing. A long moment passed.

Then he turned away from Theodora and grudgingly nodded to his friend.

Despite what Theodora saw in his visage, she felt a great silent sigh go out of her. She was accepted into the caravan—she would find her way to Alexandria.

Once there, what would come next, she could not guess or imagine. She would still be on the far side of the world, untold miles from The City. Her Constantinople. How she missed it.

Home.

She bade goodbye to Abasi, who intended to return to the Pentapolis, and who promised—at the price of another small ruby—not to speak of her to anyone, even if interrogated by Hecebolus' men. It was not certain insurance, but it was something.

He left her with the camel, having secured Haji's word that it would be returned to him.

It was only as Haji gave her a cool welcome and spoke of the caravan that Theodora realized that his Greek was quite good.

The fifty-some travelers were already preparing for the next leg of their journey. Theodora had time only to relieve herself, drink, and refill her goatskin. Once on the camel she gnawed at a hard crust of bread.

How had it come to this? she wondered. How had she come to be some wayfarer—some Odysseus wandering the far limits of the world on a sea of sand, wishing only to be home? Perhaps Hecebolus had been her siren, tempting her to destruction. She smiled to herself at the notion, a smile no one could see now with her face veiled to keep out the flying sand, if not the insufferable heat.

She could only blame herself. There had been no law to bind Hecebolus to her, nothing written, no marriage. Only trust in his promise. She had been reckless to trust him, reckless not to listen to Irene's admonitions about Pythia. She would take care not to be so reckless again.

Theodora thought back to that moment after she had buried Irene's ashes, those few moments when she unleashed the tears, when she did not think she could go on, when she herself wanted only to die.

Could she—a woman—face the thousands of miles, and perhaps thousands of lonely, frightening nights, that lay before her in her quest to return to Constantinople? What were the chances of one day having a homecoming? A woman with dwindling funds, no family, no friends?

In that moment on the bluff above the harbor at Apollonia, looking out to the great sea that separated her from home, she had thought of her mother. Her dear mother. *She* had not given up when her first husband died, leaving her with three little girls. She had gone on, calling on some unseen strength, scheming and devising and hoping so that she and hers could live.

And she had triumphed! Theodora thought of that moment in the Hippodrome when the Green faction cruelly rejected her mother and the innocent dance of three flower-bedecked children. The Blues turned the tables and embraced her family, naming their new stepfather their bearkeeper. What a glorious moment that had been! The memory of that charmed afternoon sitting on the shady side, the side of the Blues, watching the acrobats, jugglers, mimes, and the thundering chariots had stayed with her always, real and alive.

Sometimes, she thought, it *was* possible for glory to be snatched from a bottomless well of ignominy.

Haji assigned a gruff old man, Naeem, another Egyptian, to ride behind Theodora so as to watch out for her. While grateful for the hefty, crooked-nosed protector, especially because his Greek was passing, Theodora's stomach hardened at the likely prospect of having to spend another jewel at the end of the journey.

The days wore on, as interminable as the sand that stretched before them. As hot as the days were, the nights were surprisingly cold. Naeem—whose name, he told her, meant benevolence—shared his tent with her, as well as stories of his years as a merchant in the cities of the Levant—among them, Bethlehem, Caesarea, and Tyre. He spoke of the Greek influence along the shores of the Middle Sea, and—in response to his curiosity—Theodora described for him the great city of Constantinople, grateful that she could call up its sights, sounds, and smells, if only in her mind.

One day the caravan stopped at a pitiful little oasis so small no one other than a trained guide like Haji would have been able to locate it. Theodora had just filled her goatskin when she noticed not far away a man in heavy robes kneeling in the shade of a dune.

"Who is that?" she asked Naeem.

Naeem's eyes crinkled as he inspected the figure. "He's a churchman, the Patriarch of Alexandria. Most esteemed, he is."

"Indeed? Strange that I haven't noticed him until this moment."

"It's no wonder. He's not with the caravan."

Theodora's eyes widened in surprise. "He's alone—out *here*?"

Naeem laughed. "Yes, at regular intervals he's known to take to the solitary life of the hermit."

"Isn't that strange for the leader of the Alexandria See?"

Naeem shrugged and seemed not to give it any further thought.

As Theodora's camel rose from the ground with her in its seat, the gray-haired patriarch looked up at the departing caravan. Theodora had never seen a more serene face—and yet it was a visage she thought she had seen before.

Long after they had settled into their tent that night, memory of the patriarch clung to her, haunting her like a shade. "What is his name?" she asked impulsively.

Naeem, on the threshold of sleep, grunted. "Whose name?"

"His name," Theodora pressed. "The patriarch's."

"Oh," Naeem said, turning on his side, away from her. "Timothy—it's Timothy. Now go to sleep."

The name was the key that unlocked memories of long ago. There had been a parish priest by the name of Timothy in the old days when she and her sisters were very young. Her mother took them to church quite regularly then—until Militiades—her second husband and a pagan—put an end to it. The priest was kind and gentle—and yes, there was no mistaking it—the face was much the same! Their parish priest had become the Patriarch of Alexandria's Holy See.

How she would like to talk to him. If only there had been time.

Several days later they came at last into the teeming port city of Alexandria. On the afternoon of their arrival, Theodora furtively lifted the hem of her tunic, feeling for her cache of jewels. Haji had to be paid.

Her heart dropped like a lead tablet. They were gone, the emerald ring, too. She found a neat slit in the hem where someone had used a knife to extract them.

Gone! She immediately went light-headed. It took some moments for the reality of the situation to set in. All her wealth in the world had vanished. She felt suddenly nauseous, bile curdling at the back of her throat.

How could it be? Who had come as a thief in the night, for she had checked them before retiring the night before? Naeem? She thought not. He completely fit the meaning of his name: benevolence.

Haji? Perhaps. He knew she carried jewels. But, very likely, many others supposed as much of a woman traveling such a distance alone. She had slept heavily again in the cool night. And Naeem slept like the dead. Anyone might have crept in and relieved her of her jewels. After all, the hiding place was nothing original. Then, again, someone might have seen her absently fingering the hem. No doubt she was an easy mark. Lesson learned: trust no one.

She ruled out Haji when he came to collect and offered no commiseration or insincere apology. In fact, he became quite skeptical, clearly thinking she was attempting to avoid the fee. He even accused her of swallowing the jewels. Her heated denial took no acting skills.

"So," he spat, "you have nothing of value to put you closer to your home, is that correct?"

Hearing the truth so boldly stated cut like a blade. She shook her head. "I'm sorry."

"Sorry! A lot of good that does!" He bared his wolf-like teeth. "I take you on, as well as the responsibility of returning Abasi's camel! And for what? For nothing! I should have known better."

Theodora bit her upper lip to keep from lashing out—or falling into a crying fit.

"You have no one here in Alexandria?"

Theodora shook her head.

Haji seemed to apprise her for some moments. "Well, pick up your bag and come with me. Be quick about it."

Theodora recognized a glimmer in Haji's black eyes, a certain glimmer she had observed in the eyes of many men. "Where?" she dared to ask.

His eyes narrowed now, his lips parting. "What choices have you?" he asked and began walking away.

Theodora followed him, knowing—as well as any seer—what lay in store.

She stayed a week in the mice-infested hovel he called his home down near the docks. How far she had fallen—she had become a common concubine to a caravan master. Haji's lovemaking was gentle if perfunctory, and he fell asleep without thought of pleasuring her. Not that she cared enough to teach him. She lay awake nights grasping for a plan—some way in which she could gain some money and thus find her way to the next town. She knew fare on board a ship back to The City was out of reach, but perhaps money in small increments would take her winding north and then east around the Middle Sea, a city at a time. It was a grim plan, and her head hurt to think how old she might be should she even look upon Constantinople again. If indeed a homecoming would ever came to pass.

"Do you wish to ride Abasi's camel again?" Haji asked the night before he was to take a caravan back to the Pentapolis.

"No," Theodora said, cringing at the thought. There was nothing for her there except perhaps arrest and a sentencing. "Will you leave me some money?"

"And have you gone when I return?" Haji sneered. "I think not. You haven't earned out your fare yet."

"I thought I had."

He harrumphed. "You overvalue your beauty. Perhaps by the time the spring ships come there will be money for your fare—but not before."

The thought of staying there through fall and winter made her mind go numb. She would not do it. And there was nothing to guarantee he would give her the money even then. He was no more to be trusted than Hecebolus. Often, beauty could be more of a hindrance than an advantage, she realized, for men were quick to add you to their possessions, like dropping a gold coin into their purses.

By the next day when he left, leaving her nothing and confident she had nowhere to go, she had formed her plan. Little did Haji know she had been an actress and had—like so many actresses—taken to simultaneously plying a more lucrative trade. She had chosen her clients in those days of her greatest fame and chosen well—only the wealthiest and best-connected would do— but now as she ventured out into the dark narrow streets of Alexandria for the first time, she had no such luxury.

She had made herself up with kohl for her eyes and ruby rouge for her lips, adapted her good stola in what she hoped was an appealing way, and pulled from her bag the silver strapped slippers she loved. She knew nothing about the city and wandered aimlessly, wondering how she might establish contact with a rich patrician.

The hours passed. Then she stumbled upon the area she had been looking for—a little street where women made known their wares to an occasional passerby on foot or in a litter. She had no sooner put herself forward than two women approached her, speaking angrily in their Coptic tongue. Theodora smiled and tried to communicate with them, but it was all too clear what the problem was—the street and its women were no doubt regulated by some crabbed old madam, or man. Theodora was the interloper. A very unwelcome one.

A little gang of another three was crossing over now to join in what could become a very dangerous situation. They had hard faces and yapping mouths, and it was no rush to judgment to think they might be carrying weapons.

Theodora quickly extricated herself from the group and headed for the nearest intersection. Upon going closer, she realized it led to a very dark alley, dark as an open grave. She froze in place, daring not to attempt it. The women could trap her there, or chances were that something equally perilous lay waiting in the shadows.

She looked back to see the women's faces, their eyes glinting like savage cats' eyes in the night, eager for blood.

Theodora moved to the other side of the street, walking briskly, her sights set on the wider, lighted street at the corner. It was a big city. There were other streets, other fish to land. She would call to these women, tell them she was leaving them to their incestuous little trade—if only she knew the language. She felt their eyes on her back now.

She was nearing the torch-lit corner when a richly appointed closed litter appeared from behind and began to keep pace beside her. Theodora turned to see a hand at the curtained window motioning to her. She kept walking, wondering if she dared attempt to cheat the locals out of one of their patrons for a single night.

She weighed the situation and made her choice. She stopped.

The two men carrying the litter knew the game and stopped as well. Theodora quickly moved to the window as a gray-haired Egyptian drew back the curtain. She saw at once he was refined and no doubt very wealthy. No finger lacked the glint of gold or sparkle of a jewel. Here is my ticket, she thought, if not onto a ship, then at least to the next town.

At that moment, a stone struck the panel of the litter. The passenger spat out an order and the quick feet of the litter bearers started moving away. Theodora turned to see the approaching women when a stone hit her face below her right eye. Her hand moved to the center of pain and she turned back, prepared to call out for help from the patrician in the litter—or from any bystander. At that moment something from behind smashed into her head. The last thing she would remember was the hard gravel of the street coming up to meet her.

21

THEODORA AWOKE IN A TINY jail cell. She was alone. Her head felt as if the Furies had taken up residence there. She raised her hand and felt her cheek. The wound was open, raw, and it stung badly to the touch.

Her head pulsing with pain, she sat up at the side of the pallet that was placed on blocks not high enough to prove an impediment to rats, rats which seemed to come in excessive numbers—for she was experiencing double vision. For the remainder of the day, she fought to hold in check her tears and despair, trying not to think how a bad situation had become so much worse.

Standing at the bars that faced a hallway, she questioned one of the jailers on his rounds, asking as best she could—in a few words of his language and in signs—the reason for her incarceration. He leered at her and laughed, making then lewd hand gestures that she took to mean prostitution.

The women on the street had turned her in, she concluded. Their madam or a brothel-keeper had no doubt paid the local government official to keep competition at bay.

Was there to be a hearing? Would she be brought before a judge?

Theodora's normal vision returned some hours later. The days went by, each like the one before, her head clearing a little more each day. Hunger overcame pain. Bread and water were passed to her in the morning and she had to make it do until the next morning. She could hear other prisoners nearby, mostly male it seemed. Their coughing, swearing, crying, and praying went on at all hours. She saw only the guards, and even though her head and facial wounds were healing, she was careful not to wash, and kept her hair, tunic, and expression as unattractive as possible. She was grateful to have the cell to herself but knew she was at the mercy of every guard there. If they chose to impose themselves on her, they could, and if they wished to watch while other prisoners did so, they could do that, too. She could be raped and killed and it would matter to no one. Sometimes she thought she could bear no more, but she stifled the instinct to call out or cry. She would not show such weakness to her captors, but she had to gain her freedom. Each day she asked about how her case was to be heard. Each day she received no answer.

A month passed and another worry arose. She had been noticing painful tingling in her breasts but had assumed the cause was her face-down fall on the hard street. However, now she realized her usual course had not come. Her courses had always run as punctually as a water clock, and while she thought it possible her poor diet had altered her body and dried up her usual course, she held little hope that was the case.

When the morning sickness came, she knew she was carrying Haji's baby. She had always been so careful to avoid relations at the most likely times she might conceive, but she had blundered with Hecebolus. With Haji, it was different—he was the one choosing the time, and he had been uninterested in methods to avoid such a situation.

She knew ways to avoid birthing and had done so herself—successfully— and had helped other women in the theater do so, as well. The method most used was an herbal concoction that forced out the matter from the body. It made one very sick with a fever, and it was painful, but other known methods were too dangerous and disturbing.

Here in her bare cell, she had no way to end the childbearing. And she knew ending the condition must be done in the first few months. After that there would be no safe option. She would have to bear the baby full term.

Theodora thought about trying to contact Haji. Had he returned from the Pentapolis? How would he react? Would he work to get her out of jail? Would he feel some responsibility for her? For the child? She had her doubts. Perhaps he wouldn't even believe the child was his. Only she knew for certain that it was.

And what if he did wish a family, would that not tie her down as the wife of a caravan master in a foreign city? She shuddered at the thought. She would rather die.

The weeks passed, and into the fourth month Theodora knew she could not avoid having her second child. By baring her stomach and making other gesticulations she tried to communicate her condition—and plea for a hearing—to the morning guard, the only one who seemed approachable. The exchange went on some minutes. He smiled then as if he understood and disappeared.

Theodora dared to feel hopeful.

The next morning, accompanying a double portion of bread was a bowl of watery gruel. He had thought she was arguing for a better diet because of the baby and seemed quite proud of himself.

When he left, Theodora resisted the impulse to throw the bowl to the beaten earth floor. She could not afford to be so foolish. She ate both the bread and the gruel quickly, without relish.

One day, into her fifth month of childbearing, she heard someone about to pass her cell at mid-morning, usually a quiet time. She supposed it was a new prisoner being led to his cell, yet on the chance it was the sympathetic morning guard she would not lose an opportunity to ask about a hearing.

As two figures passed, she saw it was a guard she had seen only two or three times. Keys jangled on a ring fastened to his belt. Following him was a man in a clean gray dalmatic. Not a prisoner, she thought. Her gaze caught the blue badge on his shoulder and her pulse quickened.

"You!" she called impulsively. "You—please help a friend of the Blues!"

The man stopped a few feet past her cell and turned about in curiosity. He was forty, she guessed, and even in the dim light appeared handsome. The guard stopped, too, speaking sharply in his swift Coptic, no doubt a warning to ignore the prisoner.

"I am a supporter of the Blues," Theodora called. "Please help me."

The man paused, indecisive for the moment.

"Move along," the guard said, managing a little Greek.

"I'm from Constantinople," Theodora said in an intense but quiet tone. "I just need a hearing so I might go home."

The man turned, said something to the guard, and walked over to her cell.

Theodora pulled the hair back from her face and wished now she did not look so dirty.

"The City?" the man said. His forehead furrowed as he leaned forward, squinting at her.

Her hands held to the bars but she leaned back slightly so that her rank odor would not offend him.

"Yes, yes, The City—Constantinople! You know it? Of course, you do!"

Just the thought that this man was from the capital brought moistness to her eyes.

He nodded. "How did you land here?" He spoke Greek, the language of home.

That she had succeeded in getting his attention was not lost on other prisoners, who stirred in their cells. A few called out for his attention, one other female voice among them.

"I was at the Pentapolis." She knew she had but moments to explain herself. "When I arrived here in Alexandria, I was caught up in a misunderstanding and arrested. I can't get a hearing. Perhaps you can help? Perhaps you have some influence?"

The man smiled. "Wishful thinking on both our parts, I'm sure. Sorry, I'm just here to see one of my own—fully drunk he was on Saturday last.—What did you do in The City?"

Theodora bit back a lie and said, "I was an actress."

"An actress?" He cast a knowing smile but one laced with doubt.

"Yes, yes, oh, I'm a sight now, filthy and in rags, but in The City—"

"What is your name?"

"Theodora. I performed living portraits."

"You?" He sneered, took a step closer, inspecting her.

Theodora self-consciously tucked back her hair and smoothed her stained tunic, all the while knowing how little she looked the part. "Yes," she said, "at the Old Royal Palace. Did you see me there perhaps?"

Bringing his head still closer to her bars, the man let out a little gasp. "By the beard of Zeus, it is the famous Theodora!"

Theodora felt herself blushing, at first because she thought he didn't believe her claim and was mocking her, then—when she realized that he did recognize her—she wanted to die of shame for her present condition.

"I saw you once onstage." He winked. "You carried it off nicely."

"Thank you. I saw your badge. You're a Blue—they were so helpful to my family once. Are there others here in Alexandria?"

"Of course, there's a full network of Blues all along the Levant."

"Will they help me get a hearing?—Will you help me?"

The Egyptian guard, who had been shuffling his feet and making impatient noises, urged the Blue to break off.

The man's lips tightened. "I'm afraid we have no say here. We're lucky to get one of our own out."

The guard barked an order.

The man shrugged, smiled guiltily, pivoted, and moved off.

Theodora slumped to the ground, certain now that there would be no way out of this forgotten nether world.

By the time she heard the two men making their return trip, escorting the lucky one to be released, she was again grasping onto the cell bars, her knuckles white as milk.

"Blue!" she called as they passed, realizing she had not asked his name. "Blue!"

Goaded by the guard to pay her no attention, the man walked on as if he were deaf.

"Listen, please listen! Go to the patriarch—Patriarch Timothy! Go to him and tell him I am here and about to bring a Christian baby out into this filthy sty!" That she was wailing like a madwoman mattered little to her.

The footsteps were quickly receding.

"Do you hear?" Theodora let loose her best stage scream. "Patriarch Timothy—he was from my parish in The City!—Tell him!"

Theodora listened as the last two words echoed against the discolored stone walls, the sounds of prisoners mocking her, laughing at her. And one, she thought absently, could be made out applauding.

So, I think, Theodora had spent time in a cell. Five months was not five years—the time I had spent—but it was enough for her to know a little of what my imprisonment meant. Until she chose me for this project of structuring the truth of her life, had she given me any thought?

I have yet to begin my slanted version of her life. What is keeping me from it, I wonder. I tell myself there is none of the old love left and that I should begin. Her time spent in an Alexandrian prison should ignite some stories for me to tell. Oh, I have imagination enough, but if she is correct that Procopius is penning a scathing semi-fictional account of her life and times, why must I? I have little enough time to myself as it is.

22

TWO DAYS PASSED.

Theodora's gruel sat untouched. She would eat it before long, if not for herself, then for the child.

Distant noises echoed through the halls, and soon she discerned low voices, the tramp of boots and the lighter slaps of sandals on stone. Sounds from the other cells ceased, for such disturbances at odd times put everyone on guard. Perhaps someone was merely being locked up. Or perhaps someone was being summoned. The fear that ran through the minds of many, she suspected, was the fear of being sentenced. Oh, a few might one day be released, but she guessed that many would see the light of day for just the time it took for sentencing and execution.

She could make out four forms approaching. Too many for her to waylay with her pleas. A lone guard might have mercy, but in groups they would mock her—or worse.

They came closer. Two were not guards, she realized, thus the sandals. They were monks wearing austere robes and expressions to match. Dared she think—even hope—?

To her amazement, they stopped at her cell. All breath left her.

One of the guards was the one who carried the ring of keys at his belt. Up close, she saw that he was badly pockmarked. He announced in rudimentary Greek, as if in jest, "You are being claimed."

"Claimed?" Theodora dumbly repeated, thinking she had gotten the word wrong. She looked from one monk to the other. One was a bit taller, but both were slim, middle-aged, and graying—most likely Greek. And both looked horrified at the sight of her.

The guard said something, the gist of which was, "Still want her?" He smiled, pleased at his own wit.

"You are Theodora?" one of the monks asked.

Theodora nodded. "Yes."

"The actress?" the other asked.

Theodora nodded again, hoping they knew nothing of her stage credits.

"Put on your sandals and come with us," the tall monk said in a flat tone. He nodded to the guard who carried the keys.

Theodora found that she couldn't move. In less than a minute, the iron barred door swung outward. She could not guess what path she would be on now but nonetheless sent up a prayer of thanksgiving. Her eyes moved from the monks to the guards.

The guard who had been silent until now did not show the humor of the first. "Hurry up, woman," he said, all business but in passable Greek. "Get ready!"

Theodora quickly fished around for her sandals, nearly knocking over her waste pail in the process. The silver strapped sandals were still in fair condition, and as she bent to put them on she realized how incongruous they looked now with her dirty and torn tunic. She would not retrieve the stola that sat in a heap in the corner because the rats had gotten at it.

She stood, forcing herself erect, as if to say she was indeed ready. Oh, she knew how filthy—and no doubt foul-smelling—she was, but she lifted her chin in much the same way her mother had coached her when she and her sisters danced at the Hippodrome. "Walk proud as a peacock!" she would order. Head held high, Theodora did so now.

They marched down the long dark hall, the two monks in front of her, the guards behind. As they moved past cells, she felt the silent stares of other prisoners. The quiet was eerie.

At the end of the hall, they took a narrow stairway, single file, to the floor above where high, barred windows provided a diffused sort of light. They moved toward a massive iron door through which—as it opened—Theodora saw that it led to the street. In no more than twenty steps, sunshine blinded her, and as her eyes adjusted, she heard the door clang behind them.

It was just three now—Theodora and the two monks. "Come along," the shorter one said. "Don't do anything foolish like run, or there will be no one to rescue you."

Theodora tried to question them as they went down narrow alleys and tiny winding passageways, but neither one spoke. Were they taking a shortcut—or were the monks embarrassed to be seen with her on more public streets?

Within twenty minutes, they arrived at a fairly large, two-storied gray stone building with a flat roof. From the roof, above an unassuming entrance, rose a great bronze cross.

The interior was cool. Theodora was escorted—still in silence—to a small chamber on the second floor.

"You are to wait here," the short monk said.

"For Patriarch Timothy? Am I to see him? This is his home, is it not?"

"It is, and you will not see him such as you are. Place your clothing in the hall where it will be collected and burned.—Have you lice?"

A red heat suffused Theodora's face. It seemed the height of ignominy to be asked such a question and to have to answer. "Yes," she whispered, eyes downcast.

"A servant will come to take you to your bath," the monk continued, "and you will be given something to wear."

They closed the door on her now, eager, she was certain, to have done with her.

Theodora awaited the Patriarch Timothy in a garden set in the courtyard of the building.

She had luxuriated in the bath long after she had been scrubbed and de-loused by an Egyptian woman named Rashida. Her hands traced the contour of her belly, her thoughts of the child she was bearing leading to thoughts of the girl-child she had left behind.

The return of the God-sent woman—who spoke passable Greek—meant that Theodora could put away such introspection. Wrapped in a linen bath robe, she was led back to her small chamber where she found a roomy brown robe, sandals—more serviceable than her silver ones—and a little meal of cheese and flatbread topped with sesame. The woman aided her in the drying and plaiting of her hair. Before leaving, she said, "You know how to address a patriarch, do you?"

"I've never done so."

"You address him as 'Your Beatitude'."

"I see. Thank you, Rashida."

Theodora sat now, lulled by her sudden good fortune, and yet nervous to meet a patriarch. Her eyes were caught by a gray cat, slinking in and among the terra cotta pots that held a variety of plants, bushes, and miniature trees. She scanned the balconies and windows of colored glass overlooking the courtyard, wondering if she was being watched by curious eyes—or even by the patriarch himself.

And suddenly he appeared, walking toward her. His simple robe was as white as his hair so that in the sunlight he gave off a shimmering effect. He seemed to be scrutinizing her as he moved, with grace and authority.

Theodora's hand went to her hair. It was fully dry now and in a neat plait atop her head. She wondered, though, if she shouldn't have worn the wimple that had been left for her with the robe. Did he expect as much?

She stood and knelt. "Your Beatitude," she muttered.

He extended his hand to her, and she kissed the sapphire ring, still wondering if this was all a dream, if she would wake to the bite of a rat in her cell.

"Rise, child, and be welcomed."

His voice was warm and to her it tinkled a bit, like the fountain behind him. Theodora stood to find he was not tall, not much taller than she.

"Ah, you are a new bloom for my garden here, one come from Constantinople."

"Good Father, I was no bloom this morning, I can attest."

The patriarch smiled. "And so you are Theodora? The bearkeeper's daughter! His middle daughter, yes?"

Theodora's mouth fell slack. "You do remember. Forgive me, I mean, Your Beatitude."

"You are an old parishioner of mine, so please do call me 'Father.' Now—Comito was your older sister—and your younger ... "

"Anastasia," Theodora offered.

"Ah, yes! How are they all?"

"Fine, last I heard, but that was long ago."

The patriarch tilted his head. "Still Christian?"

Theodora burned with embarrassment. She could not look into his saint-like face and lie. "After Mother's second marriage, we seldom went to church." She drew in a deep breath, then blurted, "Comito and I became actresses.—Not a very Christian occupation, I'm afraid."

"I see. Is that what brought you to Alexandria? Are you in a troupe?—Sit down now, child."

Once they were both seated in high-backed wicker chairs, Theodora outlined for him the misadventures she had had with Hecebolus.

The patriarch clucked his tongue after the telling. "The Pentapolis—I'm afraid it's one of the most difficult of the governorships to manage. Always a problem. Well, that is behind you now. Will you go back to acting?"

"I—I don't know. I only know I must return to Constantinople."

"To your roots—that is understandable. Not many women travel so far from home. And Constantinople—ah! The New Rome, as they say! It is the greatest of all cities. I was never happier than in my little parish there."

"Why did you leave, Father?"

The patriarch gave a smile that wasn't a smile, and a look of pain flashed across his face. "I am a Monophysite, Theodora, and so I became anathema to the Roman church and the emperor of Constantinople. I lost my parish because of my theology and almost lost my life. Of the five apostolic sees—Constantinople, Jerusalem, Antioch, Alexandria, and Rome—only my see welcomes Monophysites, only here."

"Is it a kind of heresy?"

"To hear the Roman church tell it, it is.—You've not heard of it?"

"I have heard the name, but in the theater there is little discussion of theology."

To Theodora's surprise, the patriarch laughed loudly, his teeth glinting against a skin tanned by his days in the desert. "I don't imagine there is much interest in theology backstage."

"What is this belief, Father?"

"At its heart, it is simple enough. Monophysitism is the doctrine that states that there was but one nature in Jesus, and that nature was divine. Dyophysites believe that there are two natures in Jesus, the divine and the human."

"I see. Are the differences in doctrine so radically different?"

"I'm afraid they are. The issue is more involved than my little description."

"I wish to know more, Good Father."

"Do you?—In growing up you believed in the Trinity, yes? One God in three persons?"

Theodora nodded.

"Christ died and was resurrected to establish a new link with man. The

New Covenant. God the Son suffered and died as a man. Is it not true he was a man, then?"

Theodora nodded uncertainly.

"But," the patriarch continued, "those who worship the Trinity worship Christ as one person only. The question comes down to this, Theodora—how many natures are possible in one person?"

Theodora was unused to such questions. "I—I am not certain."

"The answer, in my opinion, is that Christ had only a divine nature. He may have lived and died among us mortals, but he was divine and therefore had the powers to take on human aspects." Patriarch Timothy continued at some length further explaining the differences between the two doctrines. He paused several times to clarify things when Theodora asked a question.

"Ultimately," Theodora said when he finished, "both factions believe in Christ, yes?"

"Yes."

"So, if there is a difference between theological thoughts about Christ's nature, isn't that merely an intellectual impasse? Must it be a heresy for one side or the other?"

The patriarch sat back in his chair, his dark eyes twinkling and widening slightly. "You, my child, have put your finger on the crux of this powerful subject that has so fractured Christianity. And you've done it in very little time. Perhaps both factions should make an effort to peacefully co-exist within one church. Bless you!"

Theodora felt a little tingle of pride rising up within her. "And when the theologians die," she ventured, "then they will find out the true nature of Christ." She had never had cause to speak of theological or philosophical things, and doing so made something in her take flight. It was a glorious thing—to converse nearly as an equal with this holy and learned man.

"Now—what are we to do with you Theodora? I was told of your condition—how far along are you?"

"Close to my sixth month."

"And the father?"

"Haji, the caravan master I told you about, is the father. I want nothing from him and nothing to do with him. I want only to return home."

"I see. Ah, on the wing, much like the cranes that leave us after the winter."

"It's a ship's passage that I need. I could work for it, Father."

The patriarch's eyes narrowed. "Are you able to travel?"

"Oh, yes, Father!"

"But are you prepared to enter your old city in your condition?"

Father Timothy's question came like a thunderclap. Things had happened so quickly this day she hadn't thought about it. For days she had pushed her condition so far to the back of her mind that each time she thought of it, it was like some new misfortune stalking her. She sat silent while his question hung in the air. Yes—how would it be to walk down the gangplank at Constantinople—penniless, husbandless, and with a big belly? She had left The City, vowing to return as the wife of a governor and a lady of prestige and wealth. Now, the thought of having been reduced to the wandering beggar she had become ran through her veins like a quick-acting poison. She couldn't bear it.

Father Timothy seemed to be studying her. "You'll stay here for the lying-in, Theodora. Bring your child into the world, and then we'll see what's to be done with you."

"You'll keep me here, in this fine place?"

"Of course, you are an old parishioner returned to me like a homing pigeon."

"Or a counterfeit nomisma," Theodora said wryly.

The patriarch laughed again.

The gray cat startled Theodora now by jumping up into her lap. Head lifted, it stretched its body, begging to be petted.

"You see, Chike welcomes you. It is no little thing—cats here in Egypt are held in reverence."

"Thank you, Father Timothy.—Thank you!"

"You are most welcome, child." He stood to depart.

Theodora set the cat down and fell to her knees, reaching for the patriarch's hand and kissing the sapphire ring.

"There, there, rise now, Theodora."

After his departure, she sat again and the cat returned to her lap, eager to be stroked. Listening to the tinkling of the fountain, Theodora obliged, whispering, "Hello, boy. Hello, little Chike."

Theodora waited out her term there at the official complex that housed the patriarch's residence, the offices of the Holy See of Saint Mark, and a clinic where monks and nuns welcomed the poor. She offered to work in the clinic but was told—considering her condition—it would not be proper.

Here she learned from Father Timothy that Justin, the new emperor in Constantinople, had been Commander of the Imperial Guard before taking the diadem.

"A soldier?" Theodora asked.

"Indeed—and without a drop of royal blood," Father Timothy said, a lightness in his tone. "Imagine that!"

"That doesn't upset you, Father?"

"Oh, his policy toward Monophysites does—yes! But that the diadem is passed to a common man? To fresh blood? No, not at all!"

Theodora would think about it later, but for now talk of Constantinople called up more immediate concerns, concerns that caused tightness in her chest when she thought of them. From the Pentapolis she had sent several letters to her mother and to Comito, but no one had written back, and now, of course, no mail could possibly find her. She could only wonder about her family. How was her mother's health? How has Anastasia adapted to her marriage? She was certain that, like a cat, Comito would always land on her feet—but what of the baby girl that had been entrusted to her?

Theodora could not bring herself to write to them now even though Father Timothy offered to see that a letter was sent. She could not bear to tell them how badly things had gone. No, she would do that in person—one day.

She spent long afternoons sitting with Father Timothy and a friend of his, theologian Severus, who had once been Patriarch of Antioch. Severus, she learned, was also a Monophysite and it was his conviction about Christ's nature that led him into exile when Justin, with ties to the Roman church, assumed power. When Severus's head had been ordered sent to The City, Patriarch Timothy offered him shelter in an Alexandrian suburb.

Theodora was neither a philosopher nor a theologian, but she listened, questioned, and learned as these men spoke of religious matters. She could not fathom how Emperor Justin could have sent good men like Timothy and Severus fleeing for their lives.

During these months, something about her own human nature came into play, something that affected her deeply, something that would change her. That these two great men welcomed her as a friend and as an equal, without regard to differences in her station or education or religious fervency, was not lost on her. They never alluded to her past. Neither was she looked upon any less for her womanhood; there was not a whiff of condescension and—most surprisingly—no hint of physical attraction or aggression.

Theodora was placed in the care of an old holy woman, Ceaseria who—Theodora was surprised to learn—was the sister of the previous emperor in Constantinople, Anastasius. Ceaseria was a confirmed Monophysite, who had left The City when Anastasius died and the persecution of Monophysites began by Emperor Justin. She was in her seventh decade, Theodora guessed, slim, and possessing of a serene, saint-like visage beneath her white wimple.

"Should I be wearing the wimple laid out for me?" Theodora had asked on the day they met.

"It would be advisable if you go out into the city, child," she said, "but within these walls you choose as to your own comfort."

"And a veil in public?"

"No, child, such a thing is not necessary."

Theodora did find that women were treated differently here in Alexandria. They enjoyed the same economic and legal rights as men. Timothy posited that this was the case because in Egypt the Pharaoh had reigned supreme, and as the focal point of worship, it did not matter whether those doing homage were men or women. Classes, however, he told her were not equal, for there were whole strata of economic classes, ranging from slaves to the very rich, among whom rights and privileges varied greatly.

Those waning days of her lying-in with Timothy, Severus, and Ceaseria were among the happiest of her life. Theodora had never been treated with such care and love.

23

I RECALL MY OWN TIME IN Alexandria and my similar surprise that unveiled women of all ages move freely about the largest and most diverse city I had yet encountered in my travels with Gaspar. The memory comes clear as glass, and it comes with a searing pain, too, for it was then that I fell in love.

I am fifteen and a virgin. Jamila is the daughter of Sabaf, an Egyptian purveyor of pelts who comes several times to consult with Gaspar on his future. I am not allowed in the wagon on the paid visits because—I assume—of the shady nature of the consultation. I am certain that binding spells are being placed on the tradesman's competitors and suppose that the man wishes no witness other than the magus. And so I am left to entertain the young lady on these occasions.

Jamila is the same age as I, and in little time infatuation leads to first love. The sweetness of her visage—so unlike the hard hawk-like face of her father—captures my heart even before her mellifluous voice and charms secure it. And yet she has a sense of adventure about her. "Stephen," she says, "let us play as spies tonight just outside the tent in which Father is meeting with your Master Gaspar."

"That's not a good idea, Jamila," I say, well aware of the malicious nature of some of Gaspar's prayers and imprecations.

Her eyes sparkle in the night. "But I think it is a most excellent idea." She is already moving to the rear of the tent where a good-sized rent in the material allows visual access, as well as auditory.

The close proximity to Jamila, her faint lotus scent, and her warm breath in the cool nighttime douses my objection and I acquiesce to her little scheme.

We watch as Gaspar uses one of his lead curse tablets against Sabaf's competitors. Sabaf repeats Gaspar's words, mimicking his intonations perfectly: "I bind Dakarai and the shopkeeper with whom he deals, Odion. I bind these two and their wives and their slaves. I bind their souls, work, life, hands and feet. Before Hermes the Restrainer, I bind all these in their graves."

My attention is drawn to the girl's profile in the diffused and flickering light, so at the completion of the curse I am not prepared for the shudder that runs through her slim body. Any illusions she had had about her father's ethics in business are shattered at once. She reaches out and grabs hold of my arm so as not to slump to the ground. I quickly lead her away.

In the following days Jamila becomes more and more emotionally distant from her father—and closer to me. We begin to meet secretly in a secluded area of a public park. Of four such meetings I will remember every minute, every word exchanged, every touch. At our fourth rendezvous the touching goes too far. We go too far.

Afterward, Jamila draws back from me, as regretful now as she had been passionate. Her regret brings shame upon me.

"Listen to me, Jamila," I say. "I will make things right. I have saved nearly enough money to gain my freedom."

She looks up at me and brushes away a tear.

"Then we shall marry," I say.

The next evening as we sit at our campfire, I make the mistake of telling Gaspar of my plans. It is a fatal error.

Gaspar stares in amazement at the cache of coins I spill out before him. "I am impressed," he says. "You have been frugal and a good businessman." His grizzled eyebrows press down above the hooded black eyes. "But even if I wished to sell you, Stephen, this would not be enough. You must be content with your life with me. It is your fortune. Oh, there will be time for women later. You will have many. For now, your allegiance is to me."

"Gaspar, I love Jamila—I do!"

"A young man like you will fall in love *many* times."

I shake my head. "No, we will marry."

"Stephen, you will not!" Gaspar shouts. "Her father will never allow it."

He is more than angry, much more. He is a tangle of emotions: at once sad, disappointed, threatened. I am betraying him; that much is clear. At first, my heart swells to think that this man—who had seemed hard and distant for all the time we have lived together—could not think of parting from me. But as Gaspar goes on speaking, I come to realize that it is not love or attachment that Gaspar feels toward me. It is something very different.

Gaspar explains in even tones, as if discussing a location on a map, how I am to be his assistant in magick, his *parhedros*, and that one could not be a true magus without such an assistant who lives with him, eats with him, sleeps with him, side by side. It is, ironically, the assistant who brings the magick to the magus, the assistant who is the teacher. The assistant helps and protects the magus. Gaspar pitifully explains to me how he had searched for such an assistant for years before finding me.

"Why me?" I ask. "Why not one of my brothers—or someone else?"

"You had the mark upon you," Gaspar says.

"But I am not special. I am not a *parhedros*. It seems to me a *parhedros* has to find *you* if it's fated. You cannot come to a mountain farm and bargain with a family for one."

The color goes out of Gaspar's face.

I speak only what is common sense, but find that I must have hit upon some truth.

Gaspar struggles for words. "Stephen," he chokes out, "you will stay—you must!" The demand is more of a plea now.

I feel great empathy for the man who has placed so much hope in me. My time with him has taught me that this magus carries magical tablets and demonstrates all the ways of the wizard to those who come to him for help, but in truth it comes home to me like a blow to the face that he is devoid of any real magical powers. Oh, he is a master of languages and has taught me Greek, Latin, and Persian, but his talents go no further. He has been relying on me to be his instrument, had been all along. "I have no mark upon me," I say.

"Not that you can see, but you are my *parhedros*, nonetheless," Gaspar insists, his eyes seeming to take on an ethereal glow in the campfire light. "There is a ritual which will bring to you powers beyond imagination. First, I am to shave all the hairs from my head.—Wait, let me show you." Gaspar brings out a papyrus now that details a strange rite involving the magus' fingernails, a drowned falcon, and a drink of honey and milk obtained from a black cow. The papyrus blurs before my eyes as he reads. To my mind it is nothing more than nonsense. I could not believe that this man has invested so much time—years—in the hope that I was somehow to become his empowering agent. My heart goes out to Gaspar.

"You will stay, Stephen. I will prepare to have the ceremony in two days. I can see now I've already waited too long."

I dwell for some time about how I will respond, not wishing to disappoint this man who has been my guardian for so long. But—at last—I draw myself up and say, "I will earn the additional money, master. I will earn it, and you will release me one day." *One day soon*, I think.

"No, you will stay. We will leave Alexandria in the morning. You will forget this girl."

I am about to deny that I could ever forget Jamila when I see white fear suddenly billow into Gaspar's dark face. He looks at me as if he can see into my soul. "Stephen ... you have not had ... relations with this girl? ... *Have you?*"

I remain speechless, but I know my face betrays any lie I could summon.

Gaspar reads it at once. He lets out a long breath. His eyes lose focus. Slowly, silently, he pushes himself up from the ground and retreats into the tent. I catch sight of a wetness about his eyes as he goes.

I lie in the open an hour or more, staring up at a star-kissed sky. I keep channeling my thoughts to Jamila so as not to feel the heartache I have perpetrated on Gaspar. I put down Gaspar's reaction to anger at the deflowering of an associate's daughter—and to disappointment and shame in my moral laxness.

In the morning, however, the true nature of his despondency comes out in a terrible tirade of curses. "Stupid, damnable boy! You are my ruin," he cries, "my ruin! For the ritual to be valid, a *parhedros* is required to be a young innocent boy—innocent, damn you!—A virgin!"

I feel sorry for him, of course, but even before he finishes his speech, my heart leaps up, for it comes to me that my days and nights with Gaspar have come to an end.

24

FATHER TIMOTHY CAME IN TO see Theodora upon hearing her labor pains had started more than a month early. "We've sent for the midwife," he announced. "The Lord will see you through this, Theodora."

Ceaseria was in attendance and openly frowned at the appearance of a man in the hastily arranged birthing room. Theodora smiled to see him as always, but now she smiled because her time was at hand and within days he would see that she gets passage to Constantinople. She would be on her way home.

After his greeting, he gave her a blessing and wished her well. Several women had been set to preparatory tasks within the small room, but he seemed in no hurry to leave. Something was on his mind, Theodora realized, and a foreboding took root.

"Father Severus and I have been talking, child, and we have reached a conclusion." He spoke in his gentle way but with great assurance, as if what he had to say was being dispensed as infallible church doctrine. "We feel that you should keep your child."

Theodora drew in a shallow breath between the pains. "Oh, Father, Ceaseria is convinced she will find a good family who will adopt it. It's as good as done."

"It's not done, Theodora. We sent for the child's father."

Theodora's breath went out of her. "You did what?"

"He is, however, at the Pentapolis now with a caravan. We will speak to him when he returns."

"But there!—You see, Father, he is a caravan master. He has no time to raise a child. I don't wish to leave my child with him."

"But *you* would raise the child, Theodora."

"I?" Her pains were sharper now, coming more frequently and in paroxysms so intense that Timothy's image blurred and his words became unintelligible, but in between the painful bursts, she managed to fasten onto the direction of his discourse, a direction fearful enough to nullify birth pains.

Father Timothy smiled. "We feel—Father Severus and I—that you must marry the father of your child."

"Marry?" The word was little more than a gasp. "Haji has no wish to marry me."

"Are you so certain? And it's not really a question of wishes, child. It is the honorable thing."

Theodora grew dizzy. Why had he waited for this moment—with her at her weakest, most vulnerable state—to say these things? "No, Father, I wish only to go home to Constantinople. You said you would book me passage."

"And should Haji wish to go, I would book passage for the three of you."

"The three of us?" she dumbly repeated as a question. "I would not make any better a parent than he!" The thought of arriving at The City with a child and the caravan master Haji in tow paralyzed her.

"I would provide you with a dowry, too."

Theodora pushed herself up on her elbow, wanting to rail against this man and his interference, his goodwill notwithstanding, but her arm gave out and she fell back against the pillow, exhausted even before the ordeal of birth had truly begun. She looked over at the birthing chair that awaited her. "Father, I wish—"

Timothy raised a finger as if to bless her, but the gesture was instead one of caution. "No more wishes, child. You will do what is right."

The heavyset midwife and her helper arrived now, crowding into the small room and shooing away the other two servants.

"I must go," Timothy said, "before I, too, am put out. We will talk after the blessed event."

Blessed event! Theodora wanted to call out that it was no such thing. She wanted to call out that death would be a better fate for her and the baby. She wanted to ask him if—for his doctrinal differences—he had not followed his *wishes* in going against the Patriarch of Constantinople, the Emperor, and the Pope himself. But as it was, he was shown out of the chamber before she could speak.

The midwife loomed over her now, her dark, fleshy face as serious as if she were at the lying-in of a Pharaoh's wife. Her wimple removed, Ceaseria stayed close by, providing a towel to the forehead and cool drinking water. After the passage of two hours, the women in the room lifted her and carried her to the birthing chair.

Her first child had come quickly and easily. Not so this one. She began to fear for the child and for her own life. She had good reason, it seemed. The midwife's tone in her directions to her helper sharpened. Ceaseria translated: "The baby's head is not positioned properly."

Theodora's heart caught. She knew the dangers of such births. Women delivering in many such cases were torn and bled to death. The midwife began to utter incantations in her Coptic language. The water clock dripped away and had to be replenished.

Below her, Theodora could feel the midwife's hands at work. She had never known such pain, and yet it was nearly benumbed by the future Father Timothy had painted for her.

At last, Ceaseria called out: "It's coming!—Oh, Theodora, it's coming!" Another few minutes passed, then: "It's a boy, Theodora—a boy!"

Theodora heard no sound and saw no movement of the baby's limbs. She was just about to ask if he was alive when Ceaseria slapped him and he let out a healthy scream. She then took the baby to be cleansed. In all, ten hours had passed.

A short while later—the afterbirth disposed of—Theodora lay on the bed, listening to the midwife and her helper take their leave. She sensed the thin Ceaseria remaining there at her side, heard what she thought was the fragile breathing of the child. She kept her eyes closed.

"Still in pain, Theodora?"

"No."

"Do you wish to see him?"

Theodora thought for a moment, knowing the woman held her baby just an arm's length away. The moment protracted. Then she shook her head. "No, the circumstances have not changed. Take him away, Ceaseria."

"But Father Timothy—"

"A pox on Father Timothy! Take the child away!" Theodora kept her eyes closed until the room was utterly silent.

Much later, Ceaseria returned, her wimple again in place. "You must sleep, Theodora.... The baby is with the wet nurse."

Theodora's head rolled on the pillow toward Ceaseria. "He won't change his mind, will he? He won't help me with passage money?"

"I think not. Men—they see marriage and children so differently. It is too bad they cannot feel what we women feel. Too bad they don't bear the children."

The comment struck a chord and Theodora managed a laugh. As much as Timothy and Severus had helped her, as much as they had taught her, they were at their core not so very different from other men she had known. She reached for Ceaseria's hand. "What am I to do?"

"If I had money of my own, child, you could have it."

"Will you at least help me to get away?"

"He's likely to put out the word at the docks—or maybe Haji will."

"I won't attempt to sail. I'll go overland."

"But that will take forever!"

"It's better than being coerced into a marriage.—Can you get me to the Blues who brought me here?"

"Yes—I think so." Ceaseria squeezed Theodora's hand. "When will you be strong enough?"

"To leave? Tomorrow."

"Too soon!"

"I have little time to spare.—Oh, Ceaseria, I love Father Timothy, and my faith has not been merely restored here, but built into something sturdy. However, I cannot mortgage my life for fear of disappointing him.—Ceaseria, do you have children?"

The woman nodded. "Two. They are grown, of course—Hypatius and Pompeius—and capable of disappointing."

"Why is that?"

"In order to stay in the capital and in the good graces of Emperor Justin, they have renounced the doctrine our family has followed."

"They stayed in Constantinople while you came here to practice your faith?"

Ceaseria drew in a long breath, her hand going to her heart. "Yes."

Theodora ached for the old woman who had kept to her faith, following Timothy half way across the world. She marveled, too, at her bravery.

Ceaseria stood to leave. "I'll not challenge your decision. I'll look in on you before dawn. You are to be ready.... Theodora?"

"Yes?"

"Do you have a name ... for the child?"

Theodora thought. "John. Call him John."

After Ceaseria left, Theodora lay back against the pillows. "Forgive me, Baby John," she whispered, "forgive your mother."

Yes, going overland would take good time. She gave it much thought. But the network of Blues that spanned the east coast of the Middle Sea north from Alexandria to Constantinople would, she prayed, aid her in her progress. She knew well enough that she would likely have to work the boards again in order to pay her way. But it would be different this time—she would hold herself more dearly in the time offstage. She would no longer play the courtesan. Despite the nature of her departure, her time with Timothy and Severus had transformed her.

And in towns where Blues were not to be found, convents that welcomed news of Timothy and Severus would likely welcome her, too. She would keep her white robe and wimple in pristine condition. It came to her how one day she might be on stage playing a sultry ingénue—and the next be entertaining a dining hall of nuns eager for news of Alexandria and the Monophysite movement. She smiled at the notion, realizing she was about to make her everyday life a life on stage.

In the morning Ceaseria came for her, and the two slipped out of the building just as the pink eastern sky turned crimson.

My own departure from Alexandria is stealthy, also, but less than willing.

On the morning after my confrontation with Gaspar, I awake to a strong hand upon my mouth. In panic, I attempt to rear up, but suddenly other hands are holding tightly to my arms and legs. Only the shortest possible cry escapes me before a gag is shoved in my mouth. Thieves! In the shadows, I manage to make out at least three men working over me before a blindfold takes all sight. Is Gaspar all right? Has he been harmed?

Once I am fully bound, I give up struggling and listen. They are speaking in Persian, saying something about the readiness of the wagon. Am I to be taken somewhere? Where is Gaspar? What have they done to him? Murdered him? And of what use could *I* be to them?

I am so slight of frame that one of them lifts me with ease. As he moves me out of the tent, I hear whispering voices nearby and strain to decipher the words. By now, I know the differences among the sounds of copper, silver, and gold coins, and it is against the jingling of gold that I hear the unmistakable dulcet voice of Gaspar. And now it comes to me: Gaspar has sold me.

25

WITHIN TWENTY-FOUR HOURS OF PARTING from a tearful Ceaseria, Theodora found herself in the company of five Blues making their way to Pelusium. Their leader, Cletus, a tall, broad-shouldered man with a military background, welcomed her. "It is a rare occasion that we host such a beauty," he said, "and—a famous actress."

The wink he gave her affirmed the suspicion that he had heard of her or perhaps seen her on stage in Constantinople. In the old days she would have been delighted, but this day she arranged her mouth into the facsimile of a smile and asked, "Will we be leaving soon, Cletus?"

"Indeed, we will."

Two hours later, they set off. From her seat high up on a dromedary, she could not help looking back now and then, fearful that someone—even Haji himself—was coming for her.

She regretted most having to leave Timothy in such a way, for he had become her spiritual father. She had disappointed him. Parting from him tore at her heart. Few men of importance—much less an archbishop—ever paid attention to women of her kind. He had guided and taught her, and even though she rejected his plans for her, she left Alexandria changed because of him. She found an inner faith she was still plumbing and came to respect and love holy men and women who had divorced themselves from a worldly life, just as Timothy, Severus, and Ceaseria had done. She recalled the stylites back in Constantinople, those men who lived out their years atop columns, praying, chanting, and exhorting people to do good. They—with their other-world voices, ragged appearances, and terrible odors—had been such easy targets of rebuke for many of the citizenry, herself included. Should she get back to The City, she would never view them the same way again.

Should she get back to The City? The thought—the doubt—had come uninvited and pricked her at once. Of course, she would get back to Constantinople. She *must!*

Theodora was well aware it would not be her newly found faith that would pave the path. While a few of the Blues recognized her because they had seen her onstage, most of them knew her by reputation and were eager to provide stage work for her as she moved north along the Middle Sea, town to town, city to city. It seemed that the network of the Blue faction, still well-connected to theater people, had grown strong in the new reign of Emperor Justin. The five accompanying her had as their final destination Antioch, where she would have to make new arrangements. She had promised to pay them with money earned on the boards along the way.

Money. Theodora had grown used to having it at the ready. She despised not having it now, despised the necessity of returning to an occupation that no longer gave anything back, other than money. But if acting carried her once again to the shores of Constantinople, so be it.

The little caravan moved along the Way of the Sea route, wending its way through marshes along the Nile Delta toward Pelusium, the gateway to and from Egypt. Fortunately, floods had receded so that they traveled at top speed, fourteen miles a day. The air was laden with humidity, the river tributaries black and foul-smelling and so slow-moving Theodora had to ask if they moved at all. In answer, the Blues seemed to enjoy putting her on edge by talking of malaria and other fatal diseases, as well as huge creatures that lurked within the marsh waters.

They eventually reached Kantara, the customs point, where Theodora declared herself a citizen of Constantinople who was returning home. The portly official looked her over curiously and passed her through, but not without a few reassuring words from the formidable Cletus. That night it was more than the humidity that kept her restlessly awake. She wished she had given a false name and destination in the event someone were following her.

The next day they took the very narrow stretch that meandered through marsh and bog, coming to Pelusium after nightfall. The city—once captured by Marc Antony—sat on a low hill, as much as protection from invaders as from the Nile's flooding. A full day was spent resting, and seeing to the feeding and watering of the camels because the next leg of the journey would take them east and then north through the Levant, which promised treacherous dunes and dryer, but hotter, air. Water and plant life for the camels' diet would be nonexistent. On the following morning, with the donkey in the lead, for camels could not be trusted to follow a path, the group set off, this time—with safety in mind—as part of a caravan of some twenty traders.

The days passed. Theodora noticed Roman-built forts on the coast each day, but what amazed her was an occasional cathedral out in the middle of nowhere, populated only by monks. They pushed on through little outposts like El Arish—the border between Egypt and Palestine—and Raphia and others so small the traders could not name them. She lost count of the forts, the cathedrals, the days. The desert stretched out, dry, barren, unending.

At about ten days out from Gaza, the terrain blessedly began to show signs of green. Trees and patches of fertile lands appeared like welcome mirages. "They have deep wells in the city," Cletus told her. "The water will be cool and fresh, nothing like this brackish stuff we've had along the way."

Theodora had never thought she would salivate at the thought of water, but she did, and it mattered little to her when he went on to say that the enclave of Blues here was strong and she would be expected to perform during a layover that would last four days. They disengaged themselves from the traders, and even before the Blues brought her to their destination within the city, she begged them to allow her a visit to Gaza's cathedral. By now she had come to realize the time and stamina it would take to return to Constantinople, and so it was there that she prayed for strength of mind and body.

News of her arrival circulated quickly. She found it odd to be back on the boards again, performing whatever living picture the theater master was able to slap together quickly and cheaply. He was generous with her, though, and she shopped at the town's market square for makeup and clothing for costumes. It was not wholly unpleasant, just strange to be doing what she thought she had put away forever. She kept her costumes more modest than in the past, however, and this puzzled some and disappointed others who had either seen for themselves or heard of the risqué nature of her performances. Too bad, she thought, upon hearing a negative comment here and there—the timely continuance of her journey would be all the more assured. No extended performances here.

Linking up with another caravan made up of mostly traders, they left Gaza after five days, passing through fields and orchards. One day brought them to Askalon; the next Ashdod. Two more and they arrived at Joppa, a lumbering port from which bound logs were sent south to Egypt. Along the Way of the Sea, wheat fields became vegetable gardens. Another day brought them across the Plain of Sharon, the sight of Mount Carmel ahead of them, passing through rich and valuable land dotted with fields, orchards, and forests. Temperatures cooled. Farmers greeted them gladly, and good water was abundant. Theodora found herself relaxing into the routine of the trip, adjusting to the ways of the caravan and enjoying the scenery.

Three days brought them to Caesarea, the wealthy capital of Palestine where Theodora was expected to perform. Some of the traders would take the inland route from there, moving up to Damascus; others would trade their linen and papyrus for iron and bronze tools and return to Egypt the way they had come. When their time was up in Caesarea, the Blues and Theodora would take a third trade route—to the north, a bit inland to Nazareth, and then back toward the Middle Sea—and Tyre.

Theodora worked a fine theater in Caesarea for a full week, taking in a purse full of coins which she shared with her five fellow travelers. Here she had to deal with wealthy theatergoers who assumed that she, as an actress, was willing to prostitute herself. When the propositions came to her, she feigned surprise and shock; effecting a few theatrical snarls on the first two nights made for an easier go of it the next few. She would work the boards because she had to earn her way back home. But the days of selling herself, she vowed, were past.

On their way north to Nazareth—in the company of a handful of traders—they passed caravans coming south from Antioch with horses purchased on the Armenian steppes and meant for trade in Egypt. When they came to Nazareth, they camped a little outside the town, where the merchants of the small Jewish town preferred to do business. The weather in Palestine remained remarkably cool and pleasant.

It was here at Nazareth, where Theodora could not avoid thoughts of the baby Jesus, that she could not keep from her mind images of the baby John she had left behind in Alexandria. Cheeks burning, tears being held at bay, she looked into the starry night sky, and whispered, "I am sorry, my baby. My John."

My captors are Persian, but their dialect is a bit different from Gaspar's. I find that I am one of eleven captives. Most are Egyptian but they are like me in their youth and in—I daresay—their exceptional good looks. At least many have commented on my handsomeness. I am the odd man, however, for when

I tell the craggy-faced leader—with some exaggeration—that I well know how to drive a camel, he orders me to take the oldest and most peevish of the lot. I approach the animal, speaking in friendly tones. He eyes me warily. I step closer, my eyes on his. "Kneel!" I command and step closer. His head retracts slightly then comes down toward me. His mouth opens and a generous bit of spittle flies out at me. As I wipe the disgusting spray from my face, several of my captors erupt in laughter. I repeat the command with more intensity and the camel kneels, then sits for mounting. Whereas the other boys ride two to an animal, I ride alone. With no one with whom I can converse, I bounce along in those first few days on the caravan trail north, oblivious to the odd, jolting gait of a dromedary camel, wondering about my future, but mostly I think about Jamila. How am I to see her again? How?

I begin to wish I had paid more attention to the curses Gaspar dispensed to his customers. Oh, I would enjoy turning the tables on him with one of his own curses, but how would that help me? The money is gone. Gaspar kept it. *Damn him.* How am I to start once again earning money so that I can buy my own freedom? And from whom—who owns me now? And if it were possible to secure my freedom, how many years would it take? Surely Jamila's father would not allow her to wait for one who had disappeared into the night. She herself would probably lose faith. How could I blame her?

No, I know that I don't have years. I must escape—*I must!* Once I make friends with the camel I call Prickly, I briefly consider using him to make my escape. But it is not an option, I realize, for most of the other camels are younger and quicker—and once caught, I could expect to be immediately executed.

My wrists are tightly tied all day except when I am allowed to eat or given time to relieve myself. I must make my move at one of these times, but I know it would do no good on the route, for the desert landscape is unforgiving even if I should manage to elude my captors. I will wait until we come to a city where I can lose myself long enough that they will give up the search.

I am not allowed to communicate with the other young men. I wonder if they know more than I—if they know their—*our* fate. I wish I could ask them, but we are prevented from speaking to one another. It seems clear we will be sold yet again into slavery—but to whom? For what purpose? One unspeakable fear persists …

I calm myself thinking of Jamila, remembering our first touch, our exploring hands, her smile as we lay together, the dotted night sky above us. I have no doubts that she sits under the same stars as I at night, thinking of me. Somehow I will find my way back to her.

Besides passing the Roman forts, the caravan comes upon several of the cathedrals that dot the Way of the Sea, and it is no surprise that we do not seek shelter there. The monks would surely question the Persians about their cache of young boys.

But then, one day we halt at a little cathedral and a run-down abbey. As we are ordered to dismount, two monks come hurrying out to meet the Persians with friendly smiles and lively talk, taking no notice, it seems, of those with pained faces and bound hands. I seem to attract the attention of one of the monks who comes scurrying over and takes my camel whip. Still in a resting position, Prickly turns his head toward the stranger, lets out the extended grunt of a typical complaining camel, and finishes by releasing his spray onto the man's bald head. I start to laugh but catch myself. The monk wipes away the saliva, all the while assessing me. As if in approval, he nods now, indicating for me to dismount.

In short order, we are gathered together and ushered into the stone abbey. I find the air inside rank, but—in comparison to the desert—cool. Each of us is unceremoniously pushed into a little cell. Mine features a monk's cot with a mattress of old straw and for that I give thanks. Once the door is shut, the grinding of gears in the lock does not surprise me.

Soon, one of the monks delivers a bowl of boiled wheat. A *large* bowl, I note with amazement. Arms free now, I try to detain him and engage him in conversation, but the monk's features go mean and a single hand gesture silences me. I take to the bowl with a real appetite. A little later I cry myself to sleep. Always in company of my captors before now, I had not the luxury of venting my emotions. Crying, I find, is even more comforting than a full belly.

In the early hours of the morning I am awakened by bone-chilling, unearthly screams coming from some other area of the abbey. I jump up and go to the door and listen as they cleave the air again, wave upon wave. They sound like the extended maddened mating shrieks of the female red fox. But I know better. They belong to one of the youngest of the captive Egyptian boys. The screams are chilling and once incised into my ears, not to be forgotten.

Then comes silence, an eerie stillness followed by footsteps in the hall, a door opening, a scuffle of sorts, and—half an hour later—another series of shrill, ungodly cries reverberating through the halls.

And now I know what is happening, what will happen to me. Oh, it's not something I hadn't thought of before. As children we were cautioned to stay close to home because young boys were sometimes captured by slavers and often enough subjected to the cutting.

I sit trembling—no tears now—thinking of my Jamila and awaiting my turn.

26

THEODORA SAT ERECT AND ALERT on her dromedary as the caravan snaked its way north through Phoenicia to Tyre, a city built on an island that skirted the coast. She thought it very beautiful with its palm trees, sycamores, and poplars, as well as its Roman architectural influences such as roads, monuments, and aqueducts. One day she visited the Hippodrome of Tyre after the racing fans had left, finding it even larger and more impressive than the Constantinople amphitheater in which she had danced with her sisters all those years ago. The memory of that day, the day that she and her family had been cruelly rejected by the Greens only to be embraced by the Blues, made her heart beat fast. She missed Constantinople all the more.

To her disappointment, the traders bade goodbye and moved on without her and the little troupe of Blues. She regretted now her own earning power, for the Blues meant to keep her there as long as she could keep the gold coins flowing in, and everyone, it seemed, wanted to see first-hand this actress from The City. It was a fortnight before they forged ahead, sights set on Antioch.

Another fortnight found the little group—unescorted now—coming upon that city, the "Queen of the East." It had prospered for hundreds of years—despite frequent and sometimes devastating earthquakes—because of its position on the River Orontes and at the junction of north-south and east-west caravan trade routes. Theodora found that she could not dispute the widespread opinion that its size and wealth was surpassed only by Alexandria and Constantinople. Surrounding lands were lushly fertile, and before passing through the city gates, the little retinue mixed with crowds of pilgrims moving through the Grove of Daphne, gazing at its bay laurel trees, cypresses, fountains, baths, gardens, statuary, and colonnaded temples. All of Roman inspiration, Theodora realized. From Constantinople to the Pentapolis and now through every step of her pilgrimage along the Levant, she observed how the Roman world stretched far and wide.

"Don't let the holy ones fool you," Cletus said to Theodora. "This is no holy city. It is a city of trade and commerce and people here have more money than they can spend but they do try, and they spend it on their pleasure."

"At the theater, too, I presume?" she asked.

"Yes, Macedonia is the owner of the most significant one—The Rose and the Thorn—and I can say that she turns a healthy profit."

"A woman?"

"A siren is more like it—or sometimes a shrew." He laughed. "Based on what we've seen so far of your audiences, I'd wager she'll try to keep you on two months at least."

Theodora gave Cletus a sharp look. "Our agreement was one."

"True enough—I'm just giving you fair warning she'll want more.—Look, see that column?"

They had just passed into a small forum on the way to the theater. Theodora took note of the well-weathered gray marble structure.

"That," Cletus said, "is renowned to have been the column of St. Simeon the Stylite."

"Really? Oh, he is widely imitated in Constantinople by men who perch like pigeons on columns all about the capital." Theodora moved close to the column. "How odd—the lower part of the column seems eaten away by something."

Cletus laughed. "Souvenirs those missing pieces are—chipped off and taken either by pilgrims or traders of saints' relics."

As they resumed their walk, Theodora returned to an old subject. "Cletus, you *will* aid me in finding passage on a ship to The City. I'll have the money."

Cletus bent over in a mock bow. "Whenever milady wishes."

Theodora gave a little forced laugh. She had hoped to return to Constantinople a true lady so that Cletus's flippant remark stung now like vinegar on an open wound.

"Ah, so this is the famous one," Macedonia said, her dark eyes—heavily made up with kohl—widening in a stage expression. Her hennaed hair framed her face like a halo of fire. "Welcome to Antioch, my dear! We are *so* in need of some new novelty here. The rich are ever bored and anxious for the new."

Theodora managed a smile. The woman reminded her of Miranda. A poor omen. "You expected me?"

"Oh, yes. News among the Blues travels fast.—I do hope the journey thus far has been such that you've forgotten your debacle with Hecebolus at the Pentapolis. And losing your friend, too? Irene, was it? Perhaps Timothy gave you some wise consolation?"

Theodora stood in the doorway of the theater office as if struck dumb. How did this woman know these things? Oh, it was likely she knew she had been in the care of Timothy. But the other—about events at the Pentapolis? She had not confided these things to Cletus and the others. "I thank you for your hospitality," she said, finding her voice. She was certain of one thing— that the woman had been quick to reveal what she knew in order to establish for herself a position of power over another actress of some reputation.

"Now, come with me. Let me show you to your dressing room." The tall Macedonia whisked past Theodora, who squared her shoulders and followed in the wake of the woman's embroidered stola, scents of powder and a musky perfume of cloves, vanilla, and cinnamon. Still dirty from the road, she steeled herself now as the woman provided her with a little tour of The Rose and the Thorn, the sultry voice declaiming the advantages of her theater.

The chamber allotted Theodora with its dressing table and sleeping couch was spare, but experience had taught her that it was more than most actors enjoyed. Someone had been put out to make room for her. "This will do nicely," she said.

"Good!"

Her eyes fell now upon a stola laid across the well-worn and once-upon white couch. She walked over and fingered the silky material.

"I left that for you, Theodora. I know others close to you call you *Thea*. May I do so, as well?"

Theodora nodded, again wondering again about her source of knowledge. For now, however, the stola held her transfixed.

"You'll look lovely in it," Macedonia said.

"But it's—it's—"

"Purple, yes."

"I can't wear that. No one is allowed to wear the purple."

Macedonia giggled. "You're not in Constantinople—not yet, anyway."

"But it's the imperial purple."

"Yes, and it comes from Tyre, where you stayed not long ago. It's extracted from the murex shellfish there. Didn't you know? The cloth of that wondrous color is somewhat plentiful here, and a few people do dare to wear it."

"Do you?"

"Yes, I do."

"Just the same, *I* will not wear it." Theodora carefully picked up the fine stola and handed it to Macedonia. "It has a lovely feel to it, I will say."

"It is up to you. I'm not afraid of a law born in Constantinople. There are two dozen other stolas in that wardrobe for you to choose from." Macedonia tossed the garment over her shoulder. "Of course, I do have some connections there that keep me safe. We'll discuss that another time. Now, they say that your performances thus far along the Way of the Sea have been well attended—but tame."

"Tame?"

"Yes. They say they lack your signature ... *verve*, shall we say."

"I was very young in Constantinople."

"Indeed? And foolish, you mean?—Well, just the same, it is *that* Theodora the audience will be anticipating. You must uncork the bottle and let her out. I want you to do *Leda and the Swan*."

Theodora swallowed hard. "I'll need four or five days."

"Three!"

Theodora gave a slow nod. "I'll have Cletus send up my satchel."

"Satchel?—Did you think I meant you to *stay* here? Oh, no! You're to be a guest at my villa! I've already had your things sent—and there are quarters there for your bodyguards."

Theodora was about to correct her regarding her relationship with the Blues, but on second thought, she had to admit that they actually were acting as her bodyguards. And one of them was passing along information to Macedonia, this much she knew.

I come down into the subterranean chamber struggling and kicking out like the others must have done—and to the same end. I am ordered to strip and when I resist, my tunic is torn away.

I am strapped in a spread-eagle fashion to the top of a large, bloodstained table. The wetness against my skin repulses me. My Persian captors move away, leaving the task to the two monks who, of course, I know by now are not real monks.

Time seems to slow, stop.

One of the faces—hard and gray like stone—looms over me. The two communicate in their Persian dialect. I am too frightened to follow it, but their murmuring tone is purposeful, efficient, emotionless.

I feel hands on me, down below. My heart surges, its hammering threatening to break through the wall of my chest. I vow to myself to hold my tongue. I will not call out. I struggle to lift my head, and before a strip of cloth covers my eyes, I catch a glimpse of the curved knife.

I feel now a tightening, a great and terrible tightening. I pray to Mithras, the god of my parents. I pray to the Christian god, as well, but because my faith in any god is weak, I am thinking only of Jamila when the pain comes.

I am unable to keep my vow of silence. My screams erupt as loud as those of the boys who came before.

27

MACEDONIA'S VILLA WAS LOCATED IN the city, and like most of Antioch's architecture it was Roman, complete with a well-planted atrium and colonnaded garden. Theodora remarked that it was a home fitting for a nobleman.

"Oh, it was indeed a nobleman's, my dear," Macedonia intoned. "A senator's, in fact. One who got himself into a bit of trouble."

"He was exiled?"

Macedonia nodded. "During your stay you'll probably feel the earth rumbling a bit—we get more than our share of quakes. But in recent history we've had no quake greater than that which erupted after Emperor Justin tossed out our Patriarch Severus, Timothy's friend. Strange timing, you might say. You've met them both—Severus and Timothy?"

"I have."

Macedonia went on to explain how the persecution of the Monophysites created a kind of civil war in Antioch. "I don't know what your religious beliefs might be ... perhaps Timothy tried to convert you?"

"No, he did not." Theodora instinctively knew to be cautious. It occurred to her now that Macedonia was mining for information. To what end? "He merely befriended me. As an actress, I've had little interest in religion."

"I understand. When you see just how hedonistic this city is, you'll wonder that religion affected anyone, but it did, and it has. So I must warn you, it's most unhealthy to sympathize with the Monophysites. There are still some in the city, but they've burrowed underground. Oh, and after the purge, people were so relieved and so tired of religious issues that revenue at theaters and pleasure houses piled upward like mountains of gold." Macedonia laughed.

"Then, again, the fact that we live in daily threat of the very ground opening beneath us leads people to live to their fullest every day."

"So Justin has ruled with his sword against this doctrine?"

"He has—and his sword is his nephew, Justinian.—I'll leave you to rest now. Remember, *Leda and the Swan*." Macedonia started to leave but when she reached the door, she half-turned and tossed off a comment like an aside in a play. "Oh, by the way," she said, "my Blues had news from the Governor's House at the Pentapolis." She paused for two beats, saying at last, "They say that Pythia woman mysteriously died, not long after you left."

Theodora felt her body stiffen as she fended off a tremble that ran through her. She managed a shocked expression and was searching for an appropriate line when Macedonia shot her a final glance and glided out of the room. Still, Theodora could not breathe easily. Macedonia was an actress, like her, not some gullible playgoer. Had she seen through her spontaneous acting? Does she know more about the death, she wondered. *Is she trying to draw me out?*

Theodora settled into her capacious room off the atrium, where a maid had been assigned to her needs. She bathed, ate a little meal of bread and fish, and slept off a great fatigue.

Three days were spent in preparation. The performances here could not be as carelessly and lazily done as some of the previous ones. On the third night when the maid awakened her from a nap, she felt refreshed and prepared to take the stage. That night, it seemed to Theodora that all three hundred thousand Antioch citizens had mobbed the theater. They had not seen living pictures before, and for the past two days Macedonia had sent out criers in the afternoon announcing Theodora's first performance at The Rose and the Thorn. It was standing room only. How would they react to these still pictures captured from mythology?

Theodora performed three multi-part vignettes, culminating in the requested *Leda and the Swan* for which she wore merely a length of translucent gauze wrapped about her in only the most necessary places. Finding someone to play Zeus, who would transform himself into a swan, was difficult on such short notice, and the amateurish actor they hired overdid it completely, moving his hastily constructed wings in a likely attempt to upstage Theodora and sending little flurries of feathers into the front rows. But the people hardly noticed the failings. They had come to see Theodora, and judging by the thunderous applause and cheers, her relatively modest rendition did not disappoint.

Theodora was relieved when Macedonia did not complain about the tameness of the performance, and as the days passed the two created eight new three-vignette series of living pictures and grew to be friends. Theodora put aside the notion that Macedonia might betray her. Or, if she had been laying a plot of some kind, Theodora had proved her worth—in gold. One night, after they had tried out a new performance, *The Three Fates*, Macedonia came backstage all smiles and sat nearby. "That was lovely, Thea! Just lovely! And your little plan for the end—to have Clotho actually *use her scissors* to cut the thread of the man's life—why it was pure genius! Everyone had come to expect not a single movement in your pictures. The crowd—a full house again—let out one huge gasp!"

Theodora sat at her dressing table removing her makeup and basking in the praise. Her stay at Antioch was proving quite delightful, and yet her quest to return to Constantinople stayed uppermost in her mind.

Finished with her task, she pivoted in her chair to face Macedonia. At that moment Macedonia's face underwent a metamorphosis as great as switching out the mask of comedy for that of tragedy. "There's a man here who wishes to meet you, Thea."

Theodora's heart froze, faltered. *What man?* Had Haji followed her from Alexandria? Or worse, had Hecebolus sent someone seeking justice—or revenge—for Pythia's death? Her pulse picked up in triple time. "Who?" she heard herself ask.

"Sergius Vitalis."

Theodora blinked. "Who?"

"He's a senator here in Antioch."

"Oh." A floodgate of relief opened up within Theodora's center. "An admirer?"

"Yes, dear. Will you see him?"

"Entertain him, you mean? *Privately?* I told you, Macedonia, that I no longer attempt to please patrons after the show."

"And I haven't asked you—until now. This would be a significant favor for me."

"Ah, so you're calling in favors in return for the hospitality you've shown me?"

Macedonia gave a dismissive wave of her heavily ringed hand. "Don't take it that way. And you need not let the assignation play out fully. Only ..."

"Only what?"

"Ply him with a few drinks. Let him talk. Enough drinks and you won't have to worry about his taking advantage."

"Talk? Talk about what?"

"Anything at first. What he thinks of your performances. His villa, should he take you there. But eventually bring the conversation around to religion, will you? If he doesn't talk about the Monophysites first, bring up your stay with Timothy."

"Spy?" Theodora let out a little gasp. "You want me to *spy* on him?"

Macedonia smiled sweetly. "It wouldn't be hard for you. You're clever, I've seen it. It's not such a terrible thing, being a spy."

"Is that ... is that what you are, a spy?"

"As a woman and as a theater owner and actress, I can provide better and more current information than any single Blue here in Antioch."

"To whom?"

"To Justinian himself, the emperor's nephew!"

Theodora sat stunned. It came to her now that the "connections" Macedonia spoke of consisted of a network of Blues who were spies. No wonder the woman knew everything about her since her days at the Pentapolis.

"Oh, come now, as good as the theater business is, do you think I could afford my villa and a staff of sixty without some other means? Justinian deeded it to me."

"And its former owner?"

"A Roman—and a covert Monophysite."

"He lost it for his beliefs?—You reported him?"

"I was but a little cog in his wheel of destiny."

"A set answer, that!—So, you have it in your power to point a finger and ..."

"A man disappears at a single word—Magick! It's a heady experience, I must say, to wield such influence in a world thought owned by men. You know, when you do return to your beloved capital, I can send with you a letter to Justinian."

"A letter?"

"He's likely to follow his uncle to the throne, but even as his nephew, he could find you a position at the palace in the blink of a frog's eye."

"Ah, so he's a frog, is he?" The two shared a laugh, then fell silent.

Macedonia waited for an answer.

Instead of a villa, Theodora would have access to the throne of the Emperor of the New Rome. It was a dizzying notion. And a ridiculous one, too, she thought. Moments elapsed.

"Theodora?" Macedonia pressed.

Theodora looked up. "I'm tired tonight, Macedonia." She turned now to face her dressing table. "I don't care to see anyone. I have no wish to be a spy—here or in The City."

Macedonia sighed and stood to leave the chamber. "If you should change your mind—"

"I think not."

In the little gold-framed mirror on the table, Theodora saw Macedonia nod in acceptance and make her exit, closing the door behind her.

Theodora was left facing the mirror with lines that drew down her mouth. She could only wonder if the days of hospitality in Antioch were over—and if she herself had foolishly aborted her chance to gain a new start in the capital.

And now there are ten. One of the boys bled during the night. No one tended to him because his calls for help were lost among several other desperate pleas. The body is being removed when I wake up from a sleep that failed to extinguish the pain. A number of the others are moaning or crying. We are housed in the large underground chamber where the cuttings occurred. It is no doubt easier for the two butchers to care for us in a single ward. Given the pain and humiliation, attempts to escape are unlikely. We are now allowed to talk and commiserate among ourselves. At fifteen, I am the oldest, but I know very little about what is happening to us.

It is the eleven-year-old boy on the cot next to mine, Zuka, who provides information. "We've been sold," he says. "And we'll be sold again. We're quite valuable now, you know, Stephen."

"How so?" I can scarcely believe the boy's blasé attitude.

"We'll be taken and traded to wealthy families. If we are lucky enough to have masters that don't beat us, we'll do well."

"I wanted to buy my freedom."

"You can put that thought away.—Other traders might have done worse, you know."

"What do you mean?"

"Other dealers cut—everything."

I thought that nothing could shock me now—but this knowledge does.

My stomach contracts and threatens to push up what little there is to vomit. Terrified that such a physical exertion would bring new pain to the wound, I manage to overcome the impulse.

During the next two days, two more boys die. The monks and traders are anything but happy, and yet they take the deaths in stride.

"It's to be expected," Zuka says. "Sometimes more die than live, I've heard. But I'm going to live, I can tell you. And if you watch the wound and make sure the tar plug doesn't get dislodged, you'll be fine, too. If it comes undone, make sure to tell someone right away before it starts to smell and you see the yellow puss. If that happens, you're done for."

"Did your family sell you, Zuka?"

Zuka nods. "Too many children. My family is very poor." He shrugs, as if his parents' decision meant nothing more than sending him out to apply for work. "I didn't mind. I have a chance at a better life than my brothers have." He chuckles. "It was a good thing for me that they are all rather plain to look at.—But then, my name means *lucky*."

"Does it?" I ask, dumbfounded by his outlook.

"Oh, yes."

I descend deep into despair. My life has been irreparably altered. Shattered, like a vase shaken from a pedestal and smashed into so many pieces no glue could salvage it. When the first boy died, I felt envious of his escape. I curse myself, wishing for death. How am I to go through life as one of the cut ones? How? There would be no marriage for me. There would be no Jamila. She was lost to me. Even if I should be given the opportunity, I would not write to her. Not ever. It would be better if she thinks me dead.

And I wish for death. With all of my heart and soul I want to be the next one to die. I think of my own parents. They could not have guessed this fate lay in store for me. At least I pray so.

As the next one dies, and the one after that, the desire for my own death fades. The boys lay pretty as dolls, and just as still, before they are carted away. What is death, after all? I wonder. What happens when the flame of life is extinguished? To what am I wishing myself? That great unknown gives me pause.

And I have another thought that takes root. To die and be buried by these Persians without a prayer or a tear—I couldn't bear it. I will not suffer such shame. I will not allow them their mindless chatter as they cover forever the remnants of a life they had snuffed out. Silly thoughts, perhaps, for I would be dead. But they are my thoughts, nonetheless.

Zuka's optimism and encouragement do me good, but it is my desire to somehow triumph over these despicable traders that makes me begin to wish myself to wellness. I vow to create a life for myself in this world. But in those moments before sleep when I cannot help but think of Jamila and a marriage that might have been, I grieve for the wife and children denied to me.

A fortnight after the cutting, the little caravan sets out for Antioch. Prior to leaving I thought I was receiving special attention by the monks and Persians, but now I become convinced of it. I have been given one of the choice, most gentle, camels and a saddlecloth softer than any other. We leave behind the butcher-monks—to other customers, no doubt—but my wound is inspected by one of the traders more often than I would have wished. The Persians see that every so often I am given an extra ration of food, and if I call for a drink, I am well attended, whereas the other boys are often ignored.

One evening under the stars, I ask Zuka if he has noticed the attention.

He has. "Well, you are older, Stephen, and perhaps better looking." He laughed. "Notice, I merely said *perhaps*."

"Why should that matter? You can scrub stone steps, milk a goat, or kill a chicken as well as I."

"True, but I may be thought too young to please in the bedchamber."

I feel the blood draining away from my face. The stars grow more distant and blurred. I have overheard little snatches of jokes the traders make that—placed in this context—now make sense. They snicker, sometimes affording me insipid, sidelong looks. Certain masters *do* use cut ones for their pleasure, I realize. I feel ill. I want to run to the latrine they dug earlier and give up my supper, but I choose not to move or speak. I am stricken with fear that I might be reduced to playing the role of such a servant—and with humiliation that a boy four years younger had to tell me.

28

AS THE DAYS WENT BY and Theodora was not asked again to play the espial, she breathed a sigh of relief. It was not that she doubted her own acumen at securing information or that she cared particularly about the would-be victim. What worked at her conscience was the fact that bringing to light hidden Monophysites seemed a terrible disloyalty to Father Timothy and to Father Severus, who had once been patriarch of Antioch. While she would admit to anyone that her own religious theory was once shallow, she now gave the benefit of the doubt to the Monophysites, along with a devotional loyalty—inspired by her time in Alexandria—that was deep as the Middle Sea.

Theodora stayed at The Rose and the Thorn through much of the summer, working hard and filling the theater's coffers to the brim. She was ever alert, however, to the waning days of good sailing weather, and when her final week was agreed upon, Macedonia volunteered to pay her complete ship's passage.

"I have the money," Theodora said. "Other than providing Cletus and the other Blues with their share, I've spent little along the way."

"Just the same," Macedonia pressed, "I wish to pay it."

At that moment Theodora made a decision that surprised even herself. "I've decided to go overland."

"Overland!" Macedonia looked aghast. "Through all of Anatolia?—You can't be serious!"

"I am! I have seen so much of the world already, Macedonia. So much. While traveling has not been easy, and at times I thought I'd die of the heat or lack of good water, I will carry what I've seen always within me. If I complete the journey by land, how many women can ever say they saw as much of the world as I?—Indeed, how many *men*?"

"You surprise me, Theodora. First, your fondness for the Monophysites—oh, don't think I didn't take note. It's my second business, you know." Macedonia winked. "And now this desire to be a new Odysseus!—Listen to me, Thea, if you take the overland route, chances are good that you will never see your capital again. It's an arduous trip and fraught with dangers. I won't allow it. I'll provide you with the value of a ship's passage in gold. A cargo ship leaves for Constantinople nearly every other day."

Theodora nodded reluctantly. "Macedonia ... it's about this Monophysite business—"

Macedonia raised her finger in a shushing motion. "You needn't worry. The secret will not follow you to the capital. And if anyone ever raises an accusation against you, send word to me. I have Blues everywhere who will do my bidding."

"Thank you."

"One more thing, I should tell you about a man who came looking for you."

"From the Patriarch? Timothy?"

"No—from Hecebolus. It was about the death of Pythia. They determined that she was poisoned."

Theodora felt an icy hand grasp her heart. Perhaps a beat too late, she found just the right stage face, one of innocence and surprise. "And?"

Macedonia smiled. "Do you recall my story about the former owner of my villa?"

Theodora gasped. "Magick?"

"Yes, dearest." Macedonia snapped her fingers. "Magick!"

That night the backstage scenario replayed in Theodora's head. Clearly, Macedonia had seen through Theodora's acting upon hearing about Pythia. More than that, Macedonia no doubt had specific information about the nature of Pythia's death from her network of spies and instead of allowing access to the man sent by Hecebolus, she proved herself to be a protector, one unafraid to go to great lengths, even murder.

On the day of departure, Macedonia came into Theodora's room and placed a rolled parchment upon the satchel.

Theodora had an idea what it was but gave a questioning glance nonetheless.

"It's a letter of introduction, my dear." Macedonia's eyebrows lifted. "To Justinian."

"Macedonia, what could I ever expect to come of that? I do appreciate the gesture—"

"Gesture! You think it a worthless gesture! It is not, I can tell you.—Yes, even the emperor's nephew owes me a favor or two I can call in at will."

"Macedonia. I didn't mean to imply—"

"Good! With your talents, Thea, you would make a perfect palace spy. Now, take the letter and be gone before I tear it to shreds. Cletus and the others are waiting downstairs to accompany you to the docks. And for God's sake, remember that Justinian carries out Justin's policy and that Justin intends to root out the Monophysites."

Christ's sake is more accurate is what Theodora thought, but she realized that Macedonia's pride had been injured. She walked over to her now, a smile of repentance on her face, and kissed her lightly on the cheek.

The ground shook only once during her stay in Antioch—on the very day of her departure. "The city is grumbling her goodbye," Cletus said with a sad laugh before he and his fellow Blues wished her well. Theodora looked at the ship that would take her on the final leg of her quest home and drew herself up, fully aware that a different fate might have befallen her were it not for the Blues. Oh, she knew that one—or all of them—had been reporting her activities regularly to Macedonia, probably since leaving Alexandria, but no ill had come of it. She moved closer to them, heart expanding. She put a forefinger to her lips and pressed it to the lips of each of the five Blues. Out of fear of spilling tears, she dared no eye contact with Cletus, who came last. Wordlessly, she took her satchel from him, pivoted, and moved toward the gangplank.

Once she was on her way, the scroll bearing Macedonia's recommendation placed at the bottom of the satchel, she gave it no thought at all.

Too late, she realized she had meant to tell Macedonia about a disturbing dream she had had the night before. She had dreamt that upon her return, Satan had taken her up to the tallest of Constantinople's seven hills. There, emulating his temptation to Christ, he had offered her the whole city if she would be his.

She shivered to think of it. She struggled to recall her reply to the devil—but she could not and a tremor ran through her again.

How odd, I think, that Theodora and I have a shared memory of the ground rumbling in Antioch on that very day. The Roman structures blurred slightly in their shaking and dust rose up from the roads as if horse-specters were passing. It scared me well enough, but I tried to put on a brave face for the benefit of—but I am getting ahead of myself.

On the day after our arrival in Antioch, another of our number succumbs to infection so that there are five of us now who are bedded down in a large second-story room in a nicely appointed villa. In the morning we find new sandals, decent tunics, and a fine meal of fried fish and boiled wheat awaiting us. By the end of the week, the other four have been paraded before buyers and sold.

"I fetched a good price," Zuka says, returning to our quarters in order to fetch his little bag of worldly goods. His smile is forced. "The man seems very rich and will treat me well—I trust."

"Why is it I have not been shown to buyers, Zuka—like you and the others?"

"I told you. They have plans for you and no doubt will place a higher price on you than on any of us. You *are* the best looking, you know. I guess I may as well say it." Zuka reaches up and gives me a kiss on the cheek. "Goodbye, Stephen—and good fortune to you."

The kiss comes as a surprise and I put my hand to the little remaining wetness on my cheek as I watch my young friend—my only friend—take his leave. I find my voice only after I hear the scuff of retreating sandals in the hallway, and it is too late for Zuka to hear the weak-voiced wish I choke out. "Be well, my friend."

I lie awake that night, certain that I will never see Zuka again. How strange it is, I think, how people pass through your life playing out meaningful roles—only to disappear forever. It is then that I think of my family—my father, brothers, sisters, and mother, my dearest mother—and the tears come on suddenly and with force.

Two days go by. My tears dry, but the uncertainty of my future holds me on edge. Then, on the third day, I am summoned to a room below. One of my captors—Bruno—pushes me toward a desk, turns and leaves the room.

Behind the desk sits a second man whom I've not seen before. He is well-fed, and his yellow dalmatic is impeccable, his nails well-filed. "Ah, the clever one," he says in Syriac. "Sit there—have you been well taken care of?"

It is strange to hear my native tongue again. I take two beats to answer in the affirmative—and in Syriac. Despite his politeness, I take an immediate dislike to him. My heart accelerates. Is this to be my owner?

"You know Persian, too, yes?"

"Yes."

"And Latin and Greek?"

I nod.

"And you can write Latin and Greek?"

"Yes, some. My master has taught me."

"You will show me." The man stands and goes to a case with criss-cross shelves that houses a myriad of scrolls.

I realize for the first time that this is a library and that all the walls are covered with such cases, floor to ceiling. Gaspar had told me about such rooms.

The man returns, unfolds a new parchment on the desk, stands to my side and thrusts a kalamos into my hand. "Write in Latin."

"What am I to write?"

His hand drops onto my shoulder. "It doesn't matter. Just write!"

He leans in close. I think of Zuka's surmise that my looks might be meant for the bedchamber of a rich Antioch patrician. The stink of garlic is strong, my fear stronger. Caught up in a moment of panic, I begin to write the opening line of one of Gaspar's binding spells.

The man pulls at the parchment, the small black eyes taking it in.

Good God! What possessed me to write *that*? The man will think I am placing the spell on him. I wait for him to erupt in anger and steel myself against a blow that might be delivered at any moment.

The man shoves the parchment toward me. "In Greek now!"

I take the reed pen in hand and transcribe the lines into Greek. When I finish, I sit back a little in my chair.

The man snaps up the parchment. A long moment passes. "They are the same?" he asks at last.

Now I understand. The man is unaware that I have written the beginning of a binding curse. He can read neither language. "Yes," I say, "exactly the same."

"You have a good hand, Stephen. Your interview is tomorrow. For your sake—as well as mine—you are to make a good impression." It's nothing less than an order. "You are dismissed."

I follow my Persian captor up to the now-empty eunuch quarters. Clever?—I am not so clever. I suppress a bitter laugh. The man whom I thought to be my prospective owner is merely the middleman merchant, a broker of slaves, of eunuchs.

My stomach tightens. So I am to repeat this process on the morrow. The sense of dread overwhelms me. I sleep little, the faces of the other boys, now sold off or dead, incised in my mind. Before dawn, the nameless middleman appears, instructing me on grooming and providing a clean brown dalmatic.

I am taken again to the library and nudged gently toward a writing table where a man steps down from a stool and waits.

"This is the boy Stephen," the Persian says, poking me in the back.

I move forward, bow. When I stand erect, I see that he is taking measure of me, allowing a minute for me to do the same. His skin tone is similar to mine, but a long, curved nose rules him out as a fellow Syrian. He is slight of build and seems frail at first, but there is spryness about him and a decided air of authority. I guess him to be close to his fortieth year. His dalmatic and sandals are brown and unassuming.

"Ah, Stephen," he says, "a healthy specimen it seems."

I am tongue-tied.

The man nods at the Persian as if in dismissal. Soundlessly, he leaves the room.

My anxiety increases. What does this one want of me?

He smiles. "I am told you are good at languages," he says. His voice is—different—that of a tenor, crisp, rich, and sonorous. His voice and something about his demeanor tells me he has been cut. He is like me.

I nod. A bit of courage returns. "I am—somewhat trained."

"Persian, I'm told. And Latin and Greek."

"Yes," I say, expecting the same kind of test the Persian had given me. A flicker of hope ignites now. Is this the reason I am of interest to him? In my years with the Persian I have learned how to judge people. I sense that this man will treat me fairly. I want to impress him, praying he will take me a far distance from my captors.

"Armenian?"

I'm certain that the blood is draining from my face as my hope dissipates. I shake my head.

"I am Armenian," he announces.

I attempt a smile. Fear rises that I have failed the test. I am not enough of a scholar to his taste.

He draws in breath, taking a long look at me.

"Do you wish for me to write in the other languages?" I pray that I am not sounding desperate.

"No," he says. His tone is firm.

My heart races, as does my mind. "I can learn your language," I offer.

"Indeed, but there is little use for it in Constantinople."

I am not sure how to react.

"You've heard of it?"

I nod.

"Well, now you'll see it. It's a wonder—Go put together your things."

"What?" I am certain I look thunderstruck.

"Surely you have another tunic at least." He claps his hands now, and the Persian appears, bowing obsequiously.

It just takes a nod from the man in the brown dalmatic and the deal is done. As I am being escorted back to my cell to collect my few things, he calls to me: "My name is Narses, Stephen."

It would be some little while before I learn, to my surprise, that he himself is unschooled.

PART FOUR

PART FOUR

29

MY HEART THUMPS HEAVILY IN the early fall of 520 as I board the *Sea-Goddess*, a merchant ship. The spaces between the beats fill with fear. I have never trusted my life to a vessel that rides the seas. Gaspar was deathly afraid of sailing so that we had always travelled overland.

The *Sea-Goddess* is fitted out with two masts; the one at mid-ship holds a large square sail while the other, at the bow, supports a smaller sail, also square. A stout hull contains wood, cereals, olive oil, and wine meant for Constantinople. I count more than a hundred oars manned by a sun-darkened crew.

The small cabin on the second deck that my new master has taken for us is decently appointed with two cots, a table and two chairs, but it is the deference that the captain, merchant, and crew show him that confirms for me that Narses is a man of some means and stature.

It is afternoon on our first day at sea, and I am congratulating myself on my seafaring endurance. We are seated at the table and Narses is questioning me about my life with my parents when the ship plows head-on into what he calls a squall. Up and down, down and up, the ship heaves, lurching to the right, then to the left, the cabin timbers creaking. My stomach follows suit.

"Why, you're as white as a bleached sail," Narses says, as if amused. "It's your first voyage, so I'm not surprised. You have yet to earn your sea legs."

I'm unable to reply. My roiling insides threaten to erupt. A gagging sensation takes hold. Using the table top, I push myself up and stumble the few feet to my cot. I sit at the side of it.

"It will do you no good to lie down, Stephen," he says. "And even a swab will hold you in poor regard if he has to clean the planking in here of your stinking spew."

I look at Narses in horror.

"Go up on deck. Do you remember where the sternpost is?"

I nod. A bitter fluid is filling my throat, rising, rising.

Narses is all soberness now. "Go!" he shouts, pointing toward the cabin door.

I fly off my cot, throw back the door, and rush up the steep ladder-like steps. I turn toward the stern and climb the little ramp to the sternpost where it is situated beneath the ship's carved ornament of a swan. I am no sooner at the balustrade than the contents of my stomach—egg, gruel, and bread—spill into the sea. When I think I am finished, another spasm at my middle disgorges the last of the bitter bile. White-knuckled, I stare into the rocking ship's turbid wake, sick and mewling like a poisoned puppy, wondering how I had come to this, fearful of where this ship—where life—is taking me.

My gut continues to convulse, triggering the gagging reflex. I hang over the side, retching, but my insides are empty. At last, my stomach settles although the sea keeps churning. As I stand, a salty sea-mist lashes my face, aiding me in wiping mucus from my mouth and chin. I open my mouth for the gathering drops to wash out the foul taste.

"Are you all right, sailor?" The voice is high, shrill, and yet musical in the loud gale.

I spin around, nearly certain I am being mocked by the young swab who empties our privy bucket and sees to our food and comfort. I am in no mood and perfectly ready to strike him down, no matter the consequences.

But there before me now, in a wet and dark hooded cloak stands the most beautiful woman I have ever seen. She is laughing, her deep-set black eyes sparkling, droplets from the mist striking her face like liquid gold. Suddenly, I realize the droplets are merely reflecting her aura, which is coming through to me with no effort on my part. And it is gold, metallic gold.

My legs buckle, my heart gives.

I stare, blinking against the sea-spray—and the thought that this is but a vision that will dissipate with the mist. Of course, she is real and I feel a fool and must look like one, too.

The vision steps forward. "Here," she says, taking something from her inner pocket, "chew on this."

I gawk at the piece of root she holds out to me. "What is it?"

"Ginger. It should settle your stomach."

"What's left of it, you mean." I reach for it. "You've taken some?"

"I have. I wish I had had some on the voyage out of The City."

"Constantinople?"

She nods. "Oh, I managed all right even through some squalls worse than this, but—others were not so lucky.—I do think the sea is settling and we'll find our balance soon."

I nod. Wanting to please the lady, I begin to chew. The salty sea-spray coming at us adds tanginess to the sweetness of the root. I am searching for words, conversation. "Was it a merchant ship, as well?"

"Indeed not! It was a trireme. A vessel that would make this ship look like a toy."

"A trireme?"

"A warship, a massive warship with three levels of rowers."

I'm impressed. In my travels with Gaspar along the Way of the Sea we did sight on occasion such huge vessels. I would wonder what they carried.

"It was government business," she explains.

I nod toward the unseen shore behind us. "In Antioch?"

"No," she replies in a clipped manner, leaving no room to pursue the topic. Her eyes suddenly narrow. "You're Syrian, yes?"

"I am."

Her lips part, transitioning into a smile. "You look it. I am half-Syrian, but this was my first visit to the province. I was raised in The City."

"What is it like—Constantinople?"

"It is both beautiful and ugly. There is the city you will see when we come into the Sea of Marmora and move toward the harbor that they call the Golden Horn. The palace buildings and many churches set among the seven hills of the city will glitter in your eyes. But when you debark and look beyond that, you will see the underside, from debris in the waters of the Marmara to ramshackle tenements to homeless in the streets.—What is your business there?"

I should have expected such a question but I have no answer. What am I to say—that I have been purchased by a wealthy eunuch? That I am to aid him some way in writing, a way that has not yet been explained to me? "It is," I say, "an adventure."

She gives me a strange look, as if she knows I am avoiding the truth. "Well, The City will afford you adventures, young man."

The way she addresses me makes me wonder how many years older she might be. Certainly not many—four? five?

That she is bundled tightly into that cloak with only the face of an angel visible prompts me to pose an impulsive question: "Are you a woman of religion? A nun?"

Her eyes grow large and she lets go of a wonderfully mellifluous laugh. "I am not!" Her hand goes to her heart. "Oh, I have found my faith these many months past, but I am no nun."

I cringe in embarrassment. The wind picks up, giving new life to the squall. Rain begins to pelt us sideways now and I say the obvious: "We should seek shelter."

She is already turning to leave, but she stops and her dark gaze finds me. "Perhaps we can meet here again? I should like to learn more about Syria." She pivots and moves away now, calling back over the wind, "What is your name?"

"Stephen," I shout and am about to ask her name, but she is quickly fading behind a thick curtain of rain—an outline—a shadow—and gone.

I reach out blindly for the rail, grasp hold, and move down the ramp, narrowly avoiding a fall on the slick planks.

Below deck I find that Narses has gone off somewhere. Scarcely noticing that the nausea has miraculously abated, I sit on the side of my cot, absently drying my hair with a towel, still entranced by her beauty—and amazed that she suggested another meeting. For me the attraction runs deep even though I know she is years older. My thoughts turn to Jamila, the girl I had hoped to marry, and at once a veil of guilt descends. I am unfaithful to her, to my memory of her.

But just as suddenly, I realize with a jolt that I can be no more to this vision of a woman than I am to the lost Jamila.

I am one of the cut ones.

"Why, you're wet through and through," Narses cries when he enters the cabin.

I say nothing to him of my experience on deck.

The next morning, with the sea calm and dawn breaking, my thoughts of the woman drive me up on deck though I have little hope of crossing her path. And yet, when I come to the ramp leading to the sternpost, I see the backside of a robed figure at the balustrade and I know it is she. I catch my breath at my good fortune. She seems to be staring out into the wake, watching the gulls dive for the cook's scraps that the swab next to her has just thrown into the sea.

I start up the ramp. The swab comes down toward me, his bucket empty and his eyes narrowing in assessment of me. He pauses just a pace away and offers a crooked smile I interpret as wicked. He disappears below and I am left to wonder at its meaning. Did he think I had designs on the woman? I consider returning to my cabin.

My feet, however, propel me forward. I give a cough loud enough to be heard over the hungry squawking of the gulls. I have no wish to frighten her.

She turns now, her lovely chin lowered, her eyes widening slightly. "Oh, it's you," she says. "Have you recovered, Stephen?"

"I have," I say, much aware that I do not know her name.

"Well, come up and watch these noisy creatures with me."

By the time I join her at the balustrade at the base of the ship's ornament, she is again facing the water. Clear weather allows for a better view of the carving. The swan's long neck of beautifully polished wood rises many feet above us, then gracefully curves down so that its head is directly behind us. I reach out and touch its smooth beak as if the decoration is a talisman.

The woman turns to me, her eyes following the movement of my hand. I had not underestimated her beauty.

"When we come into Constantinople, you'll see flocks of storks returning to the area from the warmth of Africa. Sometimes the sky over the Bosphorus darkens with them. Do you know they come back to the same nest, whether in trees or on roofs, to the same mate? And they do so for years and years."

"Really?"

"Yes, I should like that, I think. To share someone's life for what time we have. And yet, I have my doubts."

My response is a smile, a stupid smile.

"What do you think? Is that a wish of yours?"

My stomach knots up. I shrug. "Perhaps," I say. My heart catches. Such a wish is closed to me now.

She tilts her head up at me, black eyes coruscating in the sunlight. Her hood falls back, revealing long black tresses. "You're young." She winks as if sharing some secret. "Too young for such questions, too young for cynicism."

I am glad when she faces the ship's wake again because I know my face has gone flame red. The gulls persist, ever-hopeful, their wailing punctuated by an occasional exclamation of a crew member. The swish and slurp of the water provide a constant chorus as the ship cuts through the waves.

Time passes, some fifteen minutes without a word between us as we watch the sky lighten at the far seam of the sea. I become lost, content in these moments of silent beauty. Of the sea—and of the woman.

And then, out of the cloudless blue sky comes her question: "Have you ever been in love, Stephen?"

The question stuns me. "No," I say, although I think I had felt love for Jamila. "I'm but fifteen."

"Ah, of course."

I surprise myself now by saying, "Have you?' It is an attempt to turn the tables.

"No." Her answer is swift and sharp.

I turn to find her steady gaze on me. She is flirting with me, I'm certain.

"Stephen!" someone calls.

I spin about to see Narses at the bottom of the ramp. He is smiling, but when the woman at my side also turns to face him, his eyes go large and his smile evaporates.

"Come down here at once!" he shouts, his voice more of an unpleasant croaking.

My throat closes. I can't find an answer. I turn to the woman, whose eyes are moving from Narses to me and back again.

"Now, Stephen!"

Unable to speak, I offer a weak smile and nod at the woman. Then I move down the ramp and prepare to follow Narses below deck to our cabin. I pause, however, and glance up at the woman. The clouds have masked the sun and yet she stands as if in a vision, a metallic gold light outlining her body, like a foil to a jeweler's most prized piece.

I force myself to turn away.

"Must I lock you in here?" Narses asks, closing the cabin door. "Must I?"

I'm puzzled. And angry, too, for being so humiliated. "Am I that much a prisoner? You said you had fine plans for me. Am I to wear chains like the rowers?"

"I do have plans for you and they do not include the likes of that woman."

"We were merely watching the gulls. It was innocent."

"There is nothing innocent about that woman. Word has gotten about among the captain and the merchant and God only knows who else!"

"Word? Word of what? She's a woman of faith—she told me so."

"Hah!" Narses' face folds into an unlikely expression of both humor and disgust. "She's returning to Constantinople, where her reputation of previous years is not likely to be repaired by any guise of faithfulness."

"I—I didn't know. Why, I don't even know her name."

"There are enough in the capital who do know her name, despite her absence, I can tell you that. She's a woman of the circus and an actress, brought up in the shadow of the Hippodrome. Her name is Theodora."

At once, I am able to discern the meaning of the slyly licentious look the swab had given me.

At night, however, as I lie on my cot, I care little for what the swab might think, or Narses, either, for that matter. My mind's eye returns to the woman's aura that had come to me unbidden. A metallic gold aura reflects a person who is steeped in spiritual energy and who harbors a power newly awakened and activated.

For me, she becomes my siren, my Circe.

While I am not locked in my cabin for the duration of the voyage, I don't happen to see Theodora again. Narses is correct: I am not meant for the likes of that one, that Theodora. Indeed, I brood, not for her but because I am not meant for the likes of any woman.

And yet the actress is still on my mind as I stand at the ship's bow, one of a swarm of passengers huddled there as the merchant ship sails up the Sea of Marmara. I site the southern shore of Constantinople that runs for probably three miles from the land wall at the west to the headland at the east. A mighty sea wall protects two harbors, above which rises a skyline of palaces, domes of churches, and tall pillars with statues atop. The hills upon which The City was founded become more evident as we sail around the headland.

I feel a tug at the sleeve of my tunic. I turn to find Narses dressed in a silken white dalmatic that I had not seen before. The wide sleeves and hem of the robe are trimmed in gold, and small purple insignias in the shapes of crowns are sewn into the material on the sleeves just below the shoulders, three on each side in descending order. "Ah, look," he says, before I can comment on the symbols. He is pointing up, to the north. "There's the acropolis, Stephen." Then his hand comes down and he points out the Senate House. "And there," he says, directing my gaze to buildings and terraced gardens directly across from us, "is the complex of the Great Palace. Emperor Justin and Empress Euphemia reside in what they call the Daphne Wing. Now, that massive structure behind it is the Hippodrome, where entertainments, mainly racing, take place. There are two competing factions backing the teams—the Blues and the Greens. Sworn enemies they are. Oh, there are two others, the Reds and the

Whites, but they are of little influence these days. The Reds fall in line with the Greens, and the Whites cast their fate with the Blues."

"And that building?"

"The Church of the Holy Wisdom. It's one of maybe a hundred but it is the most beautiful and most stately of the lot. They say it's the largest cathedral in the world."

The site of the capital is stunningly beautiful, exceeding by far the description given by the actress.

Narses continues his role as tour guide. "Soon we will be entering the harbor of the Golden Horn. It is shaped like the horn of a stag, you will see, and protected on all sides from the wind. When the winter winds of the Bosporus and the Sea of Marmara are raging, all is calm here. Safe anchorage is assured."

He continues to elaborate on the geographical and defensive advantages of the Golden Horn, but his words recede from my consciousness. And as magnificent as the sights before me are, my eyes search the faces of the crowd about me for the woman: Theodora.

She is nowhere to be seen.

"That is to be your home," Narses is saying. A certain poignancy colors his words when he repeats himself, commanding my full attention. He is pointing again in the direction of the Great Palace complex.

I am confused. "Where?"

"There—your new life starts there, Stephen."

I stand in wonder at the sight, in bewilderment at his words. Is he amusing himself at my expense? Even though I distrust his meaning, my arms go to gooseflesh.

"We will soon be rounding the tip now where the Bosporus Sea meets the Golden Horn. You will not see much of the Horn today because we will be docking close by, at the southern end of it, at Prosphorion Harbor. Had this not been a merchant ship, we could have docked closer to our destination in that narrow harbor we passed."

"Our destination? You mean the palace we passed? You were joking about that."

"Well, not that massive building up there."

"I thought not."

"That is Emperor Justin's residence. I expect you will see that in good time, my boy. No, below the emperor's residence is the smaller one there, nearest to the water, the Palace of Hormisdas. That is where you are to start fresh."

He points to a building that is set behind huge sculptures of a bull and a lion stationed on the seawall. A large balcony facing the sea juts out over three steps that lead to a marble-framed entry. Smaller, yes, but not small. "Who is Hormisdas?"

"He's the pope of the church now. He stayed there for a while and his name became attached to it. The emperor's nephew lives there: Justinian. He has a considerable staff, including a good number like us."

"Eunuchs, you mean."

"Yes. Forgive me, Stephen, for keeping you wondering all this while about my intentions. I had to be certain you were going to be a good candidate."

"Candidate?"

"There! We are fully docked. Let us go down and retrieve our belongings."

"Wait," I say, holding to one of Narses' sleeves, "a candidate for what? Something to do with languages?"

"Well, initially, in the negotiations I was considering you for a bodyguard position."

"Your bodyguard?"

Narses gives a little laugh. "Indeed not! No, you—that is, *we*—some thirty of us, guard Emperor Justin. Excubitors we are called."

It takes some moments for me to digest this. My mouth closes tight and I look down so that my amazement doesn't make me appear foolish—especially if he is not telling the truth.

"But," he continues, "your easy skill with languages might prove an advantage. You could be considered for a higher position in Justinian's library and scriptorium."

I can only wonder *whose* advantage.

I am still not certain Narses is telling the truth when we disembark. His status evidently accounts for our being called up to the first group to go ashore. As we move through the crush of people and toward the gangplank, I scan the faces for that one perfect visage. I don't see her.

On the solid stone quay now, we make our way past noisy dock workers unloading crates and tossing sacks of grain from Egypt. Negotiating our way through a crush of rough types casting knucklebones and arguing, we pass through the Gate of Eugenios, and the sights and sounds of Constantinople envelop me. Narses hires a donkey cart for us, and we bump along through moderately busy, narrow streets. I lean out, gaping at mansions, palaces, churches and people, streams and streams of people of every variety. I hear a dozen different languages. The streets we are taking lead us to The City's main thoroughfare, the Mese, and the great circular Forum of Constantine. Statues abound but in the center, atop a tall stone pillar, stands a gigantic bronze statue. "Is that Constantine?" I ask.

"It is."

"But he's—"

"Dressed as a god," Narses said, a glint in his eye. "Apollo, to be exact. Here, Stephen, statues of the gods of old flirt with the Christian saints, just as pagans like yourself, while growing fewer, interact with Christians."

We leave the forum via the eastern entrance, moving toward the Sea of Marmara. I gawk at the variety of artisans and food sellers lining the wide avenue.

After a while, Narses directs the driver to stop at a huge square. "This is the Augustaion," he tells me. "Gather your bag. From here, we walk."

We stand in the square as the donkey cart—its driver paid—turns to retrace its steps. "There to the north is the church you saw from the ship—the Church of the Holy Wisdom," Narses says. "Here to the east is the Senate House and various palace buildings." He places his hands on my shoulders now and turns me to the southeast corner of the square so that I am facing a kind of vestibule fronted by massive bronze gates. "And that is the Chalké, Stephen, entrance to the complex of the Great Palace."

I stand speechless at the sight.

It is grand, indeed, and my eyes move up to a trio of statues above the doors. And higher yet, under an arching roof of bronze tiles that reflect the afternoon sun, glitters the most magnificent icon of the Christ.

Narses notes the wonder that must be imprinted on my face. "Well," he says with a chuckle, "you were not expecting Mithras, were you?"

We move into the Chalké without the sentries questioning us. They nod in deference to Narses. He points out a number of oratories, small prayer rooms where ordinary citizens are allowed to gather and pray. After passing barracks for the palace guards, we come to an official who recognizes Narses. When his eyes question my presence, just a few mumbled words between them allow us both to continue into the complex.

My heart seems to stall and then pound in amazement, but I attempt to hold my composure as we walk toward some five or six terraces and manicured gardens that slope in steep fashion toward the Sea of Marmara. We keep descending terrace after terrace in a southeastern direction until we finally come to a lighthouse and harbor protected by a seawall. Nearby and abutting the water is a final terrace and edifice. "This is the Palace of Hormisdas," Narses announces without missing a step. "It is Justinian's home." He turns to catch my eye. "It is your home now."

I return his gaze, heart surging.

30

THEODORA STEPPED OUT OF THE sedan chair and paid its bearers. She looked up at the house. It was certainly no mansion but the white-washed stone front was impressive just the same.

She knocked at the door, and for a long moment her heart held between beats.

The chubby woman who opened it now was not her sister. For a moment Theodora thought the woman at the theater had given her bad information. She drew in breath. "I was told that this is Comito's house."

The woman's lips flattened into a non-smile as she assessed Theodora's appearance. "Are you selling something?"

"I am not."

"You're a Religious, then?"

By now Theodora realized that the woman was a maid. "No—I am Comito's sister."

The woman's eyes went wide and round as coins. Clearly, Theodora's reputation had not evaporated with the years gone by. Part of her wished that it had. Another part reveled in the thought that the impression she made so long ago still lingered.

The maid stepped to the side, allowing Theodora to enter.

Theodora was shown to a well-appointed reception room where she paced for a quarter of an hour before Comito appeared in the doorway in a gossamer stola of pale green, her face brightening at once. "Great Hera, I thought Kleio had allowed an imposter into the house! But it's you—plainly dressed or not, it *is* you!" She moved quickly into the room, arms open for an embrace.

"Indeed," Theodora said, holding tight to Comito. "Why, you have gained a few pounds, I must say."

Comito drew back and held her younger sister at arms' length. "And you would be the one who *must* say it, yes?" She pulled one of her old comedic faces and laughed. "The fact is I have not been on the boards for over a year, so bit by bit, the pounds add up and you don't even notice them. It takes a sister to say it. Come, let's sit. You haven't written in ever so long—years, in fact. You must tell me why and what brings you back." Comito called for the maid to bring wine and some dainty sandwiches, then drew Theodora to a couch.

"You bring me up to date first," Theodora said.

Theodora listened as her sister related at some length her successes on the boards and with men. It was one man, she learned, that insisted Comito leave the theater and come live in this fine house, a wealthy timber merchant named Kastor.

"And where is your love, this Kastor?" Theodora asked.

"He's gone down to the harbor. He had a shipment arriving today. Why, I have an idea! He has this splendid house right off the Forum of Theodosius. We lived there until a few months ago. It's smaller than this one, yet very comfortable. It's empty now but—"

"A shipment of timber?"

Comito nodded.

Theodora wondered whether his shipment had been in the hull of the very ship on which she had arrived. She thought of pursuing the subject but other concerns were more pressing. "What of Mother?"

"Mother?" Comito's face went dark. "You don't know? I can see that you don't—my God! Oh, Thea, she died during the winter. Several months, now. Why, I wrote to you at the Pentapolis. A cancer of some kind, they said." Reaching out and taking Theodora's hand in hers, she provided further details.

Theodora's body stiffened and a sudden coldness came over her. She felt as if she had already experienced every word her sister was saying, every detail about their mother's last days. Somehow she had known.

After Comito finished, Theodora drew back her hand and sat back against the cushion. "And Anastasia?"

"Oh, quite the beauty these days and finding her own success at the theater. I tried to dissuade her from the life, but she would not listen to me."

A heat came into Theodora's face and an angry, deepened tone into her voice. "What of the husband? I arranged a matchmaker before I left. I paid her in full. Tasia was not to know that life!"

"Our life, you mean."

"Yes—our life. Exactly!"

"Well, she has a mind of her own, Theodora. There was no marriage. She refused to even meet the man the woman found for her."

Theodora fell silent, her mouth momentarily locked, teeth grinding. She regretted what now seemed a foolish dream of leaving Constantinople to cast her lot with a man like Hecebolus—and in so doing not being there for her mother or Anastasia. *If only I had done things differently—*

"Ah, I see how concerned you are," Comito said. "Oh, Anastasia is a bit frivolous at times, but she's made a life for herself."

"You did teach her how to—how to be careful with men."

"I did."

Theodora's breath came in one gulp. "And the baby, Comito?"

"The baby?"

"Yes, Comito, my baby. I want to see her."

Comito ran her hand through her long dark hair, her face stricken. "I thought you would ask, and then it seemed as if you were not about to do so, as if you forgot."

"Any woman who has had a child is not about to forget. Tell me, Comito … did she not survive?"

"Yes, oh yes, she was a strong baby, but—"

"But?"

"You just left without a look back. Everything was left to me."

"You said you would take care of her."

"Did I? Or was it you *telling me* to take care of her? Thea, I was in no position to raise a child."

"Comito!" Theodora cried, rising and turning on her sister, thinking for the moment that her child had been abandoned or sold. "Where is she? You didn't …"

"No, she's safe. I entrusted her to a farmer and his wife. Hyacinth is with them, not so very far from The City."

"Hyacinth?"

Comito nodded. "She was a little flower."

"How far?"

"Thea, you can't see her. And don't think you can take her from the people who are raising her. You mustn't!"

Theodora turned her back to her sister and stood very still. A full minute passed. How she longed to see the child she had made, the child of her own body. But in her heart she knew her sister was talking sense. She was still not prepared to play mother. It could do only harm to demand to see the girl, harm to the couple, to Hyacinth, and to herself. It was better to allow things to go on as they had without her. "You did give them the earrings with the three dangling pendants that I left for her?"

"Well ... I—"

Theodora turned to face her sister. "You kept them?"

"Hyacinth was playing with one of them when I handed her over. The other one I had stupidly left behind. I'm so sorry, Thea."

"That's fine. They were practically worthless stage pieces anyway. But they were something of mine to give to my daughter."

"I assure you that Hyacinth is in good health. I've seen her when the farmer brings his chickens to market."

"Comito ..."

"Yes?"

"What about Antonina? Have you news of her?" Theodora held her breath, afraid for the moment that she would hear more bad news."

"As well as can be expected, last I heard."

"What do you mean? Is she not still in the chorus?"

"No." Comito stood so that she could pantomime her explanation. "They brought back that ridiculous stunt down at the Theater of the Three Coins. You know, they fill the orchestra pit with water and the chorines are made to swim their routines rather than dance."

"I've heard of it, but never viewed such a thing. And so?"

"Well, as pretty as Antonina is with that yellow hair and blue eyes, she's no dancer and even less a swimmer. Why she nearly drowned!"

Theodora covered her mouth, still uncertain as to whether a gasp or laugh would escape it.

"With that they let her go, Thea."

"Go where? Is she destitute? I can help, perhaps."

"No, not destitute, but—"

"What then?"

Comito's complexion reddened. "Madame Flavia hired her."

There was no covering her mouth now. The gasp could not be restrained. "She works for Madame Flavia?"

"She does. Don't be so concerned, Theodora. It's a living. Otherwise, she would be in the street."

"She would not!" Theodora snapped. "I wouldn't allow it!"

"But you weren't here, were you?"

"Well, I am now!"

The conversation turned to Theodora's years away. She kept her account accurate, but not all-inclusive and not nearly as dramatic as she could have made it without exaggeration.

Just before Theodora was ready to take her leave, Comito said, "Won't you consider Kastor's house that I told you about? It's in such a fashionable neighborhood. It would be perfect for you!"

"Perhaps it would," Theodora said. "But I think I'll find something on my own." She had no wish to be beholden to Comito's man—or to any man.

At the door, Theodora halted, paused a moment, and pivoted toward her sister. "Comito, I'd like to have that other earring."

Given the splendor of the Palace of Hormisdas interior, my imagination fails at the thought of what Emperor Justin's imperial residence—the Daphne Wing—must be like.

I am given a small room on the level below the ground floor. Other tenants of this subterranean community are of various ages but all are dressed in white dalmatics that bear the purple insignias of a reed pen on the upper sleeves. Clearly, this is a brotherhood of cut ones that now includes me. Even so, I do not feel particularly welcome.

On the second day, Narses brings me up a winding stone staircase and down a long hall to what he calls a small library. I am adjusting to the stiff new sandals and white linen dalmatic I have been given. The three purple threaded badges high on the sleeves identify me as one of the royal scribes. As we move, he is at last explaining my duties.

"Your dexterity with languages might impress some, Stephen, but your knowledge is rudimentary."

He does not offend me. He speaks the truth.

"Here, your learning will increase by leaps. In time you may be asked to read to someone of importance, or to write down matters that they dictate. You will also be required to copy manuscripts. Do you understand?"

"I do." I fight off the sense of disappointment. His description of my life to come sounds tedious and regimented. My life on the road with the Persian comes back to me as one of adventure and excitement. How strange that in looking back one sometimes ignores the pain and heartache.

We enter the ebony double doors and my eyes widen at the "small" library. Lighted by tall arched windows, the key-patterned mosaic floor—in colors of white, amber, and rust red—seems to move with us as we walk. Set into colonnaded bays are diamond-shaped niches housing what must be thousands of scrolls.

"We have dozens of librarians, scribes, and illuminators," Narses says.

I mimic his hushed tone. "And which do you have in mind for me?"

"Neither. The marble columns and mosaic floor need constant attention."

When I stop dead and tug at Narses' sleeve, he turns to me with a serious expression. Then, slowly, across his face comes the faintest smile—one of his few—and I know he has a sense of humor lurking within.

I bite back my own gullibility and ask, "Am I to work with papyrus or parchment?"

"You'll be working with both." The voice comes from behind me. "That is, if you have talent."

I turn to see a hulk of a man in the prescribed white robe, one well-worn and not nearly as clean as mine. Narses introduces me to Brother Leo, the Head Librarian who entertains a smile for but moments, then continues, "If your hand is good, you'll be copying texts from papyrus to parchment which will last long after you and I are gone. Sadly, the papyrus plant comes from Egypt only, and pages made of the stuff decay. I warn you now that they cannot withstand rough handling. Parchment is made to last and, after all, animals are found everywhere. And a codex is much more durable than a scroll."

"A codex?"

"We bind parchment pages together and cover them, front and back, with heavier parchment. That's a codex. Now, when Narses finishes with you, you'll find me over there." Brother Leo points to a tall, slanted-top desk set in a bay at the front of the room. The length of the rectangular room is lined with two dozen similar but smaller desks, each with a copyist on a stool working with reed pens on what I now surmise is parchment.

As Brother Leo makes his retreat, I glance at Narses and my expression must reveal more than I wish. "Don't worry," he says, "copying is not your only task, nor, if you learn your languages, will it be lifelong. Among the beardless here, Leo will find the most proficient in each language to teach you. Also, someone will teach you the art it takes to illuminate the important codices. If you rise to the occasion, you could prove to be of use to a scholar, a lawyer, or even a royal himself, who knows? Will you accept the challenge?"

It is much for me to take in—but I nod and ask, "Are not lawyers scholars, as well?"

"Some may be—by chance!" He laughs, finding humor here that escapes me. "Now, go and have Leo show you a codex."

Narses is about to take his leave when a quiet commotion occurs. I had been oblivious to the scratching of reed pens over parchment until it ceased. Several copyists looked up from their work to observe someone just now entering. Narses and I turn toward the door. A tall, bone-thin man with shaggy black hair is proceeding down the middle of the library, his brown robe hurriedly passing over the mosaic floor as he whisks past us without a glance. No one greets him. The air in the room seems suddenly tense. He disappears into one of the far bays.

"Is that Justinian?" I ask in a whisper.

"No, that is not Justinian," Narses murmurs, his tone an odd mix of humor and disgust. "That is a lawyer of lawyers, Stephen, and a true scholar—at least to hear him tell it."

I am relieved that the disgust was not meant for what was a stupid question by me. "Seems rather sour, I think."

"And you are a quick study of people, my friend. He is sour, indeed, unless it's in his interest to be otherwise." His eyes narrow as he appraises me. "Please do as well with your languages."

"But who is he?" I raise my voice slightly to keep Narses from leaving. A copyist nearby looks up from his desk.

Narses turns back and leans in to me, whispering, "His name is Procopius. He has barely passed his twentieth year, but he is out to make that name known to the world. Steer clear of him."

Narses makes his exit now, and I am left to discover what a codex looks like.

31

THEODORA SAT IN A SMALL reception room facing a wall decorated with a massive mosaic featuring in garish colors three couples in various positions of intercourse. When Madame Flavia entered, her plumpish, bejeweled hand went to her face. She recognized Theodora at once. "When the doorman gave your name, I was certain that it could not be you."

"I've returned, as you can see."

"Indeed!" Madame Flavia smiled. "I offered you a position once, if I recall. Have you come hoping for another offer?"

"I have not, Madame Flavia. I've come to see Antonina."

"Ah, I see, old friends and all that."

"All that, yes. May I see her?"

The madame's painted face clouded. "You know she's happy here. She wasn't meant for the theater."

"Perhaps not."

"I notice that you are rather severely dressed, Theodora. Still beautiful, however, even without makeup and in a stola plain as the noonday sun. You've changed your ways, have you? Did your little adventure in Africa come to a bad end? "

"I should like to see my friend."

"You have no intentions, I hope. No thoughts of changing your friend?"

"Antonina is old enough to know her own mind."

"Antonina is indebted to me."

"Indebted?"

"I gave her a home when she had none. She had been living in the gutter, and it was some months before she was able to receive gentlemen."

"How much?"

"From the looks of you, my dear, more than you have."

Theodora had no riposte.

Madame Flavia nodded in triumph and started for the door. "I'll send her in." Before making her exit, she turned with eyes trained on Theodora. "I have no one else here with coloring like hers—the golden hair and sky-blue eyes, you know." She paused a moment, then said, "Did I tell you that Antonina enjoys what she does?"

Antonina's mask of inquisitiveness evaporated as she entered the room and recognized her old friend. "Theodora!" she cried and ran to her.

Theodora held to her, taking in the spicy scent of cypress and recalling a half-dozen memories of what seemed a lifetime past. After the embrace, Antonina went to a water clock on a nearby table and poured from an amphora, carefully watching the level rise to a specific mark on the clock. She turned about and rendered the facsimile of a smile. "Sadly, Madame Flavia has set a time limit. We have but an hour to visit." She laughed. "The room, you see ..."

Theodora nodded, realizing that the reception room had another use if the Madame was overly booked some nights.

"We must talk fast," Antonina said, biting her lip. "It seems someone is always imposing their will on me. I should like to see the day when I can impose *my* will. First, my husband and now, Madame—"

"Your husband?" Theodora gasped.

"Ah, yes, I was married shortly after you left. A regrettable choice it was."

"Where is he?"

"Dead. He got into a brawl playing at knucklebones down at the docks and someone sank a dagger into his gullet."

"I'm so sorry, Nina."

"Don't be. He was a brute. I have a child by him—Photius."

One surprise was followed by another. "Where is he?"

Antonina averted her gaze. "He's with my mother. He has bonded with her. It's for the best. I'm afraid I'm not a very good parent, Thea." Her eyes, a tearless blue, shifted back, holding Theodora's. "Is that so terrible, do you think?"

Theodora felt tightness in her throat. She could think only of the two children she had brought into the world—and left behind. She had no solace or advice to offer her friend. A thin smile was all she could afford.

They sat together on a couch and exchanged stories of the past few years, allowing the awkward moment to fade. The hour passed quickly. Theodora marveled at Antonina. Despite a tragic marriage and her current status as a thrall in a brothel, she was still beautiful, her voice still so light and musical.

"It seems," Antonina said, "that Goddess Tyche can't decide whether to smile on us or frown."

"No," Theodora quipped, "but I think she has most likely giggled and cackled like a hen."

They hugged now, laughing together as they had once done.

Antonina drew back, glancing at the water clock. The water had run its course. She stood. "I'm afraid you must go now."

"I don't want you to stay here, Nina." Theodora stood and took one of her friend's hands. "You must let me do something. I'm renting a little house off the Mese near the Hippodrome. The neighborhood is a slum but the house is nice. You could come live there with me."

"Ah, that is very nice, but the madame isn't about to release me."

"How indebted are you?"

"Three years."

"Three years!"

Antonina's eyes shifted to the doorway. Theodora turned to see Madame Flavia standing there, a smile painted on her well-rouged lips. "Antonina," the madame said, "you have an assignation."

Antonina leaned in to Theodora. "Go now," she whispered. "It's not so bad a life."

As Theodora worked her way down along the Mese toward the Sea of Marmara and the untidy alleyways that sidled up to the Hippodrome, she recalled Madame Flavia's words: "Did I tell you that Antonina enjoys what she does?" How, she brooded, might she see her friend freed from Madame Flavia?

I begin to explore this city that some call the New Rome for numerous reasons, not the least of which is the fact that it is built on seven hills, like Rome itself. Before passing from the protected grounds of the Great Palace through the bronze gates of the Chalké, I must walk past the barracks of the excubitors, the Imperial Guards. Several take note of me, and I expect to be stopped and questioned. I am perspiring beneath my tunic as I try to form my answers to an imagined interrogation.

Yet it seems my white linen dalmatic with its purple insignias—the uniform of a palace eunuch—serves as my credentials, and no one queries my destination. Narses is supremely confident in allowing me this freedom, so certain he is that I would have no better options for a life outside of the palace grounds than within. Of course, he is correct.

I come out into the Augustaion and stop in front of the Milion, the stone arch that Narses said marks the miles from the city center to all the other cities of the Empire, and from there I set out along the thoroughfare of the Mese and into the densest heart of The City of some six hundred thousand. And so I spend my day, going from one forum to the next, marveling at the mix of nationalities of citizens, servants, and slaves, their clothing styles, and their languages—although the predominant tongue is Greek. I arrive exhausted at the Constantinian Wall. At a food stand I take libation and enjoy a plate of bread, cheese, and grilled fish.

As dusk nears, I make my way back. Few take note of me although an occasional person notices my habit and offers a brief nod of deference. The poor are in abundance here, especially down the twisting, narrow alleyways that hug the area near the Hippodrome. How I long to see the charioteers race at breakneck speed the length of the U-shaped amphitheater. It is near there that I impulsively step into one of those alleyways, curious to taste a bit of The City's less fragrant flavors, but ever alert for cut-purses and cut-throats. I am taking a path against which Narses had warned me. Some yards into it, I hear a man shouting down from his perch atop a tall granite column. I stop and look up. Such holy men are plentiful in the capital. Narses calls them stylites and assures me that they often stay upon their small platforms praying and communing with their God until death claims them. This man in rags is calling out, "My basket, my basket—there it is below." People stream past in either direction, but I seem to be the only one paying attention. At the base of the column, near a ladder, is a straw basket of bread and a covered clay cup. "There, Eunuch," he croaks. "Bring it before the rats get it and I will pray for your maimed soul." My back tenses at his insult and yet I am somehow moved to obey.

I go to the offering basket, lean over, lift and place it in the crook of my right arm. By now the sharply fetid odor of feces that have been pushed to the ground from the platform cause me to gag.

I pause, stomach constricting.

A tinkling laugh comes from behind me. "If you won't do it, I will," a woman says. I ignore her, keeping my eyes on the ladder. I draw myself up and take hold of the rickety ladder. I move up, rung by rung. The stylite is murmuring something to me or praying. I can't tell which and don't much care. Why had I not merely walked by the column? I peer over the platform as I come to the top and suddenly his face is no more than an inch away from mine when he bends to take the basket, his filthy white beard grazing my hand as he takes his provisions. One of his eyes has a cast to it. He is the antithesis of a siren, but he has nonetheless drawn me in.

"You're one of the emperor's eunuchs," he says with a snarl. His mouth is but a toothless hollow in the beard, moving almost comically yet emitting the breath of a viper. "You'll need my prayers."

Repulsed, I say nothing and begin my descent, but it is trickier than the climb. A few rungs down, the hem of my dalmatic catches beneath my sandal and I nearly lose my balance. The ladder trembles—as does my heart—and it shifts to the right. I have a vision of falling headlong into the man's waste. Suddenly the ladder steadies. I look up, thinking the stylite has grasped hold of it. He is nowhere to be seen. I glance down and see two hands holding the ladder in place. I say my own prayer, pull the skirt of my robe loose and continue to descend slowly.

As I come to the bottom, the mysterious friend-in-need who held the ladder for me releases it. My sandals touch ground, and I turn to voice my thanks.

I am staring at a woman in an unbelted and shapeless gray stola, but a woman whose beauty neither garb nor dusk could sully.

My heart races.

"Hello, Stephen." It's the voice of the woman whose laughter prodded me up the ladder. *My God!* I know her.

I take in a long breath. My thoughts go fuzzy—and yet her name rides lightly on the breeze of its release: "Theodora."

"On the ship," she says, "your master must have told you my name."

I nod.

"What else did he tell you?"

"Very little, really."

"Nothing good, yes?"

Words fail me.

"I thought not." Theodora steps back, allowing her dark eyes to sweep over me from top to toe. "You've managed to collect some of Peter's filth on the gold hem of your fine robe." Her musical laugh echoes the previous one.

"It's nothing." I feel myself coloring.

"Are you to return to the palace smelling of shit?" The eyes are sparkling with laughter.

I have no answer.

"You have been given a position at the Great Palace, yes?" Theodora is not a tall woman so that she has to stretch her neck a bit to wordlessly indicate the purple emblems sewn into my dalmatic sleeves.

"At the smaller palace just feet away from the sea. It belongs to the emperor's nephew—the Palace of Hormisdas."

"As an excubitor?"

"Perhaps, if I fail at my present duties as a scribe."

"So you read and write, Stephen. Valuable assets. I wonder that they allow you to roam such alleys as this alone."

"They're confident I won't run away."

"Still there are dangers in a quarter as this. Even for you in your white and gold. However, superstition might protect you. Do you know some people regard palace eunuchs as angelic, as if they are intermediaries between God and the emperor?"

I bristle, uncertain whether she is mocking me. Ignoring the comment, I ask, "And what brings you here?"

"My house is right down this alley, just a short distance away. Come, I'll show you and I'll tend to that stain."

"No, that's not necessary."

"You didn't have to dirty yourself for a man such as Peter the Stylite. Saint Basil said, 'A good deed is never lost; he who sows courtesy reaps friendship'." Theodora's smile seems to ignite a glow about her person. "Now come along," she says.

I pause.

"Are you afraid, Stephen? Afraid of what you've heard?"

I force a smile. Fear is merely one of several emotions running through me, all demanding caution. And yet I step forward.

As we move out from under the pillar, the stylite takes notice. "Eunuch," he shouts down in a gravelly voice, "keep clear of that one!"

Theodora lifts her head slightly, looks at me, and laughs. "And sometimes," she says, "a good deed comes before an ill wind."

We brush shoulders with people hurrying to their homes before nightfall.

Her house is not far and stands out among the wooden shacks because it is newly whitewashed. A wide window fronts the street.

Inside, Theodora lights a ceramic lamp. A large vertical loom is situated at the wall, near the wide window.

"I am learning to weave wool," she says. "Nothing elaborate, as you can see, just a blanket, but I am progressing, little by little. I hope to weave intricate designs of silk one day. I can sit here and watch the people pass by. I like that."

"How is it you've managed to find a house in such short order?"

"It's a rental. I just happened upon it. Some questionable characters coming and going, but I like it." She gives a little laugh. "Don't worry, I'll protect you.—It doesn't measure up to your new quarters, now does it?"

I'm grateful that Theodora doesn't wait for a response.

"Sit there," she orders, gesturing toward the wooden chair near the loom. When she leaves the room, I turn the chair so that it faces a low table and a couch. In little time, she returns with a basin of water, two cloths, and two brushes. She pulls a three-legged stool near to me and sets to work removing the stain on my robe's hem.

In a short while the garment is clean. Theodora rises and takes away the basin. She returns with fresh water. "Take off your sandals, Stephen."

I sputter in embarrassment but I'm no match for her. I obey as she sits and begins to wash my feet. My heart beats fast. In one of the forums, Narses once proudly pointed out a lovely statue of Aphrodite. This woman's visage eclipses that of the goddess.

"You know," she says, "Christ himself washed the feet of his apostles. Some believe it was to show his humanity. It's a subject well discussed and argued in Egypt and the East, I can tell you." She looks up, assessing the confusion that must have been on my face. "Ah! Of course! You're Syrian and from the country. You're not Christian, are you?"

"No, I am not."

"But here you are in a Christian city. Do you follow Mithras?"

"My father was a follower of sorts, but since … since I was sold I'm not sure I believe in anything."

"There! Finished." Theodora looks up, her eyes seeming to study me. "I once travelled your path, Stephen, but no more. Hand me your sandals."

Again I obey. "What happened?"

She seems to think a while about her answer while working at removing the filth from the leather. Unaffected by the stench, she finally says, "I was aided by a holy man in Egypt and I came away—well, changed. One day I will tell you how holy men there believe that Jesus had one nature, a divine one and not a human one. But I can see you are anxious to leave and care little for religious doctrine."

She hands my sandals to me and I quickly put them on. I stand. "I should go. You have my sincere thanks. I do have some coins—"

Theodora rises and catches my hand. "Leave them in your purse, Stephen. You would insult me."

"No, no—I don't mean to do so."

"You can return the favor by paying me another visit one day, any day you wish. We shall be friends, you and I. I know it."

I make a quick goodbye and hurry out into the night, only vaguely aware that the snare of a true siren had been set.

I pass through the Chalké and walk past the four excubitors on duty, thankful that my dalmatic is as clean as when I departed early in the day. I sense a little stir among them, but no one addresses me.

In my windowless room, I light the lamp and arrange the desk chair so that it faces the bed. On the plaster wall above the bed is a large mosaic of a dark-haired young boy seated on the retaining wall around a pond. The light from my oil lamp makes the blue waves seem to shimmer and the golden fish to wriggle. But the boy is not watching the fish. His head is up, his face forward, large black eyes staring out, appearing to watch me.

I've already made friends with him, communed with him. I call him Jati, the honest one. Tonight I wonder if he can read my thoughts about my meeting with Theodora. I sit a long while because I am shaken and know sleep will be slow in coming. Why has Fortune placed her in my path once again? What is there about Theodora that draws me to her? She is the most beautiful creature I could imagine. No mosaic could do her justice. She was made to mesmerize men. And yet I could not remove myself from her presence fast enough.

How is it that the woman I met tonight, one who sits at a loom weaving wool and one who washes the feet of a near stranger, reconciles with the woman, actress, and prostitute of whom Narses spoke? And yet one is the other. Is she sincere in her new way of life—or has she put her acting talents to work? To what end?

I stare back at Jati as if looking into myself. I must be honest. My attraction to her is intense. I felt it on the ship, at her little house, and I feel it now. It is precisely from such feelings that an equally strong fear rises. Even if Theodora were attracted to me, I am not meant for the love of a woman. And so, with the fear of rejection and humiliation comes the bitter regret and heartache over having been sold by my parents, traded by my captor, castrated and sold again.

The eyes of the figure in the glass tesserae glisten in my lamplight as if tears are forming there, as if the coruscating water beneath the boy is there to catch the drops. Honesty breeds sorrow, I find, and tears do start to fall. But the tears are not Jati's tears.

32

DRESSED IN AN ORANGE STOLA, Comito stood in the main room of Theodora's house looking out at the passing mid-morning crowd. "I don't know why you took this sad little house, Thea. Kastor was willing to let you the lovely one off the Forum of Theodosius for very little rent."

"There—I'm ready!" Theodora said, adjusting her veil as she approached her sister. "And what if he suddenly decides I am not paying the rent it is worth? What then?"

"I would see that he kept to his bargain."

"Really? And what if he should not keep *you*?"

Comito blinked in surprise.

"Look askance, if you wish, but men are not to be trusted, Comito. I know. Besides, I like this little house. It suits me. I enjoy watching people come and go while I weave. It's like watching a play."

"A boring one—let's go."

The two left the house and stepped into the flow of traffic leading to the Mese. They walked in the direction of the thoroughfare, passing the pillar of Joseph the Stylite in the process.

"Hey, you!" the stylite called down. "Where's your eunuch today, Lady Gray? Coming later, I reckon? Oh, that's a fashionable one you've got there. An actress, I'd wager."

Theodora bit her lip, fighting the urge to call back in kind; instead, she picked up a brisker pace.

Comito caught up to her. "He called you Lady Gray, Thea—why would he do that?"

Without slowing, Theodora made a show of pulling at the sleeve of her drab cloak.

"Oh, I see. But a eunuch! What is he talking about?"

"A friend who has been to see me a few times."

"A eunuch from where?"

"The palace."

"Truly?" Comito fell silent for a few minutes as they approached the Mese. Finally, she said, "Well, he thought me quite fashionable, he did."

Theodora caught her sister's arm, drawing her to a stop. "And he also called you an actress. I can assure you that neither was a compliment. Now, do I assume we go left here at the Mese?"

"What?—yes."

Theodora bolted forward and made the turn. Her sister followed.

It took a good bit of walking before they came to an open area brimming with the sights, sounds, and, often enough, malodors of a plaza on market day, the Forum of the Ox. Comito guided Theodora to the shelter of a colonnade on the south side of the square.

They waited, watching the teeming crowd of citizens bargain over cabbages and lentils, live goats and rabbits, cheese and cereals. Nearly an hour passed.

"Maybe they're not coming today, Comito."

"They'll be here."

"It's so warm and so crowded and the place reeks of animals," Theodora complained, wrinkling her nose.

"And unwashed bodies," Comito added. "It won't be long now."

"I think we should leave."

"Do you wish to see your daughter—or are you suddenly faint of heart?"

"I do. I think so, anyway.—What makes you so certain they will show?"

"They've not missed a market day."

Theodora turned to her sister, the register of her voice high. "Do you mean to say you have watched them every market day?"

Without turning her gaze away from the forum, Comito nodded. Her face, viewed from the profile, was pinkening. "You did tell me to see to her welfare, did you not? I've watched her week by week."

Theodora had to catch her breath. Her eyes began to moisten. "You did that for me?"

"Well, she was in my care for several months before giving her up."

"So—you bonded?"

"Perhaps, but in the end, I did it for her, for Hyacinth."

Theodora was never so sure of loving her sister than at that moment, but before she could respond, Comito said, "Now look, there they are on the other side of the forum."

Theodora followed Comito's line of vision. A tall man across the square was negotiating his way through the dense crowd, bearing on his shoulder a huge rectangular wooden cage that held in separate compartments dozens of lively, squawking chickens. At his side was a woman plain of face and about his age, perhaps forty. Both were dressed in the undyed tunics of commoners. "Are you certain? I don't see a child."

"I am. Be patient. Wait for the crowd to clear a bit. You've waited years already, no? They will set up nearby and stay until the chickens are sold. There! Look now. You see!"

Theodora did see. The woman held tightly to a black-haired girl who was pulling her forward. The child was dressed in a tunic of bright blue.

"She can't wait to get started," Comito said. "She's quite the little salesman, too. I swear some will buy a chicken just to please her."

They were passing by the colonnade now and Theodora watched in amazement. The girl's animated face was not heart-shaped, like her own, but rather more round with full cheeks and a small mouth. "She's beautiful."

"Indeed," Comito said.

Theodora's eyes fastened on the little family as they moved several yards away and began to arrange themselves in front of a spice shop. Comito explained that the proprietor of the shop made sure to save them the spot, thus receiving a chicken in return.

Theodora stared in awe as the girl's expressive face, musical voice, and innocent nerve drew in customer after customer, like reeling in fish from an overpopulated stream. Her heart lurched in her chest. She—who had long ago forsworn a motherly disposition—longed to take the girl into her arms. How had she left this little angel to the whimsy of Fortune? The knot tightening in her stomach was an emotion she had successfully kept at bay for years: regret.

"The blue tunic," Theodora said, "it must have been costly."

"Indeed—you see, they have treated her well."

After a while, a lull in likely shoppers occurred, and Theodora stepped out from behind a column and down the two steps onto the concourse. Her movement was stopped at once by Comito who was at her side, holding tightly to her upper arm.

"What are you doing?" Comito asked in a hissing tone. "What?"

"I don't know. I was going to buy a chicken."

"You're not to meet her!"

"I want to meet my daughter."

"You're not!"

Theodora took in Comito's determined expression. "Do you mean to say that you've never approached them?"

"Never—not since the day she was given over. The mother, Hestia, sometimes sees me skulking about, but we don't speak. "

"But I—"

"You! You nothing. You'll watch from afar, as I have done."

Theodora's gaze went to Hyacinth, then back to her sister.

And she understood.

Theodora and Comito retreated to their spot behind a column and remained there until nearly every chicken had been sold. "Let's go now, Thea. It's time."

Theodora turned, ready to follow, but she impulsively grasped her sister's arm. "Oh, Great Hera, she looks like me and like you. Why, can't you imagine her with us when we were girls in the Hippodrome dancing for the heartless Green faction?"

"And how the Blues saved the day for us?" Comito paused, her eyes filling with tears. "How alike we are, Thea. I've imagined that scenario a hundred times. Hyacinth is one of us.—But, Thea, she is not yours."

Her sister's words struck her like a clap of thunder. Theodora stared vacantly for many seconds, then drew herself up, saying, "No, you're right. I chose this path." Her own tears were ready to spill, too, but she blinked them back and hugged her sister. "I love you, Comissa," she said, wrapping the diminutive in warmth. "Now take me home."

They walked back to the little house across from the amphitheater in silence. Blessedly, Joseph the Stylite, didn't see them.

Theodora sat at her loom. By now she had an agreement with a merchant in the Forum of Theodosius to take her blankets on consignment. Weaving basic plain-patterned blankets had become second nature so that her eyes often strayed to the right—to the street scene in front of the house. She guessed that thousands must pass by on the narrow lane each day, coming and going, going and coming. No one from her previous life in the capital visited—other than Comito, and her visits were few. Sorely disappointed that Anastasia had shirked the husband the matchmaker had found for her, Theodora kept her distance. Neither did she search out her former theater crowd, for the only thing she had in common with them now was her past. Antonina was the exception, but she was little more than a slave to Madame Flavia and would be bound to her for the next three years. Theodora longed to rescue her friend from the life she was leading, whether it was forced or not. But it would take an impossible number of blankets to redeem her friend.

Theodora had no wish to return to the Forum of the Ox to watch her daughter. Doing so was too painful. It had made her think, too, of the boy she had left behind. Not knowing what had become of him actually made her abandonment less hurtful than her desertion of Hyacinth, whose beautiful, blithesome face now haunted her.

Her eyes looked up now and then, scanning the crowd for Stephen. He was her sole refuge against a well of loneliness. They had become fast friends in a short period of time. Oh, she knew he was entranced by her, but they both knew that Fate had denied them any chance of physical intimacy. And it was this lack of a physical relationship that allowed her to open up her life to him. She found herself spilling out details of her experience on the stage, with Hecebolus, and the long journey back home to the capital. He shared, too, but she felt he held back as much as he shared.

She prayed he would come today. He never set a specific day or time. She would just see him in his white dalmatic being swept along with the stream of people. He might not come for two days or he might come on three days consecutively. She guessed he never quite knew when he would be able to get away from his duties in the scriptorium of the emperor's nephew, Justinian.

Her fingers worked at the loom mechanically now as she considered the irony of a friendship with someone from the Great Palace. In Antioch, Macedonia had given her a letter of introduction to Justinian, insisting she could become a spy for the palace. It was a ridiculous thought and often a pathway to execution or a silent knife to the heart. She had no wish to take the letter and no intention of using it to gain access to the prince's palace by the sea. It had gone to the bottom of the satchel she carried, and she wondered now if she could even find it.

Suddenly, her attention was caught by Stephen, who was making his way down the crooked lane. He gave a little nod as he moved toward the house. Why was it that he didn't look the part of a eunuch? His body was tall and slim, his Syrian face handsome, his voice masculine. He had not shared with her the events that led to his transformation. Someday, he might, she thought. Perhaps I have been too much the talker. Someday I will just ask him.

I spend my days in the airless scriptorium copying Greek and Latin texts. I know I am not the best copyist, for I find myself rushing through the text, so eager am I to improve my knowledge of each of these languages. The copying is boring. I know that I should take the time to hone my skill with my kalamos, but it is the language that I find interesting, not the execution of my reed pen. Even when I know the stout, unsmiling Leo is watching from afar, the pen moves with a fury. I look up and his expression seems to be saying, *Your days as a scribe are numbered.*

Most evenings I hide a Latin codex under the folds of my tunic and smuggle it to my room. Gaspar had taught me a good amount of Greek and it is the language most often spoken in the capital, but I am less familiar with Latin, the language of the Western Roman world, and Narses assures me that learning it is a necessity. After the evening meal, where I have little interaction with my fellow scribes, I sit at my table or on my bed studying the language in the flickering light of my oil lamp and under the glass-eyed stare of the mosaic boy.

Once in bed I share with Jati my confusion over Theodora. What is there about her that attracts me? I ask. That she is five years my senior does not deter me. Why do I find myself negotiating that wretched alley, passing that mean-mouthed stylite Joseph, so that I can visit her? What is my fascination with her? Is it her beauty? Her honesty and willingness to unveil what must be all her secrets? Oh, I know what she has done, what she has been, and yet I am fascinated nonetheless.

Into the late hours of the night, each night, I confront my reality. The faces of my parents and Gaspar come back to me. Knowing that my path had been chosen for me by others and that it is irreversible unearths anger in me that rages like a wild fire. Tears cannot douse it.

I can never be more than a confidant to Theodora. I know that. The hurt seems to grow. I vow never to see her, never to tread that filthy lane again.

But just a few hours at the copyist desk, my thoughts go to her and the vow is forgotten.

Tonight I have one more question for Jati before sleep comes: What is there about me that seems to interest her?

Jati listens patiently but he has no answer. The night invariably closes in.

One day at mid-morning, I am working on copying a Latin text at my desk, which is situated last in a row of copyists and twenty paces directly in line of the corridor entrance. I am in deep concentration, so before the sounds of a door opening and furious feet flying up the aisle enter my consciousness, I happen to stretch out my right arm in order to relieve the stiffness that invades after a few hours of writing, and it is at this moment that the thin, sinewy figure of Procopius crashes into my arm. The pain is sharp but fleeting. However, the kalamos is struck from my grasp and is sent skittering along the floor.

I've grown accustomed to his hasty entrances and exits. On the few occasions I've heard him speak, it's with a condescending, overbearing demeanor. I've followed Narses' advice to stay clear of him—until now.

Upon striking my arm, Procopius whips angrily around, his tall frame towering over me. "You struck me!" he cries. "How dare you!" His face is going red and his lower lip is curling and twitching. I call it the fish lip.

I find that I am so dumbstruck by what has just happened and his overwrought reaction that I can't speak for what must be a full minute. Pens have stopped scratching, and all eyes within the room have turned to us. I feel my face heating.

"Well," Procopius shrieks, "what do you have to say?"

Deep breath, then, "I am sorry." I apologize in Aramaic because I know that he is a native of Palaestina.

He takes this in, deep-set brown eyes widening. He is trying to calm himself but I see new anger growing. "What did you say?"

I stand and repeat my apology.

"Why did you say it in Aramaic?" he asks in a whisper.

If there is truly a devil, he enters my brain now, and I apologize in my native Syriac, then in Coptic, Latin, Greek, and finally, in Armenian, which I am currently learning as a homage to Narses. He flinches with each apology, as if each one is a slur on his mother's name.

And then he starts shouting at me in Greek too rushed—and punctuated with flying spittle—for me to comprehend.

Leo comes bustling over. "What is the problem, my Lord Procopius?"

Through gritted teeth, the offended one says, "This eunuch mocks me. I want him punished."

My mind scrambles for a defense. My initial apology in his native language was sincere, but I fear mockery crept into the ones that followed as I became more cavalier.

Without asking for details, Leo says, "It will be as you say, my lord. As a scribe here in the library, Stephen is nearly useless." Leo's small eyes turn to me. "In truth, as a scribe you *might* make an adequate excubitor." His smile tells me he has been waiting for some time to deliver his line. "Most members of the Palace Guard," he continues, "are not called upon for their writing skills at all."

So I am to be demoted.

Procopius smiles meanly, wheels about and heads for the far-off alcove where he studies.

Even as his footsteps fall away, another figure emerges from an alcove very close by, claiming the attention of everyone.

I hear one of the copyists whisper, "Justinian."

I have my first look at the prince. Wearing a brown dalmatic and brown leather sandals, he comes forward, his face as plain as his garb. I hear the heavy-set Leo laboring in his breaths. "My—my lord Justinian," he blubbers, "we did not know you had come in."

Justinian's smile is enigmatic. "I am here working more often than you know, Leo."

Justinian's words provide a caution that startles a wide-eyed Leo anew. Just a nod from him indicates his will to Leo, who lumbers off with uncharacteristic hastiness.

The emperor's nephew turns to me. "Your name is Stephen?"

I sucked in a quick breath. "Yes, my lord."

"You certainly got under Procopius's skin, didn't you?"

"I'm—I'm afraid so, my lord."

"What you may not know, Stephen, is that here in Constantinople among people who consider themselves elite the primary language is Greek so that anyone speaking another tongue—other than Greek and the Latin of Rome—

is thought to be a barbarian. And when you addressed Procopius in Aramaic, his native language—"

"He was insulted, as if I were calling him a barbarian."

"Indeed. And sometimes he is. But as a historian he will be a valuable asset to the throne."

"I see. Should I apologize?"

Justinian gives out with a good laugh. "I think you already have—several times."

The irony strikes me now. "Five or six, I think."

"Indeed, indeed!" Justinian's continued mirth draws me in and we are suddenly like old friends sharing a joke. "Tell me," he asks, "where did you come by your knowledge of languages?"

At some length, I tell him of my travels in the East with Gaspar. He seems genuinely interested.

"That's where Narses came upon you, yes?"

I want to say that that is where he *bought* me. I nod instead.

"And how are you getting along with Leo?" he asks.

"You must have heard him, my lord," I mutter. "I think I am about to get the boot, as they say. Or maybe the marching boots of an excubitor."

The comment fetches another laugh from Justinian. "Indeed," he says. "We do need good men in the Palace Guard."

I nod stupidly, thinking my transfer is imminent. I feel a cold hand taking grasp of my heart.

Justinian's eyes narrow in appraisal of me. "However, I have other ideas for a man of your talents."

33

THEODORA WORKED LAZILY, HER EYES more on the stream of people passing in the narrow lane than on the warp and woof of the loom. She was miffed that Stephen had not visited in over a week.

Suddenly, a knock at the door drew her from her thoughts. She hurried to answer it.

Dressed in a faux gem-encrusted green silk stola, eighteen-year-old Anastasia flounced into Theodora's tiny reception room. "Theodora!" she scolded, removing a white veil from a pretty face marred by too much makeup.

Theodora hushed her sister—younger by two years—with a tight but awkward hug. "There! Now let me have a look." She stepped back to assess Anastasia, her eyes sweeping up from gold sandals to the pearl pins that held her ornately piled black hair in place. She was tempted to say that her costume was inappropriate for street wear, especially for an alley bordering the Hippodrome. Instead, she smiled and said, "You're taller than I now. Or have I shrunk?"

"I'll have none of your quips, Theodora." Her face folded into a theatrical pout. "You've been here how many weeks and you haven't come to see me. You must see me perform!"

Resisting the temptation to bring up the disappointment in her sister's career choice, Theodora averted her gaze and said, "I'm sorry, Tasia. I just haven't found the time." She attempted a smile to mask the lie.

"Nonsense. You've had time to settle in this God-forsaken slum in the shadow of the Hippodrome—and time for *that*." Anastasia pointed to the loom. "What's come over you? Why, you're dressed like a beggar!"

"I've changed."

"Comito said as much but I had no idea! When will you come see me at the theater? I have not rivalled your reputation—but I have had my little successes."

"And Comito has told me that."

"I have to admit some of my initial auditions were successful only because I told the directors that you are my sister. Why, I can only imagine the excitement your return to the boards will bring!"

"I have no intention of going back to the theater."

"But you must! Thea, you are still so beautiful, much more so than Comito or I."

Theodora shook her head as if to deny the compliment. "Come, let's sit down."

Anastasia followed her to the couch that faced the window. "Why? What is this change?"

"Do you remember a parish priest years ago by the name of Timothy?"

"No, I don't."

"You were too young. Well, he went on to become the Patriarch of Alexandria. He took me under his wing when I was at my lowest."

"Alexandria? Then he must be a heretic, yes?"

"It depends on your point of view. But his beliefs *are* different from those here in Constantinople, as are mine now." Theodora knew she could hold her own in any theological discussion about the nature of Christ, but she could see Anastasia's attention already wandering.

"You must come to see me on stage," Anastasia begged. "Please?"

Theodora smiled politely, stood, and walked to the window. How was she to tell her sister that she had once vowed that Anastasia would not follow her sisters onto the stage? And yet she had done nothing to shield her from such a life. She had gone off across the sea with Hecebolus so that she was not here for her sister. I am to blame, she thought. *I am to blame.*

From her seat on the couch, Anastasia spoke at some length about the little one-act play wherein she played the Goddess Minerva.

Theodora listened half-heartedly and then stopped altogether when she noticed someone in the swell of people moving along the lane. The perfectly-pressed white dalmatic always made him stand out. She waved now.

"What do you see?" Anastasia asked. "Who are you waving at? Is it Comito?"

Another wave. She was certain he saw her, as he had other times, but he carried himself stiffly, facing forward, deliberately so, she thought, moving along with the slow pace of foot traffic.

Anastasia came up behind her now and must have detected the object of the wave. "That's a eunuch you're waving at, isn't it? Do you know him, Thea? Great Hera! How do you know a eunuch? And a palace eunuch at that!"

"He's a friend of mine," Theodora said. "Just a friend. His name is Stephen. We met on the ship coming home. Sometimes he visits. But today he seems to be oblivious. Oh wait! He's walking with a companion."

"He is, indeed," Anastasia said, suddenly drawing in a gulp of air and releasing it in a gasp. "Don't tell me you know his companion, too, Theodora?"

"No, Stephen works in the palace library. His companion is probably a scribe like him."

"Indeed not!"

"What, do you know the other man?"

"Yes. Well, not on a personal level, mind you. No doubt he's wearing the simplest tunic and cloak to avoid recognition, but I've seen him on two other occasions at parties where my director has had us perform, paying us performers a mere pittance, I might add."

"Who is he, then?"

"That, Theodora," Anastasia said, pointing, "is the emperor's nephew. That is Justinian."

Theodora looked more closely. Nearly a head shorter than Stephen, the emperor's nephew was average in height and a bit stockier in build. He possessed a round, rather plain face. "Why, it's his library," she whispered, "where Stephen works."

"Not exactly an Adonis, is he?" Anastasia asked.

At that precise moment, the man in drab brown turned his head in the direction of the window.

"Hades take him!" Anastasia blurted, dropping her arm and stooping slightly to hide behind her sister.

The man Anastasia identified continued staring for some seconds—until Stephen said something to him, thus diverting his attention away from Theodora's window. The two moved past the house now and became lost in the crowd farther down the alley, where it curved and bled into another narrow byway.

Long after her sister left, Theodora sat idle at her loom, absently watching dusk descend. She understood why Stephen—in the company of the emperor's nephew—would not wish to stop to chat with her. However, she was certain he had seen her wave. Could he not have nodded in her direction at the very least?

Another week passed without a visit from him. She stood now at the window, as she had done each day, watching, watching. Each of her sisters stopped by once during that time, and while their visits broke the monotony of her days, she realized how much she had come to appreciate Stephen's conversations and details of his life in the palace—and before, in Syria, her mother's homeland. In a surprising short period of time, an easy bond formed between the two. Has something happened to keep him at a distance? What? Her mind raced with possibilities. He was sensitive—had she said something to offend him? Certainly the on-going insults shouted down from Joseph the Stylite's perch would not deter him. Had he listened to gossip about her past? Perhaps his duties occupied his time. Had his new associations at the Great Palace eclipsed their friendship?

"What can I do?" she questioned aloud, breath catching in her chest. She walked back to the chair by the loom and sat. There was nothing to be done. She was powerless.

Late one night I am about to retire when someone knocks on my door. I answer it to find Tariq, a fellow scribe, a pleasant enough young man with whom I have shared the supper table a few times. I judge him to be just a few years older than I.

"Is it too late?" he asks in his high, pleasant voice. "I did see the lamplight beneath your door."

"Not at all. Come in."

The room is spare of furniture, so I sit on the side of the bed after offering him my chair. He's Egyptian with a bit of a hawk nose and a midsection that has started to thicken. Because he was castrated at a very young age, his body will likely run to fat in a few years. It happens that way, I've learned.

"I want you to know," he says after we exchange small talk, "that Procopius has marked you."

"Marked me?"

He nods. "He detests you, it seems. I overheard him talking to Leo yesterday. He wants to have you removed."

"Why?"

"He doesn't want anyone else on the ladder of opportunity."

"He's threatened by me?"

"Indeed—ever since the emperor's nephew took an interest in you."

"I see." The truth is, I'm well aware of the antipathy he holds for me. I'm also touched by Tariq's kindness in warning me.

"I've seen him do this before. There was a young page who became a favorite of the emperor. The next thing we know, he's gone. Like that!" Tariq snapped his fingers. "Faster than any sorcerer could bind him with an oath. Nothing left behind but gossip about what might have happened to him."

"I am hardly an obstacle to Procopius's ambition. Justinian has had me act as translator on several occasions while we walk certain quarters within The City, but I have no aspirations to—"

"Neither did Mathias, but he was gone just the same!"

A little chill comes over me.

"It is best to be forewarned," Tariq says. "Now, do you know how to play *Shatranj*?"

"I do. I was taught by my Persian master. It was played in Persia long before making it to Constantinople. My master was proficient at the board."

"Indeed?" A light comes into Tariq's soft eyes. "Then we must play, yes?" He stands to leave.

I rise. "I accept the challenge. I warn you, my master was a magus, so I too might work some magick on the board. "

He smiles and turns to go. At the door, I thank him for his concern and he leaves.

I take the chair now so that I can face my mosaic confidant, Jati. The day Justinian took an interest in me changed things for me. My unlikely mentor seemed to sow a certain timidity in Brother Leo. He no longer scolds me for my often hasty work and has not again threatened me with placing me among the ranks of the Palace Guard. I would not much mind becoming an excubitor, but I would miss my work with languages.

Clearly, Procopius had become aware that I had accompanied Justinian on his walks. I can see it in his demeanor, in his eyes when they flash at me from afar. He takes care not to travel up the aisle next to my desk again even if it means a detour to the side of the room, but the distance does not cool the heat of what I now realize is hatred.

"Well," I say aloud to my mosaic muse, "I have made an enemy in Procopius but a friend in Tariq. Shall we call it a draw, Jati?"

I think back to my first city tour with Justinian and that leads to thoughts of Theodora. I feel a pang of remorse—not for the first time—for having ignored her as we passed her humble house. *But what could I do, Jati? Introduce this one-time prostitute to the emperor's nephew?*

The oil is running low in my lamp, and as I move to turn down the wick for the night, the shadows flicker on Jati's face, enlivening it with subtly dark accusatory stirrings.

34

EXPECTING ONE OF HER SISTERS, Theodora pulled open the door to find a tall figure holding in front of his face a light brown colored board painted with black lines dividing it into a multitude of squares. "Stephen!"

"How did you know?" he says from behind the board.

"The white dalmatic is a giveaway, you goose! Now put that down."

"It's my shield. You do forgive me?"

Theodora feigned ignorance. "What is there to forgive? Now, come in."

Stephen lowered the board, retrieved a satchel he had sitting at his feet, and with the hint of a shame-faced smile, entered, closing the door behind him. Theodora went to a couch and sat. He remained standing. "I—I wish to explain. Rather, I have no explanation for ignoring you the other day."

"No need—you were occupied with an important personage."

"You knew? You recognized him?"

"No, my sister knew who he is. The emperor's nephew, yes?" Theodora raised her eyebrows. "You're finding your way around the palace grounds in short order. Do you often accompany him?"

"He's had me do so on several occasions. He seems to enjoy talking to citizens on the street, and I am more skilled in certain languages than is he. And then, I think he likes the company, too."

"I've missed your company, Stephen. You see, I've managed to buy a second couch. Now sit down, Stephen."

"Forgive me, Theodora. I've missed our—meetings." He dropped onto the couch across from hers. "This is a gift for you," he said. He placed the board on a low table between the couches, opened the leather satchel and spilled out the many black and white carved wooden figures. "These are the pieces. It's an ingenious game called *Shatranj*. Have you not heard of it?"

Theodora shook her head. "I have not."

"My Persian master taught me. You take the white pieces and I'll take the black. You have to learn the shapes. That's a foot soldier, or *pujada* in Persian."

"So many."

"Eight for each of us; they will stand in the frontline, as if for battle. Then we each have two horses or *asps*, two elephants or *pils*, and two chariots or *rukhs*. But there is just one counselor or *farzin* and one emperor or *shah*, and the goal is to protect your *shah* and capture mine. What do you think?"

"I don't like it."

Stephen's forehead furrowed. "But why?"

"There's not a woman on the board."

"No, you're right—there's not. Well, it's just a game. It's not meant to reflect life, Theodora."

"But it should."

"Look, there is but one counselor. Suppose you and I call the counselor the *shahbanu*?"

"The *shahbanu*?"

"Yes, the empress."

Theodora laughed. "You're appeasing me."

"Perhaps." He laughed, too.

"I'll make us some tea." Theodora started to rise, hesitated, and sat again. "Before we start, may I ask you a personal question?"

"You may."

Theodora took a breath. There was no good time for such a question but her curiosity got the best of her. "Why is it you don't resemble every eunuch I've ever seen?"

"Ah, you mean heavy-set and with a high timbre to the voice?"

She nodded. "And in some instances—rather feminine."

"Most are selected for their fate at an early age—before they venture into manhood. Do you understand?"

Theodora nodded.

"My Persian master, Gaspar, bought me to assist in hawking his skills as a magus while he travelled about, town to town. I was allowed to grow into manhood. However, when he learned I wanted to buy my own freedom and was not so very far from that goal, he sold me to the men who—who did the deed."

"How horrible, Stephen!"

"Many who were placed on that butcher's table did not survive the cutting."

Theodora flinched and could not suppress a gasp.

"For a while I thought they were the lucky ones."

"But now?"

His eyes, dark and revealing, held hers. "Now life has its small rewards."

Theodora smiled. "I'll make the tea."

I resume my regular visits to Theodora's humble home in the crowded alley. In Justinian's library I am considered a privileged one because of my association with Justinian so that when I say I will not be at my desk on a particular afternoon, no one demurs. In fact, Leo wishes me pleasantries. But Procopius, who holds no sway over me, seethes silently from the sidelines, eliciting a dark joy within me.

Theodora and I play *Shatranj* often and while I allowed her—early on—to win occasionally, she learned fast and actually beats me now and then.

One day, she says, "Are you still going about with the emperor's nephew?"

"Yes, two or three times a week."

Her thoughts appear to be on the board and her next move with the piece recently christened *shahbanu*—when she says, "You know, I have a letter for Lord Justinian."

I find this remarkable and all I can say is, "A letter?"

She nods, eyes on the board.

"You've written a letter to Justinian?"

"Oh no, of course not. A friend of mine in Antioch wrote it. Her name is Macedonia. She took it into her head that I could become a spy for Justinian, whom she seemed to know well enough. And so as a favor to me she wrote a letter of introduction."

"A spy!"

"I know. I didn't ask for it. It was a ridiculous idea, then and now."

"May I see it?"

"I'm not sure I can find it right now. Besides, it's still sealed."

"Indeed," I say.

She looks up from the board, her lovely face slightly pinched. "You don't believe me."

I'm caught like a dumb fish. How to save myself? "Well, I thought maybe you were joking."

"Did you?" she says as she glances down and completes her move. "Your *shah* has been pinned!" she cries.

"You are getting too proficient, Theodora."

"I forgive your skepticism. You know," she says, her words punctuated by her high, tinkling laugh, "I wouldn't have believed me, either. But it's true. And it's also true that I have no intention of doing anything with that letter. I never did, so if it has been lost with all my moving about, so be it. I'm no spy so what in the wide world of Zeus would Justinian want with me?"

One mid-morning Justinian tells me he wishes to walk the Mese as far as the Forum of Arcadius. I have little enthusiasm because we had walked a good distance the day before and I'm foot tired. But who am I to say no?

We set off, passing through the Chalké into the Augustaion, moving past the Baths of Zeuxippos and the Hippodrome. Justinian halts at the first shabby lane running parallel to the great stadium. "I should like to take this alley again, Stephen."

"For the sake of time, may I suggest we stay on the Mese, my lord?" I feel a warm rush of blood to my face.

"This will not be much out of our way. It dovetails with another alley that will return us to the Mese, does it not?"

I have no other argument to make. I nod. We turn and merge into the foot traffic. My uniform brings a few curious glances, but the unassuming appearance of the emperor's nephew in a brown robe allows him to go unnoticed.

"If I recall correctly, it was here that senile stylite berated you as we passed. What was it he said to you?"

"Just gibberish, my lord." My heart tightens. It had been some filthy comment about my visits to Theodora. *What slur would he employ today? Worse, will I have to once again ignore Theodora as we pass? This time she would not forgive me.*

While Justinian gawks up at the still figure on the platform, I sigh in relief. Joseph the Stylite is praying on his knees and does not notice us as we pass.

We move on. In a short while, I see Theodora's house coming into view.

I take in a deep breath when I notice that her window is open to the street scene. She is bound to see us. I make plans to fall a little behind Justinian so that I might give a little wave that he would not observe.

As we draw closer, I rejoice to find that she is not at her loom. Now, if I can just move us swiftly past the house, I will breathe a sigh of relief. Justinian halts and pulls at my arm. I stop, terror taking root at the pit of my stomach.

"There was a woman here the other day," Justinian says. "In that window. You didn't seem to notice, but I did. She was beautiful. And she gave a little wave."

My lips go dry. People are jostling us as they pass. "You'll find an occasional beauty in the slums, my lord, but too often the price is very high."

"Aren't you the sly one? You've come to know the capital well in such a short time, Stephen."

I gird myself for some insult about my status as a eunuch and lack of experience with women.

I start to move forward. No insult ensues. Instead, Justinian says, "This was no ordinary beauty, Stephen. Her face was exquisite. Like that of an angel."

I stop in mid-step and it strikes me now like a hammer blow that his seeing her days and days before has ignited his desire to once again tread this dirty alley in order to see her again. How had Theodora bewitched him from afar?

"It's best we move on," I say, and he seems ready to comply when we both sense movement at the window and our heads turn in tandem.

Theodora is setting a cup down near the loom and taking a seat. Above her heart-shaped, porcelain white face, now in profile, tiers of her jet black hair are piled like a crown. She begins to busy herself at the loom, her hands and fingers moving more dexterously than when I had first seen her at work.

We stand stone still in the stream of people. I reach out to tug at Justinian's sleeve.

And suddenly—Theodora turns her head to the side and looks out into the street.

35

Theodora opened the door to the man her sister had called Justinian.

Words fell away. Lacking any clue as to what she should say, she drew in breath and bowed her head.

"Are we disturbing you, my lady?"

"What?—no, of course not. It is refreshing to be called away from such a repetitive task. I'm learning to weave."

"Will you invite us in?" The voice came from behind the prince. "Theodora?" Stephen pressed.

"Forgive me—of course, you may come in." She bowed again and stepped back.

Justinian entered, Stephen at his heels, on his face the oddest expression of dismay and resolution.

"Theodora," Stephen said. "This is Lord Justinian."

Theodora gave yet another little bow. Lifting her head, she drew her mouth into a smile. "I am honored, my lord."

Justinian nodded. Theodora thought she could see some color rising to his face.

"Be seated, gentlemen," Theodora said. "I have little to offer, for I haven't been to market. Some tea, perhaps?"

"Tea would be delicious, Lady Theodora," the prince said, a hint of a smile on his lips.

As she prepared the tea in her tiny kitchen area, she considered her first impression. He was of average height, his frame a bit stocky, his face round as a coin. His gray, quick eyes reflected a keen intellect, she was certain. He seemed awkward, and she wondered at the cause. Was it walking among the unwashed in the alleys that made him so? Was it his visit to such a modest home in the slums of the Hippodrome? Or was it his meeting with her?

She completed her task and carried the tray in to her visitors. While Stephen remained seated, his back rigid as a post, Justinian stood to acknowledge her re-entry and to take the proffered cup. Theodora handed a cup to Stephen, who rewarded her with a smile that could not mask his palpable agitation. It came home to her now that this visit had been engineered by Justinian, not by Stephen.

"Stephen tells me, Lady Theodora," Justinian said, "that you have recently returned from the East."

Theodora turned her chair away from the loom so that it faced the two men on the couch. "I have."

"Where have your travels taken you?"

Theodora could only wonder what details about her Stephen had provided. She had entrusted him with a good deal of information. And then there was her reputation based on her previous life as an actress in The City. If Narses had recognized her on the ship, any number of people in Justinian's sphere might feel free to malign her, just as he had. "To Alexandria and various coastal cities leading up to Antioch," she said, carefully passing over her disastrous tenure at the Pentapolis.

"Ah—the Levant! I should like to see those places," Justinian said, a wide smile making him seem almost handsome. "Were you affected by them in any way?"

"I was, my lord. I found myself in the care of the Patriarch of Alexandria. His generosity and kindness renewed my faith in religion."

Stephen gave a little cough and shifted in his seat. Theodora glanced over at him and read a warning in his eyes.

When she looked again to Justinian, she saw that his smile had bled away. "You're talking about Patriarch Timothy."

Theodora nodded.

"You do realize that he is a heretic?"

Theodora ignored Stephen, who gave a subtle motion with his hand for her to go no further on the subject. "I know that he believes Christ had one nature that was both divine and human."

"Exactly!" Justinian declared, "Whereas at the Council of Chalcedon, the Church has proclaimed Christ had separate divine and human natures within Him."

"Is the issue so important?" Theodora asked. "Aren't both sides embracing Christianity?"

"There is a fundamental difference!" Justinian cried, his voice moving up a register. "The Chalcedonian verdict is the true verdict."

Theodora saw that the matter had upset the emperor's nephew and wished now that she had obeyed Stephen's cue.

"The emperor will not tolerate the Monophysite heresy," Justinian continued, "and I concur with him."

While in Alexandria, Theodora had learned enough about the issue that she knew she could hold her own in a debate, but she also sensed she should tread lightly in the presence of the emperor's nephew. It came back to her now that Macedonia had said Emperor Justin intended to root out the so-called heresy—and that Justinian was leading the effort. A change of subject was needed. She cleared her throat. "Stephen has most likely told you, my lord," she said, "that we met on the ship from Antioch."

"Ah, I see." He glanced over at Stephen with an expression that revealed Stephen had told him nothing about her.

For a brief moment she thought of bringing up the subject of Macedonia, without mentioning the letter that she had yet to locate. She abandoned the thought when she realized any mention of the dancer as a friend of hers would be testament to her own career on the boards. If he viewed her as a weaver making a meager living like any other honest woman, why should she reveal more? Oh, Narses had recognized her in a flash but Justinian, she assumed, had led a more sheltered existence. "My lord, how has Stephen taken to his position in your library?" She could not avoid a little smile when she saw Stephen wince at the question.

"Well," Justinian said, his tone deliberately low and sober, "he has yet to run away."

The three laughed.

"Actually, he's a brilliant scribe. Why, he *knows* the languages he is copying. That cannot be said about some of the others who have no clue what the content is that they are preserving and fostering."

Reddening with embarrassment, Stephen commented on his initial reaction to viewing the many stylites about the capital. And so the conversation turned to safer matters than that of Christ's nature.

At the end of an hour and second cups of tea, Justinian stood. "Stephen and I have business to be about, Lady Theodora, and I suspect you have a duty yourself." He nodded toward her loom abutting the wall.

Stephen stood up at once. A persistent tenseness in the lines of his face fell away now as they prepared to leave. Theodora escorted them to the door. Justinian turned to her, his expression enigmatic. "Thank you for your hospitality, Lady Theodora."

Theodora gave a little bow, her heart catching. That the prince of the empire should be addressing her as "Lady Theodora"—well, it was a wonder. She gifted him with a genuine smile.

Justinian paused, as if he were going to say something else but thought better of it. He turned to leave now, followed directly by Stephen who nodded and smiled tightly before making his escape.

Theodora went to her loom and sat, arms motionless at her sides. She wondered what words Justinian had chosen not to deliver, certain she would never know because what occurred this day would never occur again. Feeling as if she could not catch her breath, she felt a sense of dread descend. Why hadn't she mentioned her connection to Macedonia? Why? So what if Lord Justinian should think less of her? What did she have to lose? She had laughed to herself when Macedonia suggested she would make an ideal spy for the palace, but was it so far-fetched? Or—perhaps there was some other position for which she would be suited.

Theodora jumped up from her chair and dashed into the other room, searching for the satchel she had brought from Antioch. When she opened the wardrobe, she thought little about the strong scent of sandalwood. She picked up the satchel and reached in, pulling from it not only the scroll but a small bottle, as well. The scroll was damp. In no time, she had the letter laid out on the table. She stared at it in disbelief. The cork on a bottle of sandalwood perfume had come loose and the ink on the page had bled badly, obscuring most of the message and completely blurring Macedonia's signature.

Her chest tightened. She let the scroll fall to the floor. The letter was useless.

Theodora went back to her chair at the loom and sat staring out at the passing crowd. She would not give in to tears. She would never think of sandalwood again in the same way, never douse herself in its scent. And so—she laughed.

After all, what difference could it make now? He would never visit her again.

Her hands went into motion on the loom. *There is no changing my past,* she thought. *I am Theodora. I cannot, like a lobster, go backward.*

My room is in shadows but for the lamp that enlivens the tesserae that make up the mosaic boy on the wall at the side of my bed. I replay the day's happening in my mind, a happening I wish I could have avoided. How might I have altered it so that Justinian and Theodora would not have met?

I think of a dozen different scenarios. As we stood in the street before her window, I could have feigned illness. I could have invented something about her physical condition. I could have said offhandedly, "You know, my lord, the woman has the pox." Or I could have told him what Narses had said about her.

I had not thought quickly enough.

I look to Jati now. The light flickers about his mouth in what I imagine is an accusatory expression. *Why do you harbor such a wish?* he seems to ask.

And so I must ask myself: Am I afraid the emperor or others highly placed would learn that I had engineered a meeting of the emperor's nephew with a woman of odious repute? Am I afraid that Theodora would act in some untoward manner? Am I afraid that the two would find some subject over which to disagree, as they indeed did, when the subject of religion came up.

I could not answer my mosaic conscience in the affirmative. None of those fears are valid. I sigh deeply. For the first time, I must admit that I don't want Theodora's attention directed elsewhere. I don't want other men taking notice. I admit openly now, to Jati and to myself, that I love the woman Theodora. But I am still a boy. And I am one of the cut ones. I turn on my side, away from Jati, watch the lamp flicker out at last, and like the child I thought I had left behind, I cry myself to sleep.

In the morning I vow for the second time to steer clear of a certain weaver's home in the alley adjacent to the Hippodrome.

36

"COMITO SAID THAT YOU'VE SEEN the child. She told me her name, but it slipped my mind."

Theodora stopped chewing on one of the sweet dates her sister had brought with her when she arrived, unannounced. "Hyacinth," she said. "My daughter's name is Hyacinth." Theodora felt a keen sense of guilt for having left her daughter as she had, without even giving her a name. She would see her name honored now.

"What was it like, Thea, to see her?"

Theodora reached for her teacup, lifted it to her mouth but did not drink. Her hand shook slightly as she set it down. "It was like taking a dagger to my own heart. That's what it was like."

Anastasia blinked at the answer. "Shouldn't you come forward, then, and tell her who you are, who she is?"

"No, Comito was right. It would not be fair to upset the bond that her adoptive parents have established."

"Well, then, perhaps later, as the years go on, yes? I can't imagine how you feel." Anastasia gave out with a little laugh. "Perhaps that's because I don't care for children. I really don't."

As her sister droned on with a dozen reasons for disliking children, Theodora imagined an occasion in the future when she might unmask herself to her daughter. It would be a bittersweet moment. Now, though, she could not help but think of the boy she had given birth to in Alexandria. What had become of him? There was no way for her to clandestinely watch him from afar. He was lost to her forever. It was another knife to the heart.

"What is it, Thea?" Anastasia leaned forward. "Are you all right?"

"What?" Theodora asked.

"I was worried for a moment. You looked as if you were far away."

Theodora affected a smile. "I was. I was in Alexandria."

"Alexandria!—Oh, how I envy you for your travels! One day you must sit and tell me about each city. Today, however, I must fly." Anastasia stood to make her exit. "We are rehearsing a new one-act."

At that moment a light knock came at the door.

"Oh, let me answer it," Anastasia begged, already moving toward the entrance. "Are you expecting anyone?"

"No." Theodora said, thinking her visitor might be Comito or, more likely, Stephen, whom she had not seen for several days. She popped another date into her mouth as she watched her sister go to the door.

Anastasia pulled open the door and stepped back as if startled. Someone out of Theodora's view addressed her in a quiet male voice. Anastasia turned her head to Theodora, eyes wide.

"What is it, Tasia?"

Instead of answering, Anastasia directed her attention back to the visitor and effected an awkward curtsy.

Theodora stood immediately, swallowing the last bit of date.

Anastasia stepped back, allowing Prince Justinian entry. Dressed simply— in brown again—his bearing was regal, his expression serious.

Startled, Theodora drew in a deep breath and curtsied, her eyes moving to the doorway, fully expecting Stephen to follow the emperor's nephew.

Justinian smiled, speaking now as if he read her thoughts. "I am alone, my Lady Theodora."

Words seldom failed Theodora, but they did so now. He had come for the express purpose of seeing her. She felt the room spinning about her.

Justinian no doubt read the shock she felt. "Is this—is this a bad time?"

Theodora steadied herself and summoned the appearance of composure. "Not at all, my lord. Come and sit. I have little to offer, just tea and a few dates Anastasia has brought. They're quite fresh. I have no wine, I'm sorry."

"I seldom drink. Bacchus is no friend to me." As Justinian made his way to the couch, Anastasia closed the door and started to trace his footsteps over toward the couches. Theodora saw that she meant to stay.

"Anastasia was just taking her leave when you arrived, my lord. Please excuse her."

"Oh, but Thea, I can stay a few minutes, I'm sure."

Theodora reached out to take her sister's upper arm. "Ah, but you were just saying how you are to practice for that new one-act. The other actors will be waiting on you." Theodora smiled now. It was best for her to leave. She knew that her sister often said the first thing that came into her head and that could lead to embarrassment or even insult.

Anastasia winced at the tightness of Theodora's hold. Her sister's intent was not lost on her, and she returned a smile just as false. "Ah, yes," she said, "my lord, I must take my leave." She curtsied and made for the door, casting a sideways scowl at Theodora, who followed close behind.

"Don't worry, Tasia," Theodora whispered, leaning over the threshold to her disappointed sister, "I'll keep you informed."

Anastasia started down the three steps. She stopped suddenly and turned around as if to say something.

Theodora put her finger to her lips in a shushing motion and quickly closed the door.

As she pivoted to approach Justinian, she realized her heart had accelerated. *What in God's name does he want with me?* She noticed now that he sat with his hands on his knees, his fingers tapping. She had the notion that it was he who was nervous—not her—but dismissed it as laughable.

"If you will excuse me, my lord, I'll make the tea."

"Perfect," he said, as he picked up one of the *Shatranj* game pieces and sat back against a cushion to examine it.

In the kitchen area, a litany of second thoughts plagued her. Had she made a mistake in sending her sister away? Was she placing herself in harm's path? Had Stephen or another told her visitant about her sullied reputation? How was she to deter the advances of a prince, one who is likely to feel empowered, to feel superior? She had been in this position with men before, too many times, and she knew what was on their minds, more often than not. But she had never had for a caller a prince of the Empire. Did he think he could take advantage of the situation?

Justinian thanked her when she brought the tea tray. She sat on the opposite couch, noting the simple but superb tailoring of his brown dalmatic and wishing she had worn her nicest white wool stola, instead of the gray.

Justinian gestured at the board that had gone unused for several days. "I see you play *Shatranj*."

"I do—well, I mean to say that I am learning, my lord."

"Shall we have a game, Lady Theodora?" His eyes coruscated with pleasure and he suddenly seemed half his age.

The idea of sitting face to face and playing *Shatranj* with a prince raised the little hairs on the back of her neck. "I'm afraid I'm not very good at it."

"And neither am I," Justinian said, laughing, "so it will be an even contest."

Theodora sighed. "You've sprung a trap for me, my lord, as if for a woodcock."

"Ah—that bird is too easily caught. I doubt that is the case with you."

Theodora's face flushed hot, but her embarrassment seemed less than his.

"I'm—I'm sorry," he stuttered, his face paling. "It was a stupid thing to say."

"Not in the least." Theodora said, hoping to put him at ease. She stood and brought the board to a low table between the couches. Justinian said nothing as she placed the pieces on the board, the whites in front of her, the blacks in front of him, all on the sand-colored squares. Neither did he speak much for a long while. As she studied the board at each of her turns, Theodora could sense his cool gray eyes upon her. She looked up now, and he quickly looked away. *What is he thinking?*

As the game went on, she began to think that his suggestion to play the game was a subterfuge for his shyness, or perhaps even backwardness. Irene once said that men are lucky in that they don't feel the need to talk among themselves. Theodora thought now that such reserve could apply to men in mixed company, as well. Had her darker suspicions about his motives been groundless? After all, Stephen had characterized him as being a quiet soul—a scholar, no less.

Theodora knew from her experience with Stephen that early on in the game it was more important to place your pieces in a specific battle array rather than pay too much attention to your opponent's moves—as Justinian was doing. Now, well into the game, she saw a double move that she could make that would allow him to threaten her *shah*. She thought—for a good while—about allowing him to win. Barring that, she felt confident that she would win the match. One day she might regret not allowing the likely future emperor to win, but not today. She could not help it.

Justinian cleared his throat and attempted conversation. "Your sister Anastasia is an actress, then?"

"Yes, my lord, she is an actress, as is my other sister, Comito." Theodora took a breath. "As was I, in what seems a sea turtle's lifetime ago."

Oh, he might be a quiet soul most at home in a library, Theodora thought, but Stephen had said he had risen to the highest ranks in the army, so he undoubtedly knew the reputations often attached to actresses. He was near forty, she guessed, and no innocent.

Justinian looked up, eyebrows raised and eyes sparking with gray intelligence and slight surprise.

Here was the lead-in, she thought. This was her opportunity to tell him of her earlier life—before someone else did so, and with no little malice. Once the facets of her life were aired, the prince would take his leave and be glad for a timely exit. And so, yes, she would take great pleasure in her victory at *Shatranj*. After all, once she has spoken of her previous life, she was certain this would be the only game they would ever play. At the very least, one day she could tell her children and grandchildren that she once played *Shatranj* with an emperor.

"My mother was an actress, too," Theodora began. "My story started not many paces away from where you sit, my lord, across the alley—in the Hippodrome."

Justinian listened with keen interest. Her intention not to circumvent any episode of her life notwithstanding, as the afternoon and her story played out, she nonetheless found herself filtering the details so as to avoid any that might reflect too badly on her past.

The time came when she took the last of the black pieces—except for the *shah*, a move that constituted a win—her win.

The prince took his defeat at *Shatranj* with grace and left without attempting any overture or suggesting some future assignation.

Theodora sat brooding. She feared that she had chattered on and on, much like Anastasia. Oh, she had not told him near to everything, but had she said too much? She sat absently staring at the dregs left in her tea cup, feeling both relieved and disappointed. It was an incompatible mix, like water and oil.

I am in the library copying a Latin text, an easy enough task. My artistic talent at handwriting—such as it is—is improving, as evidenced by Leo's fewer glances of disdain at the flourishes on my pages. My fellow scribes have gone off to the noon meal, but my mind is set on completing this page, so I don't hear someone entering and coming up the aisle on my right. He brushes past me close enough to jolt my elbow so that the letter I am forming at that moment, a decorative *w*, is ruined. I look up. It is Procopius. He stops mid-step and pivots to face me as if he would plant a dagger in my heart. I am certain the affront was intended, but I am not moved to call it to his attention.

My silence irritates him—as I intend. "You're here more often these days, aren't you?" he says, one corner of his mouth lifting into a sneer.

It's not a question meant to be answered so I merely return his stare.

Frustrated by my silence, he continues. "What's the matter, Stephen? No more promenades about the capital with the emperor's nephew?"

I give a slight shake of my head. It's true. A few weeks have elapsed since Justinian insisted on one of his walks. In fact, he has not ventured into his own library since he last called for me to attend him. It is odd and I wonder if perhaps he has been taken ill. I miss the walks, the companionship, freedom from the library and its often tedious work.

Procopius takes a step toward my desk. "No more influence, Stephen? No more strolling down the Mese in your whites?"

"I don't miss it," I lie.

"No?—Some men of his age enjoy having a young man with passable looks about. Perhaps you didn't please him."

My thoughts delay a bit before the lurid implication comes clear. I speak through clenched teeth. "You are wrong, sir."

"Indeed?" Procopius laughs. "You're right. Oh, he used you, but not in that way. What about that miserable alley east of the Hippodrome?"

My heart catches. "What do you mean?"

"Don't play coy, whoremonger," he growls.

"What?" I feel the blood coming into my face.

"You took him there—to the shack of that reformed actress. Of course, she's not reformed at all, is she?"

"Who?"

"Theodora. You led him right to her, didn't you? You procured her, yes? Did he pay you well?—Or perhaps she did, eh? Is she still paying?"

My mouth falls open but the words come tardily. "You followed us?"

"What do you think? Not personally, of course. But I make it a point to know what goes on around here."

"We went just once, and it was at his insistence."

"An easy sale that, yes?"

His insinuation shocks me. I won't have him looking down his long nose at me, so I stand, pushing back my stool. His amber-flecked brown eyes are level with mine. "Once, I tell you. You're wrong about her. I have not been back since."

"Ah! But he has, Stephen. Justinian has—almost daily!"

I have no words. *Is it possible?*

"You look dumbfounded my friend. Hah! You'll be more than dumbfounded when the emperor and his wife get wind of this."

"You're lying!" Even as I say it, I know it's the truth.

"I'm not sure what Justin will do when he hears, but Empress Euphemia will have you pilloried. Count on it." Procopius leans in and drops his voice. "Do you know about our empress's beginnings?"

"I do not."

"She was a slave girl when Justin met her and she became his concubine and a camp follower on his various military tours of duty. Did you know that?"

"No, I am not a native of Constantinople."

"Well, he took such a liking to her that he married her. Imagine that! She shed some common name and took the name of Euphemia, as if a high-sounding name could turn her into a patrician.—Now, for all that, you might think that she'll excuse her nephew for an affair with such an infamous actress as Theodora, but think again. I know the empress. I have her ear. Oh, she's become proud and pompous. She will want no reminder of her own beginnings, no whore taking the heart of the future emperor. I can tell you that Justin may not have decided to which of his nephews he'll pass on the gold and jeweled diadem, but I know for a fact whom *she* has decided upon—Justinian."

I am thrown off kilter. How could he know these things? How could he have the empress's confidence and yet speak so disparagingly of her? "I'm sure nothing will come of Justinian's flirtation," I say, attempting confidence—even though I know firsthand of Theodora's siren-like enchantment.

Suddenly, Procopius is standing close to me, his breath foul with onions. "You had better hope and pray that's the case, Stephen." He jabs a finger into my chest. "You had better see to it. Because, if you don't, Euphemia is likely to see that *both* Theodora and you disappear." He takes a step back and studies me.

I square my shoulders, but I know my face has been drained of blood. In a palace such as this, things like that do happen.

"Ah," Procopius proclaims. "Have I taken your tongue? I must be a wizard!"

But, oh, it would be a shame, indeed, for you to lose another organ." In one great flourish of his cloak he turns and makes his retreat.

I realize he had no errand here—other than to threaten me.

37

OMITO STOOD, HER HAND GOING to her mouth, too late to cover the gasp. "How long has this been going on?" she demanded.

Theodora rose from her seat at the loom and stood before her older sister. "A few weeks."

Comito's head retracted slightly. "Are you out of your mind? The emperor's nephew! And it's not yet burnt itself out?"

Theodora aborted a smile. "Not as yet, it hasn't."

"Indeed?" Comito felt for the arm of the couch behind her so as to guide herself to retake her seat and catch her breath. "And he knows something of our—your—background?"

Theodora laughed. "Something, yes."

"Not everything?"

Another laugh. "We've had just weeks, as I told you."

"Does his uncle know? Or the empress?"

Theodora shook her head. She took good time to sit on the opposite couch. Her eyes came up and held her sister's. "So you disapprove?—I'm surprised."

"Why? Because of the way I have lived? It's not that. If he were a rich merchant or trader in Constantinople, I should celebrate your conquest."

"But not if he is nephew to an emperor?"

"Ah! So he *is* under your spell! Might the stricken lover arrive any moment? That is the game, then?"

"Game, Comito? Don't confuse my intentions with your own. Anastasia told me you've had any number of affairs."

"Aren't you the high and mighty one? No games for you? Are you to say that your feeling for Hecebolus was a deep and abiding love? Remember, I was there when you chose to leave with him only because your dancing was less than divine and becoming mistress to a governor suited you—so much so that you abandoned your newborn daughter."

Theodora bolted from her seat, nearly colliding with the little table that held the *Shatranj* board and pieces. She walked to the window and looked out at the teeming lane. "Those words are like daggers, Comissa."

"I'm sorry. I know you've come to regret leaving your daughter. But I don't think you know the danger you're tempting here."

Theodora pivoted back to Comito. "Tell me, then, good sister, what perils await me?"

"Emperor Justin is not about to allow Justinian to have a dalliance with you."

Theodora felt her stomach knotting at this comment from her own sister, but in spite of it, she gave a hesitant nod. "That might be very true. In the meantime—"

"In the meantime," Comito blurted, "you could be in danger. Things are not always done justly at the Great Palace. They might have you sent away—or worse!"

"Worse?"

"Oh, I don't know.—I do know they will not sit still to have you in his company. Do you think your reputation has not followed you?"

"I haven't given it much thought. I have a different life these days."

At that moment a rapping came at the door. Theodora's first thought was that the caller was Justinian, and a quick look at Comito's widened eyes indicated that she thought the same.

Comito stood now, her hands lifting to smooth her coils of black hair.

Theodora made for the door, but before she could reach for the handle, the door opened.

Anastasia stepped inside. She hugged Theodora, noticed Comito and hurried into the room, her face alight with enthusiasm. "I suppose Thea has been telling you about him. What do you think? Isn't it exciting? Our own sister!"

Anastasia reached out to hug Comito, but her sister took a step back, a stern expression holding her at bay. "Ah," Anastasia said, halting and dropping her arms, "you hold a different opinion, I see."

"Indeed! I think this a very poor match."

Anastasia settled onto one of the couches. "What a dark cloud you are, Comito! Must you spoil things for Thea?"

"I? It's others, much higher up, who will be the spoilers." Comito sat on the couch across from Anastasia.

"Are you telling fortunes now?" Anastasia asked. "I can tell you that I saw Justinian. I saw him look at Thea. Cupid himself brought him to our sister's threshold."

Comito turned to Theodora. "Just how far has this progressed?"

Theodora's smile masked her irritation. She sat next to Anastasia, and while she took a few moments to respond, her younger sister spoke up.

"Could it be that you're jealous, Comissa?" Anastasia asked, drawing out the diminutive.

"Maybe," Theodora broke in, "she's developed the sight that Mother claimed to have. If that's the case, she must already know how far *this* has progressed."

"Really," Comito said, "none of us inherited the sight."

Theodora let out a laugh, one with an edge to it. "So much the good for us, I say."

When Anastasia also laughed, Comito seemed to feel obliged to join, half-heartedly, in the sisterly camaraderie. A moment later. her gaze fell upon the little table between the couches. "What game is that?"

"It's called *Shatranj*," Theodora said, "and it takes a good deal of concentration."

"Really?" Comito picked up one of the carved figures. "I've not heard of it and never have I seen such game pieces."

Theodora leaned forward. "Please place it back where you found it, Comito. Exactly! The game is still in play."

"I stand corrected," Comito said, her eyes catching Anastasia's in a union of sudden knowledge.

After the black piece had been placed in the correct square, Theodora sighed dramatically. "You might as well know that that game board is as far as it has progressed."

"Well, then all's safe for now," Comito said.

Theodora regretted saying as much as she had, for her sister's tone and demeanor seemed to indicate that the conversation had been reset, much like a game can be reset. She stood. "I'll make us some tea, now."

"No wine?" Anastasia asked in a pleading voice.

"No," Theodora said, offering no excuse or apology.

Theodora's sisters stayed until dusk began to fall. Conversation often crept back to the subject of Justinian. Comito and Anastasia maintained their respective pessimistic and optimistic views while Theodora attempted to steer the exchanges to a more neutral ground.

As her sisters prepared to leave, Comito stood for a moment, staring down at the *Shatranj* board game. "It's a new game for you, Thea. So many squares, so many moves. No doubt there are pitfalls you are as yet unaware of." She hugged Theodora now, whispering in her ear.

Theodora was glad to see the two depart and hurried to prepare for her nighttime guest. How well had she disguised her desire for them to leave? Might they have guessed the reason? And—Comito could be a mystery sometimes. Her parting whisper seemed at odds with her previous stance about Justinian: "If you *must* play the game, Thea, play it *well.*"

I sit at my little table. Here, a low-burning lamp flickers, threatening darkness, but I am unmoved to adjust the wick. Above ground, dusk must be settling in. I put off thinking about Procopius. Another day will be soon enough to accede to my hatred of the man. For now I can think only of the news he has imparted.

Justinian's recent absence from the library and the discontinuing of our strolls about the capital are mysteries no longer. It seems as if you don't recognize pleasures in life until they are taken away. I had gotten quite used to his chatter about The City, its series of walls, and the ingenious aqueduct system, a product of Roman technology about which he went on and on. Oh, he staged little tirades about the conflicts between the Blues and the Greens, but his love for the denizens of the capital was always on display. His humility—no, true camaraderie—among the wildly disparate citizens we encountered was noteworthy. Indeed, that he treated me like a friend—rather than a slave—enshrined him in my heart. But now he has turned his attentions to Theodora. I am left like a lover scorned.

My heart now taps into a memory of an event that occurred when I was but seven. I had made friends with Vidal, a boy whose family had moved nearby. Vidal and I were having a wonderful time fashioning a shelter—as boys often do—in the forest. He was handier and more inventive than I, traits I admired. Our shelter was half completed when my brother Ahmed came upon us. Although he was older by three years, he set about helping us. His skills were extraordinary and in short order he was working well with Vidal. I was left standing like some bystander, my new friend stolen from me. I felt a well of emptiness and betrayal.

Of course, I have no cause to feel betrayed by Justinian. No one needs to tell me we are not equals—like brothers—or that I could ever consider intimacy with Theodora. Even if we weren't separated by five years—a difference that might lessen in significance as I grow older—I had been robbed of such a sweet communion by a forced cutting. And yet the hollow within me is worse than childhood heartbreak. I imagine the two of them together. My blood surges, pulsing at my temples. I want to lash out, strike someone, some thing, but as I turn in my chair I find the dark tesserae of Jati's eyes upon me. Is he scolding me, shaming me, scoffing at the impertinence of a slave? The foolishness of a eunuch?

He would not understand and I choose not to confide in him this night. I should be buoyed by the thought that any relationship that Justinian might have with Theodora is nearly as ill-fated as my love for her. I am not.

Nightfall is still hours away.

38

"You're late," Theodora said, opening the door.

"I've not had such a greeting since my army days."

"Forgive me. I was about to say I'm glad you're late."

Justinian entered. "And why is that?"

"I was able to rest a bit after a rather tiresome visit from my sisters." Theodora closed the door and followed Justinian into the sitting area. "You met Anastasia briefly. She is like a butterfly in human form, but Comito is full of opinions. She's taken on this big sister attitude."

"For instance?" Justinian turned about.

Theodora was glad he was no more than average in height. Nonetheless, she had the peer up at him. "She frowns on my—meetings—with you."

"Meetings? Is that how you characterized them?"

Theodora nodded. "She was insistent on knowing the nature of our relationship."

Justinian smiled wryly. "And what did you tell her?"

Theodora glanced at the game board. "That we are enthusiasts of *Shatranj*."

"And that all is innocence?"

"Indeed." Theodora could not fend off a little giggle.

Justinian took a step back, the glass-gray eyes widening as he let loose a roar of a laugh, one that came from deep within his torso, one that made Theodora flinch. Oh, she had heard him laugh before. She had made him laugh, in fact, when recounting goings-on backstage in her theater days, innocent goings-on. But she had never witnessed him laugh with as much volume and verve as now.

Theodora blinked twice, as if she were seeing a new persona coming into the light. The Justinian she had gotten to know was a conservative man with a keen, serious mind and a demeanor that was almost somber. Here was a new side of him.

Justinian's laugh was braking now, transitioning into a sigh deep enough for the stage. "Well, you are good at games, my dear." Suddenly, he stepped forward and swept Theodora into his embrace.

Wearing a *tunica intima* as sheer as gossamer, Theodora sat brushing her long, raven black hair at the little table next to the sleeping couch.

"You are so very beautiful, Thea," Justinian said, rolling over onto his side and adjusting the light linen blanket. He watched her, one hand propping up his head.

Theodora continued at her task, sensing his eyes upon her. It wasn't anything he hadn't said before—or that others hadn't said myriad times. After a while, she pivoted on her stool toward him. He was nearly twice her age. While not quite running to fat, his body was thickening in this, his fortieth year. Atop a very round face the curly dark hair appeared especially—almost comically—tousled. She knew he was not expecting a compliment in return but wondered nonetheless if anyone had ever called him handsome. She gifted him with a smile now, turned away and took to plaiting her hair.

"I want you to meet my uncle, Thea."

Theodora drew in breath. "What?"

He pulled himself up into a sitting position on the straw mattress, his back against the wall. "Yes, it's time."

"The emperor?"

Justinian gave a little laugh. "Yes, that one. Uncle Justin."

Theodora's hands dropped away from her hair. An odd mix of fear and excitement overtook her. She stared at her own slightly imperfect reflection. The box mirror on the table had been a gift from Justinian. "No."

"No?"

"It would not be wise."

"Who's to say that?"

"I say that. It's a crazy idea."

"Why?"

Theodora winced. "I would not be welcome at court. I am not a patrician."

"Is that all?"

"No—but it's enough."

"Thea, I told you my story—that I was born Petrus in the Roman province of Nish. You realize, *I* am lowborn."

"Yes, you were—until you were adopted by the emperor. On that day you were transformed."

"Listen to me. Justin is my blood uncle. Ergo, the emperor is—or was—a plebeian. He was, however, a brilliant tactician who rose through the ranks of the military. And then he got lucky. Believe me, he won't look down on you. So—maybe it's time for Fortune to smile on *you*."

Theodora turned to see a glint in Justinian's eyes and a slight lift at the corners of his mouth. He was gloating as if he had carried away one of her most important pieces on the *Shatranj* board.

"You must listen to me. You're the smartest man I've ever met, Justinian. You've led a scholar's life. You do not frequent theaters, do you? You spend your time in libraries, yes? Admit it!"

"So?"

"If your intention is to take me to court, there will be others who do remember me."

"What of it? You played the comedienne foil to your sister. Why should that bother anyone?"

"There's more to it than that."

"Hecebolus promised marriage and then betrayed you. I can't blame you for that. He was a fool to let you go."

"Do you think Hecebolus was the first man to show me attention?" Theodora moved to sit next to him on the couch. She took his hand in both of hers. "You are likely to choose never to visit me again, but I must be honest. In the years before Hecebolus, I became quite famous for my living pictures on stage. I don't regret them. Most of them were quite clever and all of them were well received. But other people with long memories will not speak well of me or them."

"But that was onstage. Those were *performances*."

"More."

"I have not lived my entire life in a library, Thea. I've spent years in the army. You mean to say there have been other men, is that it? I know that."

His comment perplexed her, and her speech faltered for several seconds. "Yes," she said finally, "there have been others. Does that make a difference?"

"No."

His quick reply surprised her. With hardly a thought, she went a step farther to test his interest in her. "And there is a child, a girl."

Justinian's face grew dark. He turned his head away and his hand slipped from hers.

In the ensuing silence, Theodora regretted her honesty. Had she alienated him? And then came an introspective thought: had she wished to alienate him?

Justinian let out an indecipherable sigh and turned back to her. "Where is she?"

"A family has taken her in."

"I see. It must have been hard for you."

"I carry guilt, I do."

"Do you know her whereabouts?"

The unexpected question cut to the quick. If she told him the truth, what would he say? Do? Would he interfere in Hyacinth's life? And how would her relationship with him be altered? "No I don't," she said, looking away. "She was adopted as a mere baby years ago, a good distance from The City, I was told."

"I see."

"My child was a fortunate one," Theodora said, quickly shifting the conversation to orphans and unwed mothers, then moving on to another subject near to her heart. "Oh, you don't know the plight of women in this city. For some, going on the boards is the only answer. They have so few options in life. Why, at this moment my childhood friend is indentured to Madame Flavia. Do you know her brothel? It's the most famous in The City."

"No."

"Of course, you wouldn't. I went there to secure her release and was told that no amount of money would buy her freedom. Three years she must remain there watching her youth slip away. She's my dearest friend."

"How do you know her?"

Theodora faced him, searching his face for sincerity. "Our friendship goes back to the day when my sisters and I danced before the Greens. Even before that."

"But it was the Blues who gave you their attention?"

"Yes, as well as employment for our new father.—Antonina was there that day." She's been my friend since I was five, Justinian. And now I find her in the claws of Madame Flavia. It's a terrible life Nina has now—terrible! Theodora surprised herself now to feel tears tracing the contour of her cheeks and spilling onto her *tunica intima*. She turned her face away.

Leaning forward, Justinian brought his arm around her shoulders and pulled her into the crook of his arm. "Wipe your tears, Theodora. Wipe them away and say that you'll come to the royal banquet on Wednesday next."

It would be later, as she readied herself for bed that she thought of her daughter and resolved to see her again, if only to watch her from afar.

Late one night a knock comes at my door. My first thought is that it is most likely Tariq here to engage me in a nighttime round of *Shatranj*, as he is wont to do several nights a week. We now use his board and pieces since I've given mine to Theodora.

And so it is a great surprise to find Procopius standing in my doorway. I find no words, but he reads my face like the page of a codex.

He renders the facsimile of a smile. "Hello, Stephen. May I come in?"

I stand aside, allowing him to pass, his head ducking so as to clear the lintel. I follow him into my room.

He stops near the table bearing the *Shatranj* board, his hooded eyes narrowing in a sweep that seems to take in every facet of my living quarters. "Not much to speak of, is it? Too small, I should think. Although the mosaic," he says, nodding toward Jati, "is exquisite." His eyes come back to me. "Will you invite me to sit?"

I nod toward the chair that Tariq has furnished, and I sit opposite, the game between us.

"How may I be of service?" I ask, my tone flat.

He ignores my question. "A scribe of your talents, Stephen, should not be housed in the bowels of the palace like an ordinary servant. Leo often speaks of your skill with the kalamos and with languages. You have impressed him of late. You should have a suite—yes, a suite, one with windows, of course."

"Perhaps one day." I know that Leo is impressed not because of my skill with a reed pen, but because I am favored by the emperor's nephew.

"Ah, you need to be more ambitious than that."

"What is the purpose of your visit, Lord Procopius?"

"It's a shame that your relationship with Justinian has reached an impasse. Or have you resumed your strolls about the capital?"

"No," I say, confirming what I suspect he already knows.

"My, he could see that you are given better appointed rooms. Perhaps a word in his ear would do the trick."

I know that Procopius's rooms are not here but in the Daphne Wing. He elaborates at some length about his suite, but when I do not respond, he moves in a different direction. "If you have not spent time with Justinian, perhaps you have seen the actress—Theodora?"

"I have not." I am becoming more and more uncomfortable. We're moving toward the reason for his visit, the reason for his bit of extortion.

"What is—or was—the nature of your interaction with her? Oh, I don't mean to imply anything indecent—that is, I know any such liaison you might have with a woman like that is a limited one."

The man has obviously come to me for information—for dirt—but he cannot help himself from delivering an insult about my manhood. He's not as smart as I figured. "We are friends," I say, my voice chilled.

"Indeed. In those days and weeks that you spent together, she must have told you about her adventures at the Pentapolis and her journey home that took her winding about the Middle Sea?"

"She did. Are you to write a report, Lord Procopius?"

"Good God, no. I am merely curious, always have been. What did she say, for instance, about the outbound shipboard experience with her—her mentor—Hecebolus?"

"She said she stood at the ship's stern in wide wonder at the playful dolphins that accompanied the boat."

Procopius narrows his eyes in appraisal of me. "Ah, what about the duration of her time in the Governor's House?"

"Only that it was a terrible thing to witness the seventeen-year invasion of locusts."

"And—?"

I shrug.

Procopius sighs. "Well, then, what about the circuitous route back to Constantinople? She must have talked about those who helped her along the Levant, those who took her in—? How did she support herself?"

By now, as we talk across the *Shatranj* board, we both know the pieces of *our* game are words. "Oh, she went on and on about the characteristics of camels. How large they are, the care one has to take in riding them, how strong they are, and how long they can travel without rest or food or water—oh, and just how far they can spit."

Procopius glowers at me. "So her chief concerns were dolphins and locusts and camels?"

"It would seem so." I laugh.

"Ah—it would seem that I'm wasting my time here." Procopius stands. "You know, I am not the only person concerned. A good many senators are, as well. And I do have influence here. If you help us nip this liaison between her and Justinian in the bud, I could see that you are given fine rooms."

I smile and say nothing.

"Listen, you don't want to have me as an enemy, trust me, Stephen. Whether the woman has changed her ways, I can't say, but she's still a whore and it is of the greatest importance that Lord Justinian's eyes be opened to the truth. With your help or without it, I'll see to it."

"Some people prefer to overlook the truth."

His retort is immediate. "Believe me the emperor and Euphemia will not overlook it."

The familiar tone in which he refers to the empress by name tells me he is well disposed toward her. It is she to whom he will go first with his gossip. I nod. "Tsk tsk," I mutter, fearing that anything more will lengthen his stay.

Procopius turns to leave. I follow, and when he pulls open the door, we are both surprised to see Tariq there preparing to knock. His gaze shifts from me to Procopius and back again. "Are we not to play *Shatranj*?" Tariq asks, his eyes like dark moons.

Procopius turns back to me. His tone is hushed but stern. "Should you change your mind, Stephen, come find me. My suite will impress you." He pivots now and pushes through the doorway, forgetting about the lintel, so that he scrapes the very top of his head as he goes. He tries his best to stifle a grunt of pain.

Tariq and I watch as he lumbers down the hall massaging his injury.

"What in the name of Hecate was he doing here?" Tariq questions as we settle in at the game table.

"Nothing of importance. Shall we begin?"

Tariq is undeterred and during our game he peppers me with questions about the self-important Procopius. I manage to put him off.

After he leaves, I sit brooding about Procopius. How far will his enmity of Theodora take him? I have not seen Thea in weeks, but my feelings for her have not waned. What can I do to protect her from his machinations?

I look around my underground chamber. Oh, how I would love to have a room with windows and natural light streaming in. But at what cost? My eyes go to the wall. "And you, Jati," I say to my mosaic confidant, "do not be taken in by Procopius's flattery."

39

"COMITO HAS ARRIVED AT LAST!" Anastasia called.

Theodora emerged from her tiny dressing area to face the audience of her sisters. Ivory in color, her long linen stola was belted at the waist so that below it draped in neat folds to the ankles. The border at the feet featured an intricately embroidered pattern of gold leaves. Her thick black hair was braided and coiled atop her head and held in place by a gold metal band. In the back, the braids escaped from under the metal and were loosened so that they fell in a bouncy display that flirted with her shoulders.

Anastasia jumped up from the couch. "There! You see, I knew it would be perfect! Oh, Thea, you will stand out."

"I'm not so certain I want to stand out, Tasia."

Having just shed her cloak, Comito walked toward Theodora, her mouth agape. "So you're going, after all? He's talked you into it."

Theodora nodded.

"Of course, she's going! Just look at her, Comissa. Just look."

Comito's eyes moved over Theodora like a search lantern. "You said you had nothing to wear and yet you come up with this incredible stola. It's beautiful. How much did it cost?"

Theodora giggled. "Nothing."

"Nothing?"

"I got it for her," Anastasia interjected.

Comito turned to their young sister. "You?"

"Well, it's borrowed, I admit. It must go back tomorrow."

"It's from the theater where Anastasia works," Theodora explained. "She bribed the costumer."

Comito's eyes went wide, sparkling with good humor. "And so you are going in theater garb, as if it's a costume ball rather than a royal banquet—how appropriate!" Her laughter began in a low register, then moved up, up into a thoroughly liberated peal—by which time her sisters had joined in.

Comito's gaze fell upon Theodora's golden necklace and dangling earrings inlaid with red and blue stones. Her laugh died away as she moved in for a closer look. She sighed now. "Theodora, I don't think the jewelry is a good choice."

Their laughs expended, Theodora and Anastasia exchanged quizzical expressions. "No?" Theodora asked.

"Why it is the best stage jewelry I've ever seen," Comito said. "Anastasia, you chose well. But the people at the banquet—nobles, politicians and the like—will be wearing the real article. The gold will be pure and the jewels will be genuine. Somebody is bound to notice and may even lack the good taste to avoid commentary. You would be humiliated. Best to wear your enameled necklace and be done with it."

"But they're real," Anastasia asserted.

Comito's eyes turned to question Theodora.

"The gold is real," Theodora said. "The stones are real. I attempted to decline the gift, but Justinian insisted."

Comito managed to say only, "Oh," her mouth remaining in the shape of a perfect O for many seconds while Theodora and Anastasia laughed.

We copyists work in silence much of the time. Most of those in the great cavernous room lose themselves in their work to such an extent they notice nothing occurring around them. I am not such a one. Of late, I find myself easily distracted. And so it is that my ear recognizes the particular gait of a figure moving up the far aisle.

I look up to see Justinian striding toward Leo's desk. To my knowledge this is his first visit in weeks. I watch the two converse, their tone light at first, then growing serious. I see Leo's head come up and his eyes shift across the room to me. I avert my gaze—too late. I resume my task, no more the watcher. But I hear them conclude their talk, followed by Justinian's steps, no longer on the outer aisle, and as he draws closer, a heat rises in my face. When I look up he is standing at my desk.

"Hello, Stephen."

I stand. "Hello, my lord."

"Leo says that I may take you aside for a brief talk. Do you mind?"

I hold down my resentment for having been ignored for some weeks, as well as a deeper bitterness—if Procopius was truthful—for the attention Justinian has been paying Theodora. I attempt a smile.

"Come along, then," he says.

I put away the codex I have been working on and obey, aware that other eyes are following us to the door. The hallway is empty but we remain silent as we move toward a far exterior door. Outside, Justinian starts to speak as we begin to traverse a long colonnade, but he stops abruptly as we observe a figure approaching us. I recognize the lankiness and gait of the man almost at once.

"My lord," Procopius says, nodding toward Justinian. He looks at me, and my identity seems to jolt him. Justinian allows no opportunity for speech, merely nodding in return. In moments we are past him.

We come to the path that takes us into the well-maintained gardens of the Palace of Hormisdas, Justinian's palace.

He stops us in front of a stone bench and turns to me. "I've missed our walks in The City, Stephen," he says. "Perhaps next week we could manage an afternoon together." His tone is light. He seems unaware that I might have been miffed or hurt by the oversight.

I nod.

"Let's sit down, yes?"

I obey, arranging myself at an angle so that I am able to observe him.

"I have a request, Stephen."

"Yes?"

"Well, first I must tell you that I have been seeing, on occasion, Theodora." Another nod.

"You don't seem surprised. She's told you?"

"No, I haven't seen her."

His face darkens. "Then who—has there been talk?"

"Just by one person," I say.

"Who?"

"He just passed us a few minutes ago."

"Procopius? A meddler, that one, scholar or no scholar." He scoffs. "He matters little. What does matter is that in the near future—providing things go as I hope they go—I will have a task for you."

"What is it, this task?" I ask, only too aware of my status as a slave.

"It's a mission, a secret mission. Can I trust you, Stephen?"

My curiosity overcomes the resentment I feel toward this man, the resentment he is too blind to sense.

40

"WHY ISN'T HE COMING TO escort you himself?" Comito stood at the window. Dusk was imminent.

Theodora was unfolding a veil that would cover her intricately braided black hair and—when she stepped from the house—her face. "I insisted that we meet there. I wanted my sisters here to send me off to the royal banquet. He would have made me anxious."

"It's here!" Anastasia cried, rushing in from the street. "The sedan chair is here. It has four bearers. Just four slaves, Thea. Impressive, I suppose, but he could have done better.

Theodora laughed. "Thank you for your accounting, Tasia. Who am I trying to impress, anyway? My face is to be covered, so no one will know such luxury is mine."

"Just the same—"

"Nonetheless," Comito interrupted, "this alley seldom sees such a fine entourage, so people are gathering and gawking."

"There, I'm ready. Come, Tasia and Comissa. Let us hold hands in a circle as we did that day as children in the Hippodrome."

"Who would have thought then," Anastasia ventured once the hands were joined, "that one day one of those poor children would be attending a banquet at the Great Palace?"

"Who, indeed?" Comito questioned.

"Comito," Theodora said with a stage sigh, "you're still skeptical of Justinian, aren't you?"

Comito's eyes narrowed. "I don't want to see you hurt. You say the jewels are genuine, but what about his feelings?"

The question caught at both Theodora's head and heart. "You do cut to the crux of the matter, Comissa. He insists that his feelings for me are genuine."

"Royals are best at insisting, aren't they? I think we have all heard that refrain before—on stage and off. And remember, Thea, princes oftentimes have little to say about whom they may love."

Theodora rendered the facsimile of a smile. "Only the arrow of time will tell."

"And time is flying," Anastasia said. "Let's get you to your sedan chair."

Theodora drew in a large breath, exhaled, and squeezed her sisters' hands, as they had done at the Hippodrome all those years ago. She released her hold now, and Anastasia helped her into a cloak matching the ivory of her stola. Lowering her veil, Theodora turned to leave.

Settling into the chair, Theodora scarcely noticed the blur of bystanders crowding around the vehicle as it was lifted and put into motion. Comito had meant well, but Theodora had to admit that her sister had echoed her own reservations regarding Justinian. Now came a moment—just a moment—when she leaned forward and was about to call for the bearers to stop so that she could return home. She knew at once that it was too late for that. Justinian would be waiting for her and with that knowledge came courage. She—like the arrow of time—was moving forward at a fast clip.

As the bearers of the sedan chair progressed toward the Mese, Theodora looked up to see Joseph the Stylite atop his column. He was leaning over his platform, staring down, eyes wide. Chuckling to herself, Theodora wondered what he would think if he could see that the veiled lady in the chair was Lady Gray herself.

Impulsively, she slowly waved her hand at the stylite. She could only imagine the dumbfounded man's expression, for in moments the sedan moved past his column.

As arranged, Justinian—attired in a vivid blue dalmatic—was waiting for her in the Augustaion, at the entrance to the Great Palace. With a wide smile, he helped her down from the sedan chair. Away from the public street now, Theodora removed the veil so as to return his smile. He took her hand and led her through the bronze double doors and into the domed vestibule of the Chalké, where the four palace guards bowed to Justinian. Her eyes tried to catch every detail of this experience. Her arms went to gooseflesh. Passing the barracks of the excubitors, they came to the long Hall of the Nineteen Couches. Inside, eighteen curved niches spanned the length of the building, nine on either side, each with three mullioned windows and a single couch, curved like a half-moon. Theodora looked to the far end where a large couch rested under the main apse. It was empty. Emperor Justin and Empress Euphemia had yet to arrive. About half of the niches were already occupied, and as Justinian led her forward, a number of people bowed to Justinian and several addressed him. Justinian was not open to conversing, however, so that they arrived at the far end in good time and settled into the niche on the right side closest to the royal couch.

Theodora had been aware of a number of assessing eyes on them as they moved, but she noticed now in the niche parallel to theirs across the way a particular watcher staring at them. It was a thin man in a plain brown dalmatic. When she returned his gaze with cold nerve, his face colored slightly, and he turned away.

Within a very short time, senators, soldiers of high rank, and men of influence, as well as female companions, occupied the couches in all the niches. For the moment, none dared to recline.

"Do you know what I've done with the dining hall in my little palace?"

"No—what?"

"Well, it was too big for any entertaining I might do and my library was too small, so I made the dining hall my library. Your friend Stephen works there. He may have described it to you."

"He has."

Justinian reached over and placed his hand on hers. "You must come live there, Thea."

It was a plea he had made a dozen times in recent days, and each time she refused. "Justinian, be sensible. Such a thing would not be accepted. We can continue as we have and one day you'll tire of me and—"

"No! Don't say that, Thea. I could never tire of you."

Now, from a side door to the left of the royal couch, came—in full regalia—the emperor and empress. Everyone stood to greet them. So costumed were they in shimmering gold cloth and jewels that little of their persons was in evidence except for their faces and hands. Theodora knew that Justin had been nearly seventy when he was crowned a few years before and that Empress Euphemia was nearly as old, but the sight of their wrinkled visages and slow gait took her aback nonetheless.

As soon as the royal couple seated themselves, the room swarmed with servants carrying tables laden with food, one for each niche. Other servants followed closely with amphoras of wine. The initial fare on the table consisted of olives, goat cheese, octopi and smoked fish. Guests nibbled at the appetizers, sipped at wine or water, and chatted, some reclining, some moving to other niches to engage friends in conversation.

"Come along," Justinian whispered and took Theodora's hand. In no more than a minute, they were standing in front of the emperor's table.

Justinian introduced Theodora to his aunt and uncle.

Her heart hammering, Theodora recalled stage business appropriate to the moment and dropped into a deep curtsey.

"Who is this, then?" Emperor Justin asked, his hearing no longer perfect. "Lovely, she is. Stunning!"

Justinian was repeating the introduction when the empress turned to her husband and said, "It's Theodora—the actress we were told about!"

Theodora could not determine whether her hissing tone indicated her impatience with her husband's lack of hearing or whether it was a rebuke of the guest. Perhaps it was both.

"I am delighted to be here, Emperor." Bowing her head slightly to Justinian's aunt, Theodora said, "Empress."

"Indeed, young lady," the emperor pronounced, "and we are better for it."

The empress's lined face went to stone, but beneath her narrow nose the facsimile of a smile broke through. "Enjoy yourself tonight. Perhaps one day the experience will aid you on the boards."

Theodora bowed her head and when she lifted her face, she could manage only a smile as false as that of Justinian's aunt. The empress's tone was undoubtedly meant to suggest that this evening would be the only one ever spent in the Great Palace and that her days with Justinian were numbered.

The emperor asked Justinian if he had recently observed the landscaping that was being done to the terraces that led down to the Sea of Marmara. As they chatted, Theodora noted that the emperor seemed to set great store by his nephew's opinion.

The empress sat, eyes averted, as if something of interest was occurring in a far corner of the chamber.

Concluding their talk, Justinian bowed and asked permission to return to their niche. The emperor nodded, flashing a warm smile at Theodora, who bowed and backed away, avoiding eye contact with the empress.

Justinian led Theodora back to their couch. Another table stood in place of the first, this one laden with fish, roast chicken, ham, bread, figs, and apples. A server was pouring wine of a different vintage into fresh cups.

Theodora was no sooner seated than she turned to Justinian. "You told your aunt that I'm an actress?"

Justinian blinked at the question. "I don't recall doing so." He reached for a fig. "What does it matter?"

"Oh, it matters. And if someone else told her, that matters even more."

"Don't be upset, Thea," Justinian said. "I have my own mind. I know how to work around my aunt. Besides, you seemed to delight Uncle Justin."

"Ah, but does *he* know how to work around your aunt?"

The two laughed. Theodora regretted having to forego the subject of who might have been talking about her, but she took the plate Justinian offered and reached with her golden fork for the sliced breast of chicken.

Later, the emperor called Justinian over for a consultation with two other men. Theodora sat absorbed in thought as she cut an apple into wedges.

Suddenly, a figure appeared before her. She looked up at Empress Euphemia. Attempting to mask her surprise, Theodora stood. "Empress," she whispered. Protocol required neither a bow nor curtsey for the empress.

"Do you mind if I sit for a few moments?" the empress asked.

Speechless, Theodora motioned for her to join her. Sitting on the curved couch, they exchanged pleasantries for a little while.

When talk of the décor, menu, and weather had played out, the empress nodded toward Justinian, who was speaking to the emperor with animation. "Justin relies on his nephew, especially in matters of law and architecture."

Something in the woman's tone placed Theodora on guard. "I see."

"We saw to it that he was carefully educated, you know.—Carefully groomed."

"Groomed?"

"Oh, Justin has several nephews, but Justinian's star outshines them all. We saw the promise long ago and we adopted him. Only Justinian has been raised to the status of patrician. He has proven himself as a military leader and, do you know, he has exposed at least two serious plots against the emperor?"

"Truly?"

"Yes, so you see, Theodora, no matter that you have amended your life, any future with our nephew is impossible."

The statement came at her like an arrow, quick, sharp, and deadly. Theodora swallowed hard, searching for a measured response. The empress was saying what Theodora herself had been telling Justinian for weeks—that a future for them was impossible. And yet she recoiled to hear it from this woman. She thought back to Justinian's recent declaration and said, "Empress, your nephew tells me he has his own mind."

The woman's thin lips curled into an ironic smile. "Ah, men do not always know what's best for them."

"Some men, perhaps."

The empress compressed her lips so that they nearly disappeared.

A lull ensued, one that Theodora allowed to go on.

The empress broke the impasse with a sigh, and then a question. "Do you know anything about me, Theodora?"

"No, not really," she lied. Rumors about her early life were rife.

"Like you, I was not born a patrician. In fact, I met Justin when he was leading the army. I was a lowborn and a slave, but we were attracted to one another. I became his concubine. In time, we fell in love, and Emperor Anastasius deemed me a patrician, allowing us to marry. My name was changed from Lupicina, a common prostitute's name, to Euphemia. A patrician's name, don't you think?—So, I can see from your expression that you are wondering why I would tell you this."

Theodora sat silent, her back stiff as a rod.

"You see, because of our similar backgrounds, I consider myself a good judge of you and your intentions. My husband can be blind to such matters."

"Indeed," Theodora said before good sense told her to bite her tongue.

Empress Euphemia's heavily hooded eyes flared. Her tongue flicked along her painted lower lip before she continued. "What makes us different, Theodora, is that at the time of our marriage, no one could have guessed that the throne would come to Justin. But—for Justinian, the throne is his destiny. You must understand that he must take a wife who has been prepared to wear the diadem, one who has worn one. It must be a marriage that strengthens and enlarges our place on the map."

"Do you have a list of possibilities, Empress?"

"Perhaps I do." She smiled now, ignoring Theodora's snideness. "But let me explain one very important factor regarding any list. Oh, your history is similar to mine. I grant you that. Come, come, we both know that a woman's magick with a man often lies beneath her *tunica intima*, yes? And I suspect you possess your share of Syrian magick."

The insult sent blood thrumming to Theodora's temples.

The empress's smile dropped away. "But there is one difference that smothers any hope you might have."

"I was never a slave," Theodora said.

"True, I give you that. But the thing that makes the difference is that you were an actress."

"So? It was the way for a free woman to make a living."

"Nonetheless, patricians are forbidden by law to marry actresses. By written law, my dear."

Emperor Justin appeared and announced: "I've come to reclaim my wife," He reached for the empress's hand, nodding to Theodora. "Justinian will return shortly. I sent him out to observe some landscaping. And you two," he said with a wink, "I trust your chat has been delightful."

"Indeed," the empress said, flashing a mean smile at Theodora.

Theodora stood as the royal couple took their leave. She willed her own smile to appear more genuine than it was. She was an actress, after all.

She sat back on the couch, her mind fraught with worry. The woman was shrewd and insufferable. Theodora knew that she now had an enemy, a formidable one that would be relentless in her desire to see her gone from Justinian's life.

Of course, Theodora knew that marriages between patricians and actresses were impossible and not to be tolerated, whether by written or unwritten law.

Several minutes passed before Justinian returned to the niche. Unknown to her, the old woman had stirred a hornets' nest. Theodora had not been thinking about marriage with Justinian.

Until now.

"I'm so sorry you're sitting here by yourself, Thea." Justinian sat next to her, his hand taking hers.

"Your aunt kept me company."

"Did she? Do you like her?"

Theodora smiled. "Justinian, I've changed my mind. I would like to see your little palace and the dining room you have fashioned into a library."

"Really? You would?" Justinian leaned into her, his eyes aglow with surprise and delight.

His expression incised itself in Theodora's heart. She nodded.

"And the suite I promised you there—? Will you at least look at it?"

"Yes, dearest."

Later, as they stood to make their way to ask their leave, Theodora glanced across to the opposite wall of niches, noticing once again the thin man in a brown dalmatic she had seen earlier. Like then, he was staring at their niche with a notetaker's eyes.

"Here," Justinian said, turning her around to face him, "let me help with your cloak."

"Look across the way, Justinian, over my shoulder. Do you know the man in the niche opposite ours? Is he still watching?"

"You mean I have competition? Let's see, the niche opposite ours. Yes, I see it. It's quite empty."

Theodora spun around. The man had gone. Something hardened in her stomach, like a stone.

"What was it about him?" Justinian asked.

Theodora gave a little dismissive wave of her hand. "Nothing, my love. Nothing at all."

Procopius comes to the side of my desk as I copy a Greek text from papyrus to parchment. He has blessedly ignored me of late so it is with some trepidation that I look up, my eyes inquiring.

"She's here in the palace," he hisses through clenched teeth.

I tilt my head as if I have no idea what he's talking about. And I don't, not completely.

"The she-devil. She's living here in Justinian's palace." Like a jackal, he watches my face.

"Theodora?" I whisper. My surprise is genuine.

"The same," he spits. "Bag and baggage. You didn't know?"

I shake my head.

"You're to blame, nonetheless."

I'm too taken by surprise to argue.

"You must persuade her to leave, Stephen."

My back stiffens. "And why must I do that?"

"Keep your voice down, do you hear? It's for her safety—and for yours."

I glance around at the other copyists. No one appears to be paying any attention. I lower my voice. "What is the danger?"

"The senators will be livid once they find out."

"Isn't there a law against her marrying into royalty? Why, then, should they worry? And what danger can *they* pose?" What I don't say is that in the time I have been here, I've learned that many of the senators have mistresses, some quite blatantly visible.

"As a group, the senators are quick to panic and quick to act. And they often act outside of the Senate Chambers, you fool. You don't think they abide only by the law? Palace intrigue often takes place in alleyways."

I am not particularly persuaded. My thought is that he himself is prone to panic. "And what danger to me?"

"You are looking at your danger."

"Are you threatening me?"

"For her safety and for yours, see that her stay is brief."

"I have no influence—" Procopius screws up his face so hideously that I stop mid-sentence.

"Just do it!" he cries, forgetting our veil of secrecy. He pivots to make his exit, oblivious to the stir he has just caused.

It is late. I lie awake wondering if Procopius spoke the truth. Is it possible Theodora is here, somewhere above me in one of the myriad chambers?

The lamp on my table is low now, the movements on my mosaic boy's image sluggish shadows. "You've not seen one like Theodora," I say aloud to Jati. "Not like her."

And now I recall Justinian's saying that if things go as he wishes, I would be given some secret mission.

I sleep very little.

41

UNABLE TO SLEEP, THEODORA ROSE from the bed where Justinian lay sleeping. She dressed quickly and moved out onto the little balcony. The late night air was cold and the marble against her feet colder. Justinian's palace was merely a pace or two away from the waters of the Sea of Marmara.

The full moon found its twin in the shimmering sea. Theodora attempted to compute how many months had passed since the ship from Antioch returned her to the capital. So few, so few. Why, the ship had passed this very building. Then it was just one of the many that made up the palace complex. Who could have guessed the future?

What is to become of me now? Amidst all the wealth and luxury, Theodora felt very much alone. She saw her current life as a fabric of so many strands, strands that pulled in opposite ways. Outside the complex were her sisters, her daughter. Inside, Justinian was her anchor, but there were his aunt and uncle, too. How would they react? Empress Euphemia had been explicit in her opinion of one-time actresses as opposed to the kind of woman meant for Justinian. Is it possible, she wondered—for the first time—that Justinian himself assumed he could make a dynastic marriage and still hold on to her? As what—a concubine? The thought made her weak. She sat down.

Someone below was scrubbing the stone patio. Ah! What of the many people that made the complex hum like a hive? She was an interloper here. Fluid as water, gossip about her was probably already rapidly flowing among the senators, excubitors, servants, consuls, officials, and couriers that made up the "Bearded Ones." And then there were those without beards—the many eunuchs that were perhaps most responsible for making the palace run smoothly; they were no less human, no less prone to idle talk.

It came to her only now: *Stephen is here. Perhaps I have at least one friend.*

Just paces from the Mese and not far from the Forum of Theodosius, I come upon the impressive stone house of Egyptian design. Its elaborate newly shellacked double doors glitter beneath a half moon window, the only window on the ground floor. Above, the narrow arched windows are plentiful enough. The edifice eclipses the smaller, more humble tenements in the vicinity, like a stout, shimmering empress in the company of beggars.

I lift the knocker and bring it down. The boom resonates to such an extent that I forego a second knock. I wait.

One of the doors opens, and a huge hulk of an Egyptian in a blue tunic stares down at me. His brown eyes and smile emanate warmth ever so briefly. He glances down, taking in my white dalmatic, gold trim, insignias. The eyes deaden, and the smile evaporates. He realizes I am not a customer. He realizes I am what I am.

"I'm here to see Madame Flavia."

"Are you expected?"

His high-timbred voice confirms for me my first impression: he, too, is a eunuch. I sense that he would like to close the door upon me. "I am not." I summon bravado from within. "It would be to her advantage, I can tell you, and to your disadvantage if you don't admit me."

His hand still clutches the handle, the eyes narrowing. His wide chest lifts as he draws in a deep breath and considers.

"Please," I say.

Suddenly, he takes a pace back, pulling the door fully open. I step up and cross the threshold of the most elite brothel in Constantinople.

Upon securing the entry, he ushers me to a small waiting room. "Be seated. I'll see if she is inclined to see you."

I sit on one of two white upholstered couches.

After a while I hear voices in the hall—his and a woman's.

Momentarily, the heavy drape is pulled to the side by the doorman, and a woman nearly as wide as the entryway enters. As I stand, the drape falls into place but no sound comes of the man's slippers, which I spy beneath the damask. He stands close by in the hall, the woman's bodyguard.

"My!" the woman exclaims, closing the distance between us and eyeing me as if I were merchandise. "A visitor from the palace, no less—and an exceedingly handsome one at that. Your name?" She sits on the opposite couch and I notice that it's long, like a sleeping couch. She nods for me to retake my seat.

"Stephen," I say, taking her cue, but my body pitches forward out of uneasiness.

"Ah! I am Madame Flavia, but you must know that." Her eyes flit to a small side table and she reaches for a dish, pulls back the cloth meant to discourage flies, captures a stuffed date, and sweeps it into her surprisingly small red mouth. Chewing with great relish, she thrusts the dish in my direction. No finger on her hand is without a ring set with precious stones.

"No, thank you, Madame Flavia."

Her shoulders lift a little in indifference and she returns the bowl to the table—but not before palming another sweet.

The madame's gray eyes narrow. "Are they sending such pretty boys now to collect taxes?"

I was at a loss for how to present my case, but she has now given me an opening. "No, I am actually bringing *you* a good deal of coin."

Her kohl-darkened eyes widen and her expansive bosom tilts slightly forward. "Indeed?" She takes a moment to consider, her face clouding. "You know I've turned down other offers to buy my—establishment—and I can assure you I will do the same to whoever has sent you. It's someone from the palace, yes?"

I nod. "But no one wishes to have you move."

"Good! I'm immoveable, as you can see." Her large form shimmies slightly side-to-side as she settles back. Her smile reflects relief.

I ignore her self-disparaging humor.

"Ah, then the favors of my girls are required at the palace, yes?"

I consider how to answer this. "The presence, rather, of one girl, yes."

The madame's head draws back, accenting her fleshy neck. "What girl? And who is paying?"

"I cannot tell you who sent me. The girl—"

"Yes? Yes? Speak up!"

"The girl is Antonina."

"Someone has good taste. A pretty one, she is. No girl anymore but she is almost as pretty as you. Should you need a position one day—"

"Such is not in my power," I say and then wonder what she had in mind. A servant? One who gives pleasure?

The woman understands. "Too bad. Well, let's get down to business. Antonina's nightly cost is—"

"Madame Flavia, I have been sent here with enough coin to release the woman from indenture to you."

"What?" With great effort, the woman pushes herself up from the couch. "I don't sell my girls."

"You merely rent them, yes?" The words are out of my mouth before thought can contain them.

Her face goes red. "You may leave now," she orders through clenched teeth.

I persist. I remove the purse from beneath my tunic and drop it heavily onto the table, causing the dish of dates to tremble.

"All freshly minted gold pieces," I say, "and twice what you might expect."

Madame Flavia absorbs my words and leans over the table, daintily drawing open the strings of the purse and peering down. With some effort she picks it up with both hands, weighing it as a housewife might check the weight of a leg of lamb. Something glints behind her eyes.

Playing *Shatranj* has sharpened my anticipatory sense. "You're thinking that if someone will pay this amount for the woman, they will pay more."

The madame tilts her head as if to question my clairvoyance.

"Madame Flavia, you've already noted I've come from the Great Palace. I don't recommend placing any conditions on this offer. I have, in fact, come from the Palace of Hormisdas." *Let her do the arithmetic.*

The heavily made-up eyes widen. "Tsk, Tsk," she mutters, "the Daphne Wing would impress me more." Nonetheless, she sets the purse down now, draws herself up, chin lifted, and calls, "Ammon!"

The doorway drape is pulled back and the bodyguard appears. I smile to myself because the name means "unseen."

"Seek out Antonina at once, do you hear! Bring her here! Now, go!"

Madame Flavia sits again. Fifteen minutes pass, her eyes moving from the purse to the entryway and back again. Ignoring the small talk I make about the weather, she pops two more dates into her mouth. "That girl," she whines, "slow as lava. Oh, she is no doubt readying herself. She's not very particular about other things, but about her appearance perfection is the goal. Her regular customers will be most disappointed if she is agreeable to what you've proposed."

I smile. "How has business been?" I cringe in embarrassment at my own question. What possessed me?

Madame Flavia's eyes brighten and she lets loose a compendium of facts regarding the brothel's continued success, its highly placed customers, and the busiest times of year, month, and day.

I nod mechanically as she draws out another fifteen minutes.

At last, the woman we await slips through the curtains in the doorway.

She is dressed in a flowing two layered stola, the top cinched at the waist, an arabesque design wrapped around the hem of each layer. It is the color of saffron. Her golden hair is coiled atop her head, a turquoise metal band holding it in place.

I stand.

She sees me at once and smiles. A light comes into the azure blue eyes. She moves toward me quickly but with grace. I notice the painted red nails on her thonged feet as she crosses the room, but my eyes move back to the light hair and eyes. I've never seen a woman quite like her. When she stops about two feet in front of me, I realize she is quite tall and must be a good deal taller that Theodora. I grant her a great beauty, but Theodora's perfect face and porcelain complexion outmatch her, much like the pure, vibrant red ruby to a stone more purplish in color.

"This is Stephen," Madame Flavia says.

I give a little bow.

"This is a pleasure, sir." The tone is all honey and roses.

"No, no," the madame cries, struggling to rise from her couch, "you have the wrong idea."

I choose to allow the madame to explain.

On her feet now, Madame Flavia turns on the golden-haired beauty. "Antonina, of all the times in the world, please don't devalue yourself now. Look at this man. Look at him! He wears a uniform of the Great Palace, no?"

Antonina gasps. "Yes—yes," she says, eyeing my dalmatic and its purple emblems on the sleeves, digesting their meaning. "And he is—he is—"

The madame nods. "He is that—so don't be a fool. He's here for you—that is, to collect you."

"Me?"

"Someone of importance wishes to purchase you out of indenture." The madame turns to me. "Isn't that right?"

"It is."

"What?" Antonina shrieks. "I don't believe a word of it. It's a trick! Some religious women are trying to do good by interfering in people's lives. I've seen that before."

"It's nothing like that," I say.

Antonina looks me up and down. "Why would someone like you tell me the truth."

"I speak the truth."

"Then tell me who has sent you. Who?"

I shake my head.

"Don't believe him, Madame Flavia," Antonina pleads. "Do not send me away—please! It could be slavers meant to send me to Persia or some horrible place."

"For the helm of Hades—it's someone from the Great Palace," the madame barks. "Isn't that enough? And no slaver would pay such a price. Now go collect your things!"

"I won't."

"Then I'll go get them. Best I do it so you don't take anything that belongs to me. I'll put Ammon on the door, so don't try anything." Madame Flavia is nearly at the door when her large form stops and quickly pivots. She lumbers to the table where the coin purse lay. Grasping it with both many-ringed hands, she hurries from the room, her tiny gray eyes dancing.

I am grateful for her exit. "I think I can tell you now, Lady Antonina, of the person behind the offer."

Antonina's eyelids rise a little at being given the deference of the title "lady." "Who?" The question is hardly more than a breath.

I lower my voice so that the unseen Ammon behind the curtain cannot hear. "Prince Justinian."

"But—why?" Fully unfurled now, her blue eyes are hypnotic.

"He is doing so as a favor to Theodora," I whisper.

Antonina gasps. "Theodora has the ear of Prince Justinian?"

I merely nod now and put my finger to my lips, knowing she'll have questions on the way back to the Great Palace.

By the time Madame Flavia returns with two satchels, a subtly triumphant Antonina takes them from her. "Thank you for everything," she tells the woman and turns to me. "I'm ready now, Stephen."

42

I N THE MIDDLE OF THE sumptuous reception room that was now hers and Justinian's, Theodora made a slow turn, her hands outstretched and upturned as if in a stage piece. "What does all this marble, gilt, and frescoes matter to me, Justinian, if I am to be a prisoner here, afraid to venture out, afraid of the criticism, afraid of *her*?"

Justinian sat on a couch, its woven ivory damask featuring a delicate arabesque. "It's only been a few days, Thea. We knew it would take time. My aunt is a stubborn woman."

"This was a mistake—my giving up my little house to come here. I can understand that it would be a provocation to enter their private rooms in the palace. But if I am denied entry even to be entertained in the Reception Hall of the Nineteen Couches, what then? It's like being held in a dungeon here."

"You miss your independence."

Unable to deny it, Theodora turned her back to Justinian. And yet, she regretted her own words as the memory of her days in a real dungeon came back to her. She had shared with him the memory of her time with Timothy in Alexandria. But she did not relive for him the terrors of her incarceration.

Theodora turned back to see that his face was drawn down in hurt. She was about to temper her words when the servant whose duty it was to light the lamps and sconces appeared in the doorway. Justinian waved him in. Theodora moved to a window and stared out. As the bald-headed eunuch went about lighting the several lamps, she sensed him trying to steal a glance at her. It chilled her, but what did it matter? By now, any number of people in the complex knew she was here, knew that the chosen inheritor of the throne had installed an actress in his palace.

"Things will quiet down," Justinian said after the servant had left. "People will get used to the idea of your being here."

It was as if he had just read her mind. Had they become so close? Theodora began to pace the room. "Even if you are right, they will continue to make conjectures as to the future. And Empress Euphemia is not about to relent. She told me as much."

"She's a woman, Thea. She has a heart, just as you and I."

"I wouldn't be so certain about that. One day you may find that she's managed for me to disappear."

"Why would you say that?" Justinian stood and went to her side. "I'll see that nothing happens to you, do you hear? Look at me, Thea. We will weather this together."

"You are an optimist, Justinian."

"Was a time *you* were an optimist, Theodora." Delivered in a lilting, teasing tone, the words came from a woman who now stood in the doorway.

The voice rang with familiarity, but Theodora had spun about to face the speaker before she could identify it. Even with the woman in her sights, several seconds were lost to a light-headed befuddlement. "Nina!" Theodora cried at last, the pitch of her voice rising. "Nina!" She looked from Antonina to a smiling, knowing Justinian and then back to her childhood friend.

Antonina crossed the room now and took Theodora into a powerful embrace. Theodora held tight for many seconds, as if the figure were a shade that might vanish, finally pulling back and holding her friend at arms' length. "But—but, how did you manage this?"

Antonina smiled slyly and nodded toward Justinian. Formality caught up to her and she bowed to the prince.

Theodora turned toward Justinian, her words coming slowly. "You did this?"

Justinian's chin came up. "I did," he said, his eyes moving from one to the other as if to gauge his success. "And now I leave the two of you to get reacquainted." He bowed slightly and left the room.

"No doubt he paid a hefty sum to old Flavia," Antonina whispered. "I saw the heavy bag of gold coins. Why, he must love you very much, Thea."

"Sweet Aphrodite! You might be right, Nina, but I am always cautious when I speak of love—or, rather, when men speak of love." Theodora took Antonina's hands in hers. "I do know he wants to see me happy. And I am so very happy to have you here. I only wish—"

"What—what is it you wish, Thea?"

Averting her eyes, Theodora released Antonina's hands. "I wish that *I* had been the one to see you freed of that life."

"Why? I'm here just the same, no?"

"It's just that I can't seem to keep anyone safe."

"But you have, dearest. You have! Justinian would not have acted unless you told him about my situation. Isn't that so?" Antonina grasped Theodora's shoulders and gave her a gentle shaking.

Theodora looked up into the intent eyes of the taller woman and nodded. "I suppose you're right, Nina."

"You know I am."

"You're to stay here, of course."

"Oh, the prince has graciously given me rooms here in his palace, but I can't overstay myself."

"You shall stay here and you may bring your son, as well."

Antonina's eyes widened, as if with fear. "Photius?—No!"

"Well, then," Theodora said, blinking at the reaction, "You will stay, I insist."

"For the present, Thea, but in time I shall have to find a means of support."

"Doing what, may I ask?" Theodora led her friend to the couch and once they were seated, asked, "Going on the boards again?"

"Perhaps."

"You know as well as I that the years are not kind to actresses. Where will that lead? To another place like Madame Flavia's?"

"There are worse fates."

"That's doubtful. If only I could, I would encourage Justinian to purchase the freedom of everyone in that house."

"That's all very nice, Thea, but within a fortnight she would have filled it up again with innocent girl shepherdesses from the country."

Theodora sighed. "Perhaps. Something more desperate must be done to eliminate such places. However, what can I do? Nothing now—but one day, perhaps. In the meantime I shall see that you are welcome here as long as I am. That way, if I am forced out by fate or that horrible Euphemia, I'll have you by my side."

"The empress—is she that terrible?"

"Well, her locks of hair may not be snakes, but she is odious just the same."

Antonina's eyes went wide, and she covered her mouth in an attempt to swallow her laughter.

Recalling a particular comment of the brothel owner, Theodora said, "Now, tell me something, Nina … did you enjoy your time there—at Madame Flavia's?"

Antonina flashed a smile, one that faded slowly as the blood rose to her face. Out of embarrassment, Theodora suspected. She had her answer, so instead of pursuing the subject, she said, "Well, I should like to have been there when Justinian went calling on the Madame Flavia. Round as a planet, isn't she?"

"Oh, he didn't come himself! He sent one of the palace eunuchs."

"Really?—What was his name?"

"I can't recall. Is it so important?'

"What did he look like?"

"Oh! Very handsome, indeed. I thought him a customer at first and was not disappointed, you might say. Tall, Syrian, soulful eyes. Not the usual kind, you know, round as a cart wheel and with a strangely high voice."

It was as she suspected. "Stephen," Theodora said. "I knew it. His name is Stephen."

Antonina tilted her head to the side, eyebrows raised.

Theodora knew she was in for questions.

Several weeks go by. I see Theodora on occasion at a distance from a window or walking on the promenade adjacent to the Sea of Marmara at the bottom of the marble steps. I rehearse in my mind and sometimes aloud to my mosaic boy what I am to say to her. Fate seems intent upon bringing us together. Once, as I am leaving the library I hear her mellifluous voice at the far end of the hallway. Is she talking to someone—or to herself? My first thought is to turn away, but I find my feet moving me toward the voice. I reach the end of the hallway, where flights of stairs lead up and down. All is silent. She is gone.

I wonder what it is about her that draws me in, like a sailor into the grasp of a siren.

The next day I come upon her on the lowest of a series of terraces leading down to the sea. Gone is the gray cloak Joseph the Stylite had mocked. Over a lemon yellow stola she wears a mantle of mint green that billows slightly in the sea breeze. Her only jewelry is a plain gold band that holds captive her coiled black tresses atop her head. I wonder if she imagines it a diadem.

"Stephen!" she cries and rushes toward me, the gold straps of her sandals catching the light.

My little speech deserts me. I find no words as she pulls me into a light embrace.

"I knew we would meet sooner or later." She looses one of her lilting laughs. "How could we not?"

No rehearsals had prepared me for this. I am still dumb when she releases me, her heart-shaped face alight.

"Have you nothing to say?" she asks.

"I am taken by surprise, Lady Theodora."

"And why should you be? You knew of my presence."

I find my voice. "Of course."

"You should be proud of me, Stephen. I am honing my skill at *Shatranj*. Why I've even beaten poor Justinian."

"Really?"

"Oh, you find it a wonder, do you?"

"On the contrary," I say. What I *wonder* is whether the game she plays with Justinian isn't a high stakes game of romance. Time will tell.

We talk for a while of the weather and the landscaping that is being done on the terraces.

"I like this terrace especially," Theodora says. "I walk it often. It is well-planted and the plane trees, young as they are, provide a shield from …" She turns her sun-mottled face away from the sea and up, toward the Great Palace—and the Daphne Wing.

"A shield from—" I urge.

"An enemy," she says.

I prod no further, but she turns those eyes on me, like marble they are, richly black but bereft of their usual warmth. "*Her*—Euphemia."

I catch my breath. Despite knowing the answer, I ask, "The empress does not approve?"

"She does not."

"And the emperor?"

"He has treated me well, but his sun does not move but by her whim."

"I see. My lady, I—I …"

"Yes? What is it, Stephen?"

"It may not be my place to speak, but you have another enemy on the grounds."

"Indeed?"

"His name is Procopius and he is determined to see an end to … to—"

"To me?"

I nod.

"What does he look like?"

"He's tall, thin as a rake, rather haggard looking. A young scholar, something of the palace historian, I'm told."

"Always in a severe brown dalmatic, always with a scowl on his face?"

"Yes."

"I've seen him. I've seen him staring daggers at me. I shall be on my guard. And now, I'm embarrassed to realize I haven't even thanked you."

"Thanked me?"

"For bringing Antonina out of the brothel and here to me. She is my dearest friend, and I shall not forget your service."

I feel a heat coming into my face. I nod and attempt a smile.

"You've helped save her from a miserable several years, Stephen."

I don't tell Theodora that Antonina in no way appeared miserable in Madame Flavia's house.

Before taking her leave, she moves in close to me. The vibration at my very core is powered by my heart. "Thank you for Antonina," she says as she leans in to kiss me on the cheek. I know my face flames red, but she is already walking away. "Oh," she calls back, "keep an eye on that person you told me about, do you hear? You shall be my eyes and ears, Stephen—my spy!"

I settle into the rhythm of life in the Palace of Hormisdas. Days move into months and months into years.

Against the expectations of many, perhaps most, Theodora creates a life for herself here in the palace complex, living openly with Justinian in his apartment. Her unsullied devotion to him contrasts with the behavior of Antonina, who by the week seems to make a new conquest among the senators and generals. By order of the empress, Theodora is not allowed in the Daphne Wing, the royal residence, nor can she take part in the feasts and entertainments in the Reception Hall of the Nineteen Couches, but she appears content. That Justinian is eighteen years older matters little, it seems, to her or to Justinian.

In truth, Justinian treats Theodora as if she has been inhabited by one of her living pictures' characters—Aphrodite.

The feverish talk of scandal that attended her installation—as well as Antonina's—in Justinian's Palace of Hormisdas subsides. Oh, there is still idle and sometimes vicious talk of how she has stage-managed the emperor-apparent with a love philter or witchcraft of some kind, but it abates with each year. The time I spent with the magus Gaspar made me highly suspect of love potions, for I never saw their positive effects. And so, with the passage of years I start to believe the bond between Theodora and Justinian is made of stronger stuff than merely his infatuation and her youth and beauty.

Despite her exclusion from all royal ceremonies and events, Theodora exerts significant influence on Justinian and, in turn, on the politics of state—and religion. She has not forgotten Patriarch Timothy and other Monophysites that took her in when her life was at its lowest ebb. As a Chalcedonian Christian, Justinian believes that Christ had two natures: human and divine. He supported the purges against Monophysites initiated by Emperor Justin but not long after Theodora's arrival, he convinced his uncle to end the persecutions. I do not underestimate the power of her influence.

I continue my work in Justinian's library, greatly increasing my knowledge of languages so that I cannot only copy texts (with some improvement in my artistry) but I can translate simpler texts, as well. I don't think I have the artistic flair—or patience—to become an illuminator of any worth, however. Theodora insists that I visit from time-to-time, most often when Justinian is away or participating in some palace function barred to her. Often, without warning, Agathe, one of her handmaidens—a very pretty one with dark features like Theodora—appears at my library desk with a note inviting me for a game of *Shatranj*. Our skills in the game are well matched now although sometimes we merely engage in the exchange of ideas. I am surprised that she finds my work with philosophical and religious texts interesting. She confides in me that she exchanges letters with Patriarch Timothy in Alexandria and keeps current with that side of the world. I have a feeling Timothy's charity toward Theodora in her time of need is being rewarded many times over. Her fortune is his fortune.

That Theodora is five years older than I seems of less importance as the years go by. My attraction to Theodora has not waned, and I still talk to my confidant Jati about it, but my station in life, as well as hers, makes me more resolute in accepting things that are unchangeable.

Just as my devotion to Theodora is consistent, so too, is Procopius's hatred of her. And yet, as a fawning sycophant to her husband, he is worming his way into Justinian's good graces; no doubt he has his own future in mind. Oh, he has learned to be careful in what he says while in my presence, but I hear from Tariq and others that Justinian's relationship with an actress of sordid background still makes him irate. He is buoyed by the belief that when, as expected, Justinian becomes emperor, the relationship will be dissolved and a favorable dynastic marriage will be arranged. According to Leo, Procopius is actively working with Empress Euphemia to that end.

PART FIVE

PART FIVE

43

524

I AM IN THE LIBRARY PERCHED on my stool when I hear the quick-fire sound of sandals on the mosaic flooring as someone rushes up the aisle. Procopius is at the front in moments, pulling Leo into one of the bays.

My eyes and ears are not the only ones on alert. The scratching of reed pens on parchment ceases as we all listen.

Procopius is furious and unable to contain his frustration and anger. I hear the words *Theodora question* as well as the names of Justin and Euphemia. After a little while, Procopius shouts Justinian's name in a less than respectful way.

What could Justinian have done? I wonder.

Procopius suddenly barges out of the bay, his face red as fire. The heads of the other copyists go down as they pretend to work, the pens moving over parchment. My eyes are riveted on the fleeing figure, however, as he races past my desk, moving toward the door, his face screwed into an angry grimace. He takes no notice of me.

The door behind him slams shut.

When Leo comes out of the bay, he realizes everyone's head has come up, their gazes upon him. He stands in front of us, his round face dark. He has no need to call for attention. He has it. "Ahem!" he says. "It is my sad duty to tell you that our esteemed Empress Euphemia has died."

A collective gasp echoes through the scriptorium.

Eugenios, one of the copyists, speaks up. "But, Brother Leo, Procopius seemed less than—uh, reverential on such an occasion."

Leo pretends not to have heard and returns to his desk.

No doubt, Eugenios and others are wondering what had made Procopius come unhinged with fury. I do not wonder. Procopius's hope that Euphemia would see to the undoing of Theodora has died with the empress. It is a stroke of fortune for Theodora, and I am happy for her.

"You should be happy, Thea," Antonina said. She sat on a couch in Justinian and Theodora's suite. "You should be *delighted*."

"Yes, I suppose so."

"You told me the things she said to you. Why, that woman was a harpy, nothing less."

Theodora chuckled.

"For how many years have you been denied access to royal proceedings? How long has she succeeded in keeping you reined in?"

"Too long." Theodora rose from the couch across from Antonina and moved to the window.

"Indeed! So it's time to celebrate."

"Still, she's Justinian's aunt." From the window she watched the pathways below, where an influx of activity among the servants and soldiers—the lifeblood of the palace complex—indicated that funeral preparations were commencing.

"And what of the emperor? What's his attitude?"

"Oh he's more liberal, considerably so." Theodora pivoted toward Antonina. "I think he likes me."

"Really?—Will you be welcome at court, finally?"

Theodora took a moment to ponder the question, the index finger of her right hand tapping the delicate dimple at the base of her neck. "That remains to be seen," she said, finally. "I suppose it may take some time."

"And why should it take time? The old nemesis is gone. You should insist upon it. Tell Justinian at once."

"What should she tell me at once?" Justinian asked as he entered the reception room.

Antonina quickly stood, her face going pale. She gave a little bow.

Theodora also rose to her feet, a throbbing at her temple. How much had Justinian heard? "Nina was just saying that I should tell you that I would like to attend your aunt's funeral."

Justinian smiled. "Just to be certain Euphemia is dead?"

Theodora suspected Antonina's blank expression mirrored her own.

"My aunt had her good qualities," he said, addressing Antonina, "but being kind to the woman I love was not one of them."

Antonina's eyes went round as blue marbles. Failing in her attempt at a smile, she bowed and started to back out of the room.

Justinian's raised hand halted her. "Antonina, I hope you will attend the funereal ceremonies alongside Theodora."

Antonina drew herself up at the surprise request, the smile this time taking root and coming into bloom. "But—of course!"

"Good!" Justinian declared. "Excellent!"

Antonina effected a self-conscious exit, her eyes casting secret rays of wonder at her longtime friend.

Theodora turned to Justinian. "You mean, I will be allowed to attend?"

"Well, your nemesis will not be able to stop you."

A heat rose into Theodora's face. "I'm sorry you had to hear that, Justinian."

Justinian walked over and embraced her, his mouth at her ear. "'The truth will out,' as they say."

Theodora pulled back to study his face. "And your uncle?"

Justinian smiled. "He has no objection to you, Thea, none whatsoever. We have no obstacles to our marriage now."

"Marriage?" Theodora withdrew from the embrace and stepped back. "I'm not a patrician, Justinian. A marriage is forbidden."

"An emperor can change that."

"If he's willing. And then there's the little matter of the law that states no patrician may marry an actress."

"Yes, there is that." Justinian stepped forward and took both of her hands in his. "Give me time, Thea. Trust me."

For the moment, at least, she did trust him. He was besotted with her. Her emotions toward him were not so easily navigated. Oh, she cared for him, but she kept one chamber of her heart under lock and key. After the debacle of the relationship with Hecebolus, she had become cautious. And the stakes here and now made the situation at the Pentapolis pale in comparison.

Kissing her on the cheek, Justinian excused himself now, pleading some business.

Theodora sat down, taking time to think. Euphemia's death would open up doors for her, quite literally, making her feel less of an outsider, less of an interloper here in the palace complex. She sensed a strange, happy tingle run through her, and it was powerful. This could be a new beginning for her. A new world. And yet her position was far from secure. Indeed, Justinian's position was not secure. She must urge him on in his quest of the throne but in delicate ways. *I must be clever this time.*

As much as she despised Euphemia, she had come to appreciate the way she set up protective barriers around her husband and adopted son, the way she handled people, the way she commanded respect. People feared her, more so than her husband, the emperor. Euphemia had reigned successfully. Manipulation, threats, and fear had worked for her—until death took her away.

These are lessons taught, Theodora thought, *and they are lessons learned.*

In her heart, Theodora could even understand why the empress—a former slave girl—objected to an actress of questionable reputation marrying into the family and one day taking her place. Their histories were too much alike. For a child, a parent always wants more than what had been her own experience.

She glanced at the water clock and stood. It was nearly noon and Saturday—by custom, the day and time she would secretly leave the complex to observe from afar her daughter at the market square in the Forum of the Ox.

Tariq makes a move on the *Shatranj* board and nods toward my wall mosaic. "Still talking to your friend there?"

"Jati?" I smile. "Yes, and I shouldn't have confided in you that I speak to a wall if you're going to mock me."

"Not I, my friend. But—it's that you say he answers you that confounds me. "

I can't help but laugh. "At least I know Jati keeps my secrets."

"And so shall I." Tariq winks. "Make your move."

I take a few minutes to consider my possibilities on the board. I make my decision and as I finish moving one of my pieces, I say, "What do you hear from Procopius? You know he avoids me."

"And no wonder since you play this game regularly with Justinian's lover. I tell you, the man is fixated on Theodora. Filled with hatred, he is. And he pretends as if he knows something no one else does."

"Like what?"

"Oh, he is convinced she's on her way out.—Is she, Stephen?"

I give a little laugh. "On the contrary, the relationship is moving toward marriage."

"Really?"

"The emperor has had her declared a patrician. No other actress has been so named. The next step is to change the law forbidding senators to marry actresses. They say Justinian drafted the changes months ago in anticipation—"

"Of Empress Euphemia's death?" Tariq gives a low whistle. "What changes?"

"So that it allows for actresses who have amended their lives for a specific duration of time to be forgiven. Theodora herself told me that in Alexandria she had found her faith."

"And has she—amended her life?"

"To hear Procopius and Narses tell what her life was before, here in the capital, she has. For whatever reason, Narses seems better disposed toward her now than he was on that day on the *Sea-Goddess* when he angrily warned me against even exchanging words with such a woman."

Tariq looks up from the board. "The reason is obvious. Narses knows that the next move in this former actress's career will be to the throne next to Justinian's—once Justin dies and his nephew is crowned emperor."

"Empress Theodora," I say, turning the words over in my mouth like the first sip of a new wine. A kind of wonder colors my voice as I think of the woman who gave me a piece of raw ginger to ease my nausea on the ship from Antioch. For a moment, my mind calls up that heart-shaped, perfect face on that wind-blown stern, and the old familiar storm of sadness, regret, and hopelessness washes over me as I think of how I loved her even then.

Tariq draws me back into the present. "Do you suppose you should warn her—I mean, about Procopius?"

"I did so once, Tariq. I told Justinian, as well, but Procopius shows a very different face to him. He's quite the confidant now."

"So it seems."

I shrug. "Like Narses, Procopius has his eye on the future. He will have to let go of his hatred of Theodora. Besides, how dangerous could he be to her?" A new thought strikes me. "Why, she might be more dangerous to him!"

44

THEODORA STOOD UP, PACED, SAT down, and then repeated the motions as she waited for the palace physician to finish his examination. Just as every obstacle standing in the way of Theodora's rising—Euphemia, Theodora's status, the law forbidding marriage to an actress—came crashing down like felled trees, Justinian became seriously ill. Two days of fever, vomiting, and extreme pain in the groin had gone by before he allowed Theodora to send for the royal physician.

Philoxenos exited the bed chamber she shared with Justinian, his face free of expression.

Theodora stood. "Well? What is it?"

The physician frowned. "I've seen it before, my lady. I gave him something for the pain. Make him drink water, plenty of water to counteract the fever."

Theodora nodded. As the physician moved briskly away, she pressed her question: "But what is it?"

Philoxenos halted, pivoted, took several moments, and gave out a sigh. "It's orchitis, a *delicate* condition."

"How severe? It will go away, certainly."

The physician affected a smile. His face ran red. "It usually does. I'll check in tomorrow, Lady Theodora." He made a quick exit now.

Theodora was left standing there, unable to determine whether he was embarrassed to speak of Justinian's privy parts—or piqued that he was being questioned by Justinian's mistress. But why embarrassment? In any case, she concluded, he was keeping something from her.

Water? It seemed too simple a cure. Nonetheless, she hurried to fill an amphora.

Narses appears at my door one evening. I'm taken by surprise, for months would go by without my seeing him because his duties and apartment were situated in the Daphne Wing of the Great Palace. His presence is not the only surprise.

He refuses my offer of wine and sits across from me at my little table. "Lord Justinian is ill," he says, "quite ill."

"I've heard as much. What is it, my lord?"

Narses' face darkens. "It's an abnormality of the testes." He allows no time for me to ask questions. "Stephen, I am here at Lady Theodora's request."

"Yes?" *Lady Theodora.* I can't help but think back to how he vilified her when I dared to converse with her on the *Sea-Goddess.*

"Lady Theodora asks that you take a position in Justinian's—their—household."

The offer causes my thoughts to scatter. Elation takes hold of me, and I suppress the urge to embrace Narses. I consider how I would be close to Theodora on a daily basis. I can barely find words. "In—in what role?"

Narses pauses. "That remains to be seen. Perhaps as a bedroom chamberlain, usher—or secretary." He goes on to detail the duties of each position.

While his voice drones on, reality sets in for me, and with it, doubts, serious doubts. "I am able to decline?" I ask.

Narses' forehead pushes back. It's his turn to be surprised. "Why—yes, it's your prerogative. At least for now. But what are your reservations, Stephen?"

I go on to tell him in detail how I have become accustomed to my life working in the library, how I enjoy working with languages, how I enjoy imbibing knowledge each day, how I enjoy the challenge of improving my artistry with the reed pen. I am quite the actor in my exaggerations.

"Ah, I might have guessed you would take to the kalamos."

"You'll tell Lady Theodora my reasons?"

Narses nods, laughs. "A shorter version, perhaps. You can supply the full text yourself, but not until Lord Justinian is safely mended." He stands to leave.

I see him the few paces to the door. "He will survive it, yes?"

Narses looks into my eyes, nods. The silence of his response weakens it.

After he is gone, I go back to my chair and stare at my mosaic confidant, cataloguing for him the reasons for my refusal. The one true reason I had avoided, I tell Jati. That I should find my days spent so close to the woman I adore would be to spend those days in torture. And yet—the thought sets my blood racing as if it were charged with mulled wine.

The girl Agathe delivers a note from Theodora to me at the library the next day. "I'm to return tomorrow for your reply," Agathe says and scurries away.

I feel a pulsing at my temples. My first thought is that Theodora was disappointed or even angry with my decision, and that she wishes for me to reconsider.

I break the seal and read. It is no such thing. No mention of the offer. Theodora writes: "Please research your medical texts for the dangers and side-effects of orchitis. Be discreet."

I hasten to the farthest bay, where some fifty or sixty medical scrolls attributed to Hippocrates' *Corpus* are stored. I move quickly through the collection and narrow the search down to three scrolls. Just as I turn to take them to my tall desk, I find Procopius blocking the entry to the bay, his eyes narrowed in suspicion.

He hasn't spoken to me in months but that respite ends today. "Ah, Stephen, I must congratulate you."

I don't take the bait. "I'm busy right now."

His gaze goes to the scrolls under my arm. "I see that. Well, I won't detain you, but I was impressed to hear that you turned down that woman's offer of a position."

I smile and say nothing. It amazes me how tightly he keeps his finger on the pulse of the palace goings-on.

"It's best you steer clear. Oh, she's to have her marriage, no question about that. But she may be in for a surprise if she has her sights set higher."

"What do you mean?" I ask.

He gives a sly smile. "Let's just say that she may be stepping onto the wrong chariot."

"Then whose—"

"As I said," he interrupted, "you made a good decision."

I start to leave the bay.

Procopius steps aside to allow me to pass—but not without a glance at the scrolls and a parting comment. "Doing a little medical research, are you?"

I return to my desk, wondering if he knows what my task is. It would not surprise me if he does.

I peruse the first two texts, all the while thinking about his intimation. Word has it that since his hope that Euphemia would keep Theodora from marrying her nephew, he has fostered the possibility that another nephew of the emperor, Germanus, might take precedence in the line of succession. Oh, Germanus seems little interested in the throne, but a covert movement bolstered by the Greens and a few senators against Justinian and his actress-wife is pressuring Justinian's cousin to make the claim. I suspect that Procopius is part of that movement. He is a man who would play both sides.

He passes my desk now, his finger on his lips. I take it as a caution—no, a threat—not to mention our conversation to anyone.

I search through the third scroll now and find what I'm looking for.

The origin of orchitis is unknown, but the condition is thought to accompany parotitis, inflammation of the salivary glands. With orchitis, pain within the swollen testes is often intense, accompanied by headache, fatigue, nausea. Prognosis hopeful and yet sometimes undetermined. Patient sometimes left sterile.

Dizziness comes over me. I take up my pen, grateful that my answer is to be in writing and not in person. It could be embarrassing for her, but I am certain it would be a humiliation for me. That this task should come to me makes me wish I followed some religion so that I could curse some power for placing me in this position.

I consider omitting mention of sterility as a possible side-effect, but by the time Agathe comes to collect the note, I have overruled the idea. Theodora would want to know and would hold it against me should I keep it from her.

Two weeks later, when I see Lord Justinian up and ambling about, color in his cheeks, I forget about the possibility of the side-effect.

During my visits with her, Theodora makes no mention of Justinian's condition. I have no gods to thank, so I thank the heavens.

45

525

"IF ONLY MOTHER WERE ALIVE to witness this, Thea!" Anastasia cried. "To see us here in the Palace of Hormisdas. What would Mother think? What would she say?"

Comito spoke now. "I was thinking of that myself, just moments ago! How she pinched every coin to dress us in simple linen tunics. And now look at the brocaded wedding stola Theodora is wearing! The daffodil yellow is stunning!"

Theodora remained silent, looking down at the jewel-encrusted bodice. Her gaze then took in the phalanx of handmaidens and eunuchs that Narses directed as they readied her for the ceremony. Her heart beat fast.

"Your complexion has darkened a bit since those days, Thea," Comito continued, "but it suits you so well."

"Oh, not nearly as dark as when I returned!" Theodora managed a smile. "You spend months travelling overland from the Pentapolis to Alexandria to Nazareth to Antioch and see if your skin doesn't darken."

"What adventures you've had!" Anastasia said.

Theodora cocked her head. "Indeed! Now listen to me, you two," she said, lowering her voice so that the servants buzzing around the dressing area of the rooms she shared with Justinian would not take notice, "you both need to give up the theater and friends you've made there. Lovers, too, do you hear? You are to live here as I—we agreed, and the time will come when I'll see you both have good marriages."

Anastasia gasped. "To a senator, perhaps?"

Comito winced. "But—"

"Don't argue with me, Comito." Theodora said, sharpness in her tone. A handmaiden was approaching to add the final touch, a sheer veil to the bride's head.

Approaching now with both hands held out, palms up, Narses carried one of Justinian's gifts: a marriage belt of gold coins that contained two large coins with Christian crosses and twenty smaller ones, many with pagan images of the old gods.

Theodora drew in a large breath at the sight, but allowed the cries of amazement and delight of Comito and Anastasia to suffice for a reaction. Her sisters set about attaching it to her lower belly area, commenting in whispers as they did so about its rumored secret powers and Justinian's expectations of an heir.

An heir? Theodora felt a tightening at her throat. She knew she should scold her sisters for their comments, but she could not help but recall that sterility remained a possible side-effect of his recent illness. She batted the thought away because suddenly Narses was bowing in front of her, his face serious as an owl's. "It's time, my lady," he said. "The procession is forming outside."

She moved as if in a drug-induced dream, stepping down from the Daphne Wing and into line. Justinian stood there waiting for her. As the line began to advance, she thought about the step—no, leap—she was taking, the man she was marrying. Justinian was different from the other men who had pursued her, especially from Hecebolus. Justinian exuded vitality, vision, activity. He was free of affectations and he listened to her, truly listened, and even though he, with his scholarly background, might prefer Latin, he spoke Greek with her. She especially liked that.

As for Hecebolus, she wondered now what he would think when word arrives at the Pentapolis that his cast-off mistress had married the man nearly certain to become emperor?

"Why the smile?" Justinian asked. "What are you thinking, Thea?"

"What?" she asked. "Was I smiling?" She recalled Narses' telling her that the empress's face to the public was to be one of serenity and so she adjusted her expression accordingly.

It seems Theodora's fortune extends to the weather, for the May sun is shining as Tariq and I slip into the Church of the Holy Wisdom. Tariq is Christian and he assures me I have nothing to be apprehensive about even if my father was a follower of Mithras and I follow no religion. About halfway to the sanctuary, we find a place on the aisle.

I have been in here before, and yet I am still awed by the interior of the rectangular cathedral built by Constantine. The inlay of marble and mosaic in the walls and floor does not surprise me, but the dozens of statues of saints and emperors shimmering in the flickering light of vigil candles under the many mullioned windows take my breath from me.

"Constantine rather favored his mother, Helena," Tariq says, pointing out three statues of her—one in ivory, one in silver, and one in porphyry imported from Egypt, its crystalline surface a dazzling purplish-red.

A swarm of acolytes appears and begins lighting chandeliers, sconces and candelabra. The church begins to fill with light, as well as with patricians, senators, generals, officers of the excubitors, and all manner of highly-ranked civil servants. A large contingent of Blues takes up one of the galleries, their presence reflecting the decided preferences of both Justinian and Theodora. The Greens are left to find their own spaces. I see Brother Leo enter, along with a host of scholars, legal and otherwise. I wonder if Procopius will appear and bear witness to the continued rising of an actress, one he despises. Emperor Justin's throne sits empty. I question whether he is well or whether he is leaving the attention to a new generation. Oh, he is rumored to be as entranced by Theodora's beauty and youth as anyone—but he had become emperor just a few years before and at the age of sixty-eight, so he might very well be reluctant to see the future flying at him too soon.

In short time, all heads turn to see Justinian and Theodora processing up the aisle, both resplendent in their robes, his gold, hers yellow. Without accompaniment, a chorus of eunuchs set into a gallery sings in high, clear voices:

> Let love and faithfulness never leave you; bind them around your neck, write them on the tablet of your heart. Then you will win favor and a good name in the sight of God and man.

"It's a psalm," Tariq whispers.

I know as much from my copying duties, but I don't say so to Tariq because I am so enthralled by the crystalline voices—and the couple as they pass. The sheerness of Theodora's veil reveals her face. She looks neither left nor right. Her head is held high.

The psalm ends. Patriarch Epiphanius appears from the sacristy and meets the pair at the stairs to the altar, his long gray beard shivering as he recites all manner of prayers for the occasion. As the ceremony—so foreign to me—goes on with billowing incense, the exchange of rings and kisses, and the holding of a large veil over the couple as they make their pledges, I wonder what the future will hold for them, for the people around us, and for the large part of the world not lost to barbarians. I wonder what influence Theodora will exert. Her power of persuasion is already evident because even though her leanings toward Patriarch Timothy's Monophysitism are at odds with the beliefs of Emperor Justin and Justinian, she has prevailed on them to cease the severe actions taken against the Monophysites. Last, I wonder how many of those present had seen her on stage not so many years ago and what they might be thinking today. I've heard few voicing their displeasure, other than Procopius. Tariq tells me that people accept rather easily the turns that God—or Fate—takes.

And now, the ceremony over, the couple turns to face the congregation and lead the recessional. The heavenly sounds of the choir's plainsong reverberate through the massive cathedral:

> Entreat me not to leave you, Or to turn back from following after you; For wherever you go, I will go; And wherever you lodge, I will lodge; Your people shall be my people, And your God, my God. Where you die, I will die, And there will I be buried. The Lord do so to me, and more also, If anything but death parts you and me.

As the couple moves, ever so slowly, their faces come into view, Justinian's alight and ebullient, Theodora's so very serious behind the veil, her fathomless, black eyes taking everything in. I have no doubt that she is aware of the significance of the moment.

They pass nearby now. Theodora's face turns, and her eyes fall on me and seem to glitter for a moment. Then comes the hint of a smile so subtle I will debate its existence over and over this night in the privacy of my room. Jati will tire of hearing of it.

Tariq is behind me and at my ear now. "She looked right at you, Stephen," he whispers, "right at you."

Before I can turn to make light of it, I have to wipe at my eye.

46

526

THEODORA AND JUSTINIAN LAY ON the wide sleeping couch luxuriating in the afterglow of lovemaking, a tamer lovemaking than that of the night before. Justinian shifted to his side, his head propped on his left hand as he studied Theodora. When she felt the fingers of his right hand moving from her breast up to her necklace, she tensed, her stomach tightening. She had meant to take it off—she usually did—but passion had ruled.

"What is this?" Justinian asked. "I've not seen this before. Is it a moon, Thea?" He leaned over and drew the object on the fine golden chain closer for inspection. "Why, yes, it's exactly that! A moon at full phase. It even has the round face of the man-in-the-moon smiling back at me."

"I saw it at a jeweler's on the Mese and I was drawn to it. It was a whim."

"Was it?"

"Yes." Theodora wondered whether he recognized the moon as a symbol of fertility. It was pagan, of course, and antithetical to Christian belief, but she had taken to wearing it often, nonetheless. Justinian seemed fascinated by it. Had the physician informed him of the possible side-effect of orchitis? Perhaps he hadn't. After all, he had not told her; she had had to learn about it from Stephen. By request, Agathe had purchased the amulet for her from a magus, along with a phallus-shaped amulet which Theodora hid under the bed. Agathe said the wizard also recommended potions of goose fat and of rabbit's blood, one more unappealing than the other.

Justinian continued his examination of the golden moon. Theodora sensed that he knew it was an amulet and that he was about to pursue the subject. "Justinian, did you speak with your uncle yesterday?" she asked, hoping to both divert his attention and learn about the emperor's mindset on the succession.

He dropped the symbol, and his eyes moved up and held hers. "We talk every day."

"Yes? Don't tease."

"Patience is a virtue, Thea."

"Indeed, but life has time limits and your Uncle Justin is getting more and more frail. I'm told the war wound is festering."

"Thea, he has just given me the title of *nobilissimus*, the highest in the empire."

"Well, nearly so," she retorted, a teasing lilt in her voice. "Is there talk of your cousin Germanus being so honored?"

"There is not."

Justinian's reply was short and clipped. Oh, he knew what she was implying. And Theodora knew when to pull back. As he was reaching for the symbol of the moon again, she took his hand, kissed it, and withdrew from the bed.

Something is on Tariq's mind. As we often do, Tariq and I are sitting on the highest of the stacked terraces that descend to the Sea of Marmara. Even here, the tangy taste of salt reaches us by way of a soft breeze. On this sunny afternoon, the views of the sparkling sea and its traffic of both humble fishing boats and fine merchant and military ships fasten our attention.

His eyes on the water, Tariq speaks, "Procopius is of the opinion that the emperor might not wish to name Justinian as his successor."

"Ah," I say, "when is Procopius without an opinion?" Tariq and I discuss the great hatred he carries for Theodora, how he is heard quite openly these days railing against the senators, the generals, and the priests for raising not a single public objection to the marriage of a likely emperor to a common actress, a whore.

"And yet," Tariq says, "he presents a false face to Justinian."

"Indeed. Now, Tariq, seriously, do you think he hates Theodora so much that he would prefer to see Justin's other nephew on the throne?"

"Ah—an interesting possibility, Stephen! Germanus has military experience like Justinian, but he doesn't bury himself in libraries going over archaic law texts and other scholarly material. And, instead of marrying a former ac-

tress of questionable repute, Germanus has married a woman from an aristocratic family."

"And, as with Justinian," I add, "he would be keeping the throne in the family."

"Exactly!"

"But does Germanus have the ambition?" I ask.

"Hard to say, I'm not so sure he does. Tell me," Tariq says, turning toward me, "You have Theodora's ear. What does she think?"

I keep my eyes on the seam where sky and water meet. I do not make a habit of breaking confidence with Theodora and so I take my time and measure my words. At last, I say, "What I can tell you, Tariq, is that there is nothing we've said here today that would surprise her."

I do not say that she believes that the emperor, her father-in-law, is hanging on to his purple mantle just as he is hanging onto life itself. She told me she would do much the same in his place. I know that she is not so much threatened by Germanus as she is galled by the fact that he has married into the most elite Roman family—the Anicii—who fled to Constantinople after the Ostrogoths invaded Rome and by the fact that his wife of such a privileged lineage has quite regularly shunned Theodora. I also know that she does have real concern for two nephews of former Emperor Anastasius—the brothers Pompeius and Hypatius—who might wish to reestablish their line. They could pose a real threat.

Theodora recognizes an enemy in Procopius, too, but knows that her husband and father-in-law find him invaluable. He is to write the history of the empire.

47

For this evening, Theodora had instructed Narses to order all the servers to leave the dining hall once the food was laid out. When other guests were present, she sat on a couch at the far end of the ebony table, a good distance from her husband's couch, but when just the two of them dined, like this night, she sat at Justinian's right hand and, from time to time, they would hold hands. Justinian seemed not to notice that they had been left completely to themselves by design.

Conversation this winter evening went to religion, as it often did, and even though they were on opposite sides of the issue concerning the nature of Christ, their relationship was such that each respected the other's viewpoint. Theodora's tutelage under Patriarchs Timothy and Severus had provided Theodora with enough knowledge and force of argument about Monophysitism that she could hold her own in lively discussions with her highly intelligent husband, who had long fostered the Dyophysite point of view.

"Justinian," Theodora said, "how is it that the man your uncle succeeded seemed at peace with those of strongly opposite views? Anastasius was a Monophysite, wasn't he?"

Justinian nodded. "The City was divided. People gathered in the Hippodrome and in the streets, ready to rebel, some crying, 'Give the Empire an Orthodox Emperor' while counter chants went up of 'Give the Empire a Roman Emperor.' Zeno's widow was quite clever and tapped Anastasius, a Monophysite, for the throne, but the patriarch at the time agreed to his succession only on the condition that he allow those who believed in the dual nature of Christ as set down by the Council of Chalcedon to follow their hearts."

"And so peace was kept," Theodora said. "An easier choice than the one David had when the two mothers went to him with one baby."

Justinian laughed. "Ah, but just as clever."

"So Zeno had no son to follow him to the throne? Was Anastasius some-how the natural choice just the same? "

"Zeno had no son but his brother Longinus had considerable political experience. *He* was the logical choice."

Theodora tilted her head slightly, eyes on Justinian's. "So—the logical choice for emperor was passed over?—It does happen."

Justinian's hooded eyes widened. "Ah, my darling," he said, laughing, "Zeno's wife was not the only clever woman to take up residence here."

Her point made, Theodora smiled, but she was not quite finished. "Now, husband, I was at the Pentapolis when Anastasius died—when was it?"

"It was in 518."

"Another emperor without a son, yes? It seems a curse."

Justinian nodded. "But he didn't marry until he was in his sixth decade."

"Another succession problem just the same, yes? How was that to be resolved?"

Justinian shook his head in amusement and dropped his linen napkin on the table. "You, Theodora, are incorrigible! I see your game. You might as well send out criers."

Theodora smiled. She had meant for him to see her game. He could be a bit obtuse at times. After all, he hadn't noticed her plot for them to be left in privacy. "You were going to tell me how it was resolved. Just how did the diadem come to your uncle?"

"The story is well known. By Zeus, it's legendary! I don't need to tell you."

"Ah, husband, then let *me* remind *you*. I've heard the story time and again. Oh, you can correct me if my facts are wrong."

Justinian sat back in his chair, resignation on his face, arms folded.

"Anastasius had three nephews, any one of whom might have taken the throne. The failing emperor could not make up his mind which to choose, and so he created a little game of sorts having to do with three couches. Am I accurate so far?'

Justinian let go a stage sigh. "You are."

"Anastasius put a badge with the imperial insignia under the cushion of one of the three couches, believing that God would direct the chosen one to the couch with the insignia that would all but anoint him emperor." Theodora paused, delighting in the telling and daring Justinian to deny any part of it.

Smiling, Justinian could not help but provide a key plot point: "The couch with the insignia stood empty when two of the nephews sat on the same couch."

Theodora laughed. "Exactly! But let me tell it! That night the emperor had a dream in which a voice told him that the first person to sit on the appointed couch the next day would be emperor. He thought it the voice of God. When the day dawned, the Commander of the Imperial Guard came into the hall for his daily report and he took—"

"The chair with the badge."

"You are the incorrigible one, Justinian. Stop stealing my thunder!" Theodora collected herself and drew breath. "And that person was—"

"Justin, Uncle Justin."

"*Emperor* Justin! To Hades with the three logical choices.—And to Hades with you for stepping on my lines!"

Justinian laughed. "Maybe I should have gone on the boards."

Theodora joined in on the mirth. "It's good to hear you make a jibe—you're usually so serious."

He stood, pushing back the table. "I guess you're right, Thea, and to underscore the point, I do have some business to take care of.—Where is Narses? Where is *everyone*?"

Theodora recognized his facial expression. It was that mix of disgust and humor he exhibited when she beat him at *Shatranj*. But she thought she saw something else in the mix now—resolve. She prayed he had gotten her point about trusting the disposition of the emperor's diadem to the whim of Fortune.

48

527

DESPITE THE DAMP COLD AND the wind whipping in off the sea, Tariq and I take a breather from the library, leaving the Palace of Hormisdas and walking up the marble steps and out onto the highest of the terraces. The inclement weather insures our privacy. We are conversing about Antioch. Word had come from that city that the land was trembling again, this coming after a disastrous earthquake the year before. I tell Tariq of my impression, brief as it was, of the city. I drop my guard and reveal some of the details of my final incarceration before being sold. "Do you know," I say, "Narses did not let on until we docked at the harbor here that this would be my home? I imagined worse, I can tell you. And, if I had stayed in Antioch, I might not have survived last year's earthquake. Strange how fate goes as it must."

"I'm glad Narses found you and brought you here, Stephen. You are a good friend."

I smile. "As are you, Tariq."

We walk to the edge of the balcony and stare out into a colorless sea and a gray, leaden sky. It's twilight.

"I can tell you one thing, Stephen. I would not like to be standing here if an earthquake were to strike Constantinople."

His tone is light and mine matches his. "Indeed, this whole palace complex might slide right down into the sea."

Oddly enough, we both look down at the layered and well-designed terraces below us and I see two terraces away what appears to be a person who has fallen and lies face down behind a little shrubbery patch, visible to us but probably not to a passerby on the same terrace.

I hear Tariq gasp, and I know he sees it, too.

"Holy Mithras, God of the Sun," I mutter and turn to go. Tariq is already ahead of me.

We take the stairs as quickly as possible, slowed somewhat by the marble made slippery by the sea spray.

One flight … then one more.

We approach the prone form. My heart is racing.

We come to stand beside the person, trampling the low bushes in the process.

It's a woman, I see at once. A wealthy woman, slight and short of stature. Her hair is tucked into a pearl-studded snood, dark wisps at the neck evading capture. The long, heavily-brocaded cloak is red and threaded with gold. Affixed to it are a thousand semi-precious stones of every hue. I recognize it.

I draw in air, my heart in freefall. "It's Theodora." They are my words but it feels as if another person is voicing them.

Tariq takes a step or two back.

I fall to my knees, find the tiny wrist. It is cold to the touch. "Help me turn her over."

Tariq hesitates. "We should summon the … the Guard."

"Damn it, Tariq, just help me!"

He kneels down and together we roll her over, toward us.

My hands come away bloodied. I see a dagger buried in her chest, the pool of blood around its brass hilt darkening.

"She's dead," Tariq says, as only someone who is seeing death for the first time can say it.

Her face is veiled and I am thankful for that.

Tariq stands.

"Wait a minute," I say, mind racing. *Who to summon? What to say?* My head is spinning.

He mumbles something. I glance up. His face is white as chalk.

My gaze returns to Thea. "Just give me a moment, for Mithras's sake! I've got to think." But I'm doing more grieving than thinking. I can't move, can't take my eyes away from the fatal wound.

Tariq raises his voice. "I said that someone is coming."

I look up and see the form of a woman in a plain brown cloak coming forward.

"What is it?" she demands.

She sees the body and hurries over, throwing back her veil as she moves.

I recognize her. My heart convulses. I look down at the dead woman. I lift the veil.

"Agathe," I whisper.

Theodora is at my side now, kneeling and bending over her handmaiden, tears coming fast.

Theodora sat at a small desk staring out the window when Justinian entered her anteroom.

"Well, the body has been returned to her family, Theodora," Justinian said.

Theodora wiped her eyes before she turned toward the doorway. "You mean Agathe. She has a name."

"What? Oh, yes.—I have ordered an investigation. In the meantime, you must be careful, extremely so, do you hear?"

"I shall.—She was a mere child, Justinian."

"Indeed. I have charged Narses to swear everyone involved to secrecy. We don't want news of this getting about."

Averting her eyes, Theodora did not respond.

"Your two handmaidens who saw to the exchange of the clothing were cautioned to keep silent."

"I'll talk to them, as well."

"Your stola was a complete loss, of course. But, except for a slight splash of blood on the lining, the cloak is still serviceable."

Theodora's eyes locked onto his. "I don't want it. The money was given to the family?"

"Yes, a tidy sum."

"Not tidy enough for the good turn she had done me. I would buy back her life with a hundred times the amount."

Justinian moved up to the desk. "About that good turn, Theodora. What was the reason for your wearing her clothes?"

"I told you: I wanted to go into The City unattended."

"For what purpose?"

Theodora knew that one day she must reveal to him that she knows the whereabouts of her daughter and that she has been observing her on market days. Uncertain of how he would react, she held back that knowledge, and now was not the time to tell him. "I didn't wish to have an entire retinue about me. I wanted to explore The City I had missed so much in my years away. I wanted to see the changes, see what remains the same."

Justinian listened, nodding. "Nothing has changed more than you, Theodora. And now you must realize that it is no longer possible to be so free. If an assailant can get onto the palace grounds, he can be out there waiting for another opportunity."

Unwilling to answer, Theodora turned back to the window.

"Do you wish to know what facts we have uncovered?"

"What?—yes." For a moment she was seized by the thought that the truth about her subterfuge had somehow come out.

"The dagger has been traced to a metal worker in the Mese, one that deals often with members of the Greens."

"I'm sure there are people close to the emperor—and perhaps to you—who would not like to see me as empress."

"Who? Who here would resort to murder?"

"Some senator, perhaps." Theodora thought of mentioning Stephen's several warnings about Procopius, but immediately thought better of doing so. Mention of Procopius would perturb Justinian, who was partial to him, and it would extend this conversation when, in fact, she wished to be alone. Instead she said, "Or a general who has already dealt with death. One more would be nothing for a military man."

Justinian took up Theodora's hand and kissed it. "I'm sorry about Agathe," he said. "You mustn't blame yourself."

"Why not?" Tears threatened now.

"In any case," Justinian said with a deep sigh, "something must be done."

"Dearest, we both know what must be done."

"Yes, but convincing an old man to share his title is not an easy task."

"I know. You are asking him to face his mortality."

"So you've seen other dead bodies, Stephen?" Tariq asks.

"I have. Eleven of us were cut. Only five survived. I saw bodies laid out side-by-side, like dolls."

Several weeks have passed since the murder. Our game of *Shatranj* has just finished.

"She—Agathe—was so young," Tariq says, his forehead furrowing. "I keep wondering why she was dressed like that. And Theodora, too, as if they had traded places."

"Shush, Tariq. We were warned not to speak of any of that business."

"But you know, don't you? You would not have lost so easily to me tonight if your mind was not elsewhere. You're Theodora's friend. You must know."

Oh, I know that Theodora somehow manages to see her daughter on market days but of the masquerade she and Agathe performed, I know nothing. I put off Tariq by saying, "Lady Theodora and I haven't talked since that day—the day of the murder. She hasn't left her rooms and hasn't asked to see me."

As fortune would have it, however, late that evening, long after Tariq has returned to his room, someone knocks on my door.

I open it to find Narses, his face serious.

"Pardon the intrusion at this hour, Stephen. I won't come in. Lady Theodora wishes to see you at midmorning tomorrow."

I blink in sincere surprise at the invitation—and that the messenger is the Commander of the Imperial Bodyguard.

I take a deep breath as the tall doors in front of me are opened by one of Theodora's handmaidens. The young woman's slow, careful movements and soft voice in announcing me tell me she is treading carefully.

I approach her couch, passing the game table and noticing that the board and pieces are untouched since we last played. Her face is pale and I wonder at how the pallid aspect actually adds to her flawless beauty. Her lips are painted pink and the corners of her mouth arch upward in a half-smile.

"It has been a while," she says. "Sit down, Stephen."

I bow, then sit on the white couch adjoining hers. "Not since—" I stop short and bite my lower lip.

Theodora's smile vanishes. "That day, I know. Agathe—poor child—was a proxy for me. She died in my place."

I nod. I, too, am treading carefully.

"I can read on your face the questions you have about that terrible day. I want to explain." Theodora sighs deeply and begins. "I've told you about my daughter, Hyacinth. Justinian does not allow me to leave the complex alone.

Agathe and I would exchange clothing on market days so that I could go to the square and watch my daughter without fanfare of any kind—without Justinian knowing I was gone. Dressed in my finery, Agathe would take to that one terrace where I am known to regularly meditate without interruption. Narses knew not to allow anyone near. So you see, I managed to be in two places at once." The half-smile returns and with it, pain, and I suspect, terrible regret.

"Has the investigation uncovered anything?" I ask.

"The guard who was to see that no one bothered me that day has vanished. And rumor has it that two Greens were seen lurking about that day. The Greens do not see me as a friend. The feeling is mutual." Theodora clears her throat. "Stephen, you have cautioned me about Procopius a number of times. You don't suppose …"

Her thought mirrors one I had at the time of the murder, one I still wonder about. "Has Lord Justinian questioned him?"

"In a manner of speaking. The two are as close as bedbugs so it was no inquisition, I can tell you. But, to the point, Procopius was not even in Constantinople that day."

"Ah, I see."

"Oh, that does not preclude the fact that he could have hired the Greens to do the dirty work."

"It is a possibility."

"I have a plan that may reveal his guilt or innocence. I shall ask you to aid me in staging it."

"I?"

"Yes, but it must wait until after the coronation."

"Coronation?"

"Yes—oh, I may as well tell you. The palace will be abuzz with it by midmorning, anyway." Theodora paused, her eyes on me, as if to raise my curiosity.

"My father said I had the biggest ears in the family," I say with a smile.

"Really?" Theodora sidles over to the edge of her couch and reaches out, pushing back the hair on the left side of my head. "Just as I thought," she announces, "your ears are perhaps your best feature!"

Whether this is a compliment or a jibe, her touch runs through me like the sweetest liqueur.

"Your father," she continues, "it seems, was wrong about many things."

I have no doubt she is referring to his decision to sell me, an allusion that dispels my pleasure and invites old pain. The blood at my temples starts to pulse. I can't bring myself to respond.

Theodora moves back to the middle of her couch. She is, I think, oddly satisfied that she has embarrassed me. I wonder if she is aware her comment about my father stings like a poisoned arrow.

"Emperor Justin has agreed that Justinian should be his co-ruler."

This had been expected for some time, and yet the reality of it comes as something of a shock.

Theodora's teeth shine white as she displays the widest possible smile. "Now," she says, "shall we finish that game of *Shatranj*? Justinian has not been inclined to play lately, so it's gathering dust sitting there all these weeks."

"Well, that explains it," Tariq says.

Night has fallen. I have just told my friend about the plans for Justinian to be named co-emperor. We are again sitting on the stone bench looking out at the Sea of Marmara, where the gentle waves reflect the sparkling of a near-full moon and a thousand stars. "Explains what?"

"Procopius's wild fit that he threw earlier today. You had gone off to meet Lady Theodora. What a tirade! He drew Leo into one of the library's niches and went on and on at high volume about how, if done correctly, something or other was to be approved by the senate, the army, and the people. He railed against Emperor Justin for ignoring such customary and formal procedures."

"Well, now you know just what rattled him. I must say that in what little I've read of the empire's history on choosing an emperor, such customary procedures are more revered in their neglect."

"Of course," Tariq responds with a hiccup of a laugh, "with his background in law and the State, he would know as much. His anger is disingenuous, don't you think, Stephen?"

"Very likely, indeed." I am tempted to tell Tariq of the suspicions regarding Procopius that Theodora and I harbor, but I hold back. An ever-bubbling stew of gossip is ever-present in this labyrinth they call the Great Palace complex. I won't add to it.

49

THEODORA SAT ON A HIGH-BACKED cushioned chair, her fingers tapping the armrests. The couches and tables in her reception room had been pushed aside so that a fashion parade could glide before her.

"Ah, you are like the Three Fates," Theodora trilled, "except that you are all beautiful, not old and ugly." Theodora's sisters and Antonina stopped before her, backs erect, perfectly coifed heads held high. "Comissa, you are Clotho in your shimmering blue stola. You, Tasia, are Lachesis in your bright yellow. And in your emerald green, Antonina, you are Atropos.—And I am Hestia, Goddess of heart, home, and family." Theodora drew a deep breath. Thoughts of how she had failed Anastasia, her mother, Irene, and two babies were always close to the surface. Now, however, she felt as if she was enabled to protect and care for her loved ones. A kind of warmth spread within her and with it the perception that she was at one with life itself.

"Oh, how *I* would like to be Atropos, Thea!" Comito exclaimed. "How divine to be the one who cuts the thread of life—and there are a few whose threads I would like to cut!"

"No doubt, considering your history, sister," Theodora said, laughing. "But I have chosen well. Whenever I need someone to cut the thread, it is Antonina I will call. She has the coin purse of a man."

"Indeed?" Antonina's face went red. "Well—perhaps."

"Coin purse?" Anastasia asked. "Do you mean money?"

"No, Tasia," Comito said with a smile and an overt gesture, both wicked. "It is the purse that makes a man a man."

Anastasia thought for a few moments, and when the dawn came, her mouth dropped open and her blush began. Tardily, her shrilly high laughter joined the peal of her sisters.

Theodora stood and toured around the three, asking one to turn this way, one that way. "I am happy with the designs and colors," she said as she returned to her chair. "And the three of you will present well on Sunday. You will be perfection. And in good time I will find you all worthy husbands.—Why so glum, Anastasia? If Comito can give up her lumber merchant to come live here, you should be able to sacrifice your life on the boards."

"It's not that, Thea. It's just that I wonder why we are not allowed into the Reception Hall of the Nineteen Couches. Especially you, Thea. Of all people, you should be there to see your husband crowned."

"It's the way it's done," Antonina said. "Emperor Justin is presenting Justinian to the senators, generals of the army, navy, and Palace Guard, as well as other dignitaries."

"Except," Theodora interjected, "the emperor is too ill with his old leg wound to attend, so it is Patriarch Epiphanius who will be conferring the crown of sovereignty upon Justinian. My time, Tasia, will come in three days." She was alluding to Easter Sunday, when she and Justinian would both be crowned by the patriarch in the cathedral.

"Dare I ask," Comito ventured, "what if the senators and the rest are not happy with the choice? What if they prefer another?"

"Oh, there may be a few who object to Justinian," Theodora said, "and more than a few who object to me, but they know not to appear with their objections. The emperor's choice is a *fait accompli.*"

"But only men are gathered in the hall now?" Anastasia asked, her face screwed up in mock disgust. "Only men? Like at the Hippodrome on racing days?"

Antonina nodded. "And—like at the Hippodrome, there are guards to keep away any woman."

"Only men?" Anastasia repeated dully, as if digesting the fact.

"Yes!" came the reply in unison from the others.

"Well—it's not fair!" Anastasia trumpeted. "I should like to see the day when more women sport coin purses!"

When the unconstrained and high-pitched laugher died, Theodora attested, "Sister, you have touched the matter with a needle. The day will come."

4 April 527

It is a sunny and warm Easter Sunday, a fine day for a coronation. I am thankful that I am one of the librarian scribes and that my skills in the scriptorium have kept me from being demoted—in my opinion—to the excubitors, guards who are charged with protecting the palace and maintaining control of the exuberant crowds. The citizenry who have turned out in untold numbers to witness the event will keep most of the excubitors from observing the history that is being made today in the Church of the Holy Wisdom. It's as if The City itself is being crowned, for the streets fairly vibrate with movement and ring with effervescent voices. Even the most raggedy alleys are decked out in flowers and garlands of boxwood, myrtle, and rosemary. Flags and pennants of every color hang from balconies, flying in the breeze rising from the sea.

Tariq and I are processing with our brother scribes up the steps and into the cathedral. The cool interior is shimmering bright with a thousand beeswax candles and redolent with the faint, woody scent of frankincense. Others—patricians of all manner—are clustered in the front. Our group is ushered into a middle section so we will have an acceptable view of the proceedings.

"Look," Tariq whispers, pulling at my sleeve and nodding to the right, "there, in those benches against the wall."

In the seating designated for the infirm and elderly, sit old men, all in the same uniform. "It's Justin's old army comrades," I say. "They could tell some stories." I look to the benches on the left side and find them filled with soldiers also, a generation younger. I nudge Tariq to look. "And there is Justinan's old unit here to see him raised."

"I wonder if they have stories about Justinian," Tariq says. "By the way, why should they have seating when most of us will have to stand for an eternity?"

"You've not fasted today. I don't think you'll faint." I give Tariq a gentle poke to the ribs.

At this moment, we observe Patriarch Epiphanius making his way down the makeshift center aisle that has been cordoned off, moving toward the Narthex, where Justinian and Theodora are just arriving in a crush of court officials and maids of honor. From our placement, his welcome to them is muffled and unintelligible. Black-robed deacons place lighted candles in the hands of the royal couple and in moments, the patriarch leads them up the aisle in ceremonial fashion.

As they are moving at a turtle's pace amid the soft exclamations of the onlookers and the heavenly strains of a hymn from a choir of eunuchs, I have time to take in their appearances. Justinian is bare-headed. His dalmatic of imperial gold cloth is bound with a sash pinned with emerald brooches. The shoes leisurely lifting the purple hem in perfect measure are of a deep red. Only the emperor is allowed red footwear. In contrast to Emperor Justin, who was sixty-eight when the imperial diadem was placed on his head, Justinian is forty-five, and though he is plain as rain, his presence emanates such radiance that he seems handsome.

It is Theodora, however, who commands the eye. Visible through the sheerest veil that hides none of her face, her dark hair is wound in elaborate fashion atop her head and studded with pearls. She proceeds, erect and poised, her gold stola, softer and more fluid than her husband's robe, hinting at the shapely form beneath. The gold imperial collar is encrusted with gems. I catch brief glimpses of her shoes in quick gold splashes as she moves. The heels of the footwear add to her height. That she has often been self-disparaging about her stature merely underscores her sensitivity on the matter.

As the couple approaches us at the middle of the cathedral, Theodora's face is all I see. Her expression is one I have not noted before—and my memory holds a veritable compendium of them. She is not serious; neither is she smiling. She is utterly calm, as if she knows that this moment in time has long been willed to her by Fate, and in that calmness her beauty takes hold of the gaping congregation with force. Tariq, leaning over my shoulder for his view, gasps. I have no breath to expel. I think of that marvelous statue of Aphrodite in the Forum of Arcadius. Theodora is that goddess brought to life in the flesh.

They pass us now and, after many more paces, arrive at the foot of the soleas area extending from the sanctuary. The patriarch steps up onto that raised platform and pivots toward the couple and congregation. His considerable height makes Theodora's diminutive status more noticeable. In strong voice he chants a litany, calling on the congregation to pray for the Empire, its colonies, its peoples, and a myriad of other concerns. To each request and with crystalline clarity, the white-robed chorus of eunuchs sings the response: "*Kyrie eleison.*"

Two deacons appear carrying the purple cloaks and imperial diadems. They place them on a table, and the patriarch blesses each one. The vestitores, a short, bald man, enters from the sanctuary to play his part in the ceremony. He bows before the patriarch, then Justinian, then Theodora. Now he takes a purple robe and places it around Justinian, clasping it with a gold brooch studded with sapphires. This he repeats with Theodora.

As the royal couple turns toward the congregation, they stand like glittering statues as the chorus sings of kings and princes who are installed by God to rule over nations, but who are also warned not to neglect their homage to God out of fear of calling down His wrath upon them. The last line repeats with the addition of the voices of the faithful: "Happy are all who take refuge in God!"

Tariq whispers, "That is the second psalm."

I nod. My eyes are on the front where the patriarch is placing the jewel encrusted diadem on Justinian's head. The great church has fallen silent but for a cough here, an audible intake of breath there. The patriarch turns and accepts the other diadem from the vestitores and goes to Theodora, whose face still radiates calmness as she removes her veil. He places the diadem on her slightly bowed head, stands erect, and sings out the *Gloria Patri* in a loud voice: "Glory to the Father, and to the Son, and to the Holy Spirit, both now and always, unto the ages of ages."

The faithful sing their reply, "Amen!"

I am not Christian, but I am moved by this moment in history.

The recessional is slow and stately, accompanied by the choir's perfectly-pitched plainsong. Rather than leading, the patriarch is following the couple this time. While Justinian's face shimmers with pride and power, Theodora, her posture relaxed, wears a mask of serenity, looking neither left nor right. I hold my breath until they pass.

By the time we arrive outside on the steps of the cathedral, the couple is ensconced in the gilded royal carriage led by four white horses. Announced by trumpets and flanked by excubitors, the splendid vehicle makes its way through throngs of cheering citizens toward the palace. The City has indeed turned out. Tariq and I fall into the crush of people moving toward the Hippodrome's entrance. Among the pushing and jostling, I hear half a dozen languages. My hand covers the purse I have secreted in an inner pocket of my tunic. A big brute of a Green manages to cross in front of me, stepping on my foot.

Justinian and Theodora will repair to the Daphne Wing of the palace, where they will pass through the small Ivory Gate and climb a spiral staircase that leads to the St. Stephen Chapel and the anterooms of the kathisma, the royal loge on the eastern side of the amphitheater.

Once inside the amphitheater, Tariq and I scramble toward the eastern side and change our seats three times, like children, each time attempting to get closer to the purple-draped royal box.

An hour passes as people continue to pour in, many with their finery in evidence, their spirits high. Women, most often excluded from the activities here, seem especially convivial, their high, mellifluous laughter subduing the prating of men, and their scents offsetting the malodor of the lower orders. After another half hour, the doors are closed. The amphitheater is at capacity: sixty thousand—or more.

We are sitting on a lower tier and face the concourse, naturally. We will have to turn around and look high above us once the drapes are drawn back in the kathisma. "Except for a wounded toe," I say to Tariq, "everything has gone as clockwork."

Tariq laughs. "Oh, it's meant to go that way," he answers. "Last year I had to copy a codex about ceremonies that was written by Emperor Constantine himself. He wrote that everything in court life should pass as if in a choreographed dance. Everything imperial is to be orchestrated with order and harmony. In this way, the court is following the order of the God-made universe."

"You must show me the codex."

A hush falls on the crowd across the concourse, presaging a great cry—no, shrieks—of joy. We see excubitors raising the imperial standards on the poles set into the spina of the racecourse—but the response is for something more important taking place behind us. Those across from us observe what we could not. We stand, pivot, and jump up onto the wooden planking of the bench in order to see the loge high above us where the gold-tasseled purple drapes of the kathisma are slowly being drawn back.

Co-Emperor Justinian and Empress Theodora are already in the imperial box. The crowd roars its approval, a thundering tumult that goes on for several minutes. When the noise lessens, Justinian steps forward and blesses the crowd by making the sign of the cross to the left, to the center, and to the right.

One deep voice calls out: "Justinian Augustus!" It is the traditional title since the time of the first Roman emperors. The crowd begins to chant: "Justinian Augustus."

A satisfied smile appears on Justinian's face.

Suddenly, the chants switch to "Theodora Augusta." Justinian reaches back, takes Theodora's hand and brings her to his side. He keeps hold of her hand as the crowd's cries and exclamations increase. "Theodora Augusta," they shout, "Theodora Augusta!" The chant for her exceeds—in volume and in length—the one given him.

My ears begin to ring with the deafening din going on about me. In a few minutes the emperor motions for silence and begins a speech thanking his citizens for their enthusiastic support. I am certain I am not the only one to half-listen, concentrating instead on the vision next to him.

Calmness still reigns in her expression. She has confided in me her past, so, as the emperor's words wash over me, I wonder: What is she thinking? What emotions must be tearing through her?

She stands in the royal loge, adored by the populace of Constantinople, here in the Hippodrome, where not so many years ago, she and her sisters danced in a pitiful plea that their widowed and poverty-stricken mother might beg of the Greens a position for her new husband. Humiliation came at the hands of the Greens, cementing her hatred for that faction.

Now, as she stands in the high loge as if on a stage, head lifted, diadem sparkling in the late afternoon light, I think of other stages, so very different, that she has played upon. How many in this crowd have seen her in the comedies wherein she supported Comito—but stole the show? How many have seen Theodora in bawdy theaters here in The City or in venues all along the Levant? How many have seen her in such lascivious "living pictures" as *Leda and the Swan*? How is it they reconcile this empress with that actress? I think of the then and the now, and my arms go to gooseflesh.

To read her face from where I stand, Theodora is not so much thinking as she is accepting, accepting that which would have been an unimaginable prize to any other young woman in the realm, and yet she collects this cup held out to her by Tyche, sipping from it as if it has been meant for her, meant to be, always.

The emperor is finishing his little oration. The crowd cries out, "Long live Justinian Augustus! Long live Theodora Augusta!" It quickly becomes a chant as the royal couple steps back and the purple drapes draw closed.

Fate goes ever as it must.

As Tariq and I leave the amphitheater, Emperor Justin comes to mind. I ponder whether his absence is because of his illness, as it has been given out—or whether he is loath to relinquish his moments in the sun.

And then—inexplicably—I think of Procopius. He has not been seen all day, not in the cathedral, not in the Hippodrome. For someone who longs to be historian of the empire, his absence is indeed puzzling.

50

THE ROYAL COUPLE IS CAUGHT up in a flurry of activities. Four months go by, months during which Theodora has not asked to see me. I begin to think my friendship with her is no more. She belongs to the empire.

On the first of August, Emperor Justin dies of a poisoning from his leg wound. After a celebratory military funeral, he is laid to rest in the Imperial Chapel next to the Empress Euphemia.

Justinian shares the throne no longer. He and Theodora are supreme rulers.

Two weeks pass without hearing anything directly from either monarch. But, indirectly, there is much to absorb. In the library we learn a good many things from Leo—who keeps his ear to the ground. According to him, Justinian's imperial plans include controlling the various barbaric hordes, winning back Rome and its lost provinces, ridding Christianity of heretical doctrines, and reevaluating and codifying laws forged in the brightest days of the Old Rome.

While these revelations raise few eyebrows, what we learn about Theodora does. In truth, I am less shocked than others. Justinian's Monday meetings with his council are called Silences because no one is allowed to speak of what goes on in the chamber. But it soon gets about that not only is Theodora being allowed to attend Justinian's Silences, but she is said to be expressing her viewpoints while Justinian commands that the councilors respect her opinions. I can't help but wonder how former Empress Euphemia would react to such a turn of events. I think perhaps the woman suspected—and feared—the power and influence an Empress Theodora might one day wield.

After another week, one of Theodora's handmaidens comes into the library to recite a message that the next day at mid-afternoon, I am to visit Theodora in her new quarters in the Daphne Wing of the Great Palace. I am anxious about doing so. We have been friends, but now she is empress. In my room, I look up at Jati and ask: "How do I conduct myself?" He is spiritless this night. The tesserae tell me nothing.

The change in palace protocol has people concerned. For the late Emperor Justin, patricians coming into his presence would salute him with a closed fist to their breasts in the Roman fashion, while other citizens would genuflect on their right knee to show their obeisance. He was to be addressed as "Emperor." For an empress, like Empress Euphemia, nothing at all was required to show homage. She was to be addressed as "Empress." Things have changed greatly in the handful of days since Justin's death, and nothing has gathered more gossip, discussion, and fiery arguments than the formal way in which the royal couple now receives everyone, including those of patrician rank. As in days of old and under emperors little revered, each supplicant is to enter and drop to the floor, face down, stretching their arms out as far as possible. Each must kiss the foot of the emperor and that of the empress, who are to be addressed only as "Master" and "Mistress." Anyone not conforming is to be strong-armed out of the room by the silentiaries.

What am I to expect when I visit this woman with whom I used to play board games?

Procopius surfaced the day after the coronation. I laugh to myself to think that he snubbed the royal couple's complete ascendency to the thrones because, other than myself, I doubt if anyone noticed his intended rebuff. Each day now, he comes bursting red-faced into the library with a new complaint about how things are changing, caring little that others will overhear what he tells Leo. One day he complains that the magistrates who used to conduct business in their local headquarters are now required to make all of their decisions within the Daphne Wing—under the close eye of the royal couple—so that hallways are now clogged with malodorous denizens of all types. The next day, he complains about the mystery of the depleted treasury, suggesting Theodora has been sending gold to Monophysites in Alexandria and all along the Levant. His tales and grievances have no end—and yet Leo tells us that he is one of a cadre of young men in whom Justinian is entrusting the future of the empire.

It is my first visit to the Daphne Wing, and I find it many more times magnificent than the Palace of Hormisdas. However, I notice few details. I am early to the assignation and am made to wait in a small chamber off the throne room. Several minutes go by, and the knots in my stomach grow worse. I start to perspire. Unable to sit on the couch, I pace, watching the water clock drip, drip, drip—until a half hour has passed. I long to escape back to the confines of my apartment.

Suddenly, a handmaiden enters, a bulwark of a woman. "You are to come with me. Mistress Theodora has just arrived."

I stand and push one foot in front of the other. "How many are in the audience chamber?"

"Oh, it is just you and the empress."

I'm not certain whether I should be happy or more nervous.

We enter the massive chamber, empty now—except for Theodora who sits at the far end on the right side of a double cream-colored marble throne. The woman announces me and backs out of the room.

I am not sure why I am so fearful of this woman with whom I have shared so many secrets—mine and hers. The gossip going around about the new ways of governing does not make me any less apprehensive. I am expecting to encounter a wholly different personage sitting under that diadem. Beneath the hem of her purple stola, her red shoes protrude, a visible sign of Justinian's willingness to share his power.

I begin the long walk, eyes on the marble floor. When I am very close to her, I dare to look up. Her smile is enigmatic.

My heart races in triple time. I go to my knees and prepare to prostrate myself.

"No, no," she—the empress—says, "We will have none of that. We know each other too well. I warn you not to be too submissive, Stephen. The submissive perish, remember that. Oh, I have learned that lesson well from admirers, lovers, consorts, men rich and men poor—and from here to Africa to the Levant and back again."

I draw myself up and bow deeply. When I bring my head up, I see that Theodora has removed her diadem and placed it on Justinian's seat. I have not nurtured my old talent for reading auras, but hers comes through to me now, unbidden. For a diminutive woman, she sits tall on the throne and I blink, for her aura is a deep, deep red, the color of power, the color of survival.

"Sit there," she orders, nodding toward a chair that sits cater-cornered from the throne.

I obey, mumbling something about being glad to see her. I make certain to address her as "Mistress."

Her small red lips fashion into a sly smile. "Who could have foretold this?" She releases one of her tinkling laughs. "In a way, I owe it to you, Stephen."

"Me?"

"Yes, if we had not become friends, you and Justinian might not have taken notice of me that day in that God-awful alley off the Hippodrome. Have you not thought of that?"

"No," I say.

Theodora is too smart not to see through my lie, but she doesn't challenge me. "When it is just the two of us, it will be like old times," she announces. "We'll have another game of *Shatranj* soon. I'm certain my skill has gone to seed."

"Yes, Mistress."

"And in private you may still call me Theodora, or Thea, as you did. We are still friends."

Relief and no little pleasure surge into my bloodstream.

"Now, today I am asking for your aid."

"Yes, Mis—I mean, Theodora."

Her black eyes hold me transfixed. "In a room not far away I have another visitor waiting. He has been waiting for more than an hour."

"If he feels anything like I did, he's now reduced to a puddle of perspiration on your lovely marble floor." Little by little, I am feeling more comfortable with her.

She ignores my quip. "I need to question this man. It is most important to me."

"Who is it?"

"Procopius." She might as well be saying, "Lucifer."

"You think he's responsible for Agathe's death?"

"Don't you?"

I take a moment. "He seems capable of doing it—or ordering it done—and yet—"

"You hesitate.—You're fair, that's good. I'll need certain evidence if I'm to convince Justinian of his guilt. Procopius has risen as primary historian of the empire and one of my husband's most influential councilors. If he cannot be proved guilty, I'll have to let it go. One must choose one's battles."

"Yes," I mutter, thinking how Procopius presents one face to us in the library and another to Justinian.

"I know you cling to no religion, Stephen, but have you had occasion in your work to copy the Bible?"

"I have."

"It has a proverb that says, 'Like a fluttering sparrow or a darting swallow, a curse that is causeless does not alight'."

I nod. "Choose your battles, Theodora."

"Oh, while Justinian and I see eye to eye on many things, the state of religion and what constitutes heresy is one thing that brings disagreement. And the condition under which women find themselves is another. Those are battles that must come."

For a second time, I see the deep red aura around her, pulsing at her arms and hands. I envision—or do I imagine?—heated exchanges between the monarchs. Whether it's the result of the seeing power, the claim of which I've often eschewed, I cannot say. I do know with certainty, however, that change is high on the horizon, like a pirate ship bearing down.

Suddenly, I realize my mind has drifted away.

Theodora is addressing me: "We're in agreement then. Yes? This is my plan. When he comes in, I'll move quickly to my accusation. I am determined to catch him off guard."

"He'll deny it."

"Of course, but if I am clever enough, his face will tell the story. I'm a trained actress, Stephen, I'll know immediately if he is complicit in the crime." She pauses. A lull ensues.

At a loss for words, I say, "If you have no further use of me, I will take my leave."

"Oh no, you won't! I need you here."

I wait for an explanation.

"When you were a child, Stephen, and did something wrong, did you ever go home expecting that your parents had somehow heard about it? And when you arrived home the curves and lines of your father's face—or your mother's—told you that you were in deep trouble? But they suddenly start talking about the meal or some such everyday thing and you realize that they did not know about your wrongdoing, after all?"

"Well, yes, you made me think of something I hadn't thought of in years. When I was seven or so, I stole an apple from a vendor on market day. He caught me and made me name my parents and tell him where we lived. I stayed away from home until evening. When I went home it was just as you say: I read it on their faces that I had disappointed them and brought dishonor on the house—but soon after I willingly confessed, I realized they had no knowledge of what I had done."

"You see!"

"What?"

"You expected that they had learned that their son was a miscreant, and because you expected to see it on their faces, that is exactly what you saw."

"Ah, I understand. You're afraid that you will read guilt on Procopius's face because you *believe* that he is guilty."

"Exactly, Stephen. I need you close at hand as a second."

"But—"

"What?"

I have concerns about providing such help, not the least of which is my own well-being should Procopius turn on me. But I address a different one. "If he finds me here with you, I will be no good in the future to—well, be your eyes and ears"

"Ah, to be my spy? I've thought of that. Look there at this screen."

To my right, parallel to the double throne, stands a black lacquered screen of Asian influence.

Theodora points. "The fine metal mesh at the top will allow you a good view of his face without his seeing you."

"But he is likely to know someone is behind the screen."

"So what? All the better for him to wonder about it, as long as he does not know it is you, especially if he is capable of murder."

I'm glad the design gives her confidence, but a chill runs through me. Is the worth of my friendship to her little more than the value of a spy?

Theodora rings a little hand bell. The stout handmaiden soon appears.

"Eurydice, you may go fetch the other man now."

I realize I am not being given a choice in this little murder play.

"An interesting name, Eurydice," Theodora says when the handmaiden lumbers away. "The goddess of that name sometimes drove Apollo's chariot."

My laugh is spontaneous. I nod toward the door through which she retreated. "Somehow, Theodora, I can see it."

The empress lets loose a laugh that is both sudden and generous. "Ah, Stephen, I have missed you!"

If I am reading her face correctly, her words are sincere. Or am I reading only what I *want* to see?

Theodora cuts short her amusement. "Now, go behind that screen at once."

I obey—without a moment lost, for Procopius is entering. He is wearing his signature brown dalmatic, cleaned and pressed as always. His face is a blank canvas at first. Through the metal mesh, I think I see pride and an attempt to appear cool and incurious. But I am unsure. This will be more difficult than I thought.

Procopius comes close to Theodora's throne, standing still for a few moments. "Mistress," he says, bowing in a perfunctory manner. When his head comes up, I see movement behind his eyes. He knows what else is expected and it is contrary to every bone in his body. He is not about to receive the waiver I had been given. I hear his sharp intake of breath as he kneels down, pauses a moment, then falls to the floor prostrate, his arms spread as in the crucifixion, his head to the floor. "Mistress," he mutters again. I've heard him complain aloud about the changes to palace protocol, but I wonder if she hears the contempt coiled in that word.

He looks up and he realizes he has misjudged the distance between him and the empress by a full foot or more. There is an intake of breath again, and he shimmies like a snake to the throne. His head drops and he kisses her proffered red shoe.

"You may rise," Theodora says. "Take that chair."

Procopius takes the chair I had vacated just minutes before. When he sits, his head comes up and he sees what is almost directly in his path and what I had not noticed: the screen.

An icy hand takes hold of my heart, and I take a pace back. One sandal creates a tiny scraping noise. My heart pounds.

His eyes narrow in perusal of the screen.

The empress distracts him. "Procopius, I sometimes wonder where you were on April the fourth." She sits stiffly, her spine aligned with the back of the throne.

He and I are both taken aback by the question. So I was not the only one to note his absence on the day of the royal couple's coronation, as I had thought. What is there that escapes the notice of this eagle-eyed woman?

"I—I was unwell that day, Mistress," he says, a gargling in his throat. "I took to the country for the good air."

He is lying, and I see it as if it were tattooed upon the stressful lines of his face.

"Indeed?"

"Yes, Mistress."

Theodora sees the lie, too. I hear it in her tone and see it in her expression. She allows the matter to drop.

"And what about the days since?"

"Mistress?"

"Have the days since the coronation been pleasing to you?"

"You would not want to hear my quibbles, Mistress."

Fool! The man is not as clever as he would have people believe. He has slipped into her web.

I recognize Theodora's laugh as false. "Oh, but a good empress must hear every quibble, don't you think?"

Procopius's hands, palms down, slowly trace his knees, forward and back, back and forward.

"Come now, Councilor, tell me your quibbles."

Even from my distance, I can see that he is paling. My task will be easier than I imagined.

"On second thought, Mistress, I have no quibbles to speak of."

"Indeed? What about your friends in the Green faction? Have they quibbles? They do, don't they?"

"I have no friends in the Green faction, Mistress."

The bold lie registers in his dark eyes. I imagine him a kind of Judas disowning his friends.

Theodora springs her trap. "You hired Greens to kill me, did you not?"

My eyes narrow as I study his face, taking note of every nuance. His eyelids flicker a bit, but his color stays steady.

"Not I," he says.

"You did and my handmaiden was killed in my stead. Can you deny your complicity in this murder?"

"I had nothing to do with it, Mistress. Nothing at all."

Theodora holds him like a fish on the line with a few more probing questions before closing her course of interrogation.

I have made my own determination regarding the question of his culpability.

Procopius clearly thinks he has permission to leave. "Mistress," he says, bowing and beginning to back up toward the door.

"Wait!" Theodora orders.

His head comes up and his eyes go to the screen. He knows someone is behind it, watching. The pace of my heart picks up.

"Procopius," Theodora says, "I noticed you misjudged your placement before me when you offered obeisance."

"I apologize, Mistress."

"You had to wriggle like a worm to find my foot. Why, in front of a crowded audience you would not like to be seen doing such contortions, would you?"

A long pause. "No, Mistress."

"I should like to see you do it again, Councilor. I was an actress, you know. Of course, you know. You've been heard talking about my time on the boards."

Procopius's head draws back slightly, but he has no words. He swallows hard.

"Well," Theodora continues, "you may be sure that I learned then that proficiency comes with practice."

"I shall do better, Mistress." His tone could not disguise how it pained him to use that epithet.

"Indeed," Theodora snaps.

A tense lull ensues.

Theodora's mouth flattens a bit and her teeth flash white as she orders, "Now!"

Procopius is a beaten man. He drops to the floor and executes his prostration perfectly, but when he goes to kiss her shoe, she withdraws it just enough so that he does have to slither toward it.

He kisses the red toe of the shoe now and stands quickly. He averts his eyes from her, stealing a glance at the screen in doing so. His chin is trembling. He bows toward Theodora as if his body would collapse in on itself. "Mistress." The hated epithet comes in a whisper before he backs out of the room.

I stand immobile until Theodora cries out, "Well? Stephen, have you gone to sleep?"

I come out from behind the screen and move toward the throne. "And miss the drama?" I dare to say.

"Well?" she repeats, ignoring my quip. She stands and takes a step toward me. "Is there not an execution in his future? Am I to request it of my husband at once? Speak up, Stephen."

I take stock of my options. I read his facial reactions as if reading my own writing in a codex. I think back to his face and bodily stance at the key moments of the interrogation. What if my answer is not the correct—true— answer? What is *her* judgement? *And what if I go against it?*

"Stephen!"

I draw in a long breath. "I saw no guilt, Mistress—Theodora, I mean to say. The strongest emotion I read was humiliation. No guilt."

Theodora's eyes grow large, her shoulders settle slightly, and she pivots so that her back is to me.

A long minute passes, my heart thumping. What have I gotten myself into? Am I to regret the day I met her on the merchant ship? It would not be the first time.

Suddenly, she reels about, her face pinched and pale. She stares at me as if reading me.

I want to turn away but cannot. Perspiration collects at the back of my neck and trickles down my spine. Long moments pass.

Her face relaxes now; her color returns. "I was an actress," she says. "A fine actress and I know acting. I know that when the face may appear to be delivering truth, the eyes always reveal the lie—always."

I am unsure where her words are leading.

Theodora's black eyes sweep up to me. "You are right, Stephen. We are in agreement. Procopius is innocent of Agathe's death. God rest her soul."

"Amen."

Theodora looks to the door through which Procopius had made his exit. She sighs. "At least he will be gone from The City for long periods."

"Why is that, Thea?"

"My husband is to name him adsessor to Belisarius, the general who is to go on campaign to restore control over Persia."

"Really—as a legal adviser? I thought he wanted to write history."

"Well, the law is his area of expertise, but if you hear the emperor tell it, Procopius has this absurd notion that he can become another Thucydides writing about historical events witnessed firsthand. Those military histories are not the histories that give me pause."

"So—he will be gone more than he is here."

"Yes, Stephen, but he bears watching, nonetheless," Theodora's hand goes to that dimpled area of her collarbone at the base of her neck and restively massages the area. "I can't help but think that that man—so beloved by my husband—will do great damage to this empire. And to me."

51

I AM SITTING IN THEODORA'S PRIVATE reception room where we have just finished our game of *Shatranj*.

"You've been working, Stephen?" Theodora asks.

It is the question I have been dreading. "I have."

"Is it finished?"

"Not yet, Theodora." I cannot bring myself to tell her I have yet to write of her reign of twenty-one years, that I have yet to detail the Nika riots, her influence in the naming of a Roman pope or a hundred other things that would have to be mentioned.

"Nonetheless, I will read it—or better, you will read it to me."

I stave off a shiver. "No," I dare to say, "the draft is too rough."

Theodora laughs. "Like my early life, yes?"

I nod. "Thea, I have a nagging question relative to your early life."

"Yes?"

"You've not told me what happened to Hecebolus after—"

"After I became empress?" Her smile is immediate and a bit of color flows into her pallid face. She seems young again. "Oh, how I wish I had been there to see his face when he found out. I would have sacrificed my diadem to witness it."

"And?"

Theodora's hooded dark eyes, still dazzling, narrow and fasten on me. She gives a little shrug as the smile fades. "It seems he vanished, Stephen."

"Vanished?"

"Yes." She snaps her fingers. "Like magick."

I had planned to ask her about Mikos, also, the man who had so violently taken her virginity—and who seems to have mysteriously disappeared from Alexandria, where he had been stationed—but she has closed the subject, and I know her well enough not to probe deeper.

"You will return next week with the manuscript." It is not a question.

I swallow hard. I stand, dizzy with the impossibility of the task, frightened, too, at her reaction to what I have been able to write—despite the fact that she herself is the source.

Theodora is growing weaker. "Yours will be my story, Stephen. You are my friend. I trust you."

I nod again, fighting off sentiment.

"It is strange, Stephen, the way life plays out, is it not?" From a table near her couch she picks up her diadem, places it in her lap, stares at it. "I do know that Procopius is proceeding with his history of the empire and that his bias against me is great. I found out five years ago and confronted him. He denied any such writing to me and to Justinian. My husband believed him. I did not. The lie was in his eyes. And I soon learned that he was attempting to interview people from my early days, the days before the Great Palace." Her eyes sweep up to hold mine. "You possessed knowledge that I couldn't allow him to have."

And so it is only now that she alludes to my five-year incarceration. My stomach tightens. I will not allow the moment to pass. "But there are others who knew you then."

"Of course. But only you knew that my childless marriage to Justinian is the result of the fever he had early on. That physician that warned me about his likely sterility has long since died. So—you alone possessed that knowledge."

Her distrust runs through me like a swift sword to the heart. "I would not have revealed it—and it would not be such a terrible thing to come out."

"Oh, but it would! I had to protect my husband from that knowledge, that hurt. Why, anything having to do with succession to the throne is important. For an emperor, it is everything! I wanted him to go on thinking that our childless marriage was my failing, not his. You see, Stephen, his boundless love for me is such that he forgave me. Had he thought that the failing was his, he would not have forgiven himself. It would have doomed our marriage."

I attempt a neutral tone. "And so I was locked away."

Her black eyes soften. "There was the other matter, too, of the child. Oh, Justinian came to accept my daughter Hyacinth.—But only you, Stephen, knew the details of my son, my secret son. No one else on this side of the world knows the details of his conception."

"And that he came here as an adult to meet his mother."

Theodora's face pales. "And were it not for—well, he might be the successor to the empire." She takes a breath. Her eyes well with tears. "All of this, only you knew."

"Am I not to write about that ... episode?"

She sighs, clears her throat, and blinks back the threatening tears. "You may do so, but you must promise me not to make the codex public until after Justinian is laid to rest beside me."

"You'll trust me to keep that promise, Thea, but five years ago you dared not trust me."

Theodora draws in breath, turns her face away for a moment, turns back, the line of a single tear visible on her nearly translucent cheek. "I have done countless things as empress that I would not have entertained as a woman—and as your friend."

Is this her apology? I wonder. It comes preciously close. However, I want her to say the words. Does she expect forgiveness without my hearing the plea?

"The irony is, Stephen, that I had you—sequestered—so that my story could not be told. And now I have had you released so that you *will* tell it, so that you can tell it without slant."

What I think is, *If your days were not coming to an end, would I still be in that dungeon cell below us?* What I say is, "That means the truth, Thea." I resign myself to the fact that she will not apologize. As she pulls herself up so that her shoulders touch the back of the white damask couch, the deep red aura becomes visible to me once again, its pulse weaker.

"Yes," she whispers, nodding slightly. "The truth—but you must promise me something else—promise me that—after I am gone—you will seek out the manuscript Procopius is writing, find it and destroy it." She draws in a hard-fought breath. "Promise me!"

I nod and affect a smile.

"Say it, Stephen!"

"I promise."

A week passes, and I sit in an anteroom with my unfinished manuscript waiting to see Theodora. I am told she is not well today but that she insists on receiving me sitting in a chair in the royal bedchamber. Her handmaidens are aiding her from her sleeping couch.

Too proud for me to see her abed. I wait. An hour passes.

I think of the false story of Theodora I had in mind after my release, my companion piece to her version of events. My revenge. I realize now that if I do as she requests, and paint the real woman, in flesh and blood, virtues and flaws alike, my need to invent her misdeeds and sins is unnecessary. And—if she is correct about Procopius's writing an exaggerated and scurrilous account of her life, that would preclude any attempt on my part to depict her life, writing it slant, as she says.

I look to the water clock. Another hour has passed. Will she ask me to read? I wonder. If so, my hope is that we will not progress so far into the story that she will realize how much is left to write—or how much the truth of her story will sting.

A soldier enters and crosses the room. I should think it's odd that it's not a silentiary or one of Theodora's handmaidens, but my mind is sluggish. I rise, ready to follow him into the royal bedchamber. I stoop to gather up the manuscript, and when I stand I am surprised to find Narses, motionless as a sculpture in front of me. He is a general now, a most successful one, and his well-decorated dalmatic and gold cuirass bespeak his status.

"I—I am to see the empress," I say.

Narses shakes his head. His eyes are lifeless. "No," he says, "she will have no need for you today."

And I know at once. "She's—gone?"

He nods, eyes brimming. Mine was not the only heart she had won.

I swallow hard, unable to speak, my hands reflexively crushing the manuscript. I want only to escape to my room. I turn to leave.

Narses grabs hold of my sleeve. "The Mistress asked about you."

I pivot and search his dark eyes, heart in freefall. "What—what did she say?"

"She said for you to 'persist.' Do you understand the message?"

"I do." I can scarcely breathe. "Thank you." I bow to Narses and turn to take my leave before I break apart like an old woman.

"Stephen," Narses calls just as I get to the door. "And so, *will* you persist?"

I stay in motion as if I have not heard.

AFTERWORD

Truly–I never planned on two books for Theodora. However, as I'm sure you can bear witness, she was bigger than life, and once Stephen entered the story, one book was not enough. Please be patient. This will not be a long series. It's to be a duology. Stephen has yet to relate how Theodora becomes involved in conspiracies, inserts herself into the naming of a pope, and almost single-handedly saves the empire.

This author would so appreciate it if you would write a little review on Amazon, B&N, KOBO, Smashwords, i-books, or Goodreads.

And stay connected in order to learn more about the second and final Theodora novel: *Too Soon the Night: A Novel of Empress Theodora.*

PLEASE subscribe to my rather infrequent **Newsletter** about progress on the second book, as well as freebies, bonuses, booksignings, contests, news, and recommendations: **http://jamescmartin.com/announcements/**

LIKE me on **Facebook**:
https://www.facebook.com/AuthorMan/

Follow me on **Twitter** @JConMartin

Follow/add me on **Goodreads**:
https://www.goodreads.com/author/show/92822.James_Conroyd_Martin

JConMartin on **Instagram**

READING GROUP GUIDE

1. How is it that a massive crowd in the Hippodrome—commoners Theodora has left behind—comes to wildly celebrate the rising of a lowly actress/prostitute to the pinnacle of power?

2. Like a Gemini, Theodora demonstrates traits at odds with each other. In her past she railed against people in power over her, yet once she becomes empress she revels in power and protocol, even bringing back the archaic practice of ordering suppliants to lie prostrate before the royals and kiss their shoes. How might these opposites be reconciled? Are there any other opposites you've noticed?

3. An old adage says, "Past is prologue." In what ways do some of the details of Theodora's early life before taking the throne foreshadow her life afterward?

4. An early feminist? Theodora is considered by many to be the first leader to recognize the rights of women. In what way might we see the seeds of feminism at work in this book?

5. Before Theodora became empress, what lasting effects might her interactions with men have had on her?

6. Can a seminal event in childhood, like the sisters' dance in the Hippodrome, have effects that last a lifetime?

7. They say a middle child—like Theodora—tends to be easygoing, innovative, independent, self-motivated, loyal, protective, strong, level-headed, tenacious, and successful. Which traits apply to Theodora? Which do not? Additional middle child traits?

8. What do you think causes Stephen to go silent about the loss of his first love, Jamila?

9. Just when Stephen recognizes his love for Theodora, he wonders what there is about himself that piques her interest. Thoughts?

10. After his five-year incarceration, Stephen plots revenge on Theodora and considers his "old love" for her dead. How realistic is it that he might come to truly embrace forgiveness?

NOW~ A GLIMPSE AT
TOO SOON THE NIGHT

A NOVEL OF EMPRESS THEODORA

28 June 548

THE EMPRESS IS DEAD. THEODORA—DAUGHTER of a bearkeeper, actress in living pictures, concubine to Hecebolus, lover to many, supporter of Monophysitism, and an equal partner in power to Emperor Justinian—is no more.

On the day of her death, a Sunday, I am called to the women's quarters of the Imperial Apartments at Emperor Justinian's request. He is a man overtaken with grief. His face is red, his eyes wet and little more that slits, as if he is trying to shut out the world. What could he want with me, I worry, as I make my way up the stairs from my suite. Years of my life flash by. How has a Syrian boy sold to a travelling wizard come to live in the Daphne Wing of the Great Palace, one might wonder. The father that sold me for a few coins no doubt would.

"Ah, Stephen," the emperor says, "you must do your lady one last favor. And it is for me, too, this favor."

I have no words—and not a clue as to the meaning of *his* words.

"Her women are dressing her now." He pauses, averting his gaze. After a long moment, he turns toward me, half-hidden eyes holding mine. "You loved her, too, don't think I don't know that. Now, hold out your hand."

I obey.

He places in my hand a needle already threaded with translucent thread.

"I am so ashamed, Stephen—but I just can't do it." With his head so low that his chin touches the top of his rumpled purple tunic, he hurries from the room.

And so I am left to perform the task that only a loved one is allowed to do. I am holding hot tears at bay and shaking like a sapling in storm when I screw up enough courage to go into Theodora's bed chamber to bind her mouth closed so that her soul would not escape into the night.

In my room I sit at the desk in the alcove that serves as my office. A breeze from the Sea of Marmara stirs the curtains of sheer silk at the balcony door and sets the flames of my lamps dancing. Two weeks have passed since Theodora's magnificent funeral, the ceremony so regal and elaborate that the Augusta herself would have approved.

For years Theodora held me enchanted, in some ways not unlike Circe's spell on Odysseus. Upon being reprieved from five years in the dungeon beneath the imperial quarters, I had promised Theodora that I would write the story of her life and tell it true. "Others will tell it slant," she said. Despite the wrong done to me, she trusted me not to embellish the facts.

I look down at the pages I have written of her early life, pages created before her death at forty-eight. Cancer, the doctors said. Oh, I was tempted to emblaze her life with wicked fiction in requital for my lost years, but something held me back, that which I came to recognize and admit as my enduring love for this very proud and complicated woman in whose veins compassion and cruelty comingled.

Am I to continue with this quest to set down the truth? Why should I spend the days, months, and perhaps years that would consume my life to satisfy the wish of a dead woman? Merely because I promised her? I recall the hours and hours of interviews wherein she described in detail every important event, every thought and emotion that accompanied them. I wrote it all down so that her story could be told. The many shelves of neat manuscripts in my study bear witness to her life. Oh, the promise weighs heavy, and yet I consider renouncing it and living my life for myself. It is a weighty temptation.

Suddenly the breeze from the sea escalates into a strong wind and several stone oil lamps sputter and go out, except for a metal one stationed on a stand here in the alcove. Lazy shadows play in the darkened room. You may call me superstitious, but I feel her presence. Oh, how she and I—both of Syrian blood—would trade gambols about which of us possessed the second sight, neither of us with any conviction.

The wind rises again, the current this time invading the alcove, chilling me and extinguishing the lamp next to me. My arms turn to gooseflesh.

And suddenly I recall her reasoning, passionate as it was, for leaving behind an accurate accounting of her life. Her spies had told her that Procopius, her nemesis in life, was writing his own—false and base—version of her life.

It is enough to set me in motion.

It is quite late and the hall, lighted at intervals by sconces, is eerily quiet. I pass the doors of the imperial apartment. The sleepy palace guards—excubitors—stationed there nod soberly as I move toward the stairwell. Justinian has not shown himself in days, so great is his grief. The two—emperor and empress—had become as one and for now he is lost.

I exit the Daphne Palace, the Imperial Wing of the Great Palace complex and make my way down the stairs set into the escarpment bordering the Sea of Marmara, descending from one terrace to the next until I reach the Palace of Hormisdas, where the salty scent of the Marmara is sharpest. I come and go at all hours within the complex of the Great Palace, and so I am admitted entrance without question. I move noiselessly. This was Justinian's palace when he was a prince, and it was also where I lived and worked upon my arrival in Constantinople. I have with me a torch and lighting it now from a sconce, I pull open the high double doors of the one-time great dining hall that Justinian had fashioned into his massive library.

I move up the middle aisle of the high desks of copyists. It was here that I worked in the early years. I excelled at languages and my skill made possible a rise in stature that I—a slave and eunuch—could not have foreseen. In time, even my handwriting became adequate. Others will say that it was my relationship with the empress that led me up the palace ladder—and there is truth in that, too.

Fronting the rows of copyists' desks is a row of bays that are lined with crisscrossing shelves of manuscripts. I come to the last bay, the one commandeered by Procopius for his own manuscripts. I take a deep breath and enter, knowing he would have me flayed alive if he knew I trespassed on his sacrosanct domain. As long as a guard on his rounds does not interfere, I feel comfortable in my stealth, for Procopius, in his role as adsessor, has been on campaign with General Belisarius and his army.

I place the torch in the holder on the wall and begin my search. I know what I'm looking for, what I've been commissioned to find, but I don't know for certain if it even exists. Theodora's spies were insistent that Procopius was recording her life in the most unflattering way imaginable.

Working my way around his desk, I rifle through the codices and scrolls on all the upper shelves, thinking he would want it out of reach. Nothing but codex after codex about the military campaigns in which he had accompanied General Belisarius as his legal advisor, secretary, and historian. I search the middle shelves now, wondering if he would be so confident of his privacy as to place it in plain sight. Half of an hour reveals only manuscripts detailing the architecture that Justinian has initiated in the capital, and the smoke from the torch is irritating my lungs. I go to my knees, crawling from one niche to another pulling out dusty scrolls and replacing them after quick inspections. A number of them pertain to the governance of a large bureaucracy. I come to the last shelf, find it empty and sit back against the shelves, defeated. Does he keep it in his apartment in the Daphne? I had feared so from the first, but how am I to enter his locked, private residence? Or perhaps he has it on tour with him, anticipating a moment when his dark imagination would ignite and spew out calumny. Again, I ask myself if Theodora's spies were wrong. Perhaps he did boast of such a lurid venture—but was it just that, an empty boast? Did he really follow through on it?

Like my own energy, the torch sputters. From my sitting position on the floor, I glance up to see it will go out in a matter of minutes. So what, I think, I'm finished here. As I bring my gaze down, I notice something strange. Attached to the middle of the underside of Procopius's desk is a large square object. It is visible only from my position on the floor. The desk I had worked at in the early years had no such thing. Neither did, as far as I knew, any of the other ones belonging to copyists.

I go to my knees, stoop under the desk, and examine my find. The hidden receptacle slides along metal rails and comes free in my hands. I set the secret drawer on the floor and take from it a manuscript. I unroll it and observe Theodora's name. Moving down the scroll, I see that it occurs again and yet again. I don't have enough light to read it here, so I roll it up and plant it in my voluminous sleeve. I replace the drawer on its rails and stand, feeling victorious just as the torch dies completely.

It is of no concern because I know my way about the library in the dark. I take the dead torch and leave the bay, moving toward the copyists' desks.

A noise.

I halt in the middle of the large chamber. Through the seams of the double doors a light appears. Is it a guard making his rounds? I hold my breath, praying he will pass, but the light does not move away. The sound of the door handle breaks the silence. My heart accelerates. I am about drop behind a desk when I think again, assuring myself it is a guard to whom I would owe no excuse. I steady myself and wait.

The double doors open now, abruptly as if to admit someone of importance, not a guard. A man enters.

When my eyes adjust to the light of his torch, I see that it is someone of—self-importance. Procopius looks up with startled eyes to find someone in the darkened room at this late hour.

I freeze. Fear runs like a poison through my veins. He could have only just arrived in Constantinople. I would have heard otherwise. Some malignant force has contrived to bring him here first thing. I curse myself for not having hidden.

My thoughts are lost in a mist. I attempt a smile. Our relationship has always been adversarial.

His surprise dissipates at once and he arranges his face into one of annoyance. "What in Satan's name are you doing here?" he demands.

My fear accelerates. I realize that my right hand has gone to the sleeve that secures my treasure. I am without words, heart pounding like a kettle drum.

Procopius marches up to me. "I asked you a question!" He thrusts the torch out, toward me, as if to burn me at the stake.

I am trying to formulate some story when he says, "That's your old desk, isn't it?" He moves the torch as a way of pointing. "The one you worked at before *she* brought you up in the world."

I look down. I hadn't noticed but he's correct. It is my old work station. I take his observation as evidence that I must have been an annoyance to him then. "I couldn't sleep," I say, ignoring his comment, "I often walk about the palace grounds."

"Indeed?" His eyebrows move up in a show of skepticism. "And you come here out of—what, nostalgia?"

I thank the gods in whom I hold no faith. Procopius has supplied me with the excuse—however weak and unlikely—I had been searching. "Exactly," I say.

"I don't believe you."

"It's true," I insist, my stomach knotting as his gaze flits past me toward the library bay I had just left.

His eyes come back to me. "You've been here a while if your torch has spent itself."

"Ah—I heedlessly picked up one that was nearly spent already." Without allowing him time to respond, I wish him a good evening and hurry past him.

I pass through the double doors and in taking care to close them behind me, the stolen scroll slips from my sleeve and falls to the floor. I reach down in the darkness, recover it, and hurry toward the exit.

Having no religion, I am at a loss to whom I should pray that Procopius does not discover the theft tonight.

Dawn is pinkening in the East in those moments before the sky runs a scarlet red. I usually savor the sight from my balcony in an attempt to consign to oblivion my many days spent without natural light. Initially, the effort works but proves fugacious once the red bleeds from the sky and day fully breaks.

Today, however, having calmed myself from my encounter with Procopius, I sit at my desk with his manuscript before me.

I begin to read, marveling at the neat flourishes of his pen.

Theodora's spies were not mistaken.

Procopius has done more than exaggerate. The manuscript has a sprinkling of truth, but it is little more than a compilation of falsehoods. He writes, in general, of Theodora's cunning and misdeeds as she conspired to seduce Justinian, not with charm, but with charms. Oh, I've heard such malicious gossip before, so I feel an argument such as this will be a waste of time. And then too, I am much aware of Theodora's imperfections. As I read on, however, a coldness takes hold of me at my core, moving through me like hardening ice in winter. I have born witness to many shocking things in my forty-three years, but I find his libel concerning Theodora's sexual bent so disturbing and disgusting that, even sitting alone, I feel hot blood rising into my face and to the roots of my hair.

I am thunderstruck. The account is unimaginable, repellent, scurrilous.

An hour brings me to the end of this manuscript.

Like her spies, the empress was not mistaken. Given his quest, Procopius would see to it that Theodora's place in history would be vilified in unspeakable ways. The lies are monstrous.

If ever I was hesitant in writing an accurate account of Theodora's life, I am no more. Procopius's philippic eclipses any bitterness I still harbor for my five years of incarceration at her whim and brings to the fore the loyalty—and love—I still hold for her.

My hands involuntarily tighten on the manuscript. I am struck by the intensity of my own feelings, staring at the document, wanting to tear it to pieces and set it ablaze. But there's no destroying it now because he would know. With Procopius's proximity to Belisarius and Emperor Justinian himself, his steps to see me punished would be extreme. He would see me banished—or worse.

I take a breath, think. My head begins to clear. One thought breaks through the fuzziness: this is nothing but a fragment. I must see it returned to that hidden drawer. The whole manuscript has to be found. Only then can I take my own steps. No joy accompanies the notion that I am now a sleuth.

A double burden has fallen on my head now: to bring an end to Procopius's story—and to continue with Theodora's story, beginning with the early years on the throne.

Lacking a means to act on the first task, I partake in a solitary meal of bread, cheese, and dates, before settling in at my desk and beginning the latter one.